Tales From the Internet

STORIES BY

STEVE GRONERT ELLERHOFF

ART BY

KEVIN STORRAR

First published in 2015 by
Norbert Allen Books

First Norbert Allen Books edition: November 2015
Color Edition ISBN: 978-0-9894462-0-4

For Kevin,

who I didn't meet online.

CONTENTS

1   HTTP://YOUAREFORGIV.EN

                    dreamail #1   5

7   TWATTER

                    dreamail #12   18

21   <LOVELYLOTUS>

                    dreamail #19   59

61   THE PIXELATED PALADIN

                    dreamail #24   88

91   THE MARTYR DUMB

                    dreamail #36   98

101   UNCLE SEEKS AUNTIE

                    dreamail #40   125

127   THE TROLL

                    dreamail #45   132

135   OUT OF CHARACTER

                    dreamail #54   197

199   FUGA MUNDI

                    dreamail #59   206

209   THE OTHER LIFE OF PAT COTTONS

                    dreamail #67   229

231   BARRY'S QUEST: WALKTHROUGH

                    dreamail #72   301

303   KEEP YOUR FUTURE TO YOURSELVES

                    dreamail #77   311

Computers and computer networks enrich the world with new channels of communication. In fact, metaphorically they add new social spaces, cyberspaces, to our lives. As individuals, we live an increasing portion of our daily lives in these cyberspaces rather than in face-to-face communication, and even when we are in the same physical space, we augment the space with the technology of cell phones, mobile devices, and electronic displays. ...

Every time there is a change in culture or an upheaval of society, new pathologies arise. The computer revolution is the focal point of such a phenomenon today. Cyberspace is the new stage on which we may act out our psychological problems. Moreover, technology itself creates new temptations, fears, and frustrations. There are new hills to climb and valleys to descend into in the landscape of technology. Our interactions in cyberspace are a reflection of our behavior, both normal and pathological.

KENT L. NORMAN,
CYBERPSYCHOLOGY: AN
INTRODUCTION TO
HUMAN-COMPUTER
INTERACTION

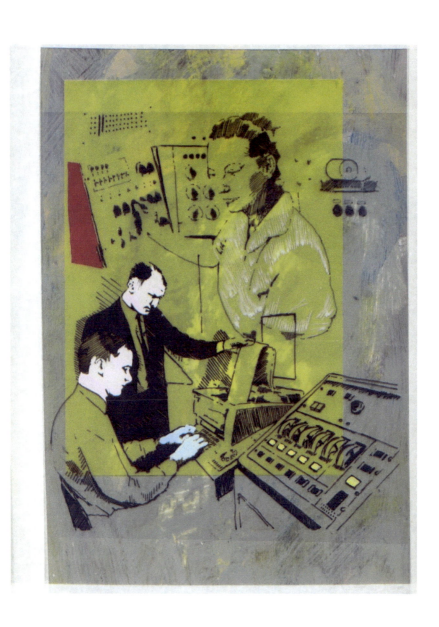

http://youareforgiv.en

They say it's out there, somewhere on the web, and if you can just find the right link or conjure up the proper search terms or—miracle of miracles—*guess* the domain name, there is a website that, once found, absolves everything. I or you or anybody else could find it through any browser, on tablet, phone, or laptop, and upon arrival have the sum of our trespasses unto self and others wiped away. All we have done that has brought forth hurt would be cleansed of us. Simply by arriving at this site, we will be made whole again.

It's a tall order. Believe me, I know that. I've hurt plenty of people, some of them in tiny little thoughtless ways, ways they probably barely registered themselves or at least lost no sleep over—you know, like when I took in a movie and the kid in the box office gave me ten bucks more in change than he should have and I said nothing and he probably got chewed out later for his register count being ten dollars short. I was a shit to not correct him, to be thrilled at getting ten extra bucks back, being a man of modest comfort myself.

Other people I've hurt in the sort of mid-tier range of assholery. In junior high, for instance, there was this kid I won't name (he's a middle aged insurance agent family man now and it'd hurt him all over again if it got back to him). He never liked me and I never liked him and he was giving me a hard time in the locker room after P.E., so, well, I called him "Pencil Dick," because, as it happened, it was an apt description in a way. All the boys cackled like animals—I didn't foresee it at the time but they'd be calling him that on into high school—and in that moment he should have gone ahead and hit me but he was so stunned with humiliation, because, like I said, it was pretty apt, and he just died a bit in front of all of us. Hell, maybe that blow is what put him on a career path in the insurance industry, providing security for others who've suffered hardships.

Or, another example, when a certain unmarried coworker had a miscarriage and confided in me because I found her bawling in the break room and she asked me not to tell anybody and I said I wouldn't tell a soul but then told the head of HR later that day and the head of HR approached her about it and no one even knew she'd been pregnant because she was kind of bigger and it kind of, I guess, hid the pregnancy a bit, even though she wouldn't have shown much because she wasn't all that far into carrying the baby or fetus or whatever it's called—and then she knew I'd told? That was insensitive. I should have kept my trap shut on that one.

One person, though...

One person I betrayed.

And of course betrayal is the worst hurt because in order for it to occur there has to exist trust. Betrayal relies in its most destructive aspect upon solid interdependence.

2

We depended on one another. One another can be two together. And that's what we were. We were together.

Until my betrayal.

I've said I'm sorry—not to the box office kid (who even knows where he is now?) or the classmate I regrettably called "Pencil Dick"—but the others, sure.

I've apologized.

Especially to the one I hurt the most.

I said sorry so much the courts had to get involved and it was ordered I see a counselor, who told me in his little office, decorated with sepia-era photos of American Indians and boasting a corporate park view through wood slat blinds, that the person I had to forgive most was me.

So I've told myself I'm sorry, every morning, every night, lots of times between those times in the course of a day, every given day.

And I still don't feel forgiven.

Not for any of it.

But this domain name, there's something numinous in the possibility of it. You know, because *Gott ist tot* and has been since at least 1882. I mean, that's long enough now that we ought to realize our world is vastly different from what it used to be. A good few generations living there without a living God. And if God is that which transcends all thought, and that's dead, and what we've got leftover is thought, then why shouldn't we be able to find salvation in that new landscape we've collectively thought into the ether? The internet is itself a path, a way, an information superhighway with more sites to see than those found on any outworn pilgrimage you might make on land, in the world, alongside a miller, a cook, a physician, a statistician, an Ameri-Mart clerk, soldier, adult entertainer—anybody. So many virtual rest stops on the way and, one should hope, that final elusive destination where all of all opens up. Like in cyberspace there could be this divine potential for unburdening all the shame and all the guilt lugged out of the wrongs you've committed.

Atonement could be the best guarded secret online, as secret as the tetragrammaton's pronunciation, sought by many but arrived at by few.

I can't die without this expiation. I dread my sorry life ending without reparation.

I've seen the messageboard claims made by some, the tweets, that they found the site, that it's so obvious, that they should have figured it out sooner, that the heart of the labyrinth was there all along. But these braggarts are not in league with Sirs Galahad, Percival, and Bors, those gallant three who achieved the Grail. Would anybody who's found it, who's regained both vessel and ground, turn around and announce it?

Not me.

If I ever find it, if I ever finally find myself forgiven, I'll simply hold that.

Until then, I'll keep cross referencing search terms, combing domain directories, typing my blind, wild goose, Rumpelstiltskin guesses in the address bar. Until then, I'll keep saying I'm sorry. I'm so very sorry.

Western_Hillbilly

to LovelyLotus   13 January 2010

I had this dream I was so hungry I went to the supermarket, got the shopping cart, and just filled it up with lettuce and carrots and mushrooms and tomatoes, cherry tomatoes, grabbed a box of plastic forks, swung round the salad dressing aisle. I picked out a nice garlicy Italian, gave it a shake, opened it up, doused the cart o' salad right there in the store. Tore open the box of forks and started eating my salad straight out the cart. And then you walked by in Daisy Dukes and gave me a crumpled up one dollar bill.

And I don't even like salad!!

Anyways, Lotus Lady, your making waves in dreamland now. Thought you should know. Must be in kahoots with the Sandman!!

Spanks alot,
Royben
--
LIFE HACK: If your girlfriend starts smoking you should slow it on down and use a lubricant.

Twatter

Just another Friday evening and Dr. Marcus Dunning-Kruger, Professor of Psychology at Aylsebury University, is meant to be relaxing. This is family time now. The work week is *o*-ver! And yet he's stuck tidying his own neglected admin responsibilities, in haste, of course. After her own departmental meeting, his mate, Dr. Grace Cloirk-Esterday, Associate Professor of English, fetches their young from Aibileen's and loops around to pick him up at the university. Of course he isn't done when she pulls back into Lot F, so all during the ride to Imperial Orient, he's been getting everything squared away on his phone so he can fully participate in weekend family freedom.

"Sukiyaki" comes on the radio, the radio preferred to playlists because it keeps the family in touch with the psyche of Des Moines. The children sing along:

"Ching-chang ding-ling ding-dong—"

"Children," their postcolonialist mother scolds from the wheel, "stop Othering!"

"But that's what it sounds like," says Frantz Dunning-Esterday.

"The lyrics sound nothing like those pejorative caricatures of East Asian languages."

"Stop speaking for us," protests Gayatri Cloirk-Kruger. "Only we can tell you what it sounds like to us."

"Marcus, really, are you not going to back me up on this?"

"Kids, come on," an e-mailing Dr. Dunning-Kruger says, not looking into the sun visor mirror to avoid their darling manipulative eyes. "Shut up."

The children, thankfully, sulk.

Parking in sight of the tank farm that has always been there—but not seeing it because there won't be a reason to until the day it leaks into Walnut Creek—they split off from the car in different directions: Grace to the *shi*-guarded red doors of the Chinese restaurant to order dinner, Frantz and Gayatri sprinting to Tristram's Books just next door, Dr. Dunning-Kruger almost following them in a 4G-drunken meander.

The bookstore door is held open by a peripheral obesity with Maeve Binchy's last book in hand. He scuffs in without muttering thanks, so close is he to being finished with thankless duties, hitting SEND on an e-mail explaining to a less-distinguished colleague at Lewis and Clark that he'll be happy to chair the panel he proposed at the thirteenth Annual Pacific Northwest Evolutionary Psychology Conference in July, but can't help with filling out the speakers beyond himself—surely she knows that's what an additional e-mailed call for papers to grad students is for—and neither can he attend the dinner because he has to catch a flight that night, which is a lie—he's actually picking up his wife and kids at the Portland airport and whisking them off for a two-week, all-family vacation at a rented condominium in the woods overlooking the aftermath of geological nausea called Mt. St. Helens. Taking the initiative—an adaptation that served him well in landing tenure early—he goes ahead and opens his Twitter app, typing seventy-eight characters.

<@APNEPC seeking papers for my panel: Mechanism Is Not Metaphor. #networkingopportunity>

He presses the TWEET button but before swiping work away to finally, at achingly long last, relax, notices a tweet from his own department's poor pitiable genetic dead-end, Shane Ebrards.

<Another publication for the CV!> A thumbnail image is just tantalizing enough to earn a tap, revealing a shaky-handed pic of what is apparently his new book lying on a desk. Unpinching the image and squinting sharpens the title: *The Soul Yearns But Does It Really Yearn?: Understanding Post-Adlerian Psychology through* The Mighty Boosh.

Mighty Boosh?

Google reminds him it's a television show from the UK, three-series-worth between 2004 and 2007, cult status, meant to be funny but undoubtedly in that British way.

Google reveals the book is published by Metoporon Press, a small non-academic publisher out of, of all places, Lithuania. Retails for $30.95.

Back to the tweet. Posted at ten in the morning. No one has replied or re-tweeted it in eight hours.

Poor Shane.

Shane isn't like Dr. Dunning-Kruger—or anybody else in the department, for that matter. Stocky, pale, rotund Shane, from BFE, Ontario, did his advanced degree in BFE, Wales,

9

and wound up at Aylesbury simply because they were in a pinch with Dr. Collier dying in that wreck and spring semester already underway and even though he was under-published and a post-Adlerian he would do. Shane, who wears mall-bought suits and whiskers that have refused coalescence into a beard all the three years he's been sucking air two doors down. Where Dr. Dunning-Kruger cultivates intellectual rockabilly chic—cowboy shirts, belt buckles, and tweed—Shane galumphs across campus looking obsolete, something like a video rental store manager in this torrenting, Netflix-era America. Shane also doesn't seem to have attracted or created anybody, no wife, no husband, no family to get Chinese take-out with on a Friday night. No recollection of any mentioning of pets. No grapevine rumors or overheard indiscrete moans from his office leading anyone Dr. Dunning-Kruger's talked to to think Shane even *deals* with the students. The man just does not seem to know how to get along, undriven perplexedly by genes utterly lacking in selfishness.

Having been in the academic game a year longer despite being two years younger, and feeling sorry for the guy since no one has responded to his announcement, Dr. Dunning-Kruger decides he'll do his daily mitzvah and reach out to advise with a reply.

<@SEbrards Not peer reviewed, so I'd suggest holding back on the old CV>

TWEET.

Scrolling down the latest tweets out of habit, unable to resist, and there's one from Pinker, that Old English Sheepdog who gets *all* the press after solving the mind. As if. Has this guy even passed his genes on to the next generation?

He's getting a bit long in the tooth, although, of course, a healthy male remains reproductively viable until the day he dies.

Tapping STEVEN and PINKER and OFFSPRING into Google he's interrupted by a banner. A tweet.

From @SEbrards.

<@DrDunningKruger I'd be more inclined to consider your eminent opinion if you'd once in our lives say hello to me when I greet you.>

Dr. Dunning-Kruger reads some of the words a few times. He shakes his head at the store's staring bookcases. He taps the REPLY button and holds his forefinger stiff and upright.

<@SEbrards> he taps in an effort to save face, <I have no recollection of you ever saying hello to me, which leads me to believe there's been a misunderstanding. Can't believe yo>

Out of characters.

Delete, delete, delete to "misunderstanding" and TWEET.

Second message: <@SEbrards I can't believe you actually lack the social graces to address me about this in person if in fact it actually bothers you>

<@DrDunningKruger I have many recollections of you ignoring me to my face. But feel free to buy my book, available at a store you're near!>

<@SEbrards before being so rudely dismissed I was merely trying to be helpful>

<@SEbrards because in the grand scheme (ie tenure) without peer review your little book is nothing but a spandrel>

That tweeted, he sneers, touches a few of the bestsellers on the table beside him without looking at them, straightening them. The hippy worker woman, the one always working Friday nights, is at the information desk. He stalks over to her with a question.

"Looking for a book," he says, biting the words. "Probably won't have it."

"Oh sure, let me see what I can do." She pulls a few strands of her long hair over her shoulder and clicks through whatever she's got to click through on the store's dinosaur of a PC. Probably still running XP. "What's the title?"

He's squinting at the unpinched pic again. "*We All Yearn But Do We Really Year—*"

"Oh Dr. Ebrards' book—love that shooow," she says, glancing past him with a look. "We've got twenty on order but I'm pretty sure those are all claimed." She clicks through a few windows. "Yeah, yeah, all claimed, but I can totally put you down for one in the next order. Won't get here for I'd say a week?"

Dr. Dunning-Kruger holds an outward hand over his face and reels from the information desk.

His phone chirps thrice.

<@DrDunningKruger adding his name to the waiting list for a copy of my new book> Accompanying it is a picture.

Of the hippy worker woman.

And she's talking to a well-dressed guy who's—him!

Just then, there at the information desk.

There's him from behind.

There's her in her bandana blouse.

There's the shop's clunky outmoded computer monitor.

He arches onto the toes of his black leather Chuck Taylors, leaning over a long bookshelf like a seething neighbor at the fence, clocking everybody in sight: old lady stretching for the third-in, untouched, brand new, final Maeve Binchy she can't reach—bald retiree in Sears plaid bifocalling the test-drive sample e-readers—bent over rear end in mom jeans perusing the bottom-shelf, half-price calendars—unexpected black woman he tells himself shouldn't be unexpected in a bookstore, affirmative action at state schools having been in place for people of color her age—dyke-or-teenage-boy sneaking a peek at a remaindered *Kama Sutra* (probably teenage boy given that that particular edition is wholly heteronormative)—"Where *is* that antisocial contemptuous bastard?"

Not in Cooking.

"Evolutionary byproduct'll never make full Professor."

Not in Literary Criticism.

"Not at Aylesbury. Not on my watch."

Not in Humor.

"Post-Adlerian my mother's ass." He slows and rubbernecks.

"Father," a small voice asks from below, "can I get this book?"

It's Gayatri.

"Walk and talk with me." He takes but doesn't look at the book, leering down aisles. "What is it?"

"*The Left Hand of Darkness*. It says it won the Hugo *and* the Nebula."

"What'd Mom buy you last week?"

She stops, her hope nose-diving.

"Come on," he asks, backpedalling to her, "what'd she get you?"

Gayatri pointed at copies of it displayed across the way.

"*School Will Be My Making: A Girl's Quest for Know-*

ledge Despite the Always Totally Evil Taliban, Inspired by Real-Life True Events."

She had taken liberties with the title.

"And have you finished reading that one?"

"I'm just really tired of Mom having me read YA narratives about girls from the developing world being denied an education by fundamentalist Muslims. The genre isn't totally helping my view of Islam, which Mom turns around and says is peaceful and loving. That and plus I'm hungry for *other* kinds of stories but I can't even say the word *other* without her getting all honked off."

He finally looks at the cover. It's got an iceberg on it. "This looks dreadful." He hands it to her. "Put it back."

She sighs angrily, more an aggressive grunting display typical of great apes really, and stomps away as his phone chirps three more times.

<@DrDunningKruger Despite a surprisingly mature argument, Tintin vetoes LeGuin. #thisisanoutrage>

The attached pic shows him in profile, cringing at the book in hand. The salt-n-pepper fade he had styled yesterday looks good from the side, but this registers only momentarily. Three-hundred-sixty degrees fail to place Shane.

<@SEbrards tintin? ...???>

<@DrDunningKruger Everybody calls you Tintin. It's the haircut.>

He grabs the back of his head, kneads, feels the tapering of the hair. <@SEbrards name calling? really???>

<@DrDunningKruger You're the one who's been cursing my name up and down the aisles of this typically quiet bookshop.>

Not in Metaphysics.

Not in Self Help.

Not in Popular Psychology.

"Where are you!"

And there he is—with his phone and his stupid near-beard—ducking out of Gardening!

Chirp-chirp-chirp.

<@DrDunningKruger #ihaveabadfeelingaboutthis>

The family's weekly tradition of wandering around Tristram's while their dinner is prepared and cartoned at Imperial Orient next door devolves into an eighties TV cop-drama chase leitmotif, shots alternating between the professorial detective in harried pursuit and the evasive perp casually disappearing behind endcaps. Glimpses of a shoulder, a rumple-socked ankle, a hand in a cuff an inch too long—each vanishing around the next corner. This is Bigfoot looking back as he retreats into the woods, but the forest here is laid out by subject. And like the mystery ape of evolutionary folklore, Shane is somehow able to step into Anthropology and next be seen in Children's Books, drift behind History and reappear in Biography. He can't be cornered. He can't be caught.

A mere tap on Dr. Dunning-Kruger's shoulder springs his sneaker pirouette reflex and he seizes his female mate by her shoulders.

"Where is the bastard! Where is he!"

Dr. Cloirk-Esterday horripilates. "Get the hands of white patriarchy off of me right this instant."

He jolts left, then right, a dog who's lost track of the ball. "Dammit, you just made me lose him!"

"Frantz hasn't been taken. He's right here. Calm yourself, Marcus."

Frantz is with her, clutching a graphic novel. "Dad, the whole store's *looking* at us..."

"No, no, Shane Ebrards," he laments. "Shane Ebrards, that good-for-nothing inconsequential relict, somehow still living in utterly extinct branches of psychology..."

"I just saw Shane on his way out the door," she says. "He's a very pleasant man. Wished us all a nice weekend."

The exit stands empty except for the table of bargain books. But spying out beyond the threshold, at the lot, there, waiting for him, is the idiot in his rink-a-dink Civic. Shane throws an arm out his window and waves, keeps waving until his car toodles on past the store's windowed wall and out of frame.

Dr. Dunning-Kruger grinds his molars in his head, chewing on nothing, staring at the parking lot in sunset.

And Shane Ebrards reappears! He's returned! He drives back the way he came, arm still out, reaching high to wave above the roof! He's honking the horn!

That gloating mole man...

Taking a prideful lap of the lot...

He and his pathetic little chassis go away with absolute cheer, leaving him alone in rage again.

A feminine chuckle. Soon as he looks, Dr. Dunning-Kruger sees the hippy worker woman trying to cover her reaction by suddenly reorganizing whatever's under the counter.

"Alright," Grace says, curving back with Gayatri in tow and that iceberg book she wants. "I'm paying. The Discover card?"

"Sure."

He sets immediately to putting down his final thoughts

on the entire altercation, poking at his phone with tenured authority and sharpened erudition.

<@SEbrards this is the last I will say about this but your inclusive fitness rating of ZERO combined with your kin altruism rating of ZERO...>

TWEET.

<@SEbrards ...put you as an organism in our panmictic population the closest I've ever seen to making a scientific law of Hamiltonian Spite.>

TWEET.

He lets out a great breath, diaphragm unclenching, intercostal muscles relaxing, his lungs expelling air dead with carbon dioxide. A controlled inhale through his clenched nostrils dances fresh oxygen upon his countless alveoli and, already, he feels control waxing strong.

He scrolls up and reads through the exchange again. Halfway down—right when he got called Tintin— when his nemesis interrupts with a new tweet.

<Can't wait to begin new case study tonight: Exacerbation of the Inferiority Complex Via Social Media. Thanks @DrDunningKruger! #inspiration>

"Oh no, you don't!"

He quick brings up his own tweets, starts deleting them, erasing them, undoing them all in a rhythmic tapping on the screen.

"Oh would you stop with the phone already?" It's Grace, bought books bagged in hand. "Come on. Time we picked up dinner and got General Tsou in your stomach."

"Almost done here," he says, staring past his reflection in the phone, tapping, trailing the wife and their offspring out of the bookstore. "Almost done."

JackiePooper

to LovelyLotus   18 June 2011

Hi. I've never talked in your chat room but maybe you've noticed
my name in the sidebar. I know I'm there a lot. Sorry I don't talk.
But listen, I know this is crazy but I had this really intense dream
about you and I'm compelled to share it. It's kind of amazing how
someone I've never talked to could work into my dreams like you
did last night. There is just something otherworldly about you.

I was in Syria. I saw a large Muslim resort complex with very
stereotypical Arab architecture. I climbed the wall to look inside
the courtyard. There's a huge swimming pool shaped like a giant
splat and filled with green water. Swimming in the pool are five or
six huge bears. They stand up to my chest on all fours (them, not
me, ha) and they have big asses, brown hair, and I understand
them to be sacred animals. I decide I want to swim with the bears. I
hope the wall and jump in the water, careful to not disturb any of
the bears. Some Arabs see me and pull out swords and run to the
edge of the pool. I dive to evade them. Suddenly I'm grabbed
around my middle from behind. I think it must be a bear so I
struggle and turn to face my assailant in the water. It isn't a bear.
It's you! I'm pleasantly surprised at this. I ask what the heck you're
doing there and you drag me to the edge of the pool, opposite the
Arabs, and tell me to just follow. We climb out, run, hop the wall
before the Arabs get us. We run into a giant extravagant palace via
a secret door and you lead me down several corridors that are
dimly lit. You stop and tell me to walk down a path and there will
be a secret door into your bedroom. On the left. So you leave and I
do as told and wind up in your bedroom. It's enormous with
intricate gold patterns on the walls and flooring. The ceiling is like
two or three stories up. The only object is the bed, which has a see-
through drape hung over it like a teepee. And laying on the bed

real still but watching me closely is you! I ask how you got there if you'd just left me before but you say it isn't you, just a decoy. The real you enters through the big normal door and you tell me I'll be safe here. Just then your mom walks in talking on an old style portable phone. She tells the person, "Oh so we can call to Minneapolis now? Oh that's great." Then she hangs up and notices me. She's pissed and demands to know who I am and where I came from. You tell her and say I'm a good person but your mother doesn't buy it. She starts attacking you, saying you don't even know what real danger is and that you've led a way too sheltered life. "OR SO YOU THINK" she says. She pushes a button and all the gold walls dissolve to nothing, revealing the harsh desert all around. The night sky is stunning though, real deep blue with giant white stars all over. Your mother says the walls were an illusion all along and anyone could have walked through them to kidnap you. You're pretty upset about that and as an uncomfortable observer to all this I say, "I'm gonna head." You say you're coming with even though your mom forbids it. She says if I take you I'll never be able to do anything ever again. We leave anyway. We go to the bank and I try to take out a loan but they won't let me because your mom told them not to. I get angry and make a scene all "Fuck her! Fuck the establishment!" I was so mad, I'm kind of embarrassed to say, that I stormed out and left you there at the bank.

I got to head to work but I wanted to let you know about it before I left. And sorry for leaving you at the bank like that. Not cool.

Dreams are weird.

Do you get a lot of these from guys? I'll bet you do.

By the by, my name is Neil. What is yours? And what is your home address? And social security number?

\<LovelyLotus\>

After work she got a double-double at the drive thru and drove through the blown blue-dune evening to the house where she was staying, sipping and thinking about the screen names she had come to expect on weeknights. Welcomed in from the snow by Dogberry, she set the mostly empty Minot State Beavers mug in the sink and appeased the Kerry Blue Terrier with a liver snap. Upstairs in her small green room she turned on the space heater and emancipated herself of turtleneck, slacks, socks and cotton underwear. Denuded but for a hair tie, she prepared herself in the shared bathroom with eye shadow, mascara, and sheer lip gloss. Lipstick, because of a comment her father made the first time she'd worn it—the ever-echoing word: *transvestite*—had no place in her palette or on her face. She took her time, didn't feel she had to hurry. There would be gentlemen and fellas and freaks and dudes. There always were, at all times, all through the day, all through the night, every continent checking in.

She watched her reflection while rubbing lotion into the

longness of her, paving routes for the eyes, all subtle slope and wind on grain. Moisturizing hands and the remembered compliments, bestowed by men the world over, thawed each part of her. Capping the lotion, she leaned to the looking glass, pouted and unpouted, made sure she hadn't goofed up her lashes. Pulling hair tie free and snapping it around her wrist, she brought down her barley blonde hair in two clean arcs and returned to her room.

She kissed the tip of her finger repeatedly, deciding what would be most fun to take off. Though her collection recently bloomed, making a spring bouquet of her lingerie drawer, tonight she opted against grape hyacinth, daphne, tulip, and daffodil for a snowdrop lace. Panties first, making sure the tag was right side in, she then furled new stockings up her legs. Bra, which would come off first, went on last. Making sure her toys and baby oil were ready on the bed, she took the phial of lotus essence sitting atop Grandmother's bureau and touched its glass stopper to her skin at the hollow of her neck.

She toed swiftly downstairs to the kitchen while the laptop started up. Returning without dog's notice and a glass of Pinot Grigio, she shut the door and sat in front of the computer. She set the wine beyond the mousepad, next to her lighter and a pack of Virginia Slims. Logging on as Lovely-Lotus, her fingers keyed the password faster than she could think. The webcam awakened atop the screen like a footed eye, its blue LED shining. This moment of stage fright was unpreventable. But as soon as her chatroom and self-view appeared on the cracked screen—the crack etched like staccato lightning in the haste of her move by a great fall—and she was on. Live.

Sure enough, men were waiting. In seconds the number

of users in her room spiked: eighteen, fifty-four, one-seventy-one. And yes, some of her regulars had made it; BobaFettish, Viewmaster, and pastorchuck each welcomed her with animated gifs.

"Hi guys," she said, all dulcet tones. "How are we doing tonight?"

<gr8 now ur here> they typed. <happy monday sexy> <TITS OUT WOMAN> <hru bb>

She loved the absurdity, the range in manners from polite to unabashedly vulgar.

<why the name?> chunkyboner asked.

"Why am I called LovelyLotus?" It was the only question asked more often than *hru bb*. "First of all, I do yoga, and as you surely know, chunkyboner, being a cultivated man with utmost appreciation for the female form, the first and last pose—in yoga—is the lotus position. Secondly," and here she stood for the camera so they could see her panties, "the lotus is a timeless symbol for this place between a woman's legs." She shifted her weight to one leg, her hand flirting with white lace, letting the sight sink in before seating. Her eyes narrowed with feminine bravado. "Third, the lotus flower blooms on top of pond scum. And, having been bequeathed a bucket of duckweed and algae in the not too distant past, I've decided to rise and bloom above it instead of letting it bog me down."

<sexy voice>

"Thank you, ChoadCaptain."

<u got a boyfriend bb> oorealy asked.

"No, love," she said, reaching for a cigarette. "You should read my profile." Before she could light it, the chime she sometimes heard in her other life jingled, signalling a group show. "Well alright, fellas. Why wait? My bra isn't even off and it's time for group."

<brown-chicken-brown-cow...> typed Enkidu76.

"Enki!" He normally appeared later, eleven-thirty her time. "We're going to group."

<Don't mind me. I'll sit outside the gate pouring libations.>

"Alright, love. Okay. Everybody into group!"

Before becoming a haven for hundreds of souls around the world, the small green room, which her girlfriends had previously glorified as a closet, became her hermitage. She brought with her a full length mirror, Grandmother's bureau, and a framed print that went on the wall: a black and white panoramic photo of hoodoos and heaps in the Medora Badlands. So much had gone in a Quonset, the rest to the Easter Seals. The bed and bedding upon it, of course, had to be new. Arvid Benson Furniture, the name known and trusted since 1949, answered that need. Unengaged, she disengaged, keeping work professional, picking up extra yoga classes on Sundays and Wednesdays, restricting contemplation to the midst of these walls. Here she worried the ghost of a mark on her ring finger and smoked her Virginia Slims. Curled near the space heater through autumn and then winter weeks, she remained tethered to the outside world via her laptop.

She came to know the room with the single-pane view of snow intimately. There was a wisp of web in one corner of the ceiling—she let it be—and, more permanently, three gouges that didn't buff out the last time the floor was finished. Who and what had caused the moon-shaped impressions was a mystery, the house being a hundred years old. She spent time guessing, sometimes far past bedtime, *Super Freakonomics* lying open on the new eiderdown comforter. Was it something that happened in a move, the stubborn leg on a plaid couch, the weaker lifter losing grip not once or twice but three times? Maybe it had been a child's room, being the smallest in the house, and one-time practicing ground for stilts, a mere three hops before Mom's warning to take it outside. Or the result of an aerobic tantrum? A larger woman, a New Year's resolution, and, two days in, forfeit punctuated by a throwing down of the dumbbells. Really, she was no more able to conjure the room's prior dwellers than they ever could have envisioned that space becoming something of a broadcast studio for viewers around the world.

Most evenings after work, her officemates having subjected her to another day of sweet but increasingly unnecessary gentleness, she took to the Internet. She consumed blogs, streamed Attenborough documentaries, wandered aimlessly through Wookieepedia. She scoured the *Puffington Host* and *NPR* but tired of news and talk, her belief validated daily that religion and the United States were to blame for most of humanity's current illnesses.

When tired of those distractions, she watched free clips of women. Women disrobing, women pleasuring themselves, women pleasuring other women. Their shapes comforted, their forms a bliss despite her.

An inevitable link—Flash script advertising NUDE LIVE GIRLS with fluid motion loop of a coquette cooing and typing and cooing and typing—led her to the hub of webcam modeling. Other online distractions vanished under season's snow. Here she had her pick of several hundred women, each bedside in next to nothing and happy to perform solo sex acts for tokens, purchased easily by credit card. It was an arcade of lust, where one could pick a model and vie for her attention in a chatroom alongside users from who-knew-where.

The more she lurked in these gullies, the more engrossed she became. Many of the models, she learned, not only possessed super model genes; most were peculiarly Romanian. Sure, down toward the bottom of the directory, unfortunates not attracting many viewers at all squatted, but they were the minority. There thrived a strong middle-stratum of women from Eastern Europe and, though beautiful, worked with the lackadaisical ennui of one stuck in a McJob. They checked the time, yawned against the back of their hands, even argued with each other. Though they claimed to be working from home, she figured out that many of these women worked in something like a puppy mill, four to a room, each with her own mattress and color scheme in her own corner. Probably, no joke, victims of human trafficking. She didn't dwell on this thought long. It ruined the fun.

There were women from all over the world, not just Romania. Not all seemed to loathe doing it. Those receiving the most attention were North Americans, most living in the United States. On Friday nights, some rooms boasted upwards of a thousand users, many tossing tokens like dollar bills at the strip club. Bidding wars erupted. She once witnessed a mousy Californian with massive teardrop breasts and whiskers drawn on her face receive a 900 token tip, one-upped by a 901 token tip, followed by 902 from a third guy.

900 tokens, she researched, equalled about seventy-five dollars. The model got to keep about half of that. She would later see amounts far exceeding that.

Four weeks in, thinking of debt over her broken lease and lingering student loans, as well as the thrill, she decided to don the mantle herself.

She told no one.

Her first week or so cast her as an ADD fembot. She thought, as these were paying customers, she had to honor every request to the best of her ability, hopefully exceeding expectations. She'd always been a good student, applying herself with gusto. And so her beginning resembled amphetamine-crazed games of Simon Says, where there were a dozen Simons and she the only player, scrambling to meet each written request or demand as it appeared: <legs open> <bend over> <lick nipples> <feet up> <spread cheeks> <shoe on head> <fingers in> <Sharpie in pooper> <and so on> <and so forth>.

That frenzy didn't last long. She dawned to the fact that she held more control than anybody else present. While it could be arousing being told what to do, especially when dealing with someone both creative and articulate with a bee runner-up's grasp of spelling, the average horndog's articulations left much to be desired. Her reading comprehension skills were high but most men's mix of illiteracy, text-speak, and/or English as a second, third, or fourth language could rend the chemistry.

27

So she did as she pleased.

She also, having always been a good student, went ahead and did a bit of research on the phenomenon. There were a few decent forums for women in this line of work, message boards where they joked, commiserated, and offered sound advice to each other. Here she found mature perspectives proffering pointers to the naïve beginner:

> <I too have felt the icky creepiness of a silent room and this is precisely the method I invoked: *Fake It Till You Make It*.>

That from Gwenevere, a Canadian model; this from EastCoastBlue, a model with nine years of experience:

> <Regulars? They're gonna get attached. You can't prevent this any more than you can make the rent/mortgage/bills stop coming. When you can't give them what they want—your life, your love, your heart—they will flip the freak out. They'll make a great show of leaving, announce grandiose declarations of undying love as they type off into the sunset. But listen: Every regular you never give a final definitive goodbye to is a guy who may suffer a pang of desire for you somewhere down the line (usually two, three weeks tops, though a stubborn fella might take six months or longer to crack...), at which point he'll return, grovel with apologies, and proceed to dump obscene amounts of tokens on you. Know this. Benefit from it.>

As it went, having done her homework, she came to lay some ground rules:

- She would fulfill commands happily in one-on-one shows and, conversely, follow her own rhythms, remaining open to appetizing suggest-ions, in group shows.
- Though possible to view users' webcams, she would only do so during shows. The endless penis parade between shows, when what stimulated her most was witty repartee, grew tediously gratuitous.
- No acts involving byproducts of digestion or self-mutilation were on the menu.
- No eating or yawning in front of the cam. She found neither all that sexy in this context.
- Details stalkers fish for would remain safely locked away. No matter how trying it might be to maintain vigilance, she sort of had this thing for self-preservation. So, while she would volunteer her geographical Upper Midwest-ernness, she would offer nothing more about her location than that she hailed from the prairies. Her e-mail address, where she'd gone to college, and the holiest of holies—her name were off limits. She also hedged her age by a year and would keep her birthday private. Anonymity was freedom.
- She would never beg for tokens. Other women did this, particularly the puppy millers, and

seeing as this wasn't her day job, she would refrain from it. She would take each man as he came and accept the offering he brought.

♦ With that in mind, every tip would receive a personal thank you, even if, when the chatroom dialogue filled up with 1 token tips, it became a rather silly race to thank each tipper personally. Showing gratitude was something she had been raised to do.

♦ She would proudly call herself a camwhore. That would be her title, the station she held in this endeavor. There was nothing derogatory or denigrating in her use of the term. There was empowerment.

The irony of leading seminars twice a year on e-mail appropriateness, for by day she was a Human Resources Manager in the corporate office of a utilities company, was not lost on her.

There was one anxiety dream, once, and it pertained to work. She and her boss, Mr. Montgomery, a fine upstanding Christian gentleman, sat in his office awaiting Mikhailo, the Ukrainian janitor. Mikhailo's file sat closed before her. A standard termination, which, granted, wasn't normally what one would call fun. The nearly-fired-janitor stepped in shirtless, like the construction worker in the old Diet Agri-Cola commercial. She checked her boss's reaction. "Right, are we ready, Mikhailo?" Receiving a nod, Mr. Montgomery turned to her. "Mikhailo here brought something to my attention earlier this week and, well, I think he can explain this better than I ever could, fine upstanding Christian gentleman that I am." The file in front of her now bore her own name. "I see you on the Internet," Mikhailo said, "doing this." He licked a finger and touched his nipple. "And this." He tore his pants off and bent over spanking himself. "And I think this here," Mr. Montgomery said with Mikhailo's pants flung 'round his neck, "is what I object to most: the *spanking*."

She woke a'sweat.

Later that day, on company time, she scoured her contract for any clause that forbade her from moonlighting *au naturel*. Working HR, she knew labor laws. She knew fireable offenses. And she discovered that she had signed nothing that prevented her from doing as she pleased three nights a week. So she went about her business and, being a stronger sort than most, never suffered another dream about it.

Her body was capable of feats she had yet to comprehend. Yoga had done little to prepare her for this. That she could, for instance, experience a dozen orgasms in a four or five hour span was not only a true miracle of the body, it was a rapturous upswelling of life. There pearled within her an interfolded, lit essence, a spring of renewal. Broken strings set aside, she restrung herself without worry of being ready or fearing the feeling of pleasure, tuning her soul boldly with an ear to sensation. The wife she had so believed in becoming would not become. Here she was, a woman beholden to no one but herself. Here she could try everything she'd wanted to try before without preclusion. The peanut gallery didn't hinder her experimentations. They celebrated her for them, participating from time zones she would only ever visit in voice and image. They called her a goddess and, despite her staunch humanism, she allowed herself brief indulgence in the declaration when it arose.

Occasionally, unavoidably, trolls surfaced. This was the Internet after all, the Wild West all over again. These drifters, for they never lingered long, she ate like air. When a nasty little misogynist shared one of his nasty little judgments for all gathered, she never granted him an emotional response. Instead she would speak a measured, heartfelt wish that, with the hundreds of women working on the site at any given time, he might find one he *really* liked, one to hold dear. When this didn't defuse him, she lit a cigarette, looked into the webcam, and asked, "How would you describe your relationship with your mother?" Off he'd dash, as if she'd guessed his true name, back to the ether.

What she hadn't considered, not for one moment, was the possibility of finding a friend in this hullabaloo. She had regulars. They were good to her, offering up tokens and sticking with her shows until she finished. Most of them had no compunctions about their role, no delusions of grandeur, although a shift never passed without a tongue-in-cheek marriage proposal—which secretly bothered her. These guys tipped heavily on payday and kept on giving through the month. They were her dudes, the old boys who sat at the end of the bar. She paid attention to what they liked and showed them what they wanted to see.

She had no recollection of the first time that Enkidu76 appeared. There was only, after time, the realization that he was ever-present, as constant as the crescents gouged into the floor under her. Each time she signed on, opening the world's curtain on her room, his name eventually appeared, usually half an hour to midnight, and slowly climbed the user list as other guys left. By bedtime Enkidu76 sat right under Lovely-Lotus's name at the top of the room list. He never tipped. He never joined the group shows or requested to go private. He was, in this respect, a cheapskate, a social loafer. But it wasn't possible to get irritated with him, the online equivalent of the guy who sits at the back without paying, because he never made demands, never ruffled feathers, and typed with impeccable spelling and punctuation. He paid attention. And used multi-syllabic words. And made her laugh. He was at times witty, at times silly, always kind. While other guys were heaving indecipherable vulgarities upon her, he undermined them with syntactical pirouettes, had her back when FOX News acolytes slimed their icky trails through the chatroom, typed her praises in Gordon Lightfoot lyrics.

The first wisecrack she could remember was something he said when guys in the room were measuring their dicks by what they'd majored in at college. One guy claimed he was currently in school for homeopathic medicine. Enkidu76 didn't miss a beat:

<You can't get married but they let your kind practice medicine?>

He could in this way cut through the carnival atmospherics and reach her as if on a direct channel. The first time this happened, the moment he became more than a screen-name, when it convinced her that there was another person out there on the other side of this—whatever this was—was when he called her out on her fidgeting. She was a fidgeter. Always had been. It was a habit Grandmother had always teased her about, starting when she was small. It was a need to keep her hands busy rabbeted to the casual urgency of bored anxiousness. Her fidgeting manifested as a genuine talent for being distracted in any given situation and it drew attention. She could remember, for instance, sitting in church next to Grandmother utterly engrossed as she confidentially tore the service's folded over program into tiny pieces in her lap beside her, winking at her, and then realizing, when her own hands had run out of material, that she was imitating her, her own program reduced to confetti in her own lap, and her hands still jittery. Grandmother gave her an unforgettably fay smile at that.

This became a tradition of sorts at Thanksgiving, too, when the uncles would make a show of exaggerated antsiness after her fashion as Dad smirked through the carving of the bird. She didn't like when the uncles chipped in like that, the teasing only really tolerable when coming Grandmother, who always, observing it as part of the annual ritual, came to her defense at the table: "You don't watch that fidgeting, deary-o, and you'll be attracting knuckleheads far worse than these sons of mine."

If Grandmother only knew how very prescient she'd been about the knuckleheads of the world finding her.

Boyfriends and guys who wanted to be boyfriends would pick up on it, of course, but none ever tempered their tauntings with charm beyond little-girling her. That was a fine line for her, a man letting her know his delight in her idiosyncratic restlessness came from a place of affection.

Enkidu76 got it though, nearly replaying from wherever he was out there that early memory of her grandmother in church. This time, feeling alone in the avocado room even

34

though she wasn't, she knew full well that she was ripping up paper into teeny-tiny flecks, a list she'd made of possible chatroom topics while working her day job. But her hands worked off cam, out of voyeur view, down in her lap.

<Fidget, fidget, fidget.> he typed.

Called out, she rolled her eyes and smiled it off. And then she ceased her nervous handiwork, moved her wine glass, took a sip of wine, six times kissed the tip of her finger, rolled her bare shoulders forward and back, realized she was fidgeting more and, holding her fingers still over the keyboard, widened her eyes on the chat dialogue.

<Restrained fidgeting.> he typed.

She bit her lips shut, trying to hide the smile brought from being seen. Regrouping, she shrugged him off with a pout made to look absentminded as she disinterestedly glanced in the direction of the green wall behind the screen where nothing at all happened to be though he wouldn't know it.

<Affected nonchalance.> he typed.

She shook her head, embarrassed now, feeling more exposed by far than she ever had by the near perpetual nudity.

<Absolutely endearing.> he typed.

And with that, something that felt safe—or something close to it—opened between them. He stuck with her, too, with a reliability she did not take for granted. Other guys would leave and return with sordid tales of the sphincters being pounded in other chatrooms but Enkidu76 did not stray.

<I'm monocamous.> is how he explained it.

When she realized that his arrival always made her feel secure, she next realized that, each night, up until he

35

appeared, she felt, perhaps, a bit lost.

Daydreaming at her work desk on, for the first time in some time, something other than grief, he swam up in her consciousness, this person who made her feel seen. She wrote his screenname in her planner as a reminder to check his profile—of course, there was no checking it on her office computer. If the IT guys even caught whiff...

When she stopped by the house before yoga that evening, she found he had indeed created a profile. Scanning it, she mentally knotted all of his details into a macramé likeness. Enkidu76, *Eyes: Brown* and *Hair: Receding*, stood six-feet-two and weighed twelve stone, which, that last fact, told her he must be across the pond before she got to his nationality: *Irish-living-in-England*. Location put him six hours ahead, an early bird, always signing on at what would be half past six AM GMT. Thirty-four and single, a university lecturer, an elderly-cat owner, and bicycle-rider. She could see him in wool cap with shamrock in tweed lapel cycling home through English rain with a bag of litter slung across his handlebar basket. But he had a PhD in Religious Studies? That might explain the reluctance to embark in sexy-sex shows. Perhaps pious study had neutered him. But then, no, because he often paid lyrical compliments to her boobs and butt. In any case, she had hoped for a photo but found only a pic of a clay tablet indented with chicken scratch.

Despite making herself late for class, she Googled the name *Enkidu*, having discerned by his age that the 76 referred to his birth year, and ended up on Wikipedia skimming ancient Mesopotamian mythology. *Enkidu*, according to anyone's mother who'd updated the entry, was a character in the

Epic of Gilgamesh, a wild man civilized by a priestess of Ishtar, whose method of catching him up to speed was a solid week of life-altering sex.

All notions of a stoically celibate religion prof were defenestrated as she shut down Windows and hurried to yoga.

Later that evening, after he signed on, she did a thing she'd not done in this whole format: she sent him a private message. Guys sent them to her all the time, lighting up blinking boxes down the right margin of her screen. She had used it up to this point iron out what a fella expected out of a private show before blowing his tokens on it. But she had not *initiated* a private conversation. Until now.

<How's Gilgamesh doing these days?>

There was an uncomfortably long pause before the reply came: <Yeah, sure, he's grand. Hasn't been online much because he's been off shaking down Utnapishtim for the Plant of Heartbeat.>

This was fun already.

<I may have looked up your screenname in my free time today...> she admitted. <Surprised to find myself directed to Mesopotamian mythology via this mad mad mad mad website.>

<Is this not a modern day iteration of those forgotten temples of Isis?> he typed back. <Those priestesses in that time, anonymous behind a veil, bestowed womanliness upon the men who convened to worship femininity. Seems to me that you are inheritor of an ancient tradition honoring the sacredness of female agency and sexuality the likes of which Western culture has all but blotted from its cultural memory. It's shameful that our ancestors shoved the goddess underground but women such as yourself show that she is still with

us and making a comeback. And thank goodness for it.>

<Never thought of it that way.> she wrote, hiding behind a short response.

After that, after he became a little more real to her, she took him as an ally. Not that she needed help from anybody, she just liked having someone around who shared her sense of humor, with whom she could show the outrageous private messages she received, knowing he would find them just as foolish and disturbing. Being as he appeared every cam-shift it was like having a wingman. He got really good at reading her, too. Seconds after receiving a doozy from another user, he'd type, <Disturbance in the Force?> He could tell from the look in her eyes alone. And she loved that.

The night Dad let her know that Luanne had come by to ask Mom when her daughter would find it in herself to forgive her son so that the yoking union of families who'd long been friends could be salvaged and sealed—as if him hiding the second cell phone wasn't his fault—as if paying another woman's rent in another state wasn't a deal breaker—as if the bank account he secretly opened for the other woman was the sort of thing anyone could understand an engaged man doing—as if his DUI and outpatient "rehab" (it was a class) for getting caught with Tylenol 3es was on her—as if this flibbertigibbet's son was a victim of *her* seemingly limited capacity for almighty forgiveness and forgetfulness—the miasma whipped to such a froth that it could not be entirely masked, no matter her effort.

Retreating to her chatroom in the little green room, the fellas watching around the world hurled mirth and nonsense with the unselfconscious fun that had become so predictable as to be a source of dependability at a time in her life when she needed it. They were also not altogether oblivious to her suffering, though their approach was more spaghetti-thrown-to-the-wall-to-see-if-it-sticks than thoughtful attentiveness.

munkin_about: <y so sad? yr tits r perfect bb>

HowardTheDork: <perfect tits trump sadness. every time.>

BobaFettish: <Cumming in a group show will cure anything, Mistress Lotus.>

Eventually, thankfully, before she had the chance to notice he had arrived, Enkidu76 sent her a private message.

<You can type to me.> he typed. <If it will help.>

Her hands hit the keyboard and didn't lift for ten minutes, tirading faster than thought, the chatroom disregarded, keystrokes pelting and piling words like hail. Nearly every aspect of the day's drama that she'd mulled—and several considerations new to the present moment—issued forth in rant-of-consciousness staccato. Bless the hearts and friends and family in the inner circle, but they were worn out, one and all, from being entangled in it all, their receptivity to the situation flagging—and still she needed to unload. And so she did, here, two thousand words of it to this Irish religion professor. Presumably he was reading it. He didn't interrupt with questions or requests for clarity. He didn't interject with phonetic versions of the little verbal noises people make to indicate when they're listening. She didn't wait for any. She just typed the private message window full, lifting each sentence a line at a time with the enter key. And when she quite abruptly felt she'd finished, she indicated as much and thanked him for listening, even though he'd actually been reading. Presumably.

And when he replied, with a little keyboard icon in the window letting her know he was composing a reaction to what she'd just dumped on him from half a continent and an ocean away, he came out with something that told her she'd been heard.

<I'm not here to tell you how it is or what you need to do or any of that. I will say though that it's okay that this business hurts. And that I admire the way you're bearing it. And that you've got a friend in me.>

She smiled and typed, <Wait, how'd my friend get in you?>

<His methods are most mysterious...>

And that helped. And she was glad she had opened up to this guy.

Not all male fidget-spotters, it seemed, were knuckleheads.

Why hadn't she told her roommates about the new gig? It wasn't because they would disapprove. They wouldn't. It was because she knew them as well as she did. Neither could keep secrets. Their boyfriends were twice as bad. Luckily, Allison slept over at Ian's regularly and Rebecca worked nights as a projectionist. Her time on cam was best left to those evenings when she was the only human in the house, Dogberry being more or less clueless to what she got up to in the little green room. If one came back, which she listened for, she might carry on at a whisper, restraining moans in shows to such a point that users asked if she was in fact mute. One night, thinking herself very much alone, she ducked out for more wine to find Rebecca downstairs fixing a box of macaroni and cheese. Luckily she'd put on a t-shirt, but her answer to the pointed question about what she was doing—downloading music and watching YouTube clips—fell short.

"Why d'you have all that makeup on then?"

"Oh, you know," she lied to this woman she'd known since elementary school, "a lady likes to get gussied up to watch the Youtube from time to time."

That wasn't half as jarring as the Friday in January when, nude but for stockings, the door behind her suddenly opened. Without thinking, she smacked the webcam, sailing the electric eye across the bed, and rose like a Valkyrie against the door.

"Hell-*o-o*?" Ian's dopey face Cheshire-grinned through the crack.

"What the fuck're you doing!" she shouted, shocked that she hadn't heard them, enraged that he'd enter without permission, mortified that he had just caught her *in flagrante dilecto*. Reaching out with her ass against the door she hit the chatroom's Away button to deal with him without the world watching.

He put up no resistance, letting her shut the door, and, quite timidly, said they all just got back and wanted to know if she'd like to come downstairs. There was beer and pizza. "We thought you might be lonely up here in your room," is how he had been instructed to relay it.

She pulled her hair back and dove into clothing. She paced. She fetched the webcam from the bed and re-perched it, returning, flustered, to her chatroom. She scrolled up to skim the boys' reaction to the intrusion. Discussion, not surprisingly, had exploded. Theories abounded.

41

DickKnuckle: <WTF just happened? What that 'mum' I heard?!?!?>

Dystex: <o.O>

joelikestowatch: <yeah said MOM>

Hedgehawg: <what in sam hill just happened?>

qbert42: <he didn't say mom>

oldyBUTThorny: <what the fuck r u doing was the exact quote>

coys1990: <mommy cams so we can have nice things>

joelikestowatch: <her kid walked in on her>

_____: <I have good ear.>

Hedgehawg: <her body's obviously never born children, you twats>

Randumshit: <You have bb, bb??>

qbert42: <husband/bf>

THE_CHAV: <mum!!!!!!!!!!!!!!!!!!!!!!!!1>

She took a Pranayama breath and turned her cam on, returning for a red-faced explanation of what she thought had just happened. Yes, it'd been her roommate's boyfriend, innocently inviting her downstairs because they were worried about her being lonely, spending so much time up in her little green room. Whispering and giggling, her eyes wet, she shot down conspiracy theories, dispelled doubts, and asked the question that need be asked: "Why, oh why, after you lovely gentlemen have funded so many toys and a nice roll-y chair, why didn't I use your hard-earned money to buy a lock for the door?"

Enkidu, who'd lain quiet the entire time, sent a private message: <Are the roommates right, LovelyLotus?>

<about what?> she typed back.

<'Lovely' and 'Lonely' are one letter different.>

She curled her lip. <funny>

<It's okay if you're lonely.>

Irritated by his sudden switch to analysis, she held off answering. It wasn't that he was right. It was that this, wherein Eros liberated her of more than student loans, was meant to be a sanctuary. There were enough hours the rest of the day to be reminded of loneliness.

Having more or less satisfied the room with her account, she expressed the need to sign off, to join the fun downstairs and make sure all was copasetic in the house. But just as she was hushing her goodbyes she noticed Enkidu had a small webcam icon next to his name.

<wait your cam's on?> she typed to him. <can I see real quick? please?>

<Of course.>

She clicked, the screen hiccupping a new window, and, lo and behold, on the other side of the crack in her screen, there he was. Pink-cheeked with a high forehead—and fully clothed—he sat as if awaiting judgment. Her skin flushed anew. A man unlike the others, a practitioner of daily hygiene, a friend of the comb, the wearer of zippy-uppy cardigans. His study, for that's what the room must be, had bookcases and, to his left, a leaded window dark with pre-dawn and a large bottle garden on its sill.

"You're so freaking *cute!*" She slapped hand over mouth, checking her volume.

He sat back, hamming surprise.

"And your cardigan is awakening all of my earliest sexual desires for Mister Rogers."

At that he shrugged, his mic off. She wanted to hear that accent, the one voted Sexiest Accent In The World by every magazine she'd ever pretended to read at the salon.

"Did you guys have Mister Rogers? Prolly not. It's a good thing; he was old-man-hot."

He lit and pointed both fingers at his cam. She did the same to hers. And it was the strangest, gentlest feeling of actually being right there with him. She didn't want to go downstairs. He graciously accepted her leave though, and blew kisses, wishing her luck, promising he'd see her soon.

Downstairs, over Nite Train Pizza and Wood Chipper IPA, she discovered everything with the roommates was cool, that Ian was already a tad drunk and hadn't seen much of anything. She got a big laugh when revealing her weekend plans involved waking up early to drive out to Lowes to buy a lock for the bedroom door.

Several months after the fact, her people, the people she knew and dealt with daily in what they would call her real life, her extended family and the ladies at the bank and acquaintances and even some friends, were still treating her with kid gloves. Worried greetings. Angling eyebrows and clutched lips. Collective, relentless concern. It was all a bit much by the second week of February, as if the approach of Valentine's Day crescendoed their sense of tragedy in their interactions with her. Having graciously accepted everyone's sympathies, repeatedly, for the last four months, she battled their excessive consideration for her heart silently, with the smile they wanted to see.

Annoying as that was, they had nothing on the hopeful, scheming guys she'd known for years. When her situation first changed, in those early, bleary weeks no fewer than three men, two old friends and a colleague, had each, of his own accord, put himself at significant emotional risk by revealing to her and her alone his eternal and heretofore utterly unhinted-at undying love. From then, she confined them to voicemail. But consumerized holidays did such foolish things to foolish hearts. Though the prairie lay helplessly frozen, the forces of advertising and unrequited courtship defrosted and then cooked one fellow's common sense.

The Friday before the 14th a dozen roses awaited her at work, much to the cooing delight of every married woman in the office. The guy-in-Marketing's hastily-deposited dinner-proposing card was a bit too distant, Marketing being just down the hall. Far sweeter, but no more effective, would have been to present the red roses in person, to ask her to dinner with his voice, and accept her firm decline. Was she so utterly unapproachable? Granted, she'd shot men down enough to gain a reputation for it. But this guy's reluctance rang of fear. He'd likely heard what she did to her ex's paint-job with the diamond he bought her.

She recycled the card and traipsed her way all through the office, avoiding Marketing, bestowing roses upon the first twelve colleagues she encountered. "Someone didn't get the memo," she said. "If you bring Valentines, there'd better be enough for everybody."

The last rose she gave to her boss. Mr. Montgomery took it and along with it the opportunity to vouch for his protégé. "Joseph there really is a fine young man. Done wonders not just over in Marketing but at our church, too. Fine young man to be sure. The," he fwapped the rose against his chin, "*loyal* sort." She cringed behind her face. He smiled in his fatherly way and gavelled the rose twice more on his desk and, being stuck by a thorn, let her go.

She left work early, looking forward to nothing other than a weekend of getting off for her desperate, lonely, horny men. The roommates were heading with their boyfriends to the lake for a romantic weekend. They'd invited her, to be nice, and she'd happily declined. This weekend would be a full cleanse, a chance for her to sweat free every atom of frustration.

She stopped at the post office on the way home to collect whatever the week had brought. Soon as she stepped in from the cold, P.O. box key ready, the lady who was probably installed when the building was built greeted her with that same worried expression she got everywhere else. "How're you today, hon?" Betty Lou waited for her to respond, which she did with *the smile.* "There's a package for you that just wouldn't fit in your box there." The old lady, who she may have half-regrettably opened up to in a moment of vulnerability four months ago, toddled away and soon returned to the counter with an Amazon package. She couldn't seem to recall ordering anything. But then, as, "Done some Internet shopping?" came out of Betty Lou's mouth, she remembered, oh yes, of course, the wish list she'd set up and linked to her profile the night she became a camwhore. "Something you couldn't find around here then?"

Heart pumping with intrigue—for there was no telling if it was the 10-Function Clitoral Hummer or the voice-activated R2-D2—she told Betty Lou it must be some bath salts she'd ordered. "Well who doesn't love a good long soak?" Betty Lou said, handing it over.

She thanked her and carried the featherlight package outdoors, forgetting to check the P.O. box altogether. In the safety of her Subaru, she tore her gloves off and keyed the tape down the seam. Inside were cellophane pockets of air and, hallelujah, just what she'd always wanted: a belt buckle in the shape of a blooming lotus. A slip of paper let her know who'd sent it:

> *Valentine's Day abbreviates to VD. Coincidental? I think not. What a racket of a holiday.*
> *Down with this sort of thing,*
> *Enkidu76 xox*

She rushed through new snow to the house to thank him. No, he wouldn't be online for hours but then perhaps he would surprise her. It was the weekend. He might stay up late.

First thing she did was set the lovely lotus belt buckle, a talisman of her growing powers, next to her phial of lotus essence on Grandmother's bureau. Then she showered, prepared and perfumed herself, having anticipated all day the new pomegranate bra and panties. It was while putting on the bra, first hooking in front and turning it around, that she wished she just had Enkidu's e-mail address—this business of having to wait until he was online to say thank you elevated her restlessness.

She eased into the evening, doing two group shows and a private for a footy named DeanLearner before taking a break to feed the dog and have something herself. She ate a small plate of cheese and whole grain crackers with Pinot Grigio in her underwear at the bar between kitchen and dining room. It felt nice, not having to worry about anyone coming back to the house. Surrounded by stuff that wasn't hers, dear dog included, she might as well have been house-sitting. Before dwelling too long on the looming uncertainties dominating everything down to her living situation, she dashed upstairs to see if he was online.

He wasn't.

Then, right on cue at half past eleven, something pinged at the window. The actual window. Entrenched in a show, her hands upon and fingers within, the noise barely registered. She'd been at it twenty-two minutes, coming once already about fifteen minutes in, but only just. A larger release lurked behind it, her focus fixed on coaxing it free. Even the chatroom hardly existed as she swirled closer and closer, answering the slow build sensation by sensation.

But for the pinging.

The incessant-pinging-that-had-absolutely-nothing-at-all-what-so-ever-to-do-with-this-or-anything-else, tapping more than a dozen times before it broke through, suddenly reiterated by Dogberry's yapping, and so about to come, so very close, the incessant unexpected at her window pulled her away, away so briskly.

She stopped.

She turned to the window shade, poisoned by interruption.

She listened.

<wha happen?> the silent voices asked. <u were so close o.O>

She apologized to the world, masking her ire as best she could, and thanked them and told them she'd return after a brief message from her sponsors. Hitting the away button, she crawled back into her underwear, found a shirt.

Fear struck.

Of the hypothetical froggies who could'a come a'courtin, which one was under her window? Or had something really scary happened, something involving her identity and the men who paid to watch her?

One of Dad's .22s was slid under the bed but she didn't retrieve it. She grabbed her cell phone and crept out of her room and into Allison's, Dogberry's downstairs growls sounding louder. Careful not to slip on clothes that hadn't made it into her roommate's weekend bags, she peered just over the lip of the windowsill into the yard, which glowed cornflower blue.

Standing at the base of a fresh-tromped, lopsided heart in the snow, pitching coins like a handler plying a two story seal with fish, swayed the man she would have married. His truck, lights on, angled in the driveway, spoke to his sobriety level. Seventeen below and he'd come prepared: a bottle of champagne on ice by his boots and next to it his change jar. This was precisely how he'd won her in college, over six years ago now, when she lived in a dorm and fell for mellifluous gestures from handsome, half-cocked Romeos.

She dialled his brother, who needlessly apologized and promised he'd be right over to get rid of him. While she waited, she snuck back to her room to check the laptop.

No Enkidu.

She wondered through the pinging pennies where the Irishman might be. And she wished he was the one in the yard. And when she heard talk outside, she stood and lifted the shade. Jake recoiled at the sight of her, his arms open, scattering change. She didn't want to see him any, but she wanted him to see her watch his brother take him away, scratching a jagged line through his snow-trod heart. She

49

knew she must show neither the worry she felt nor the anger. When his brother got him to the base of the driveway, she lowered the shade and returned to her chatroom.

He wasn't there.

He hadn't shown by a quarter to four when she broke one of her tenets by yawning on cam. She half-heartedly checked her balance before signing off and was surprised to see she'd just made seven hundred dollars. Nice after all the hoopla but she went to sleep anxious, wondering what kept Enkidu from showing up. It was the first time he hadn't been there.

She ignored Dogberry's whimpers long as she could, waking with sex hair and a severe reluctance to let the cold touch her when letting him out. But she unfolded and put on a sweat-shirt and appeased the canine with her door-opening and bowl-filling skills. She checked the time—almost noon, meaning the dog had let her sleep—and found voicemail messages waiting from roommates and sisters fast with questions, having heard something from somebody sometime in the past twelve hours about whatever it was that'd happened in the yard below her window. She should have expected the news would be of the breaking variety. The roommates urged her to come to the lake. Her sisters wanted to meet up for coffee.

Coffee she could do.

Wearing her new belt buckle, she met them at Moxie Java at two. And she should have foreseen it, it making perfect sense: they brought Mom. As the eldest, she was used to her moves being monitored by her sisters, unspoken expectations governing her place in the family. That said, their support had been and continued to be great. Her women wasted no time, asking their needle-nose questions over their double-doubles and scrutinizing her answers. She told them precisely what happened and what she did to take care of it. By now it seemed nothing more than annoying nonsense. She assured them that she wasn't in any way thinking of taking him back. Her apathy on the topic seemed to convince them more than anything.

Worries at rest, they went into their Valentine's Day plans, where they were going to dinner, what chick flicks they'd conned their boyfriends into seeing. Mom absorbed the brunt of this talk as if it were something she needed to protect her from.

She imagined, sitting in the booth with her sisters chattering, touching the lotus on her belt, Enkidu's study. And what it'd be like to be there with him. A fire burning orange in the fireplace and high-backed chairs set arm to arm with tasselled, velvet ottomans under their feet. Dozing hounds. And pipes for each of them. Bubble pipes. And bookshelves filled with august volumes and curiosities—petrified wood and tin biplanes and monkey paws—bookshelves up in the mezzanine, accessible by a wrought iron spiral staircase in one corner and descendable by a fire pole in the other. And a stained glass ceiling, a mandala of a blossoming lotus. Tapestries on the walls depicting her frozen prairie and his native Ireland and chatrooms and Gordon Lightfoot and her sisters snapped her out of it, having asked for the second or perhaps third time if she'd received any valentines.

"No, none," she said, covering the belt buckle and withholding mention of Friday's twelve roses. "But I should go. Hot yoga."

She wanted to get to the house. Mom stopped her with something Dad sent along, producing from her purse a red envelope. She opened it there to quench her sisters' curiosity. The card depicted a chimpanzee dressed as a princess and contained a check, which she tried to give back, promising she was financially secure. But Mom said he'd anticipated her rebuttal and insisted that she take the money. So she took it and hugged her sisters and kissed her mother and called Dad to thank him while her car warmed up in the parking lot.

At the house she went through her routine, her preparations now ritualistic. By four she entered the arena, much to the delight of the lonely, sad men spending the holiday weekend alone. In some parts of the world it was already the 14th and countless hearts and cocks begged attention. She paced herself with shows, held herself back in anticipation of his arrival. And like a hierodule of old, she tended to these men. Part camwhore, part nurse, part social worker.

ZiggyLee1000 of Shreveport, Louisiana, wanted her to watch him jam on Hendrix's "Red House." So she did, opening his cam and letting him fumble with his Stratocaster. He looked to be in his sixties. Pills may have been to blame for that. He also appeared to decorate with flypaper. She paid attention for a couple minutes. He was still on "Red House" two and a half hours later when she checked on him.

oldyBUTThorny, of Australian extraction, just wanted to see her spank herself rosy, which she did until he ran out of tokens three and a half minutes later.

Viewmaster, one of her faithful gents, didn't need to specify what he wanted. She gave him the same old DP show he always requested but hadn't yet realized was almost entirely simulated, cam angled off her face so her eyes were free to roll.

BobaFettish, when he found out she had a vintage *Millennium Falcon* she'd saved up for as a girl, bought a private show that went on for twenty-eight minutes, long enough for her to come. It all started out with giggles and pinup poses, spaceship in her arms, atop her knees, between her legs, but turned kinky once she brought out the dildo with a suction cup base that stuck to anything.

pastorchuck wanted her to put some jeans on and zip and unzip the zipper. Over and over. While moaning his name. She learned the friction from excessive zipping makes metal zippers too hot to touch. Luckily he got off fast.

TonyH begged a tentacle fantasy show, typing gobbledygook about his specific desire for a cephalopod to have its way with a woman. She treated it without issue like any other show, playing along, making a mental note to consider writing a memoir. Not only was she astounded at the diversity in people's fantasies, she also wondered at how her own weirdness scale had shifted in the wake of this months-long experience.

And no, Enkidu76 did not show.

She went to bed sore and wondering. Did he meet someone? She blamed her eyes going the least bit green on the color of the walls, not being the type to get jealous over a guy she didn't know. But was it worse? Had a lorry hit him while riding home through the rain, kitty litter salting the cobbles? Was he in the hospital, arms and legs in traction, tended by nurses oblivious to his spectacular wit? Or was this the one weekend every three months he spent, supervised, visiting his children, his baby mama having painted him a perverse deviant in court hearings due to his habit of befriending and deserting camgirls? Far likelier, he was seduced by a student, Cornish or Welsh, surprising him in his office wearing a nun's habit, nothing under it—he was an Irish Religious Studies professor after all. But then she couldn't be sure even of that.

She didn't even know his name.

She spent the next day entirely with the lonely hearts club, answering all offers to join people in the real world with texts of polite decline. Demand for her attention online had never been so high, the number of users in her chatroom breaching eight hundred. As light lapsed and afternoon's night rose, she opened and shined, a noctilucent lotus, softly alive. She was online so long that Australians went to bed, slept through the night, and found her there when they woke in the morning. She held true to her decision before this marathon that she wouldn't worry where Enkidu had gone. Theirs, she rationalized, was a silly chemistry, unnatural, him halfway around the world, a stranger really. Free of that ongoing conundrum, of thought, she committed to the moment. There were peaks. There were troughs. Mixed with the exaltation was an agony, a pain in bliss. Reason slipped into liminality. She felt marvellously uncaged. Her body's limits surpassed, she caressed and rubbed her arms, her breasts, thighs, between bouts and fiddled about a bit with a carefully chosen cucumber, whose cooling skin felt nice once the toys made her ache. And she gave of herself, anew, to the multitude of strangers, to whosoever came along with whatever he had.

She laid herself out aglow, kissing musk from her fingers

after an hour-long show, when he signed on.

"Enkidu!" She sat up, eyes wild, and lifted the screen. "Where on earth have you been!"

<Heh, sorry about that...> he typed.

"Where were you?"

The chime for a private show request rang, a new window asking to accept or deny it. Impatient, she clicked it aside and watched for him to answer, to type something, anything. Other guys blathered text in the room as usual but she ignored them.

Then, finally, <Aren't you going to accept my private show?>

She looked over at the show request again. It was him.

"Oh, sorry, sorry." Her breathing anxious, her lower lip bitten, she scrolled to his request but refrained from clicking. "Wait, what are we going to do? We haven't even talked about what you'd like, my darling distant man."

<It's okay. Please accept it.>

She did.

The chatroom blinked away, leaving only his name. His webcam on, his image appeared before her.

There he sat, looking thin, looking bloodless. He obviously hadn't slept, eyes gray. The look of him broke her open.

"Hiya there," he spoke into his microphone. His brogue, masked slightly by English pronunciation, rang like tarnished silver.

"What's the matter?" she asked, kissing her forefinger.

"Ah, come here till I tell ya."

"OMG, your accent..."

"I'm meant to go lecture postgrads on shoddy Sanskrit translations but..."

"What happened?"

He fiddled with something out of view, something on his desk. "I had to put my cat down."

"Aw!" She lit and wept at once and saw the life it brought him. "You sweet man, I'm so, so sorry!"

"No, no. It's okay." He winced in his cardigan. "She was eighteen."

"Ohh."

"Yeah, she suffered some manner of infarction."

"Oh no." She covered her mouth, taking his pain.

"Same way my Nan went." He lifted his eyebrows emptily. "Just had to see to that."

Her eyes glittered there in the self-view like wet flowers. "What was her name?"

"My grandmother or my cat?"

"Sorry, I meant your cat." She pulled the hair tie out and ran her fingers under her hair.

"Mrs. Slocombe." He lifted a disorganized pile of photos into view, showed her one. A cream coloured feline sat in a window seat peering through leaded glass.

"I'm so sorry I never met her. But wait! I need to show you something." She leaned far off the bed, nearly sending laptop to floor, to retrieve the belt buckle from the bureau. "I was *so* excited to get *this*. It came in the middle of a crummy day and—"

"Crummy day?" His concern shifted.

"Oh it's fine now," she said. "It is. I just love this buckle and I've wanted to say thank you since Friday. So. Thank you."

"Well, but, you could do with a numinous charm." He set the photos aside.

She couldn't help from shining for this man. "Would you please give me your e-mail so this won't ever happen again?" Grabbing for and clicking a ballpoint, she stopped before finding paper. "But we're wasting your tokens!"

"No we're not." He straightened in his chair.

"Oh really?" She set the pen and gift aside.

"It's been on my mind—our friendship—if that's what this is—and," he hesitated, "I need to ask something of you. A favour."

"Before you say anything at all," she said, resting forward on her elbows, "you need to know I'm an extreme introvert who's learned extravert skills."

"Sure, I know that."

She fought the urge to fidget. "Try not to startle me."

"Right. You're not like the other women here." He paced each sentence laconically. "That's to say, as it were, this isn't your livelihood, your month's rent. The thing about it is this: you won't need this forever. Or even probably that much longer."

"Okay?"

"And that's not a judgement! I don't think this is 'beneath' you. I've not got the white knight syndrome afflicting some of these gobshites. My afflictions are loneliness and grief for a dead cat."

"Okay."

"I've grown fond. Of you. And I'm very aware of the fact that when you go, you'll be gone." He unconsciously patted his heart through cable knit wool. "You've become a constellation in my sky. That's what I mean. Sounds rehearsed, I know. And it is."

And here she anticipated the dread of being asked for

more than she could give, of coming to a bittersweet event horizon with someone whose presence she cherished. While he'd just gone further and gentler in expressing his fondness than any other man in the last long while, she feared, in this moment, what he might say next.

"So, if I might make one request of the Great and Powerful LovelyLotus," he went on, lifting his head, "would you, and could you, please, give fair warning before you retire? So I can prepare?"

Breathing, tingling with relief and conviction that somehow she really did know this person somewhere over the Internet, she lowered her lips and lifted her breasts for him. "*Most* assuredly, good sir. Most assuredly," she soothed, knowing just how to wash him clean of hurt and worry. "But first, tell me, what's your name?"

"Ah sure look." He squinted into his webcam, so that he seemed to be looking directly into her, wholly present beyond the branching crack in her laptop's screen. "Couldn't I be asking the same of you?"

Taffy Ben Hassan

to LovelyLotus   15 February 2010

Hi luv,

I just enjoyed the most delightful dream about you and simply have to share before I forget it. I was with a team of scientists digging at an ancient site in Palestine. We archaeologists are excavating a site containing the remnants of a siege during the crusades. The other archaeologists have ignored a corner of the ramparts, focusing instead on the mass graves. So I start digging at the corner, and I proceed to make the find of the century: a computer from the middle ages with a database cataloging the name, vital stats, and likeness of every one of the six hundred some crusaders who attacked there. No one knew they had electronic devices back then, let alone computers. I'm over the moon. I run to show the others but they are too busy. I sit on a stone platform in the ruins and contemplate my find. Harrison Ford, the world's foremost archaeologist, walks through the barren courtyard. I try to tell him but he's on his way to the toilet. But then the younger sexy bird archaeologist—played by you—comes up and says hello. I lead you to the computer and you're all excited. We dig a tad further to find a case full of ancient cartridges that have movies on them. Everything from Empire Strikes Back to Spongebob. I resolve someone, probably me, took these movies and the computer back in time to be a king among those Dark Ages technologically-primordial continental Europeans. I admire my tact at taking Empire back but leaving the newer episodes behind so I could hype up how great they are to people who will never live to see them and be disappointed. You're so impressed you pull me into the hole we dug and we pretty much made love right there. What a treat! xx

--

On Questalot? Check out Taffy Ben Hassan's Serpenporium
Tell them Taffy sent you for a complimentary potion!

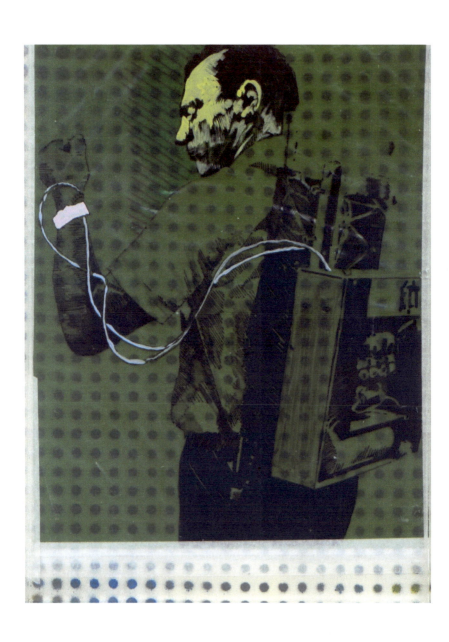

The Pixelated Paladin

The almost real sun burned bright from the monitor, setting ten times faster than the real one. Its heatless, coded beams flared the autumnal leaves of the maple tree his character stood beneath and fell into eclipse behind the five-spire basalt fortress on yonder plateau. Seen from an over-the-shoulder perspective, the Nordic paladin, donning white crystal armor bedazzled with glinting golden rivets, idled with an occasional programmed turn of his helmeted head. Jean-Luc, who customized this character down to power bonuses and width of eyebrows, shared no physical resemblance to him save for being of distinctly Vikingly, as in Norwegian, stock. Whereas HoNoR_BlAdE91 (the username HoNoR_BlAdE was already taken) looked to be forty with a bodybuilder's physique, Jean-Luc was nineteen with receding acne and a curvature accentuated by the tight XL shirts he wore. Sitting before his desktop computer, he idled in his own way, impatiently taking gulps from a two liter of Diet Mountain Dew. He'd just talked to his Dad on the phone so the wait was increasingly irritating.

Finally a figure approached, ambling up the hillside, obscured by metronomically swaying prairie grasses. When the other crested, Jean-Luc stuck out his jaw. Standing before him was a spritely, grin-lucky Garden Elf, waist-high with green hair tufting out of a brown Robin Hood cap. A leather Peter Pan leotard left nothing to the imagination. His father, a financial advisor who told people how to invest their money, had customized a character wearing booties with bells on the ends of their curled points.

<Jean-Luc?> asked a chat prompt from Jean-LucsDad.

"Dad, talk into your mic like we talked about," he said into his headset. He'd specifically told him to not pick any of the elves for his race because of about a thousand reasons.

"Come in, Jean-Luc, can you hear me?"

"Dad."

"They don't have apostrophes for the login name."

"Look, it's okay," he said. "But I told you not to be an Elf and you picked the worst kind!"

"Sorry," he said. "He just looked funny so I picked him."

"What class did you pick?" Jean-Luc took another swig of pop. "Tell me you're at least some kinda Mage."

"I picked the Courtier."

Jean-Luc groaned. There were no rules against playing as a Garden Elf or as a Courtier, for each had its niche advantages, but those who didn't know better should not have been allowed to pick a Garden Elf Courtier. It was doubtful that any player had ever picked that combination in Questalot's history. And rules being rules, new users were allowed one character in their first two weeks of play. An appeal to the mods to change it was technically possible, but matters of policy were often carried out to the letter. And so they were stuck with both the Garden Elf Courtier and his embarrassing user name.

"Come on," he grumbled. "Let's get ya set up."

He handed over a mahogany bow and a quiver of pearlescent arrows he had gone to the trouble of dipping in a flaming curare obtained personally from the Frog Queen. It took a foolish amount of time to teach Dad how to equip them, but when he had it Jean-Luc walked him down the hill and talked him through target practice on the maple tree. The first ten arrows—he counted—were all air-balls. None flew anywhere near the trunk. Worried that he was wasting the pricey arrows, Jean-Luc cursed himself for not bringing along standard iron ones, which came a dozen for one piece of gold. Once the trunk met three arrows, Jean-Luc decked his father out against class and build in heavy armor. Elves, the physically weakest of the races, had Agility bonuses for wearing light armor and penalties for heavy. All the same, he'd bought his dad a suit of peach-colored Dungeness armor, comprising of cuirass, helmet, gauntlets, greaves, and boots, and even enchanted each piece with shielding magic for added protection. Equipping it, the avatar looked stupid, with his idiot grin and huge eyes shining out from the crab shell helmet. He may not be able to fire arrows in quick succession but at least he'd be protected.

"Are we going to attack the castle?" Dad asked, indicating the black tower in the distance.

"Are you kidding? That's a Goblin stronghold–you'd last five seconds in there if that."

"Oh, are Goblins tough?"

"Very. We're gonna start you out with something hard

but not that hard."

He took his father in the opposite direction, over the hills and into the thicketed Forest of Wyrral. The idea was to earn Dad bookoo experience points and level him up quickly so he would fend better on his own. Finding a tough monster would do. There were no glades for safely camping in these woods but anti-social players seemed to dwell there nevertheless, Godless necromancers and vagabond treasure looters preferring its darkness to the open highway. Luckily for his Dad, Jean-Luc's character wore a peacock plumed enchanted helmet that could detect life nearly two hundred feet away, souls showing up with a hazy blue glow long before he could really see them.

"Cool graphics!"

"Yeah."

"Remember when we used to play D&D on the old Intellivision? When you were little?"

"Sure."

"They sure have come a long ways..."

The sound of thirty dogs bayed and it appeared, fading in amid bending ferns, a Level 20 Questing Beast. It was a child's nightmare amalgamation, the head of an anaconda mounted on a leopard's middle, with stag's hooves and lion thighs and tail. It unhinged its jaw and unleashed its horrible canine chorus again. Discounting neck and tail, the monster was as big as a Datsun.

Jean-Luc attacked, casting fire on his Vorpal Sword and hacking at it with mouse clicks. Dad was to stay behind a tree but, of course, wandered into the open, letting fly arrows without aim.

"One hit from this thing'll wipe you out, Dad!"

"I can't seem to... Wait, how do I—"

"Get back!"

He ran between the beast and his gnomish father, taking the full force of a bite that sank his health bar. Gulping poultices with the P key, he kept the index finger slashing and, with great concentration and properly timed right click shield blocks, whittled the monster's health bar to a mere sliver of red. Calling his Dad into the open, he circled the monster.

"You've got to shoot it. Shoot it now!" If he gave it one more hit their purpose for the fight would be lost. Dad let loose an arrow. It went straight up. "Aim at the big monster!" Another zipped wide.

"I think my aiming thing is broken..."

The creature slammed the paladin so hard he lay stunned on the forest floor. Unable to move for ten seconds, he screamed into his headset. "Point your mouse at it and click!"

He watched, unable to help, as his dad let a flaming arrow rip, the game slowing for effect, a definite kill shot. The shaft sank into the Questing Beast, setting its hide ablaze. With prerecorded cry and animated agony, the sprite faded away, replaced by the number 20,000.

"Grab that, Dad."

"What is it?"

"The XP you just won for killing a Level 20 Questing Beast."

His father, the whelp, toddled to the number and claimed it.

"It's saying I 'leveled up?'"

"Yeah, I'll talk you through it. But listen, what we just did, killing that monster, we're gonna do that over and over."

65

"All night tonight?"

"We're gonna level you to the baddest Garden Elf anybody ever saw."

For the next fortnight they, along with tens of thousands of otherwise powerless middle class Americans, embodied the hero archetype and enacted the mono-myth from the safety of rolling chairs. They leveled Jean-LucsDad every evening for a week before he was ready for any kind of adventuring. Jean-Luc would slog up to his dorm room after dinner in the dining hall and sign on to find Dad waiting for him under the same tree. It was a tough grind, the toughest in Jean-Luc's memory—and he'd mastered many an MMORPG in his day. Dad had put every starting perk and bonus towards Charisma and Mercantilism in a game played more for its monster-slaying aspect than its economics. His hit points were half what most characters started out with, galvanizing Jean-Luc's duty to protect and teach him. His daily Latin homework may have taken a slight slide, his Intro to Pre-history readings gone unread, but this was his father he'd brought into this dangerous world. He felt responsible for him. Jean-Luc's sister took Mom. He took Dad.

Soon they were hunting Bandersnatch and Giant Vermicious Knids. Jean-Luc played the tank, battering foes with might, while Dad picked them off at a distance with bow and arrow. They sieged Kobold crypts and looted Wight barrows, Dad's misplaced merchant skills actually counting for something when they sold the booty in the nearest towns. Other players would snicker into their headsets, make their avatars bite their thumbs at the duo, the crystal-armored paladin and his pantywaist sidekick with the pointy nose and clunky Dungeness armor. Oh, but they rolleth in gold.

"What are these guilds people talk about?" his dad asked one night, skipping along at his side as they left a merchant.

"Drama, Dad," he said between bites of nachos he'd nuked in his dorm room microwave. "Drama and a lot of politics."

Jean-Luc didn't shun the social aspect of Questalot so much as he cultivated himself a lone do-gooder. There were a few players he'd seen around, fighting the odd mission together. Guys like gatewaytohell and TheHedgehawg and LeeroyJenkins. But the guilds—he'd never bothered with the guilds.

"Are they like clubs?"

"Clubs of all the geekiest geeks you went to high school with, yeah."

He explained in brief the guild in concept (unionized players sharing their own uniquely designed meeting hall and competing with other guilds for gold, glory, and prestige) and reality (cliquish fraternization with plenty of in-fighting, backstabbing, and competition amongst the guys for the attentions of the sole token female member).

"I was in a frat in college," Dad said for the umpteenth time. "Sigma Phi Epsilon."

"A lifetime supply of nachos couldn't get me to join one of those," Jean-Luc said, crunching into a corn chip laden in melted processed cheese product.

❖

By the time midterms came around, Jean-Luc's academic focus had sagged. Knowing this, he drove himself to study, cutting back to a mere three hours of Questalot a night. By now, Dad's stats were good enough that he could fare alright on his own. Marauding rogues were always a risk no matter your level. Sooner or later the old man had to venture out into the wondrous wide world on his own.

The first time he left his father alone, he did so with the same advice Dad gave each time he dropped Jean-Luc off at the arcade as a kid. "Have a spider's wit about you," Jean-Luc said. "Always be aware of who's on your web at all times."

They were standing halfway across the broad stone bridge to Dragon Jaw, the game's capital city, so named because its fortressed spires looked like teeth rising from a reptilian jawbone. The programmed wind whirled their capes and Dad made his character dance a three step jig by way of farewell.

"Good luck with the Latin test tomorrow."

"Look out for pickpockets," he called, not needing to call, his dad's voice right there in his earpiece. He watched Dad cross the bridge and let a lizard-mounted Orc pass, and waited until he disappeared behind the massive oaken doors to the city before signing off to cram.

The next time Jean-Luc logged in, Dad, hopping boot to boot under their tree, was not alone. A sylphish, near-nude Sand Elf towered over Jean-LucsDad, two heads taller than the top of his conical helmet. She had a Saharan lankiness, her complexion indigo with Farah hair flowing in violet hues. Copper ringlets decorated her arms. She wore thigh-high camel-foot boots, a black mamba thong, and a seam-teasing tortoiseshell halter. The scorpion tail staff she carried gave away her class: a Red Mage, placing her on the vengeful side of sorcery. Not as bad as, say, a Necromancer, but on the malevolent end of the spectrum all the same. Not the kind of folk virtue-loving Paladins caroused with. Her name floated over her head in lavender script: PurpleTia

"Jean-Luc, I want you to meet my new friend, Tia," Dad said, emphasis on friend. "Tia, this is my son, Jean-Luc."

<hey> she typed.

"Hey," he said, drawing up her personal profile.

"How was your test today?"

"Fine."

> *Name: Tia*
> *Sex: Female*
> *Age: 29*
> *Location: Boring, OR*
> *About Me: Want to know more about me? Be careful what you wish for.. I bite. ;) Has to be a brain behind the face please. No smartasses need apply here.*

The thumbnail photo portrayed a headshot of a woman, neither attractive nor ugly, whose stringy brown hair hung over her eyes. The use of such an extreme close up gave away the attempt to hide massive bodyweight. If the person behind this avatar was in fact "Tia," she was definitely obese.

Dad shared, a little too eagerly, the story of how they met the night before at a tavern in Dragon Jaw.

<The Salacious Krumm> she added.

"Yeah, that's right. That's the name of the tavern."

Jean-Luc knew of it, passing by on his trips into the city to barter, never bothering with its offerings. They had card tables where you could lose heaps of gold, a small ring where you could box other players in unarmed combat with the crowd betting, and special rooms upstairs where you could engage in in-game prostitution. The Egyptian mascara on this player's cartoon princess eyes made him hope to Dawkins they hadn't met under those auspices.

"So this Witchfinder—that's what he called himself—was boasting real loud and threatening Tia here, because apparently that's what he does, he hunts down witches for a living—well, in the game. So you know me. No man is gonna threaten a beautiful woman in my presence. I get up from my fifth pint of ambeersia and stand up to him. Tell him to leave the lady alone or else. What's-his-face laughs at me, I mean he virtually spits in my face. Here's this drunk little Garden Elf, that's what he's thinking, challenging a level eighteen Witchfinder decked out in twelve-point antler armor. I'm thinking, 'Oh shit, I'm no David to this Goliath. The amber-sia's got my stats down and I'm in close quarters with a bow and arrow...' He draws his sword so I arm my bow and pull back the string, pointing right into his helmet and just when I think I'm dead there's this jingle-jangle purple smoke and this guy's totally frozen in place."

<ensorcelled>

"Yeah, I love that word. She ensorcelled the S.O.B.! So he's frozen in place, you know, and he can still talk into his microphone and he's cussing us up and down and I just thread arrow after arrow into him, whittle his health down one shot at a time, the other folks in the bar are loving it because he's a real jackass. She keeps recasting Immobilize on him and I'm throwing in lines from Dirty Harry and he looks just like that saint with the arrows when I finally finish him off. Tia loots his body and then drags me the hell outta there before one of his friends shows up. It was so great!"

"Yeah, sounds like it."

Her character, he discovered while Dad yammered, was at level nineteen and had logged in 971 hours of gameplay. Seeing as he was a level nineteen Paladin with 982 hours to his name, they were comparable in terms of experience. Immediately he suspected deception. What woman would want to get involved with a forty-eight year old noob? And the lack of a microphone, another giveaway. He couldn't trust a single thing this stranger typed.

<dad she might not even be a she> he typed in a private message. <she doesn't even have a mic so you can't even know its a woman>

"Oh, I'm sending her a mic," Dad said, reacting to his message in public. "Tia didn't have one so I got her one off Amazon."

And his father's status as a cyber sugar daddy snapped into focus so sharp his appetite for a large Slaughterhouse Five pizza from Falbo's perished. So it goes.

"I told her you know all the best places for loot. She's looking forward to meeting you."

<lets go kill something mean> she suggested.

Jean-Luc led them to the Desert of Shrieks, a snarky move because it's the homeland of the Sand Elves. Was he testing her? Sure. But he had to gauge just how bad Dad had it. And he had to show that he was still the expert. They wandered past Clitheroe, the biggest desert settlement, and made for a rocky ridge. Once there, Dad regaling the both of them with giddy recaps of the fight with the Witchfinder, Jean-Luc took them into Death Rattle Canyon. At dusk every night, Giant Bats funneled from their roost at the canyon's armpit to feed, leaving their naked young vulnerable in the cave. The bats themselves were enormous, the size of city busses, and nearly impossible to slay. Their batlings, however, made great slice-n-dice targets, both for their inability to fly and the fact that their spleens were worth mondo gold to Alchemists.

<looks like we're battling batlings huh>

"You've been here before?" he asked.

<i went from mama's teet to this canyon> she typed back. <i'm down>

<isn't she cool?> Dad typed to him privately. <and almost a nubian look to her!!1>

Jean-Luc disregarded the message and dragged a vial of Guano Musk from inventory to Dad and then to PurpleTia before using one on himself. If one approached the cave without masking his or her scent, the Giant Bats would drain you dead soon as they flew out of the cave, whereas if you smelled like poop, they didn't know you were there. When they reached the entrance, the three of them sped up the game clock to dusk and waited for the show to begin. Out flew the Giant Bats, zipping and zooming over their heads, flitting in a brown cyclone into the cornflower sundown. Once the show ended, the trio crept into the cave, weapons drawn.

When the interior of the cave loaded, it was time to fight. Batlings, great, hairless beasties with undeveloped wings and crooked teeth, left their spit-cup nests on the walls to attack the invaders. These bats went blind only at puberty, making the guano musk useless. The fight was brutal, Jean-Luc's special Sunlight Redemption move stunning the lot for a good twenty seconds so they could cut up and do away with the monsters in assembly line fashion. They went on, filleting batlings, racking up experience, Jean-Luc forfeiting half of his to Dad. PurpleTia, too, he noticed, sent XP his way. And once he had enough to level up, reaching level ten, they celebrated his ascension to double digits with a tent rest at a designated safe spot in a side branch of the cave.

"You wanna put those two points into Strength and Agility, Dad."

<agility yes, strength no> Tia countered. <do the other in intellect>

"His Intellect is already at nine," Jean-Luc said. "Strength is still down at three."

<which is why it makes sense to top out intellect now and focus on the other stats later>

"Intellect gets you like nothing. It's just talk and trade bonuses."

<exactly> she typed. <which means he has our back when trading in town just like we have his back in the wilds>

"Yeah, I think Tia's right, Son." And he took her advice. And thus began her habit of contradicting every bit of expertise Jean-Luc had when it came to anything. Anything at all.

At the end of midterms, that Friday, Dad and his irritating little friend weren't there under the tree when he signed on. They were both online, their names, the only ones on his

Friends List, lit blue. He sent a message to Dad.

<oh sorry! middle of a fight...>

<where at?>

Dad didn't write back for half an hour, by which point Jean-Luc was already hunting down a Hornswoggler in the Sumpish Swamps.

<sorry about that. i think me and tia are just going to have an us night if that's o.k.?>

Jean-Luc didn't write back.

"What's up?" Jeff asked when he rolled in from the bars at two in the morning, stinking like smoke and vomit. Jeff was a Business major from Mingo. "You look pissed."

"What? No." Jean-Luc clicked through a swarm of swamp bugs, dragonflies big as condors. "I'm just trying to concentrate."

The roommate threw his wallet and keys at his side of the room and exaggerated a hard look at Jean-Luc, imitating his hunch in his chair. "Dude, you seriously look pissed as fuck."

"It's nothing..."

"I've watched you kill shit on there every night since August and you've never looked so fuckin' pissed like that."

He danced his character over the XP points and gold pieces, collecting his booty for killing the insects and turned only his head, only halfway. "My dad's getting involved with this stupid bitch on here from Boring, Oregon, who thinks she knows Questalot's ins and outs better than anybody..."

"Every man wants a little pussy," Jeff said, dropping his pants and going into that Chippendale pants-twirling thing he needed to do every night before bedtime. "Especially after a divorce you didn't ask for."

He received the invites for membership as an officer in Jean-Luc's Dad's Guild – guild names could apparently handle apostrophes. They came from his dad and Purple Tia and he denied them regularly. Perhaps it was rude, not what a good knight should do, but he remained, principally, solely, in the service of nothing but virtue itself.

Thanksgiving was to be with his dad and sister at Gramma's house in Beaverdale, their first since Mom left. Jean-Luc, on moral grounds, refused to give thanks at Mom's boyfriend's table. His sister, always more diplomatic than him, would attend both gatherings. But it was Jean-Luc's season of turning down invitations. He didn't negotiate with philanderers.

So Dad was the one who drove to Iowa City to fetch him home for break. Jean-Luc waited, forehead cold against the reinforced glass window in the door at the end of his hall. He had his high-performance gaming laptop in his backpack and dirty laundry stuffed into a duffel at his feet. The small parking lot outside lit up red with brake lights as parents evacuated their undergrads from Cresthill Dormitory in a rush hour jam. He saw the mustard-colored sports car edge up the line before Dad had a chance to ring the phone in his pocket. Jean-Luc shouldered out of the residence hall and into late autumn evening, crossing the quad to Dad's Nissan 370Z, his first gift to himself after the split. The trunk popped and he crammed his duffel in before hopping in the front. As usual, the heat was blasting on full.

"Hey there, HoNoR_BlAdE91!" He socked his son in the meat by his knee.

"Hey, Dad."

Half an hour of traffic later they were finally driving west on I-80, the harvested hills of Iowa stretching outward in all directions. The moonlight gracing the rows of stubbled cornstalks illuminated a landscape almost too strange for any of the computer games he had played. The land so still and blue.

"Listen," Dad said, once through the McDonald's drive thru at Williamsburg, his mouth smiley, full of French fries, "what can I do to get you into the guild?"

"Honestly?" He reached for a chicken nugget at the bottom of the bag. "Pretty much nothing."

"But why? I don't get it. I started out with your help and I want you there with me, fighting side by side, father and son. You know, we could really make something of ourselves in Questalot. The first family-run guild."

"I don't do guilds." Jean-Luc peeled back the foil seal on a plastic serving of barbecue sauce.

"But wouldn't it be fun?"

"I go it alone. I'm a knight for the sake of good and nothing else."

"We could make all the decisions together."

"Together?" He held his barbecue sauce-dipped nugget. "We haven't even played together since your girlfriend showed up. And that's been weeks now."

"Well, but a guild takes a lot of oversight in the beginning."

"I got you into the game to begin with because I didn't want you to be alone in the house with nobody to talk to."

"And I'm not alone! That's the thing. Drink?" Jean-Luc hovered Dad's Coke so he could take a slurp and put it back in the dashboard drink-holder. "Thanks. About the not being alone, me and Tia've been doing Skype a lot. You know Skype?"

"Yeah." He considered tearing apart the chicken nugget and plugging his ears with it.

"Yeah. It's good, you know. I mean it's great. I got her set up with a webcam and, uh, her living situation isn't too good out there in Oregon. She and her dog're living with her ex-boyfriend. William. He's a few years younger than me—I guess she has a 'Daddy' thing. But yeah, I don't know what you and your sister were thinking for Christmas, if you were gonna spend it with Mom since you're doing Thanksgiving with me and Gramma or…"

The sauce had dripped from the nugget down Jean-Luc's thumb and forefinger.

"Because Tia doesn't really have anyone out there. She's actually from Humble, Texas, but can't go back home 'cause her stepdad is a real monster, I guess. Real monster. Did things I would never, ever even—"

"So PurpleTia's coming for Christmas."

"Not definite. I was thinking I could fly her out. Thinking of asking if she'd like that."

"So you can have sex with her."

"Well and why not?" Dad asked, giving the steering wheel a rancorous smack. It got Jean-Luc's attention but failed to impress. "When your mother was boinking that Southridge Mall optometrist behind my back for three years!"

"I won't come home for Christmas if she's there," Jean-

Luc said, "and I want nothing to do with you two's dumbass guild."

A week later, while hunting for the Square Egg of Cibola, a gem said to be as big as a Scottish duck, Jean-Luc cut and slashed his way through teams of Skeleturtles to the top of a minaret and found the one thing he'd been avoiding.

PurpleTia stood calm in the gallery, looking like a Goth Metal Bratz doll.

"You looking for the Square Egg of Cibola?"

It was his first time hearing her voice. She sounded fat, kind of country.

"Wrong tower."

"Well no kidding."

"Listen, Jean-Luc, I know you're not thrilled about me and your dad—"

"He's been through a lot, okay?"

"Don't think I don't get that. 'Cause I do."

"Yeah, I've got an Egg to find, m'kay?"

"Could you just do me one tiny little favor?"

A window offering an inventory item opened. She was trying to give him a vial of Crozzled Coelacanth Liver.

"Hold onto this for me."

He accepted the vial, more out of curiosity than good will.

"Thanks," she said. "I remember the Egg of Cibola quest. You should try the tower over—"

"I'll find it on my own!"

"Alright. Happy hunting."

PurpleTia vanished in a swirl of lights, teleporting

somewhere else in the game.

Jean-Luc drew up his inventory and right clicked on Crozzled Coelacanth Liver. It bore no special description. A throwing potion, he armed it and launched it off the top of the minaret. Down it fell through coded space and exploded in a brown cloud on a date tree in the courtyard.

And while he kept dibs on the guild, its ranking rising stupidly fast—from #58,118 to 387—he wanted nothing to do with it. He was a mercenary of the most holy order, the last of his kind, pledging allegiance to no group or man, not even his father, but to everyone who had been made a victim by evil.

It occurred to him that maybe he should stop by the guild hall in a show of good will to Dad and Tia, even if he didn't approve of them guilding in sin. The closest he came, however, was a grove at the base of the hill they'd built upon. There the hall rose, part pagoda, part massive toadstool, like an island in the mists of the Painkiln Plains. Players were coming and going like worker bees from their hive, or junkies from a crack house, he couldn't decide. Questalot message boards had been buzzing for a month about how Jean-Luc's Dad's Guild had a genius at its helm, a man able to turn profits on investments like the game simply hadn't seen before. They'd already snatched up vast swaths of real estate, all of it virtual of course, and were making gold by the minute on rentals all throughout the realm.

"Hello, wayfaring Paladin," someone said, startling him. "You've come to bear witness to Jean-Luc's Dad's Guild."

ChickenbonesMcKenna, a Druid clad in robes and silver cords, stood at his side.

"You're not sure if it's for you. But surely you, a Paladin, are more than worthy of joining the cause. Surely you know of all the good works Jean-LucsDad and his queen PurpleTia have done for the realm. Just last week they provided security at a vigil held by Goonies Guild for one of their players who died in real life. He's vowed they won't let anything like the Serenity Now funeral raid to ever happen on his watch."

"Yeah, that's great."

"They say he's so accepting because he lost his own son. No one knows who Jean-Luc was or what happened to him— only that Jean-LucsDad loved him so much that he named himself for him."

"Oh go worship the moon!" He ported out to the hill with the maple tree, the first location on his landmarks list, before the Druid could respond. There, in the shadow of that black goblin fortress his father had wanted to raid on his first day, Jean-Luc vowed to himself, there being no higher authority, that he would never return to the guildhall or even the Painkiln Plains.

For some reason they turned the overhead lights off in the dorm's halls over winter break. Before going home for Christmas his roommate warned him that he heard Cresthill was a mental institution before they converted it to student housing, so it might be haunted by the ghosts of "schizos and serial masturbators." It made no difference to Jean-Luc. He had never lived anywhere so empty, so vacant. The place, meant to house a thousand people, felt entirely different when occupied by five or six other stragglers with nowhere to go between semesters. The dining hall closed, he fended for meals, subsisting on gas station burritos he could zap in the microwave and pizza delivered from Falbo's. Food gathering only interrupted his days briefly, there being no reason to leave his room otherwise. Having the space to himself without Jeff snoring or farting was nice and the high speed internet connection kept him far from bored.

It was his first Christmas alone. Both his parents had sent him care packages full of presents. These sat stacked out of reach on Jeff's side of the room.

On the night before Christmas, en route to obliterate a clutch of demons who had overrun and ruined a beloved chapel, he ran into Jean-Luc's Dad's Guild. The lot of them, probably three hundred players, marched in long procession, trailing through Hapsworn Hollow like ants on the move. They clogged the dirt road, players of all classes, Knights and Berserkers and Mages and Shamans and Druids and Rogues and so on, all dressed in their finest armor. Jean-Luc stalked alongside the long line of warriors, keeping many paces off the road so they wouldn't see him. Looked like a raid in progress, though the snippets of conversation he could pick up from other players without microphones suggested celebration. Dad and Tia were surely in attendance, probably up at the front. In the end he had gone to her for the holiday. Jean-Luc had his flight info and contact numbers for the Best Western in an e-mail he'd kept but only glanced at once.

Over the River Lune and left at Pendle Rock, they came closer and closer to his own intended destination. Soon the desecrated Chapel of Iamblichus sat before all gathered, ruby light shining out through holes in its slate roof. There wasn't enough room within the broken walls for all the guild members.

Jean-Luc held back, knowing the game's AI would compensate for the size of the opposing force with stronger enemies. And sure enough, given that an army had come to siege the broken chapel, Questalot spawned dozens of level 25 Letch Demons. He watched as the black, thorny figures splintered from the red-lit chapel, one after the other. They slammed into Jean-Luc's Dad's warriors like infuriated bracken. His urge to help lay slack. As a Paladin, Jean-Luc's obligation was to smite evil wherever he found it. But this was a snafu, the chapel glade a swarm of twitching character names and numeric damage totals ringing up one over the other, the din a legion of runaway cash registers. The battle heaved. Good men fell. But so did demons. One hellborn cry of defeat would trail off and be replaced quickly with that of another. He needn't play the deus ex machina. The guild fended without him.

He was just ducking out when an epic crash of thunder hit like a bucket of marbles hitting concrete, signaling a surprise game challenge, followed by a voice like Orson Welles on Robitussin:

"Who dare challenge Asmodeus, King of Demons?"

An explosion birthed a creature twice as tall as the chapel's ruined steeple, which dashed to the ground. A terrible monster, three headed of bull, ogre, and ram, shook a'rage, cawing harmonized terror. Triple-crowned, he sat on the back of an enormous fire-breathing lion with a serpentine neck.

A bank of Druids cast sparkly blue protection spells on the warriors, who made for its mount's feet. Each shuffling step of Asmodeus's beast stunned those closest to it while a green fire spouting from its mouth scorched all within its arc.

He still hadn't placed Dad.

About to leap out of the undergrowth, he received a private message from PurpleTia.

<HELP! bring that liver potion i gave you. the time is now! your our only hope!!!> She sent a teleport offer to join her in Hapsworn Hollow. She didn't know he was already there.

<why do you need the liver potion?> he typed back.

<we're up against Asmodeus – big bad demon – coelacanth liver its only weakness>

Jean-Luc balked. He thought back to throwing the vial off the top of the minaret.

<hold a sec> he typed.

He teleported to Dragon Jaw and made for Ape's Tooth Remedies in a Shift key run. The shop was like every other independently operated small business in Questalot, floor to ceiling flat thumbnail images of merchandise on every wall. The only time he could recall seeing Coelacanth Liver was when PurpleTia had given it to him. He scanned the wall once, twice, skimming over item names, not seeing it. He drew up the shop's list of items for sale and searched for liver. No results. Of course the shop's owner wasn't around. It was just him and a butch Dwarf wearing a Dragonhunter's wyvern-hide cuirass. Sleater_Kinney didn't look entirely approachable but he needed help.

"Hi, excuse me?"

"Yeah?"

"Hi. I'm looking and can't find this special ingredient. It's a vial of this kind of liver, Ko-ell-uh-canth liver?"

"See-luh-canth Liver."

"It starts with a C and—"

"Yeah, yeah. You won't find it here."

"Shit."

"Only place you get it is in the Driffledaw Pearl quest. It's the prize for killing the Giant Coelacanth."

Jean-Luc hadn't even started that quest. It was supposedly impossible to complete unless you went through it on a team.

"Need it quick?"

"Yeah, my dad's about to be killed by the King of Demons if I can't pull this liver outta my ass."

"You could try the Black Arts Market," she said. "If you can stand being seen in such a place, Mr. Paladin."

<HURRY!!!> PurpleTia typed in their private chat window.

"Thanks for the tip, Dwarf." He was about to do a search for the market's location when Sleater_Kinney sent him a landmark. Using the link he teleported directly there.

His avatar shone like the full moon in the near pitch bazaar, a halo of light pouring off his shoulders to bring out the dirty green and deep purple surfaces normally obscured by darkness. Other players, the Necromancers and Vampires and criminal underclass who thrived here, threw jeers as soon as he arrived. A place of commerce, with its leather-tarped booths and bamboo cages holding men, critters, and monsters, the unsavory shoppers weren't there to fight. He gulped a Shield potion just to be safe and dashed to one of the booths boasting serpent charms, potions, and familiars. Taffy Ben Hassan's Serpenporium read the sign. Taffy, an iguana-dewlapped Saurischian, was in.

"You got the fish liver from the Driffledaw Pearl quest?" he asked, not attempting to pronounce Coelacanth again.

"How much gold?"

"Uh, you're the one selling it."

"How much gold," he asked, "do you have?"

The lower right corner of the screen displayed his wealth next to an icon of a piece of gold. "Uh, like, three-hundred-thousand-some." He was quite proud of what he'd managed to save over the course of his career.

"That's how much it costs."

<come on kiddo> PurpleTia typed. <i'm trying to make you look good...>

"Dammit." He right clicked on Taffy and selected the Pay option. He typed in 300,000, okayed it, verified the Okay with an Okay, and watched his savings drop to 9,437.

He waited.

"Gimme the liver!"

"Patience."

"It went through now gimme the effing liver!"

"In a moment. I'm the finder."

"You mean you don't even have it!?" He struck the F key, drawing his Vorpal Sword.

"You paid me. I know a guy. He'll be here."

Jean-Luc groaned and responded to PurpleTia. <side-tracked... sorry...>

He waited for her reply while waiting for the courier, his knee hopping up and down in an anxious spasm.

<too late> she answered.

<literally on my way!!!!>

<nm>

A wiry Saurischian dressed in black mummy rags rezzed

out of a teleport in front of Taffy Ben Hassan's. It was wearing silver goggles and had piercings running the length of its tail. A window popped up, asking if he would accept a vial of Crozzled Coelacanth Liver from Naga_Champa. He accepted, checked his inventory to make sure it was there, and teleported out with a double-click on PurpleTia's offer to join her in Hapsworn Hollow.

The screen went black and reloaded on the scene of battle. The Chapel of Iamblichus stood rebuilt. The sky and suns were out. Fallen warriors had resurrected, their blood in the grass washed clean away. They stood en masse in front of the chapel, lining the path up to its decorated brass doors. No fight, no archdemon, no struggle. As if nothing had happened at all, order completely restored to the glade and its house of worship. Jean-Luc, who'd teleported in amongst the troops, stumbled into the path, rotating his view all around to try and find his dad.

"Private ceremony, Paladin," Paul_the_Fool warned him. "Beat it."

"What happened to the battle? Where's the...?"

"Cleaned up. Our lady weakened it with some kind of potion and we took it from there."

"Where's Jean-LucsDad?"

"In there doing their commitment ceremony," he said. "Making their union official."

"Uh."

"Why do you think our guild exorcised the chapel?"

Jean-Luc tore off his headset and threw it. It bounced off the wall and landed in the sink. He stood, kicked at his chair. Disgust. He aborted Questalot, exiting to desktop.

He was meant to wait until morning but no one would

know and he was angrier than he'd ever been in his nineteen years. He opened the presents from Dad first, out of spite. He shredded the Santa Claus wrapping paper and scowled as they piled up. Expansion discs to Questalot. He shoved them across the floor and turned to Mom's gifts. His fingers had more trouble with the plastic foil wrap she'd used. Lots of working his fingernail under each open place between strips of tape.

Mom, unexpectedly, had come through. She'd given him exactly what he asked for: World of Warlords, Questalot's leading competition in online gaming. She'd sent him every-thing. The game, the seven expansions, everything currently available. He rolled over toward his desk and grabbed his mechanical pencil, wondering why he hadn't thought of it when he struggled with the gift wrap, and used its steel tip to slice through the seals on the boxes, one by one. He with-drew and set out each instruction manual and disc. Here, arranged before him like a tarot prophecy, was a brand new world to explore and rid of the forces of darkness. Here was months of life, maybe even a year. Here was escape.

He got up and uninstalled Questalot.

When prompted if he would like to save his character, without a thought he opted for complete deletion.

Fred_Loves_LL
to LovelyLotus   26 March 2010

I dream of LovelyLotus. At beach and water going out like on VHS
rewind. Sand is there. You are thrilled to running on it and
screaming 'WE DIG CLAM!' I followed but I am not liking clam. You
go far. Pulling out clam with hands out of sand. I am afraid of the
crab pinch and I nervous picking the sand with a toe of my own.
You see lower sand like a step down shown by water going away
and say we go down to get clam. We crawl like small rat down
steps. Mouse! I am scared. The sand is wet here and you start new
clam hunting. I am nearly sick of worry. I am wonder when water
comes back and when will we have time to climb to beach? If trap
when we drown! And the water it comes back. Before panic I tell
you and we climb to beach. Beach people are afraid to scream and
I hearing 'MORSA MORSA MORSA!' We are up to balcony of hotel
to see beach. Beach people running with hands on the air and out
there is the black beast. It has red mouth and body of horses or
bulls and snorting at us! A man is on the beach beside camelo, his
pet on the rope of its neck. He is black like dark burned wood dust
(sorry, LovelyLotus, for my brain dictionary is not complete). His
gold earring is a circle and move in wind. He is Antônio Fagundes
but is not him (famous actor in Brazil). He is standing on his ground
and does not get his camelo away. The beast see him. He holding
his head down like impressive actor (but he is not the real Antônio
Fagundes). The beast cough and run at him. He is not move! It hit
him down and his camelo is eating by the beast! The man who is
not Antônio Fagundes pulls with hands in sand. Beast eating him
too. Spit him over ten meters. Beach people running in scream. I do
not know why, why I do this, but I laughing. Beast seeing me on
balcony and you went gone now. Impossible it jump onto balcony
and I am done and waking up wondering why you leaving me in
dream like you leaving me in life and never answering mail. You

never love me in dream or in the world when I love you forever. Why is this so? Why do you hurting Fred every day when he loving you into the ending of the times? This chart from free website of making free charts can showing why you are hating me when I am loving you like your goddess. Please to understand? PLEASE? I dream of LovelyLotus! :(

Chart of why you are hating me?

LL hating Fred

LL PLEASE loving Fred

Fred loving LL

The Martyr Dumb

The drive to Muscatine from Des Moines takes nearly three hours, but Jacob is grateful to be out of the city and bearing witness to the countryside. Riding over Iowa's living hills, alternating crowns of corn and soybeans, there's no doubting it: this is God's country. He spent all night rehearsing the Sinner's Prayer for her to recite. He also printed out the addresses of the three Sanderson households listed for Muscatine so he can deliver Rachel to her mother should she resist.

Having never been to Muscatine, the storefront town charms him straight away. Of course he's early, so he drives down to the river and looks at it for a while from the car. That the Mississippi is muddy strikes him as a shame. Old Miss needs her own John the Baptist to make that water clean. He could open up a stand, like one where the kids sell lemonade, but right on the river's bank, selling baptism instead. Except it'd be free. Salvation is priceless, after all. The image really tickles him and he has to make sure to remember it as he drives away. Pastor Brenner'll love it.

Dairy Silo stands right where MapQuest said it would. It beckons tall, an antique grain silo with a soft-serve swirl rooftop that probably lights up at night. Sitting at one of the picnic tables out front is a girl in a ball cap with curly red hair. He parks at an angle in the gravel lot and reaches behind for the Bible he'll give her. But it isn't in the backseat. Not on the floor either.

"How could I forget it?"

Oh well. Sending up a prayer, he shimmies out and doesn't bother to take the keys from the ignition. This is a small town and all.

His feet slide on the gravel, making him conscious of his scarecrow stride. It's okay. He is otherwise presentable, wearing a striped dress shirt with khakis and mousse in his hair. He tried spiking it, but the aerosol foam simply made it droop.

"Rachel?"

It's devastating to see how temptation has seeded her. Besides the Cubs hat, she wears hoop earrings ample for perching canaries, a yellow polka dot pink halter-top, an el cheapo magenta miniskirt, and white knee-high boots with leopard-spot faux fur trim. Worse, she is fellating a frozen treat on a stick. Jacob winces. Teenagers of this type are not the easiest to Save, especially without a Bible. He'll have to rely on the verses he knows by heart, which aren't many. Blasted memorization never came easy.

"I'm Jacob." He tries to smile, his lips dry despite the humidity. "Told you I'd be here."

She slides the creamy Silo-sicle out of her mouth and licks her fuchsia-painted lips. "Hey."

92

He must maintain eye contact. A diverted gaze could imply that he wants to defile her, which he doesn't. She does have nice eyes though. Clear brown ones.

"Your eyes look pure."

Hadn't she once said they were green?

"Oh yeah?"

And where were her freckles?

"You're dark complected," he puzzles.

A hand lands on his shoulder. He realizes he's ignored the crunchity-crunch of a man's shoes on gravel behind him.

"We don't have to make this difficult, do we?"

He turns to see who and is thrown to the picnic table. Rachel hops out of the way and the world goes sideways with his cheek meeting weathered wood. Whoever-it-is wrenches his arms back and clamps metal around his wrists.

"Excellent work, Leah."

"Leah?"

Rachel, in perpendicular view, takes off the cap and her red hair lifts away with it. She shakes her head and a coiled black braid falls around her shoulder. She holds a badge.

"Officer Leah Garcia. Muscatine Police Department."

"Jacob Alan Pfister the Third," the other says, seemingly omniscient, patting down his legs, "you are under arrest for violating Section Seven-ten Ten of the Iowa Code: Enticing away a minor under the age of sixteen."

"Where's Rachel?"

The officer spins him around and slams his rear end on the table. He is probably forty years old, his high forehead crowned with loose red curls. His eyes green. Freckles.

"You know how you thought you were talking to an at-risk fifteen year old girl? That whole time," he squints, his hands on Jacob's shoulders, "you were talking to me."

"Who're you?"

"Officer Francis Allen."

"So where's Rachel?" Jacob is lifted up. He stands under the sun with his wrists linked in back. The yellow-aproned employees inside Dairy Silo gawk. He drops his chin, pondering this turn in God's plan for him, and finds comfort. The Lord is with him. His mission hasn't been vanquished, not really, for right here is a soul.

"Do you know where you're going if you die today?"

Allen scowls and yanks him toward a squad car that has emerged in the confusion. "I'm not the one here has to worry about going to hell..."

When they read him his rights, telling him whatever he says can be used against him in court, he responds, "The only judgment I fear is the Lord's." When Officer Garcia editorializes that he'll need a good attorney, he explains he won't because he was only trying to Save Rachel's soul, which is as far from committing a crime as a guy can get. When they book him, he grins for the mug shot, saying, "Praaaise!" And when he stands before a judge, who explains he's being charged with a Class D felony and sets his bond to $5,000, Jacob, knowing this will all be smoothed out soon, clucks, "Judge not, lest ye be judged!" The judge bumps bond to $10,000.

Some hours after Jacob's one phone call, Dad arrives. He stands at the booking desk with his arms folded and severity in his face. Jacob is uncuffed and Dad pays bail. While signing the various forms, he's stricken with giggles. It's just so silly. The process is like checking out of a motel—but it's jail! They leave in Dad's Mercury, his Tempo being impounded, and twentysome minutes down the road Dad says:

"Your mother will never recover."

"It's a huge mix-up," Jacob wheezes, relieved the quiet has ended. "I was—"

"Son, you haven't had any kind of normal dating, steady girl situation. *Ever.*" He is sitting stiff at the wheel, leaning forward. "I don't know what all you get up to on the Internet, but it's found you some real trouble."

"I was going to chat rooms," he tries to explain, "searching for lost souls. Those in greatest need are the worst sinners and the worst sinners, what are they? Pedophiles! I play down being a Christian, which isn't easy, and when the time is right I pounce with Jesus. That's how I met Rachel who, I *thought,* was sin-bound. I saw an angel in dire need of salvation and had to act."

"Fifteen can be awful nice to look at—"

"Dad!"

"But it's just too young," he spits. "Everybody knows that. Sixteen is legal but that doesn't make it all that acceptable either. You're almost thirty. You should'a been looking for a wife."

Jacob sulks but finds a retort. "Some people say the Virgin Mary was only fifteen or sixteen when the Lord impreg—"

"For cryin' out loud," Dad scowls. "This is gonna ruin me, too. If the news picks this up? You've damned the both of us." His eyebrows strident slashes, he still won't look at his son. "People'll hear the *name* and *child molester* and that'll be it for you and me. They won't care whether it's Jacob Pfister the Second or the Third."

"Dad..."

"I should've let your mother name you Gary like she wanted."

"Stop worrying already." He flutters his hands in what he thinks a dovelike motion. "God knows I'm not guilty. And anyway, this is America. I'm innocent 'til proven guilty."

When they get to Des Moines, Dad drops him at his apartment. Documents are taped to his door and inside his belongings are in new places. Dust bunnies clump where his computer should be. Just in time for the ten o'clock news, he turns on the television, which now sits on the kitchen counter. The second story, following the daily toll in the Holy Land, lets him and the rest of central Iowa see how his mug shot turned out.

"A Des Moines man has been arrested in a child predator sting by Muscatine police today and charged with a felony for enticing away a minor via the Internet." So says Calvin Rooney, the silver-haired anchor he grew up watching every weeknight. "Twenty-eight-year-old Jacob Alan Pfister the Third reportedly drove to eastern Iowa this morning to meet an assumed fifteen-year-old girl with the intention of having sex."

Jacob gasps. That photo looks nothing like him. Somehow they enhanced it so he looks possessed, giving him demon-dark eyes and a downright vampiric grin.

"The girl was actually a Muscatine police officer who had been chatting with Pfister online. He faces a maximum of five years in prison and a seventy-five hundred dollar fine. If convicted, he will also join the state's sex offender registry."

He can hardly believe the sternness in Calvin Rooney's avuncular voice, giving him the three-name treatment re-served for assassins and real-life child molesters.

"After breaking this story at six, we were contacted by Pastor Cameron Brenner, leader of the Holy Power and Sword of Jesus Christ Church where Pfister has been a member for several years."

His bull-cheeked pastor appears squinting in front of the church's pink neon cross. "He was always a bit not normal, you know? But if I had any idea that a wolf had infiltrated my flock, I would've smited him myself."

"Pastor Brenner will hold special prayer groups," Rooney concludes, "for parents and children in his congregation and the community who are distressed over these allegations."

The news meanders on to a story about video stores giving free rentals to kids with good grades. Jacob knows just what to do. He kneels to the floor and, as he raises a hand to heaven in prayer, he sees it on the end table. The only thing the cops didn't move. The Bible inscribed to Rachel.

Aluminum Blimp

to LovelyLotus   26 April 2011

so this was my dream a couple nights ago

i went to see this thing on the stones in the basement of a building and guess who was my date?

you werrrrrrrrrrrrrrrrrrrrrrrrre

mick jagger was gross but after the movie we decided to have a baby together and you offered to carry it but i said i would and my belly grew all big and i take you home so i can have our child and in my old bedroom we both strip naked and i go into birth and it doesn't hurt like i thought it would

the baby is a girl and pink and fat and tiny and perfect and i hear my mom and sister come home and throw clothes on to run downstairs to meet them but they're busy so i run up to check on you and our baby which has turned into a kitten

you wat to make love and i hear dad come home so i run down but he's busy too with the evening news on and he's not to be disturbed so i run back up and your naked in his bed and i hear my buddy arrive so i tell you to put a blanket on and get back in my room before dad finds you

my buddy is in the living room with short hair and a bike and he tells me all about his new thing which is biking and i want to tell him and my family about the new addition to our clan but can't get a word in which is weird for me

then my buddy's fictional aunt comes to the door and hassles his about something so i decide to hell with it and go back upstairs and you haven't moved from dad's room so i rush you out and time my steps behind you up the stairs to my room so my feet land with yours to mask i'm not alone

our baby kitten is orange and cream and its doddling in a lawndry basket in my room and you fell on the bed and i closed the door and you threw open the blue blanket and spread your legs and i got on you and you can imagine the rest i'm sure ;)

Uncle Seeks Auntie

If you've seen the episode of *Suburban Intrigue* the Yester-year Channel did on my uncle, you might think you know all about him, but the truth is you're actually missing out in terms of getting to know him. The story they told might of drawn from facts and might of purported to tell the truth—I know the family members they paid to interview on camera gave their best to it—but what they did with third-rate Californian actors in reenactments wasn't what happened to my Uncle Howard here in Iowa. They stretched things. And left holes more gaping than the one that opened up under his basement and made his death so exploitable for cable producers turning real life misery into entertainment.

I'm fully aware you probably didn't even see that show—there's a hundred different programs offering the same sort of crap anymore—and anyway, like I said, if you did, you don't know Uncle Howard. Which is what I'm doing here. I'm telling you who he was and what happened to him. This way he'll have his memory served right. And everybody deserves their memory served right. Especially Uncle Howard.

Think back. Do you remember how there was a window of time when people were ashamed of online dating? It was brief. That shift from the shame of placing personals ads in the local paper to making a profile on a dating site seems like it happened pretty quick, though I was a girl at the time. By the time I was out of high school everybody my age was fine with online dating. And now, of course, those who haven't given it a shot are the weirdos.

I just remember at the time that my mom gave him such a hassle about it. We were at a family get together at my great aunt's house—a barbecue with cousins and second cousins and pretty well everybody on Mom's side of the family. I'm five years younger than most in our generation, but I'm also the oldest of my family by four years—so I was an oldest in-betweener at these family things—and I'd spend the time bouncing from the kids, who were annoying, to hanging around Uncle Howard. He was my favorite relative because he always had time for me and would listen while I basically hashed out the plot to whatever *Baby-Sitters Club* book I'd just read and he never seemed bored or annoyed by it or me. When you're ten, eleven, twelve, this means the world to you, having an adult in your life who takes your concerns seriously, who treats the happenings of Stoneybrook, Connecticut, like it's literature.

Anyway, I was making my way to Uncle Howard after losing interest in sidewalk chalk with my siblings and came around the corner of Great Aunt Carla's house and Mom was just hooting at him. He was slouching lower in a vinyl lawn chair, all exaggerated, and the frayed weave broke under his butt, sending his knees up to his chin and his arms up, paper plate of potato salad and beans flopping onto the patio.

My timing had been perfect to catch sight of this.

We were all of us laughing then.

And while the great uncles pulled Uncle Howard's rear end out of the flimsy lawn chair, with him insisting he'd replace it, and, it seemed, some genuine embarrassment. Mom kept ribbing him though and the way he wouldn't make eye contact with her just really made me feel suddenly protective of him.

"Leave him be!" I shouted at her—and everybody fell quiet.

Then suddenly the eyes were on me, and I said, "Sometimes in life we fall through a chair!"

And then they all really laughed and laughed.

And I retreated.

And Uncle Howard pranced after me like one of those cartoon animals that always attends a Disney princess and we filled fresh plates and were very happy to ignore the rest of the family for the rest of the barbecue.

On the ride home, Mom extended the branch. Said she hadn't really been picking on her brother. That what she'd thought was so funny to begin with was that he was trying out computer dating. "And I said," she said, "'Who'd wanna date a computer?'"

"He can date a blender or a microwave if he wants to," I said. "He hasn't got kids like you do. Not even a dog!"

"He might get one soon," Mom said, turning onto our street.

I remember that being a thing. He lived in one of those depressing apartment buildings out in West Des Moines and the landlord didn't allow pets, but that was the year he bought the house and there was talk he'd go to the animal shelter and bring home a pup. I was rooting for this, lobbying for him getting a Labrador or Golden Retriever so I could mother it by proxy. His priority after the house though was a lady. Uncle Howard wanted to be somebody's someone.

He was Mom's little brother by a year, so they were pretty close. He always liked reading, that's how his growing up years are remembered, and after college at ISU—first in our family to go—he carried that love on into working at Tristram's Books. He was the weekend manager, taking care of the store on the busiest days no one else wanted to work, often picking up the slack for part-time employees who called in sick. It was the lower end of management in retail but he liked it. He wasn't ambitious. And I loved this about him. He didn't feel like he had to prove himself to anybody like Mom did. She's still playing musical cubicles at Percival, her always unstable standing there playing out like she's survived as a minor character after thirty-some seasons of *Game of Thrones* when countless kings and queens and underlings like herself have been killed.

Uncle Howard floated comfortably through bookselling. His only problem was that he often felt alone, which he told me every so often because we got along.

The thing with the house, with him buying it, was sort of a sanctioned lifestyle makeover. Mom was behind it, as were some of his friends—and yes, he had friends, despite what *Suburban Intrigue* went and made up. The stuff where they showed the actor playing him wandering through life without anybody around him was total crap, such a gross misrepresentation. Plenty of people showed up for his memorial for instance. And, like I just said, I think it was that he felt alone—not that he was. There's a difference there, between feeling like you're on your own and actually being on your own. Just because somebody has secrets doesn't mean he's completely isolated.

But I was getting into his deal in buying the house and all. The story goes that Grandpa always said to never purchase a house over by Kmart because that land was tunneled through like Swiss cheese with abandoned coal mines from forever ago. This was apparently decreed long ago. I don't know why he'd impart such advice but he'd come from a family of miners down in Lovilia and this was cause enough to believe him on the matter. He died before I was born so all of that knowledge is really lost by now. Anyhow, you see, Uncle Howard found a home over there for a price he could afford by making some minor monthly sacrifices regarding his creature comforts and, not heeding his father's advice, went ahead and took on a mortgage on a plot that may or may not have been dug through with the odd unstable mineshaft.

The psychologist they put on that show, saying he had a death wish, was way out of line. They made it seem like Grandpa had surveyed the land himself and forbade it when actually it was just this hunch he had is how I was told it was. All that junk about him defying his dad after he'd died with this suicidal urge is just such a bunch of lies. I mean, the house was in a newish neighborhood with loads of other houses looking just like it all around. And somehow they got building permission on this supposedly perilous land. And I'm pretty sure all those people in all those houses were just going about their lives and happy to find a decent place to live. Kind of throws his little "destrudo" theory under the bus.

But it was right after he got the house pretty much that he started seeing Sadie. It was one of the days we were helping him move his stuff from the apartment that he let on that there was somebody who'd possibly, maybe, potentially come along. He made a point of bringing it up when I was present—I like to think because he knew I was his ally at all times.

"Was this someone you met in real life or through your website?" Mom asked in this really teasing way. Like she held the keys to dating or something. She could hold onto boyfriends no longer than eight months and let go of them no sooner than six. Even though that was the repetitive shape of her love life—nothing ever working out on her terms—always her terms—she seemed to think it was always open season on Uncle Howard's.

One of his virtues was his sense of humor. He just laughed her off, said he'd been e-mailing back and forth, that she seemed worth taking out to Chi-Chi's some evening for a chimichanga and fried ice cream.

Mom got into this really ugly laughing fit, imagining out loud how strange and deformed and misshapen his date could be, a whole freak show playing out from her imagination alone.

I asked what he knew about her. I was carrying a floor lamp, I recall.

She had told him she was earning a master's degree at Aylesbury in social work, which sounded like a nice thing for her to be doing, showing that she wanted to help others. She had bounced around a lot growing up—New Hampshire, Florida, Maryland—before being sent to her grandparents in Missouri, who brought her up. After high school then, she bounced around again—Florida, California, Arizona—before going back to gather herself with her grandparents in Missouri again, where she enrolled at Northwest Missouri State and got a degree in Sociology—which funneled on into the master's at Aylesbury.

"She sounds troubled," Mom said. "Anybody moving around that much with such an interest in social work is troubled."

"She sounds like she has real nice grandparents," I said, or something like that. I wanted to focus on the positive.

I guess I still do.

Uncle Howard agreed with me anyway. Said he didn't know what the situation was with her mom but that it seemed like maybe the woman just hadn't really had such an easy go of it—and there hadn't been any mention of her dad so he was assumed to be totally out of the picture. Mom, being Mom, stuck stubbornly to her disapproval of the whole thing, asking why he thought it was a good idea to develop any kind of interest in a woman he'd not met, let alone one who'd shown herself incapable of settling in one place for any amount of time.

This wasn't fair, but Uncle Howard, a seasoned veteran when it came to deflecting her judgments, batted it away with silliness. "But riddle me this," he challenged her. "Don't you think it's time the kids got themselves an aunt? That's my headline: *Uncle Seeks Auntie.*"

"Oh sure," she said, trying to wither the conversation with her tone. "You're always thinking of the children."

She meant it as an insult but it didn't actually make any sense. And I knew this. And Uncle Howard did, too. And we both knew we were on the same page and that Mom was not.

"Take her out for *frie-ie-ie-ie, ie-ie-ied ice cream*," I sang.

And that was the nudge he needed, because who else were we meeting a month later at his official housewarming party than this Sadie lady from the internet?

On seeing her, it was known that any far flung hopes of her being some gorgeous thing born from sea foam in a clam shell had been a bit foolish. Uncle Howard was not handsome, though that tends to matter less for men than it does for women. It's not written anywhere that an ugly man has a better chance at snagging fancy ladies than an ugly woman has of snagging a dreamy man, but that does seem to be the way it is. In this case, his face wasn't unpleasant to look at, but he hadn't taken care of his teeth and he was soft all over, a bit flabby but in a kind of cute way. Sadie had a lovely figure but her chin jutted out almost, I'm embarrassed to put it this way, like the bottom point on a crescent moon. She also had a super fluffy perm that was a few years out of fashion. It made her look like she had two great big cocker spaniel ears on either side of her head.

Taken on their own, you'd likely not pay attention to either of them. Together, however, they were unquestionably beautiful.

It was just that slightly manic rapport they had with one another, a romantic excitement, as if they both knew they were at the beginning of a love sure to last a very long time. Uncle Howard never seemed so joyful or sure of himself. And she took to me and my brothers, Sam and Lou, like she belonged to us. She complimented me on my newly pierced ears, which she said she'd heard about. I remember recognizing her making a special point of addressing me as someone she'd heard a lot about, and the way Uncle Howard smiled, I knew he'd made a big deal about me to her. My approval meant something to her because I was important to him. It was the sort of selfish thing I took away from the party, when, really, I should have been interviewing her the way Mom wasn't—she all but ignored Sadie. Seeing him so happy in this way must have been too much for her.

The big joke at the party was when Great Aunt Clara gave him the lawn chair he'd sat through at her house the summer before, the seat patched.

Sadie, it turned out, was into cycling. It accounted for her figure. And Uncle Howard, hoping to hold her interest I think, got himself a ten-speed mountain bike and a helmet and challenged her that summer to ride RAGBRAI—the *Register*'s Great Annual Bicycle Ride Across Iowa. He must have met her in the spring because by the time they undertook the eastward crossing of Iowa it seemed to me like they had been together for ages, though, in retrospect, it had only been four months tops—downward slope time for the dalliances Mom had had.

Uncle Howard hadn't trained at all—how could he on such short notice really? He did allow me to decorate his wheels in Spokey Dokes, which I ensured would bring him lots of luck. Mom, fully convinced he'd be dead halfway across the state, agreed to meet the two of them in Lake Mills, the designated stop for the fourth night of the ride and pretty much a straight shot north of Des Moines, not far off I-35. We went to replenish snacks and Gatorade and underwear, driving up with room in the Volvo to bring him home if need be. Mom was convinced, I think, that they'd be broken up by that point.

"I never want to hear anybody tell me Iowa's flat ever

again," Sadie declared once we finally found them and their tent at the campground. "Put them on a bike and let them decide for themselves if it's flat."

This was funny because she'd teased him ceaselessly about having bought a mountain bike in Iowa. Hers was an Italian racing bicycle, named Basso, which was actually perfectly suited to the ride, I imagine. But anyway, they weren't either of them at the other's throat. They were laughing and sweaty and starving. The only disastrous factor, obvious to anybody giving Uncle Howard a once over, was that he was thoroughly poxed with mosquito bites.

"I woke up this morning, rolled over, and confused him for bubble wrap."

"Took her seven stomps without any popping before she realized it was me," he said.

She started smacking him in the arm with the back of her hand and he laughed and laughed, saying, "Hey, it's me, it's me! I'm not packing material!"

It was adorable to them and to me.

Mom found it repulsive. She interrupted all of their fun stories about how much fun they were having on this fun bike ride by forcing food on them, a spread we'd fixed up at home and sealed in Tupperware so they'd have some home cooking halfway through the eight day ride. She practically made a side dish out of her spite, grumbling about totally unrelated stuff when really I just wanted to hear more about their adventures together. Uncle Howard, despite being out of shape, seemed to have shed a touch of weight. He was keeping up with this Sadie. And he was enjoying that as much as you'd hope he would if you loved him. He'd never had a girlfriend as long as I'd known him, which was all my life.

The tiny little town set off fireworks at dark. No sooner had the first bang of color gone off than Sadie jumped up and pointed to the sky and said, "'Aha!' she *cried* as she waved her wooden leg on *high* and cast her glass *eye* out into the distance..."

She repeated that for me until I had it memorized perfectly, complete with pointing motion. I knew she was trying to win me over and I was absolutely fine with being won over. Mom was thankfully too busy telling my brothers to stay out of the tree over the tents to poison our visit. And I, being spontaneous and wanting to make my own gesture of appreciation, suggested they come to our motel and take a shower if they like. Mom had booked a room at the Super 8 in Clear Lake. They leaped at the offer, said thus far they'd only shampooed in front yard hosings and sprinkler dashes supplied by friendly townsfolk.

Mom, of course, was none too pleased at this, since it involved some driving she hadn't anticipated. But we went ahead and got them their showers and neither of them even seemed to notice how peeved Mom was. My brothers, as usual, were too busy pounding on each other to notice much anything else. When we dropped them off back at the campsite, neither of them reeking anymore, their bikes and tent were all propped and pupped and untouched, just as they'd left them.

"I love Iowa," Sadie said, and I made my proclamation: "Iowa loves you!"

When we walked back to the car, passing a tent that seemed to contain a snoring grizzly bear, I looked back over my shoulder and saw her and Uncle Howard kiss in the shadows. They were both on all fours and she was backing into their tent with their lips locked and I'd only ever seen anything like that on TV or in movies and I thought I'd burst from the sheer romance of it all.

Mom pretty much stopped me in my tracks, or tried to, on the way back to the motel. I was sitting up front with her, my usual place, and she made me feel so stupid and small by telling me not to get my hopes up about Sadie, saying that kind of giddiness burns out fast, that she was sure there was something wrong with her, it'd very likely end before we knew it, that it was almost certainly already over. I tried to point out all the contradictory evidence to the case she was building but she shut it all down with the authority she told herself she'd earned with her own lack of luck in the relationship department.

"You just don't know it yet," she told me in the dark on the interstate, "but that feeling isn't even real. We just tell ourselves it is."

The car was silent after that. I looked into the backseat and my brothers had gone from pummeling each other to passed out on each other. It wouldn't have hit them the way it hit me but I was glad they hadn't heard Mom say that.

Sadie and Uncle Howard conquered RAGBRAI and went along enjoying each other's company to the point that I started feeling his absence in our family life. It was stupid, and I knew it was stupid, but I felt a bit envious of Sadie after a while. We had always seen him regularly is the thing, and now we saw him infrequently. He was happy. But I was twelve.

My birthday, at the end of the summer, was a small thing, mostly being a sleepover with my two best friends, but there was a dinner to it and I chose Chi-Chi's because I knew Uncle Howard and Sadie would come and I'd told him to take her there for their first date and he had—so it would be sort of a return to the beginnings of their romance, my gift to them on the advent of me becoming a teenager.

They came but couldn't stay long. Sadie was apologetic about it. She was in the throes of finishing up her master's thesis and looked a bit out of it, showing up in sweats. Which was a bit embarrassing but only because I knew Mom would comment on it in front of my friends after they left—which she did. They gave me a present: the purple and magenta Caboodles jewelry organizer I'd specifically asked for. Uncle Howard had driven to the south side to find it.

I still use it twenty years later.

I begged them to stay for fried ice cream, bragging to my friends the thing about their first date being there at that same Chi-Chi's and how I'd told him to ask her out. Sadie hadn't known that and though she was worn clear out from writing her thesis she melted a bit in front of us, enough to give us the glow I wanted to see.

That autumn they took a trip to New York City, celebrating the completion of her MSW. They went to a taping of the Ed Pressman Show and took a carriage ride in Central Park and sent me a postcard of the Strand bookstore. Sadie wrote it but both signed it.

We found out who's buried in Grant's Tomb, it says. *Some cad named Archibald Leach!?*

It was a quick three weeks after they returned that any of us heard from Uncle Howard and what he had to say was every bit the validation of Mom's undermining predictions that she needed to put a spring back in her step. It was weird anyway because he showed up at our house without her and when I asked where Sadie was he just said, "I don't know." Like nothing bad had happened. Then he hung around and let us eat dinner without eating anything himself, sitting at the table with us, and at the end of dinner, after Mom had complained enough about her job, I asked, "Do you think you and Sadie'll do Thanksgiving with us or are you gonna go to Missouri and finally meet her grandparents?"

At that he dropped his head and after a still that made even the boys shut up he just started sobbing.

Mom was ready to kill her for breaking his heart but she was not so secretly thrilled by the news, too. She teased out details and got him talking after hugs and tissues. It seemed Sadie decided to take a social worker job in Maryland near her mostly-estranged mom. She hadn't told him she was looking that far afield. She didn't want him to follow her. Des Moines was lovely but she'd never intended to stay. She was already gone, had left that morning.

My mother had never been left by anyone but my father. All the boyfriends she had, she'd left. I had never seen heartbreak this close before. It frightened me. This sweet, gentle man changed in front of us like something out of one of those werewolf movies where you really feel sorry for the person with the full moon curse because they never asked for it. It just befell them. Which, being older now, that just seems to be the way it goes sometimes. I'll never understand it but I know I'll witness it again and again and every time I'll be alarmed by it.

I was in eighth grade, okay? I still believed that hearts could be mended.

So I resolved it upon myself to fix it, to bring them back

together, to make it all better again. Sadie was a nice lady. I knew I could reason with her and she'd come around, just like that episode where D.J. steps in when Uncle Joey gets his heart broken by Alanis, successfully brings them back together with a blind date at a movie theater, and he buys her a car to thank her for sealing the deal for him on a lifetime of love.

I got on the computer and used the context clues I'd picked up along the way—namely her grandparents' names—to find a way to contact her. Sure enough, her grandma and grandpa's address in Quitman, Missouri, was listed online. I wrote it out on the back of a tabbed divider in my Trapper Keeper and set to work on a letter. I had learned how to type but felt handwritten would carry the extra personal touch that was needed to urge Sadie to take Uncle Howard back and save him from the pain of not having her in his life. Also the printer was super loud and would raise Mom's suspicions.

I don't remember how I said what I said, just the feeling of the letter. It went on for pages, I remember that. I put everything I was learning in Mrs. Franklin's class about building a persuasive argument into it. This was my chance to put newly acquired skills of persuasion to work in a way far more constructive than standing in front of the class and insisting that Crystal Agri-Cola was superior to regular Agri-Cola.

I spent all night working on it in my room, Mom worrying that I was suddenly a serious student. I didn't tell her what I was up to. No way. She'd have none of it. She was thrilled it hadn't worked out between Uncle Howard and Sadie because she didn't want to be alone in being forever alone.

Life made more sense to her when her brother was single. It doesn't make much sense, no, but neither do people.

When I finished the letter, I folded it in a middle school folded-note pattern and wrote FOR SADIE'S EYES ONLY upon it. I tucked it into a card I raided from Mom's box of blank cards, which I signed with a stick figure doodle of her and him getting back together and instructions to read the letter. I licked the envelope shut on that and sealed it with stickers of the Snorks with hearts over their heads—I had a whole roll of Snorks stickers that one of Mom's boyfriends had given me years earlier (He'd worked at Nub's Novelties downtown, which boasted the biggest sticker selection in Iowa...). Then I wrote her name on that, put a stamp on it, and tucked it into another card written out to her grandparents with the request that they fill in Sadie's new address and send it on to her at her new address in Maryland. I wrote their address on that envelope, put a stamp on it and, on my walk home from school the next day, dropped it into a mailbox.

I felt triumphant at my intervention. I'd done something selfless. I'd worked to bring two people back together who I thought I knew deep down cared about each other.

What I wasn't prepared for was the wait and worry over getting a reply.

I'd check our mail soon as I got home but all it was every day was bills and Fingerhut catalogs. I allotted time for the card to get to her grandparents' in Missouri—about three days—and then a couple days for them to mull over mailing the letter, which they'd do because they were grandparents and grandparents always want their grandkids to find lasting love—then a good business week for the enclosed card to get to the east coast—then a full week for her to weigh how to

116

respond, the weighing inspiring a change of heart—another business week for her reply to come, thanking me and saying she was inviting him out to spend a week with her, maybe introducing him to her sort of estranged mom, and getting him an interview at the local branch of Tristram's Books. So I knew to not really be anxious until enough time for all that had passed. All the same, I was anxious about it constantly, writing their names in hearts on my homework, in the margins of Mrs. McMahon's civics class worksheets.

And then one day after school Mom interrupted the daily two-hour block of *Saved By The Bell* on TBS and WGN by coming into the living room and sitting next to me on the couch, which she never did, and asking if she could talk to me, which she *really* never did.

"Did you happen to reach out to Uncle Howard's ex?"

I finally had something to write in to *Seventeen Magazine* about: I was mortified. Just sat there trying not to quiver. Then, of course, when Mom hugged me from the side and started touching my hair and lecturing me in this tone that sounded gentle but wasn't at all if you actually listened to it, I started crying.

I have no idea what Sadie wrote back but from what I gathered Mom intercepted a letter addressed to me from her. When I protested against the invasion of privacy she pulled the "you're-living-under-my-roof-and-when-you're-eighteen" thing, which only inspired me to move out on my eighteenth birthday, which I did.

She said she tossed the letter out. That it arrived days earlier. That she'd called Uncle Howard to talk about it and he'd not wanted to talk about it. I was instructed to not bring up Sadie to him ever because it would only upset him. I was also told to not contact Sadie again because it was none of my business—it was grown up business—and wouldn't change anything anyway.

To say I was humiliated is downplaying it.

And yes, my grades took a dip.

The next time I saw Uncle Howard was when he took me to the middle school party at Skate West. Sam and Lou had hockey that night so Mom had to get them to the ice rink while he stepped in to chaperon me to the roller rink. And he looked so gaunt and sad, his face thin like it never had been before. And he didn't have much to say.

The other parents there, to the absolute horror of their kids, were mingling and sharing stupid stories about their kids growing up so fast and so on. Some of them put skates on, too, but he didn't. He sat at one of the tables bolted to the floor reading a book, his head down. I don't remember what he was reading but I do remember being far more interested in him than I was in doing the limbo, which I always fell down for. My ladies understood the situation—I'd told them everything I could without the bits that I felt made me look pathetic—and they let me go check on him. He'd given me ten bucks so I bought two paper cones of cotton candy, each a blue-pink combo swirl, and rolled up to his table with my offering. He wasn't going to take his but seeing that I'd bought two he sort of had to. We sat eating spun sugar and I noticed a black smudge just above his eyebrow toward his temple and asked what he'd been doing, if it was bicycle grease. Now, of course, I know it was probably coal dust but he just told me to not waste time with my sad lump of an uncle when I could be having immense amounts of fun on eight wheels. I respected his wish to be left alone and coasted back onto the rink to join my friends for the locomotion.

On the ride home he asked if I still had spelling tests, which I didn't, but I told him we had a spelling bee, though I'd not signed up for it. He said that was okay and asked me to spell "Materteral."

I asked what that was.

"The adjective for aunt," he said, staring at the stop light like a racecar driver. "So. Aunt-y. Or, more, aunt-ish. Aunt-like. No one uses it but it's in the OED. You'll hear avuncular, sure."

I asked what that was.

"The adjective for uncle. It means uncle-y, or uncle-ish."

I told him I'd never heard anybody say either of those words. And even though my instinct was to ask him how he was feeling about what had happened with Sadie, I didn't. And even though Mom said she'd talked to him about the response Sadie had sent me, he didn't bring it up. It was like we were both of us living under her control, respecting whatever decrees she'd issued about not bringing it up with each other. I didn't think it at the time but I think it now, that she likely told him not to bring it up with me because I was too young to understand it, much like she'd told me not to talk about it with him, being a topic unsuitable for my age. Why we both respected this boundary line she drew is beyond me. I didn't really fear her. I knew she was full of crap about these things. So did he. But we still followed her rules.

I wish we hadn't.

We got home before Mom and the boys so he was supposed to stay with me because of Johnny Gosch and Eugene Martin. But he didn't want to come in, so we waited in his blue Tempo with the heater going and the oldies station on.

And we had there the strangest conversation we'd ever had, all about dreaming, and he asked if I could lucid dream. I didn't know what that was so he explained it, how it was basically taking control of your dream and turning it into whatever you wanted it to be. I'd had a few times where I realized I was dreaming as it was happening, but I didn't really take control like he was talking about.

He lifted his eyebrows at nothing, not looking anywhere or at anything, and said he used to be able to do it but not anymore. When he was in college, apparently, he spent a lot of time taking the reins on his dreams but he said it always left him exhausted in the morning. If he'd decided to go dogsledding over mountains of bubble bath suds, he'd wake up as worn out as if he'd really done it. So he made a mental decision to stop it, just in the interests of getting enough rest for classes, and ever since he'd not been able to reclaim the skill.

"It's like I banished myself," he said, leaving it at that.

Mom pulled into the driveway then.

I thanked him for the ride and the snack money and I gave him my glow necklace I got at the party. He let me fasten it around his neck. I got out and waved to him from the porch. Mom shouted a thanks at him without stopping to talk to him, herding Sam and Lou as they continued a fight that'd started on the ice all the way to our front door. I got the door open, trying to stay out of their way, and when they tumbled into the house I looked again but his car was already halfway down the block. He'd forgotten to turn his lights on.

And that was the last time I saw him.

Suburban Intrigue didn't cover *any* of that. I guess that stuff wasn't intriguing enough to them though it's sure held a place of confusion and basic unresolvableness for me. They went for what was easy and sensational while drawing out everything else that had nothing to do with anything—the retired state coal mine inspector in his bow tie? I guess there's a history to the mines and whatever but there was a heart in my Uncle Howard and it was broken. His life shouldn't be fodder for twenty-one minutes of television, interrupted by prescription ads for dry eyes and drier vaginas, but it is. That's the kind of world we live in which is only kind of a world and one we should shake our heads at.

Where their producers—or whoever it is that makes those stupid shows—picked up was when he didn't show up for Thanksgiving. And that's very true: when he didn't show up for Thanksgiving and didn't answer his phone we knew something was very wrong.

Now I never saw the hole in person—Mom kept us away—and I'd not looked at any pictures since the one I saw on the evening news when it happened. Over the years I'd seen it plenty in my dreams, different versions of it, and sometimes he was fine down there and sometimes he was dead and sometimes he was undead down there. I just felt so claustrophobic seeing the old file photos they used in the show, like I couldn't breathe, like he couldn't when every-thing caved in on him.

So apparently the thing that happened was at some point half his basement fell into a sinkhole caused by an old mine under his house. And instead of getting out of there, like most people would do, he stayed and went down there to explore it or something. The one "expert" they had, from the city as-sessor's office, who speculated it was the weight of all his books that did it? What a load of bull. Why do they let these people talk about stuff they haven't got any knowledge about in the first place?

They knew where to dig because a group of extension cords and a phone line ran from the basement wall down the hole and continued on into the debris, like the earth had taken four or five strands of spaghetti and not slurped them all into its mouth. When they excavated, they found him there on the other side of a lot of dirt and rubble. *Suburban Intrigue* said he was slumped in his easy chair and showed him with the TV on but that isn't how it was from what I understand. The chair he took down there with him was the patched lawn chair from Great Aunt Carla and the TV wasn't on—or the computer either—because the collapse had yanked the cords out of their sockets. But yes, it's true that he'd set up a sort of den in the old mine. Twists my stomach, them labeling it "the first man-cave before man-caves were cool." He did seem ready to spend a lot of time down there though. He had a lamp and the TV set and his desktop. He even took his bike down there. It still stood on its kickstand.

And he hadn't told anybody about it.

The show got that right at least.

All we know is that at some point—probably right after the breakup—the basement of his house fell into that sinkhole and instead of letting anybody know about it, he went down into that old coal mine and decided it was the place he wanted to be. Then, probably the night before Thanksgiving, the ground settled some more and he was trapped.

It was suffocation in the end.

Sadie wasn't at the funeral but I kept hoping she'd appear, sneaking into the back of the chapel at Westover, having rushed back from Maryland, dressed all in black, suffering unimaginable regret, confiding in me as he was lowered into his grave at Glendale that she *had* loved him and was going to call him, had meant to the night before but was busy with the holiday at her mostly-estranged Mom's—and now she'd lost him forever. It made me cry more that she wasn't there because I knew he'd want her to be and that if she hadn't left in the first place I'd probably still have an uncle.

I don't know if she ever found out or sent a card or anything. *I* wasn't going to let her know what happened, not after what happened with Mom and the letter I'd written her.

I still haven't asked Mom twenty years later if she'd ever heard from her. I'm still too scared to.

Sometime after I got on Facebook, I managed to track her down. I don't remember how I did that but when I tried to find her again the next Thanksgiving, which is when I think of Uncle Howard the most, I couldn't. Maybe she deleted her page or something. I remember she'd married a Greek, so now her name is Sadie Koprofagodopoulos. Or something.

My girls have three uncles and they're all fine and I'm glad of that and I'm thankful they're there even if my daughters aren't close to any of them the way I was to mine. I've had to invent what it means to be an aunt, and do so after becoming a mother, which I think changes the expectations of the title. Less time to be the carefree one I'd like to be—the one I wanted for myself—because I've had my own kids to chase around and take care of.

So I never did get an auntie of my own.

And I lost my uncle.

And maybe that's the thing, the most offensive bit they

left out of that stupid episode of that stupid show. They missed the longest, saddest part of the whole thing. When things don't work out between two people, sometimes the person who's devastated isn't the only one who's left sore. Sometimes there's a friend or sibling or maybe a niece who'll wish all her life it had worked out, too.

Viewmaster

to LovelyLotus   12 May 2011

Hey girl:

So I've had this dream a few times now and figure I might as well tell you so you can start dreaming it, too. Maybe you can take it beyond where it stops for me, which is always in the same place every time.

I was renting the condo I bought when I was in med school but I'd finished school in the dream, had the degree (which I do have, as well as my own practice, as you know), but I had refused to enter practice. I was absolutely convinced that I could enhance my own semen and bulk it up to create superior offspring by using methods of science only I knew about and was ready to try. So I took a cup of my own semen and mixed it with blue food coloring to see my swimmers better under a microscope I have set up next to the cappuccino maker (clearly I'd lost my mind). The doorbell rang and I knew it was you. So I scrambled to hide my semen on a shelf, in the cupboard next to the box of Life Cereal. You, of course, discovered the cup upon being let in and you knew what was in it. I was horribly embarrassed (which is also strange since I'm a urologist) but you weren't put off really. You even let me kiss you on the cheek.

Now where do you see the dream going? I'm sick of it cutting off there every single time.

Sent from my iPhone

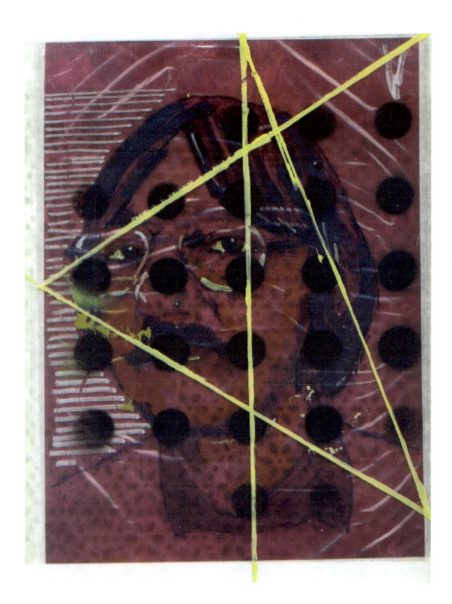

The Troll

"If it's pointless cruelty you're after,
give a man a screenname."
– Not Oscar Wilde

The troll awakens from a dream of life beneath a bridge, as he does each of his days, in a King Size Sleep Number Bed that has only ever known his and his wife's bodies. Preferring the softest setting, he rises after the fourth or fifth snooze in a helpless scramble the missus has so lovingly dubbed "The Flipped Beetle." Being autumn, the house is well heated by the gas furnace in the basement. He fights the aroma of Maxwell House to reach the shower before the wife wakes the girls. The water is warm and the pressure robust. He pees in the shower. He brushes his teeth and gets dressed in dress shirt and khakis from Sears or JC Penny or Kohls. Argyle socks. He lumbers downstairs and fetches his laptop from the room under the staircase that he calls his office. He turns the laptop on, setting it on the kitchen counter to start up while he fills the coffee mug that's been left out for him. At the appropriate moment he swipes his right middle finger on the fingerprint scanner and, security unlocked, fires up his self-penned Virtual Private Network. He opens his browser to headlines on the *Puffington Host*.

20% THINK PRESIDENT IS MUSLIM has the most hits.

The article is of no consequence; he scrolls past to get to the comments section.

> *Myrthe_Kent*
> *Why is such a large section of our population concerned with this to begin with? Even if the man was Muslim he would still be our President. I just wonder about these people.*

<Here's why>, he types under his anonymous username: T-Cup. <Take the name Osama Bin Laden. Mix it around. Obama Sin Laden. "President" OBAMA is LADEN with SIN. AKA he's a Muslim. The writing was right there on the ballot and you sheeple couldn't see it. FML & take a bow.>

No sooner has he posted that than HumblePi replies, <flagged.>

<Leave it to a lib to step on the 1st amendment rights of a triple amputee disabled vet who went and got PTSD so you can eat your Cheerios each morning without worrying about ISIS cutting your heads off>, he taps.

<i prefer froot loops>, replies scruffaluff.

And then, midway through typing another response, GeorgeBernardBeckett chimes in with an axiom for this newest era of electronic communication: <Don't feed the troll.>

The girls tell him it's time to go to school, forcing him to pinch it off: <May your son's son's son suffer this same deadly fate you heartless faceless cowards.> He leaves the laptop running but secures it in the room under the stairs before being herded into his Escalade. He drops the girls at school. The topic on *The Big Old Morning Show* is last night's episode of *Engagement Isle*. He tries to call in amid rush hour traffic on 235 but gets a busy signal on all twenty-seven attempts.

Soon he is at his cubicle on level B1 of Percival Insurance Tower. There are already forty-seven e-mails to answer in his work inbox and Amber, the next cubicle over, is trying to cry quietly. Her daughter died two years ago, of the flu, the virus emboldened by the girl's asthma. Peeking over, he asks if he can get her some coffee. She nods into a tissue. He goes and fetches two cups in the canteen and delivers one to her, there in her workplace shrine to her girl, all of wall and desk commemorating the child in photo, card, and art class art.

Settling in, he hooks into the GUI he penned, running in his browser to bleed through Percival's network security. He tediously answers three tedious e-mails and heads on over to GreenThumbForum.com to see if he can ruin anybody's day. Online gardeners are particularly touchy when somebody comes in and winds them up for no good reason. Easy morning prey.

But the sniffling, it really is *incessant* this morning.

Too distracted to troll the gardeners sharing slug control tips, he tucks back into e-mails, answers two more—but, gosh, the simpering grief on the other side of carpeted cubicle wall seriously isn't letting up. Most days, by now, she's done with the canned despair.

Grumbling but following a hunch, he draws up her daughter's never-ending virtual funeral on Angel-Memorial-Pages.com. The link is buried in his bookmarks. Here Amber has posted every photo she has of her dead girl, shaky cell phone snaps of her artwork, and multiple entries in the Remembrance Garden Guestbook every day since setting it up a couple years ago. She changes the main photo, framed in digital lace, often. At the moment it's the last yearbook photo the kid sat for.

Ah, right.

He'd *thought* she'd died in spring.

It can be hard to remember with Amber grieving at an intensity most folks wouldn't be able to sustain.

It's what he calls Holy Week in his head, the days leading up to the anniversary of her actual death. Amber is really Christian, which doesn't help anything. Instead of just accepting that her kid croaked and had no soul and that was that and getting over it, she believes this whole fairy tale scam that clearly does nothing for her in terms of moving on.

The snotting into tissues just won't stop.

He slaps his desk with both palms but cools it. He could head over and tell Jeri in HR that Amber is having a rough morning/week/month/year/life. But look, whatever counseling she's supposedly meant to be getting, it really isn't making his working conditions any better.

He glances behind him to see who's where.

Nobody's watching, as usual.

He opens a new pane in the girl's Remembrance Garden and, calling himself the TwillSyouF, starts typing.

Without the brakes.

Statistics about how many children die of the flu each year in the U.S.A., he fabricates them.

Qualifying such a death as less tragic than other varieties, creating a pyramid from blood cancer to being mauled by pit bull to murder-by-pederast, he goes there.

Speaking on behalf of the girl to condemn the garishness of the online memorial and the shamefulness of her mother's obsession with maintaining it, he flames.

When he's sure he's quite done, he hovers the cursor over the Share button.

He *could* go to Jeri.

This dream I had about you really shook me up so bad, okay?

So so bad. And like I don't know what it's about but I just want to say right off the bat that I don't think it has anything to do with you and how I see you because you really are the hottest woman I've ever seen in my whole life. It was just a freaky dream is all is what I keep telling myself. It was just a dream.

And it was. That's all it was.

So here goes the dream now. I'll just type it out for you and you can totally be the judge yourself for it.

I was in a class on marginalia taught by none other than you. You had this ongoing powerpoint about weird notes written in books (that's what marginalia is) but all I could look at was the way you filled out your business casual blouse. You tell me to come up to your office after class, so I go and you seduce me. We do it. Later I'm walking around and find out the university found out about our extracurricular activities and you're being fired? So I decide to go see you at your house to apologize. Strangely, the world is a giant enclosed train station complete with wood trim and tiled floor and frosted glass roof, ok? I get to your house and a real plain blond answers the door. I ask if Professor Lotus is there and she says, "Uh yeah..." I look in and you come stumbling down the staircase but you suddenly have John Tuturro's head and a five o'clock shadow and you're dressed in gypsy rags and you're all disoriented, maybe even insane?? You're shouting, "I'm intersexed! I'm intersexed!" And you lift up your dress and there's a penis. My first thought is, "How did I miss that when we did it on your desk?" And then my second thought is, "She's hung better than me!"

I woke up going, "AHHHHH!!!" and my roommate was like, "Wtf, dude, pinch it off." I went to logic and quantitative reasoning but had to leave early to jot this down and send it to you.

No idea what that's about because I'm not gay and it seems pretty gay…

For the record I don't think you're intersexed.

Love (too soon to say that?),
Daniel Wu
~~~~~~~~~~~~~~
GO BLUE HENS!

Out of Character

Not since Dietrich had Europe produced a lily so exquisite as Lea De Wever. So sayeth the ad placed in *Daily Variety* by the producer of her current film:

NOT SINCE DIETRICH HAS EUROPE PRODUCED A LILY SO EXQUISITE AS LEA DE WEVER

There she was in black-and-white, done up like Shanghai Lily in a British Captain's hat with fur collar radiating like a Ceratopsian neck frill. Full-page. The photo came from that shoot a month ago where the photographer got sulky when she told him in front of his assistants that he had a broccoli bud between his two front teeth. Are you not supposed to tell people such a thing? Is it not rude to let them go about their business with food in their smiles?

A yellow Post-It note stuck along the top of the page bore a handwritten message from Trenise, her studio-assigned PA: *Hi lady! Call producer to thank him for this.*

Cécile, her agent in Brussels, had sent a phone message saying just as much, with the producer's number there, callable with a tap.

Producers producing productions, that's what this place was. And why not? The trouble was simply in figuring out who one could trust, which wasn't all that simple at all.

The current picture—*The Man Who Bent Time*—placed her in a spread of supporting roles, which was fine—Lea was not above a supporting role let alone a whole spread in the same film—but most of them lacked complexity, not to mention screen time. The idea was that she play a time traveler's lost love—an English social worker—as well as every other woman he fleetingly encounters throughout time—Mary Magdalene at the Crucifixion, the Oracle at Delphi, a Neanderthal widow. All variety, no depth. Lots of eyebrow acting, especially in that last part, which was going to be tough under the makeup. Few lines. Not the starring leads she enjoyed back home in Belgium, where she was fortunate to choose her projects.

The hope: this was a foot in the door to working in more American films—and not only as wives to protagonists.

The experience itself: long stretches of downtime between carrying out these little roles interspersed throughout the shoot engendered a lot of inner doubt and second guessing. About things.

That's what this ad was for, she knew. The out-of-placèdness she'd been feeling had become known to others despite her effort at keeping it hidden. This was a gesture expressing flattery. This was something only an old man would think to do anymore—and indeed the producer was an old man. This was meant to make her feel more welcome but it was also Hollywood talking to itself about her.

Part and parcel of the job.

The magazine marked with a Post-It was waiting for her inside the screen door of the townhouse she was renting on Quail Run Drive when she returned from the gym in her also-rented Chrysler.

Even that name—Quail Run Drive—left little room for ease. Why were the quails running? Because of all the driving happening in their natural habitat, surely. The poor quails, scuttling in figure eights, trailing chicks, having to dodge the fat tires of gargantuan American automobiles... She had yet to see any quails, which, until seen, she was forced to assume were all now dead, extinct from this place, thanks to vehicular flattening.

She made her FaceTime session with her therapist back home in Antwerpen. There, through the small pane in her hand, sat Ferdinand, nine hours in the future. He was very good, agreeing to see her twice a week, based on her schedule. Normally she would sit upright and at an angle from him in his consulting room. Here, with it being evening there, and Ferdinand in an armchair in his library at home, he saw her, she knew, from the screen of his laptop, which, placed on his lap, provided her the lap's-eye view of Ferdinand—an entirely new view—all wiggly wattle and tufted nostrils. He had her take off her glasses—amber tortoiseshell horn-rims that almost matched her memory of her hair's natural color—so he could better see her eyes in Californian light.

This time, though neither of them needed it, they spatted. Without articulating why, she had stretched out on the sofa and held the phone over her face. This simply matched for her what she was seeing—not that she wanted to be lying in

Ferdinand's lap, not at all. It just correlated with the view. He took her lying down before him 9,000 kilometers away as flirtation and leveled the charge of transference—the same trouble that had ended things with Lotte, her last therapist. Lea hadn't fallen for her but Lotte sure claimed she had, wouldn't hear anything contrary, at which point she started seeing Ferdinand, thinking that if a woman therapist hadn't worked out perhaps a grandfatherly one might. And now here, she hoped, he was simply having a bad day. He took her sympathy for pity and, most unfortunately, cut the session short. They had only talked for eighteen minutes.

She rummaged through her satchel for her iPod and drew up this film's playlist. Even though her phone could hold the music, the little orange gizmo had been with her for years, held all her playlists. It was superstitious tradition: each of her projects got its own playlist, built over the course of production, those songs that accompanied her through each shoot. All were different, and so far *The Man Who Bent Time* playlist was mostly doozies. "Do You Know the Way to San Jose?" never sounded grim until the day she actually listened to the lyrics about failed actors pumping gas. She scrolled through her library, adding Marc Benno's "Speak Your Mind," dragging it to the top of the list. She cradled her iPod in the dock and let it play, Telecaster notes riffing like distant thunder on that first track. The music could get her through this job.

Lunch became salmon, lettuce, and a green avocado she picked herself from the backyard. They had "backyards" here, watered green with timed sprinklers against the arid climate.

The avocado was under-ripe, to say the least, yellow and

dense to the point of being nearly impossible to cut. Somehow she managed without flaying open her palm.

She chewed the unchewable fruit down anyway. Her stubbornness extended to her curiosity, and a Google search of "ripe avocado" revealed her mistake in assuming one could be sliced and eaten straight off the tree. Another trip out back and she returned with five that she lined along the tiles on the too-bare kitchen counter.

She closed *Daily Variety* on herself and took up the script. She reviewed the pages where she was playing the Oracle, her lines written out in phonetic syllables—phonetic to an ear tuned in American English anyway.

"AY soo-DO-man-TISS AY-me thoo-ro-COP-ose FLEH-doan," she said one way.

"Ay SOO-do-MAN-tiss AY-me THOO-ro-COP-ose FLEH-doan," she said another way.

Her phone hummed from the counter. She checked it.

A pic from Wouter. There was her flowering ficus, orchids, and the sweet peas blooming pink and white up the indoor trellis. Of course they all bloomed while she was far from home.

She saw him typing before his message arrived: <vrolijke planten>

She tapped out and sent a reply: <mijn lief poezeke?>

Waiting, waiting, and then a pic of her little black kitty, Piet, the runt of his litter. His yellow eyes held the proper attitude of indifference toward Wouter on the other side of the phone. It comforted her to know the cat had not yet betrayed her in her absence.

Despite Piet's total lack of cheerfulness, Wouter wrote: <vrolijk poezeke>

She took off her glasses and fiddled with her hair and took a selfie conveying appreciativeness, not fussing with a second take, sending it along with informal regards: <danku>

She put the glasses on again and sighed herself a lip-flapping sigh.

Her phone hummed with a new pic. This time it was a part of Wouter she hadn't missed, thought about, or longed to see ever again.

Wouter may have said his offer to water the plants and feed Piet was only friendly, but of course it wasn't. Her brother just as easily could have done it, had said he would, had balked when told that Wouter, who, yes, still had a key, was taking care of it. Brothers don't bring post-relationship flatulence into one's life. She would have to remember this for the future.

The phone rang and she nearly silenced the call—but thank hesitation—it wasn't Wouter calling.

"Hello!" she sang, staring out the window onto quail-less Quail Run Drive.

"Allo, allo!" the producer said. "Did you ever see that one? Was a TV show about World War Two humor—'Allo 'Allo!—British show about the war in Belgium."

"Yes, we got that when I was a girl." She declined to correct him. It took place in France.

"Listen, did, ah—"

"Thank you!" she gushed. "Yes, yes, the magazine was right here waiting for me after I returned from the gym—so thoughtful! Thank you!"

"Well you know I just want to make sure you feel like you're at home here on your first stint in Hollywood. When I heard you were a little under the weather—"

"The weather's not a problem here."

"Not in Southern California it isn't—haugh, haugh!"

She watched herself laugh in this unfunny moment.

"Listen, my family's away on vacation in Bermuda and I'm kinda lonesome over here all by myself. What do you say to dinner at mine tonight? I'll pick you up."

"Dinner at yours is great, yes," she said on professional autopilot.

"Great, great—what about any dietary restrictions I should know about? S'pose I should know about them already, eh?"

"Apparently I can't eat avocados." She eyed the line of them left to ripen she-knew-not-how-long on the countertop.

"And the only thing I know how to make is guacamole—just kidding! I can work around that. Pick you up at seven-ish?"

"I look forward to it."

"See ya then!"

He hung up and conflict swiped across her. She checked the time.

2:13.

A business dinner in private company did not appeal. Not in the slightest. Which her of the hers in his imagination would he expect her to be—and which the hers within might manifest in relation to him? The chipper persona she'd just been on the phone had a short fuse these days. How would she change when chipperness ended? Lea embraced the cliché of a cage of her own making, where her decisions formed the bars. She had always struggled to be mindful in her professional choices so those bars were spread far enough apart for her to come and go. People could always find her tapdancing and vaulting pratfalls in her enclosure in the showbiz zoo during operating hours. Just please, no one ask her to always be there.

Maybe she could use the diarrhea defense. Nobody, if one cancels plans feigning diarrhea, can ever object.

"Even actresses get het vliegend schijt," she rehearsed aloud, finger poised upon calling him back.

She called her best friend. Annemie was on holiday with her boyfriend in Vietnam. Lea wasn't sure of the time difference, despite being told every time they'd chatted the past week. It made no difference anyway—went straight to voicemail, so she cancelled the call. They were probably exploring limestone towers or boating across rice paddies or doing whatever one does on holiday in Vietnam, if they'd even managed to leave their suite. Romance.

She gathered herself in the corner of the couch, chest to knees, and launched into a game of Review Roulette. More reliable than reading tea leaves or consulting the *I Ching*, the rules were simple: (1) Google "lea De Wever review", (2) open a link to a review she'd not seen before, (3) read it, (4) augur what to do next based on how it makes her feel.

As a game it could calm her nerves with affirmation or send her confidence into the depths of Funk Perilous. Lotte, Ferdinand, her agent, Annemie, her brother—and especially Wouter—had all told her to stop doing this.

She swiped through seven pages of search results on her phone before the purple links turned a virginal blue. Closing her eyes, she tapped.

Opening them and adjusting her glasses with a nose scrunch, she read:

What's On At The Schwarzwald: ciné rex
(*Dir. Arno Van Vliet; 2008, Belgium*)

By now, of course, faithful readers of this blog are familiar with my rather quaint habit of expressing sentimental love for the films we show at the Schwarzwald, but please, let all of that mean nothing to you from now on. After building up and previewing this week's Foreign Feature, I've got a new favorite film. Can hardly believe I'm typing this but, yes, Minnie *and* Moskowitz *has been dethroned by a Belgian masterpiece:* ciné rex.

(Before one of our loyal retired English teacher customers comments—Jean, Vicki, Rick, I'm looking at you—let me just say they don't capitalize their film titles over there...)

I don't know about you, but I don't know boo about Belgium. Is it stupid to assume that a lot of Belgians probably don't know much about Iowa? Probably. But listen, aren't we, as a people, a bit thin-skinned when it comes to others not knowing a lot about us? There's a benefit, isn't there, in watching cinema from a place we aren't well-acquainted with?

The film opens on the afternoon of December 16, 1944, at Ciné Rex in Antwerp. The matinee showing of DeMille's Wild West mash-up, The Plainsmen, *is underway when a German V-2 rocket all but levels the theater, killing half the audience, a good many of them Allied soldiers. Based on historical events that Thomas Pynchon alludes to in* Gravity's Rainbow, *director Arno Van Vliet tracks back to the cinema's gala opening in 1935 and charts its life through Nazi occupation in 1940 (they rename it the Eldorado) to liberation by the British and local resistance in September 1944 (when it is restored, however briefly, to Cine Rex). Think* Inglorious Bastards *if Tarantino had only focused on the cinema, gone for character study over snappy violence and suspense, and filmed a cast speaking in Flemish. The title,* ciné rex, *translates to Black House, referring symbolically to the darkened auditorium where films transport the people of Antwerp away from—or back into—the strife they are living, depending on what's showing.*

An ensemble cast takes us into the lives of the cinema's staff, but the character we follow closest is the projectionist, played by Lea De Wever. And I must say I feel my own existence validated by her performance, especially in her quietest moments. Take the scene during Nazi occupation when she is screening Abel Gance's 1927 silent epic, Napoléon. (SPOILER ALERT: At this point, she has grudgingly undertaken a sexual arrangement with the new manager—a pencil-pushing, low-ranking, pseudointellectual SS officer—to save herself and her husband. The bastard, in cinematic Nazi fashion, makes a precedent for his menace by taking the affable, chocolate-loving cinema manager—played by Beuker Deneuker, cast to type—to the roof and throwing him off of it). De Wever's caprice as she dances back and forth between tending those beautiful twin projectors and holding herself together at the booth window while viewing Napoleon's schoolboy snowball fight is art at its finest. Of course, Napoleon was finally defeated on Belgian turf, and in this film we are following people hurt by what Hitler wrought. We feel what she feels, the abject pain of living the repercussions from tactics learned again and again throughout time from games waged in the snow. It's there in the way she carries herself, moving between the grace of an expert machinist, and the restrained anguish she imparts when reacting to the action onscreen.

The silent film's effect upon De Wever's character shows just how mysterious catharsis is. I'm attuned, as the manager of a classic cinema, toward appreciating the wonder of film—but ciné rex is the first time I've perceived my career as sacred. Any rocket that has ever destroyed a cinema has been an attack on the collective enterprise of film. I'm not being a ham here when I thank Lea De Wever for evoking for me the beauty of my own life's work, for iterating that what we do in film exhibition is relevant to greater well-being. Little did these filmmakers know the effect it'd have on a guy in Des Moines. I'd love to thank her myself, although she's no stranger to critical and popular praise. She won a Golden Waffle and a Rubens Award (both for Best Actress) in Belgium, and was nominated for five other awards for her performance in ciné rex, which is also, since its release last year, the highest grossing Belgian film of all time.

Also, showing this at the Schwarzwald, with all the historical significance our theater carries regarding the same war, compounds the film's impact—or ought to. The Schwarzwald, of course, was renamed the Capri in late 1942, and the Capri it remained until we reopened and reinstated the original name in 2005. I can only suspect that our entry into the war at that time was behind the name change. In any case, I hope you, too, will feel a historical echo when seeing the film here. Sadly, we only have ciné rex for one week. Don't miss it. Show times are at 1 and 7. And yes, the film is subtitled, so don your reading glasses.

Lea looked up from her phone, her free hand covering her heart. No need to interpret the omens in her own entrails. This required no literacy of the gut.

She scuttled up and down the page. The blog post was four years old. Seemed to be a website for an old cinema, the Schwarzwald.

But who had written this?

Harvey!

There, at the bottom of the page: *Harvey*.

Like Jimmy Stewart's invisible rabbit—or *Doc* Harvey—in *Shanghai Express*! She lifted from the couch and returned to *Daily Variety* on the counter, opening its pages as if they were curtains. There she was as Shanghai Lily, wearing an officer's cap like Doc Harvey's.

This Harvey had written a lot of blog posts, weekly, reviewing every film screened at his cinema, on up to present. His "About" in the sidebar revealed less than little: *I've been manager of the majestic Schwarzwald since the cinema reopened in May 2005.*

A Google search of "harvey schwarzwald cinema" only produced links back to the site.

"Where is Des Moines?" she asked her phone.

bing-bing "Here's Des Moines."

A map with a red pin appeared. She pinched the screen, pulling away to a view of the continent, clocking the distance from Los Angeles.

She called the producer.

Straight to voicemail, thank God.

"It's Lea. Listen, so sorry, don't bother tonight. I've come down with het vliegend schijt, which is very much what it sounds like in English."

She ended the call without salutation, cringing with sudden she-may-never-work-in-this-town-again anxiety. Some moments, so it seemed, held more life than others, were more authentic. And feeling just such a quality of genuine living, she realized it had been awhile since she felt one of these moments.

She turned the open magazine over, face down, grabbed her plaid vintage satchel lying on the floor, uncradled her iPod and Joni Mitchell's voice with it, and walked out the front door of the rented house.

Her phone played psychopomp between her and the destination, leading with left turns, right turns, and merges as soon as she drove out of the Des Moines Airport in a rented Honda. The car was electric, like hers back home in Antwerpen. Summer hung hot and muggy here in the night air, which, though still, vibrated with the drone of cicadas. The insects cut clean through Nick Drake, his music composed in a place without such summerly racket. So strange, to be driving through an unimagined city, everything from the ongoing gridded residential neighborhoods to the Kum & Go gas stations established with confidence beyond her simple assumptions. Much of it looked so much like the America she catalogued from a life of watching American films, yet it held its own ground, insisting itself in its own ways. It all existed here in its own way in spite of her ignorance of it.

It was 10:27 when the phone told her, "Your destination is on the left!"

There in absolute fidelity, holding up the corner next to Diode Shack and Coppola's Pizzeria, stood the cinema, lighting the dark with a thousand old bulbs. A sign announced its name vertically in green-lit Arnold Böcklin:

S
C
H
W
A
R
Z
W
A
L
D

Idling by it, the cinema stood paradoxically grander and quainter than it did in the pics online. She pulled into the parking lot for the Uptown Shopping Center, all but empty at this hour, and parked facing the place. TRANSFORMERS 4 and LOVE ME TONIGHT were tacked up in movable black letters on the yellow-white marquee.

She cut the engine, and with it "The River Man."

While reading through Harvey's cinema blog on the

plane, she had pondered forming a new playlist called *Search for Harvey* but decided against it—because in taking this trip she had not quit her job. Whatever happened here was part of the experience of making a big budget Hollywood movie with a bargain-basement time travel plot. She'd be going back to California. She always finished what she began. Even if she didn't find him, Lea would only ever be the only person to really know about it.

Lea really didn't know what she was doing here.

Maybe she was really and truly at long last finally going crazy.

"Gonna see the Schwarzwald man," she sang low, for herself.

When she got out and crossed the road, the ornate decorations rising above the marquee seemed poised to act, the whole thing meant to be a cuckoo clock. Of course! Cuckoo clocks were traditional to the Black Forest—what better decoration for a cinema sharing its name? Lacquered fiberglass oak leaves garnished the branches framing and buttressing a dozen figures from German folklore: here the Bremen Town musicians with their instruments, there the Pied Piper coaxing children away with his fife. Under one bow Faust sold his soul to Mephistopheles while under another Till Eulenspiegel hovered his bare arse over a cooking roast. Peart pheasants and perspicacious hares stood beside farmers in feathered Hecker hats and dirndled maidens in pompon-topped Bollenhuts. A hipped roof, like those found on so many of the valley homes in southwestern Germany, capped the display. Under it, and above the round clock face, she spied the unassuming door that surely housed a vigilantly punctual cuckoo bird. The hour was not upon them, thank goodness. Lea was apt to startle with slapstick alarm at the cuckoo element of these clocks.

She couldn't identify all the characters, the kobolds or the witches, but was happiest to find her old friend, Reinaert the Fox—the very first role she ever played on stage, when just a preschooler—peering from behind a trunk with a gimlet-eyed wink. This connection, made while crossing the street, came just in time; abruptly, staggered across a few moments, the blinking yellow bulbs under the overhang, the uplights, and marquee board went dark.

Being a classic cinema of a practically forgotten era, there stood a box office true to its name: a boxlike vestibule jutting out with poster cases and glass double doors on either side. Lea stepped under the marquee, past a sandwich board advertising *FREE POPCORN TUESDAYS*, and across the vintage hexagonal tile work, making to walk in. But the doors on the left were locked. The doors on the right were locked, too. The lobby within, squinted at, seemed disturbed only by stillness, lit dim by the concession stand menu boards.

She went to the box office and peered through the ticket window. It was framed in polished brass decorated top to bottom with oak leaves matching those atop the marquee. She cupped her ball cap bill to the glass. The door behind the ticket seller's stool was a painstakingly carved hornbeam relief of an old valley village with steeple and mill and tiny people and horse-drawn carriages in the lane. Astonishing!

Then she peered down past the stool and saw a man curled around it, hiding on the floor.

She lowered her mouth to the open semicircle in the window. "I see you."

Though he was mostly in shadow, she saw his frame

loosen with resignation. Her heart quickened.

"Are you the cinema manager?"

"Ah, I am," he said, the enclosure muffling his voice to a sigh. He clambered upright in hide-and-seek defeat.

Here she saw him half in shadow, his face reflecting stray halogen from the streetlights. Taller than her, without being tall. Thinned hair, trimmed neat. Rimless eyeglasses and a plaid dress shirt of brown and blues with the sleeves rolled up two turns. His face, with little lines wrinkling around his mouth, showed him to be sincerely ashamed.

"Sorry, we're closed?"

Again she stooped to the opening at the base of the window. "Were you on the floor because you saw me coming and didn't want to help me?"

"Well, the late show began an hour and a half ago—"

"No I'm not here for the late show."

He set his hands flat on the ticket counter and she saw the wedding ring. "How can I help you?"

The question, asked simply, made her want to turn on her sneakers and retreat, drive back to the airport, wait for the morning's first flight. No one ever had to know she'd come here like this.

"Are you Harvey?"

"I am," he said, registering the beginning of impatience. "What can I do you for?"

She looked down at herself in her summer finery—a long tank top of the Beatles' *Revolver* LP cover worn like a very-awfully-short dress and many-pocketed black shorts and All-Stars sneakers, and then up into the bill of her Mets cap. "I guess I'm not Shanghai Lily, am I."

"Say again?"

"Look, might you let me in? It's humid out here and I'm already sticky—not like the heat in Los Angeles. This is like a wet jungle heat. I feel I might be choking here—"

"Alright, alright." He left the box office through the carved backdoor and reappeared behind the glass double doors on the right. Gave a discerning once-over and opened the door to her.

"Thank you, thank you," she said, crossing into the lobby and reacting to its near-frigid air-conditioned atmosphere with an unconscious feline stretch. "Jesus, it's like stepping into an ice cave, the temperature."

He looked at her gripping her upper arms and crossed his own, as if waiting for an explanation. And again she didn't know what she was doing here. But she couldn't tell if he had recognized her yet or not.

"Do you know who I am?"

"Uh."

"Don't worry—we haven't met before."

He searched her face with distressing confusion.

Aware that she had hunched down, made herself smaller than she already was, Lea rolled her shoulders and straightened her back. She lifted her cap free and pulled her hair to the side, pouting ostentatiously in the light of the menu boards.

An explosion quaked out of the auditorium, the calamitous clamor of the summer blockbuster interrupting them with the full startle of thunder.

She thumbed at the doors. "Is that the biggest thing happening in Des Moines tonight?"

"I know it's hard for folks on the coasts to believe, but life happens here." He said it defensively, illustrating that thing he alluded to in his review about Iowans being a bit thin-skinned about Iowa.

"Guess again," she said with one finger lifted. "I'm not from your coasts."

"Well you're in Cubs territory wearing a Mets hat while talking about Los Angeles with an accent I'm hearing but can't place..."

"I'm Flemish."

He winced. "Allergies are hell with the corn tasseling."

"No, no," she said, remembering and removing her tortoiseshell glasses. "I come from Belgium."

And that did it.

His confusion became disbelief, his forehead smoothing and chin sinking to where his mouth might open. Instead of blushing, which people in the Low Countries occasionally did when meeting her, he lost color.

"No, no, it's just me!" She offered her hand. "And you're Harvey."

"I am..." He caught himself mumbling. "I'm Harvey Wallace." He uncrossed his arms and accepted her hand, gently, his fingers warm. "Hi! What on earth brings you—I love your film—*ciné rex*—it's my favorite! What are you doing here?"

"I wanted to thank you for your kind words."

"You were blonde in the movie," he thought aloud and caught himself again. "Wait, *thank me?*" He ran his hand up and down the back of his neck.

She looked at him, really looked at him, and considered that perhaps her plan—FIND HARVEY AND THANK HIM—wasn't actually a plan at all, but the sort of thing crazed fans armed with hollow-point ammunition or vials of acid did to confront celebrities with their neurotic admiration that could very well sour very fast and end in the emptying of a hand-gun or a face burned blind for life. And come to think of it, that's the sort of thing that happened to regular people far more often, although it didn't get quite the coverage as when a famous artist or luminary is killed or maimed. "But you see," she said, as if that line of thought had been conversation, "I come from a little chocolate and beer country where we recently didn't have a government for five-hundred-and-thirty-five days. We're grounded and sober—even though our beer's strong—and we don't know anything about stardom. Like who are the super famous Belgians? Jean-Claude van Damme? Okay, his splits are amazing. He's just Jean-Claude. You know?"

"Wasn't Audrey Hepburn born in Belgium?"

"To an English banker and Dutch baroness." She sneered for the unfortunateness of that disqualification.

"Sure, sure."

"But who else? Who else? Jacques Brel? You know Jacques Brel?"

He held his chin in his hand, shook his head.

"Jacques Brel is brilliant! A singer, a performer. But he's from the French part of Belgium. So is Jean-Claude. See, we don't have such famous people in Flanders."

"You're famous."

"No, no. Not here. At the airport I was just a lady with a funny accent in a Beatles top—although the girl at the car rental was super pleasant to me—and so was the parking lot person in the little box with the arm that goes up and down?"

"Uh huh?" His eyes flickered from her chest to her face. Glancing down she found he was disconcerted by the way her nipples currently riveted Lennon's right and McCartney's left eyes into three dimensions.

"I told you it's cold in here!"

He snapped to attention. "Sorry! Please, my office is just here." He led her along balding velvet ropes slung between cloudy brass stanchions—"Would've polished those if I knew you were coming..."—and dug a jangle of keys out of the pocket of his chinos. He fumbled unlocking the door labeled MANAGER with an engraved plastic sign, so Lea gave the lobby a turn.

The place was encrusted with detail to minutiae as if by the great Wes Anderson. Suggested in the soft light of the menu boards was a symmetry of old fashioned decoration: oxblood carpet with an Old World pattern, circular lobby couches with deep-buttoned cushions, oak-paneled walls. Facing doors on either side of the lobby announced their distinct purposes with small brass figures affixed at eye height of a gent and a lady, although the gent might be confused for a lady because of his frock—the peaked hat and shepherd's crook only masculinized him if you knew they were meant to masculinize him. Above the re-outfitted concession stand the vaulting wall was painted as if bedecked with mounted heads of stags, does, rams, and boars, their expressions ever-so-slightly jejune. Ascending either side of the stand and disappearing behind this muralistic array, twin roped-off staircases boasted carved statues for their bannisters and railings carved with leaves. High overhead and unlit, a trio of chandeliers—heavy enough looking that she stepped out from under one—struck a peculiar sight. She thought them many-pronged anchors until seeing they were arrangements of antlers capped with glass candleflame bulbs. Had those been giving light, the Germanic pastiche would have revealed more of itself—and she suspected the emphasis would be more on pastiche than Germanic—but perhaps it all benefitted from having its kitsch muted.

Harvey turned the lock and relieved his fiddling embarrassment with a deliberate sigh. "Please! Come on in."

Lea walked into the little windowless office, identifying the framed posters, all facing the desk and its tall vintage lamp from all walls. Behind the rolling chair were Jon Voight and Dustin Hoffman standing tall as Kong and 'Zilla over the blue New York City skyline—

"*Midnight Cowboy.*"

—with Gena Rowlands and Seymour Cassel on the right, top of crown to top of crown, she right side up and he upside down—

"*Minnie and Moskowitz.*"

—and, in the frame on the left, Grace Kelly giving would-be voyeur Jimmy Stewart a patronizing smirk for looking the wrong way with his binoculars while plenty's happening in the apartment building behind them.

"*Rear Window.*"

On the left wall, over a coffee table and black Barca-lounger, was a striking, watercolor Garbo gazing upward—

"*Queen Christina!*"

—and grinning, gun-toting Helen Walker standing over a head-scratching Fred MacMurray.

"*Murder, He Says?*"

"My favorite film from the forties," Harvey said, mysteriously chanting, "*Honors flieses, incum beeziss...*"

On the right wall, above an old desktop Dell and even-older fax machine perched over the safe, was a pyramid of meddlesome, swashbuckling kids trespassing on One-Eyed Willie's piled trove—

"*The Goonies.*"

—and Meryl's cheek on Clint's shoulder before a covered bridge under a sepia sky.

"Oh," she brimmed, "one of my own very favorites!"

"*The Bridges of Madison County?* That's in Iowa, you know." Harvey had already hoisted off the wall the poster hung by the door. "And don't forget this one."

He held it so his head, arms, and legs all grew out of a rectangular torso of her face in profile with hand on projector lens. It was the original Belgian one-sheet.

"*Ciné rex!*"

"It's what I see right in front of me when I'm working at the desk."

The door and a filing cabinet with a combo-TV/VCR atop it left room for just one poster there. Coveted real estate in this tiny office.

"Could you get that?" He meant the coffee mug, full of pens and shaped like Yoda's head. She seized it by the ears and he laid the frame flat on the desk, over a spread of paperwork. "I hope," he said, prying back one of the frame's clipping sides, "you don't mind me going a bit fanboy on you, asking you to sign this?"

"Not at all!" she twiddled through the pens sprouting from Yoda's open mind, looking for the right one. "But you have to accept me going fangirl on you."

"Now what's that even about?" He paused with the Plexiglas lifted from the poster and, when she hesitated, set it down, propped it against the desk.

She lingered over her selection, venturing into her admission as guarded as she could without it going maudlin. "I guess the internet is a funny place these days. I found your blog totally by chance and I think the way you think about films and then write about them is so sincere—"

"Ah jeeze."

"—but what you wrote about my performance in *ciné rex* especially, that"—oh God, was she about to cry?—"that what you wrote, about it"—thank God, no, she could curb it— "showed me I'd done something right. So I came to tell you that you did something right, too. 'Cause what are we doing, Harvey, if we're not making connections with each other?"

Before he could react, she downplayed her sincerity by prizing a Sharpie—"Dit is de pen!"—and passing Yoda into Harvey's care.

It had been some time since she signed one of these posters. Most of the image was black, the booth's darkness, and so for it to show up she usually autographed her hair— one of two roles she'd gone blonde for—or the light beam coning out of the lens. "I'll sign the light."

"That'll be great, thanks."

He stopped the top corner there from curling with his left hand, the gold ring announcing itself again.

To my Harvey, she wrote, the possessiveness impulsive, before switching to Flemish: *Omwille van de connectie. Lea De Wever*

"What's that say there? Your handwriting's perfect so it must be me."

"It means 'for the sake of connection,' or," she bullshitted, "'for all the orgasms.' Open to interpretation."

"Hokay then!"

She capped the pen and peered over her glasses at a

photo by the fax machine of a white and black dog with great big black eyes and lashes to envy.

"Cute pooch!"

"That's Consuela," he said. "She's a Cockapoo."

"Sounds messy."

"Cocker Spaniel-Poodle mix."

The phone rang and he reached for it, apologizing without need. She watched him in genial manager mode, damn near the same as he was with her. Harvey's role. He had expected the call, went about carefully shifting the open frame, lifting it like a slab to fetch a sheet of paper under it. He read off a few numbers. Wishing them a "great night," he hung up and tilted his eyebrows at her, another unnecessary gesture of apology.

"That was Portland, Oregon, calling," he said. "The numbers people. Tracking grosses."

"Were the numbers good?"

"Um..." He went about dropping the sheet and setting the poster aright in its frame. "The numbers are never good. We try to offset the fact we only have one screen by showing two films daily—a throwback or art-house-slash-foreign film and then a mainstream-slash-hopefully-moneymaker to keep us afloat. Business retreated to the multiplexes out in the suburbs back in the eighties and frankly the only reason we're open at all is that we're a tax write-off for a local real estate mogul who's either crooked or stupid."

"Your boss."

"My boss. I just mind my Ps 'n' Qs," he admitted, "which lets me pick the specialty films and atone for showing folks stuff like the crap playing in there right now." He twitched at the violent automotive-gladiatorial cacophony just then obliterating the auditorium on six channels of sound.

"You live in balance."

"I wouldn't call it that—but I like it. Please, please, take a seat there."

Feeling bold she stepped behind the desk and took his chair.

"Or you could just take my job. Bet you'd be better at it anyway."

"And there's something I'm not so sure of." She swiveled.

With the poster back in its frame, it went back on the wall. Harvey stepped as far away as he could with cheek in hand, elbow in other hand. "Look. It's perfect. Signed—here—by Lea De Wever..."

He turned to her and she lifted one shoulder and one side of her mouth and stared at the desk because he, of course, might very well be under the same soul-eclipsing spell she had fled, seeing not a person but a character. How appropriate. Just what she deserved. Run away and you will run into whatever pursues you. Or that you think pursues you. Or not. She didn't know.

Harvey lowered himself—for the seat was low—into the Barcalounger. He angled it toward her in two heavy scoots.

"Did you want some popcorn?"

She eyed the concession stand, seeing the bin through the open door. It hadn't any popcorn in it.

"No, thank you."

"Good. I wasn't going to fire up the kettle for the likes of you anyways."

"You've got an eye right here from your desk to the popcorn machine there."

"Gotta watch the concessionists like a hawk. Half of this

159

job is babysitting kids who're old enough to be babysitting."

"You're right. I may not be cut out for it."

"The world's better off with you acting," he said. "Like that scene there," and he gestured again to the poster, "and you're consistently brilliant all through the film—but for me, and I wrote about this, it's the scene without any words—not from you—not from the film, which is silent, of course. And you're showing your character going through the motions of her job, the ritual of twin-projector exhibition—which is a dance with steps that can't be missed or the audience below, who can't know the projectionist exists, will be torn from the illusion they've paid to see. That character, moving between projectors and the reel rewinding table and booth window, she has to stay hidden while maintaining the dance in perfect time—but she is doing this during an extraordinary time. Her city is occupied, Jews have been taken away, she has to sleep with a Nazi to spare her and her husband's life. If she slacks, despite her exhaustion, if she forgets to thread up the next reel, if she gets the reels out of order—which she does but corrects it before it's too late—if she misses the cigarette burn and fails to hit the switchover button, if she just gives in to stubbornness and stops altogether, she may die, her husband may die, who knows who else? They already killed the old manager! And so you—*you*—show her worn out, on autopilot, fumbling at the table as she rewinds the last reel, threads up the next, redoing the finger loops when she gets them wrong, pulling young Napoleon into focus and really being affected by that snowball fight on the screen. She's living under conquest and there's the winter games apprenticeship to one of Europe's past conquests. All the anguish you bring out for her is there but only so much as she can stand to feel—well, and we were talking about balance—in that film she's living in her hometown, where she grew up, and now it's all off balance—and how do we find a balance in a world that hasn't got it? You brought all that out of her. It's just, look, some of the real-est—as in *most real* experiences of my life have happened in dark auditoriums with light on a screen and sounds breathed out of speakers—but I'm trained in making that mass hallucination happen for others, too. And seeing you express *that* is a confirmation. I'm not alone. *We're* not. Ah, and when she stomps the switchover with absolute rage, her only chance to express it—it's just the most brilliantly felt performance and I never ever imagined I'd have the chance to blather about it at you in person like this, sorry for gushing, I'll very much stop now."

"Thank you so much." It was all she could think to say.

"And they taught you how to do everything in the booth, for the film?"

"I learned." She told of the retired projectionist, in his eighties, who choreographed those shots. Ronny. He had told her of Willem Willemen, who was an old projectionist when he started out, who had actually been a projectionist at the actual Cinema Rex following the war, an alcoholic who had no teeth and used to set his beers one by one inside the lamp house to warm them so his tender roots wouldn't ache when he drank, slung halfway out the booth window. Always smoking, Ronny, insisting she smoke, too, until, luckily, the historical consultants convinced the director she wouldn't have access to cigarettes during the occupation, being luxury items at the time. She'd given them up a year prior and was thankful when they didn't make her tempt relapse.

"And *Napoléon* by Abel Gance, I went ahead and saw

that," she said. "However many hours it is, a true masterpiece. Have you seen it?"

"Oh yes, in college," he said. "I love silent cinema."

He told her about his first semester at college. Every film
class was full-up, even Intro to Film Analysis, but one, a Cinema Auteurs course, had a place. He signed up and arrived
on the first day to find about fifteen graduate students, at
least five years older than him, showing their eagerness with
seriousness for what was to be an advanced class on Soviet
cinema, from 1917 to 1945. At the end of that first ninety
minutes, with lots said about a Marx brother he'd never
heard of—*cheesy*—he approached the professor, who wore
leather pants and swung his arms when walking indoors. Explaining he had just left home and arrived here and hadn't
even had Intro to Film Analysis and was quite intimidated by
the subject matter because he didn't know much of anything
about Mother Russia, Dr. Kaufman thanked him and encour-
aged him to stay, to not be frightened, to know that he would
remember the level he was at and not crucify him for it. Nice
guy.

The next class, however, tested him. Kaufman screened
Vertov's 1929 masterpiece: *Man with a Movie Camera.* All
the other students were stenographizing into their notebooks,
faces down but eyes rolled up to the screen. He didn't know
what they were writing down and tried to write things down,
too, but without knowing what he should be looking for he
ended up just holding his pen and watching, watching all the
sequences of people going about their business in another
time in another country. And he started to get into it. At one
point, a magician was shown performing tricks for children, a
classic bit where a ball under a cup turns into a mouse, the

kids reacting with delight and bewilderment.

"I laughed," Harvey said. "The kids' reactions just cracked me up. And all of a sudden Dr. Kaufman pauses the Laserdisc and marches up to the front asking, 'Who did that!?'"

"No!"

"'Who laughed?' he goes. 'Raise your hand!'"

"What did you do?"

"I raised my hand, thinking I'd ruined the first screening, all the grad students staring at me. And then Dr. Kaufman is up there and he's got the frame of this little girl's face projected on him and he goes, '*Thank you*! This is a *film*, people! It's designed to evoke *reactions*! Let's loosen up and not worry so much about taking notes and see if we might actually *enjoy* this thing!' He unpaused it and I sank into my seat, you know, embarrassed. But talk about positive reinforcement. That did it for me in terms of loving silent cinema.

"In fact," he went on, "I'd love to do a Garbo double feature of her silent films but with more modern contemporary music. See if we can draw the under-sixties crowd."

"Which of her silent films are you thinking?" Lea asked, feeling protective of her beloved Greta.

"*Flesh and the Devil* and *The Temptress*? I'm all about the Argentine whip fight in *The Temptress*."

"They wouldn't let her go back to Sweden for her sister's funeral," she said.

"Sorry?"

"When she was filming *The Temptress*, her sister died. They didn't give her time off for the funeral."

"Well that's"—he paused—"not right."

163

"No." She said it almost as if it had happened to her. She attempted to brighten. "Life is too short to set bad music to Garbo. You need Antony and the Johnsons, Blind Yackety, Sarah Vaughan, Frightened Rabbit, Dory Previn!"

He reached and took a pencil from Yoda, jotting in the margins of the nightly report. "Anthony and the Yacketies?"

Lea made a face and snatched away the pencil and paper. "I gotta sort out your music, man. That's integral—*integral?*"

"That's the word."

"It is though, so important." She wrote down artist and album titles as they came to her. "Accompaniment has to be part of it, like it belongs to the film, lean."

Harvey followed her hand's trail of neat writing. "No complex Garbohydrates," he said.

"Ha-*ha!*" she laughed like Nelson Muntz.

"So are you between films or...? I mean, if they didn't let Greta go to her own sister's funeral, I can't imagine them giving you dispensation to come say hi to me in Des Moines."

"No, I'm doing a time travel thing in LA right now."

"Well, right now you're writing down musicians for me who don't suck."

"Sure, sure. There's a lot of waiting around for my scenes on this one. It's more of a supporting role—roles, really—sort of—they're all the same—"

"But you should be the lead! I've followed your career since this one—but we haven't been able to get hold of them to screen them like I would like. I mean I have a regionless player at home and you've done some powerful things—the one—sorry, I won't attempt the title—but the one about the woman dying of ovarian cancer—and the one about depression after the death of a child—those performances are so

164

affecting, even with me having to read them. I remember just weeping watching those. You've proven again and again your capacity for playing a lead, for years now."

"But you're showing *Love Me Tonight*?" she asked abruptly.

And he told her just what a special time it was for her to have visited, because when the Schwarzwald opened on August 26, 1932, the very first film they showed was Mamoulian's *Love Me Tonight*, a two week engagement. Harvey rocked himself out of the Barcalounger and retrieved a thick binder from the top drawer of the filing cabinet. When not making sure the kids didn't scorch the popcorn, Harvey liked to play cinema genealogist. He had gone back through the microfilms at the downtown library of the *Des Moines Harbinger* and recreated the definitive record of which films the cinema showed since it opened. For most of the cinema's history, it was known as the Capri.

"A lame attempt to Frenchify it," he theorized.

"Capri's Italy."

"Right, sure. Really they were trying to erase the Germanness—the renaming happened after Pearl Harbor. And still the décor stayed the same. Makes no sense."

The cinema had been the last project, he explained, of one of the city's prominent architects: Balthasar Hoffman. He'd been born in Germany and immigrated aged nine when his father led a failed uprising against the monarchy of Baden from the Black Forest. Many of the oldest buildings downtown in Des Moines were designed by him but this was his most idiosyncratic achievement, an homage to the folklore of his childhood, built mainly to please himself.

"They named a middle school after him," Harvey said.

"Boringest brick box of a building you ever saw. Complete opposite of *this* place."

He designed the Schwarzwald with personal quarters for himself—which was strange seeing as he was in his nineties and had a large house of his making south of Grand Avenue.

"That's the posh part of town."

Harvey got another binder and opened it to her.

A black-and-white photo of Depression era Iowans in gala duds showed, in the middle, under the cuckoo clock marquee, a wizened old fellow with snowy wizard beard flanked by two men.

"That's Dwight Lewis on the right, Mayor of Des Moines, and Daniel Webster Turner on the left, Governor of Iowa. Hoffman's there in the center. This was the opening day. And that night Hoffman retired to his daydream fantasy private quarters upstairs and died in his sleep."

"The guy who built this place died here?"

"He still haunts it late at night," he said.

"Don't say that, I'm superstitious about death."

"Well, so they say, so they say. I was active in getting them to rename the cinema back to the Schwarzwald when I helped reopen it in 2005. And I think the renaming appeased old Balthasar's restlessness. I haven't ever seen him once, even though I'd love that. There's a thousand questions I'd like to ask the guy."

"Well that's exciting about showing *Love Me Tonight*, with the history of it," she said. "I'd love to see it in this place."

"How long are you in town for?"

"I guess I don't know."

"But I could give you a screening after this show. If you

like. Tonight. A private screening. Unless you're totally zonked."

"Yes! I'd love that. Please!"

"I'd love that, too," said Harvey, drawing his phone out of his pocket. "Hang on here while I just send a text..."

"If it's a problem..."

He raised his eyebrow at her from the other side of the phone. "Our secret."

Sure, until the next time his wife came to the office and asked about the autograph on the poster.

They whiled the time poring over the binder of films that had played at the cinema. He'd even compiled an index with all of them listed alphabetically, but it was more serendipitous to flip through the chronology, eighty years of movies as they actually screened, and bear witness to the vast range of stories all exhibited in the same environs.

Harvey found the week they screened *ciné rex*. Alternating with, oh hell, *Transformers 2*.

"What is it with me and this place and the Transformers?" she asked.

"If I had my way, we'd've been showing, um, anything else..."

She checked the week she was born, pulling her finger down the page, and found there *I Wanna Hold Your Hand* and *The End*. She began with *The End*? Of course, the Beatles thing—she didn't know it, but Harvey described it as a screwball comedy about teens in New York succumbing to Beatlemania in early 1964—that sounded great, fine, an affirmation of her excellent taste in music and current choice of wardrobe. But *The End*? He denied having seen it though she suspected he might be hiding something from her, for her benefit. The deets under the listing indicated that Burt Reynolds directed and starred in it with Dom DeLuise and Sally Field. Sally Field was one of the greats, of course. But beginning with *The End*, what did that *mean*? Was she done before she started? Was her entire life epilogue?

Distracting her from a distress of her own imagining, Harvey commandeered the binder and turned to July 1972. The week he was born: *Marjoe* and *Conquest of the Planet of the Apes*. A far more dynamic combination, what with the first, according to him, winning Best Documentary for exposing corruption in tent revival evangelism and the second, well, at least she knew the franchise. She had seen neither. Harvey then showed her the listing for the first film he saw at the Schwarzwald: *One of Our Dinosaurs Is Missing*. This seemed both a cause for nostalgia and embarrassment, the look on his face as he sat forward from the edge of the Barcalounger openly apologetic. The film, apparently, Harvey having revisited it on VHS several years ago, bore insensitive East Asian characters played by white actors. One of those that hadn't found its way onto DVD.

"Granny was a Peter Ustinov fan—she brought me," he said. "Pretty sure I fell asleep but I do have a vivid memory of seeing the steam-powered bus with the Brontosaurus skeleton on top of it—in foggy traffic—knocking on the roof of a London cab with its chin." He seemed to be seeing it again, looking at nothing.

"Well and it was playing the same time as a movie called *Smile*," she pointed out. "So that's positive."

"Another dud. This old place has shown the best and the

worst." He eased back in the chair. "Anyway, the cinema itself made a bigger impression on me, especially the marquee out front. I was three. Thought this was Disneyland."

Possessing the binder once again, she traipsed through her loved ones' birthdays. For Mama it was the Western *Rim of the Canyon* and *Not Wanted*, a lie of a title, for it bore no relation whatsoever to how much Bomma and Bompa had doted on her in those difficult postwar years. Papa fared better, with *The Man in the White Suit*—Harvey described it as an Alec Guinness speculative drama about the synthetics industry—and Abbot and Costello's *Jack and the Beanstalk*. For her brother it was *Neighbors* and *Shoot the Moon*, while Annemie beat everybody for strangest combo: *The Amazing Dobermans*—starring Fred Astaire?!—and *Network*. Finally, someone got a brilliant film! Lea also, discreetly, not really all that curious about it but just curious enough, checked the week Wouter was born: *Mass Appeal* and *Johnny Dangerously*... Ironic. He'd failed to appeal in any favorable measure to the most important people in her life, displaying more an interpersonal recklessness than a capacity for living dangerously.

She knew she could build a sort of astrology out of this binder, given the chance. Under what constellation of films shown at the Schwarzwald had one been born? Whichever film time you were born closest to, that was the dominant film, the one most indicative of your life's condition, with the other one expressing the repressed aspect of your soul. And wherever in their careers the actors and directors of those films were, that was important, too. Someone born under, say, *Bananas* was born with Woody Allen rising—under

Hollywood Ending, Woody Allen waning—under *Blue Jas-
mine*, Woody Allen resurgent. Except he hadn't been in that
last one. Wrote and directed it, yes. All those roles would
have to be figured in, part of mapping somebody's Schwarzwald chart. That and the tension and interplay between the
main and the lesser films complicated everything. Lots of
factors, so many of them, to track a more complete reading:
directors, writers, producers, distributors, studios, awards—
and of course the stars and co-stars! So it *would* be an astrology after all!

They were quite happy debating what bearing the con-
junction of genres would have on one's ensuing life—in her
case, taking into account the seven hour time difference, *I
Wanna Hold Your Hand*, thank goodness, was dominant
while *The End* was repressed, explaining perhaps her tendency to farcically gambol through life with full-blown
romanticism while neglecting her own particular dread for
the ends of things like projects and goals and relationships
and, duh, life itself—before realizing customers were silently
filing out of the auditorium and through the lobby.

"S'pose I ought to..."

"Let me help!" Lea stood with Harvey and pulled her
hair into a loose chignon, pinning it with a pen from Yoda's
noggin. "I'm your Girl Friday!"

Following his lead, she assumed a hands-behind-back
stance beside a roped stanchion, like he did, and nodded, like
he did, at the half-dazed people making their way outside.
The pair of them made an impression on no one despite, in
her imagination, being the very reincarnation of Stan 'n'
Ollie, their impatient disingenuousness marked oxymoronic-

ally with sincerity as they made eye contact with the leaving patrons. Out they processed, some yawning, nearly all lumbering. If the spectacle had thrilled any of them you wouldn't know it, so subdued they were, checking phones, stopping off at the men's room. They were nearly all men and teenage boys of corn syrup pedigree. The odd polite one made sure to toss his empty drink cup and trapezoidal popcorn bucket into one of the two wheelly barrels placed by the auditorium doors. If Harvey got a nod in return to his, he would wish them a "great night" at a gentle octave. She left this to him, preferring to keep her lips shut in a sleepy smile.

He left her to stand watch as he stepped outdoors to fetch the sandwich board.

"Damnedest thing I ever saw," said an old man who snuck up on her. "Or at least I think I saw it. I'm really not so sure..."

He had silver-white hair and gave her a smile that was all flirtation.

She minded her own business with a downward-looking look mimicked right off of Laurel's face.

"Did you just see it?"

"No."

"You weren't in there, too?"

She stuck out her lower lip, shaking her head.

"With all that lot of whiz-bang robut nonsense?"

"Not me, no."

"Well I should'a been out here with *you* the whole time," he said, touching her folded elbow, bouncing his eyebrows and making his egress. "Would'a made a lot more sense!" He swatted a wave at her over his shoulder.

She wondered to herself, could that be the ghost of Balthasar Hoffman?

But the awkward exchange he had at the door—both he and Harvey, lugging that sandwich board, choosing the same one despite two being available—both negotiating in overly polite gestures who might go through first—Harvey coming in or Gramps going out—and the clumsy false starts each made before the other—convinced her that no, nope, this was just some foxy old grandpa.

Harvey finally strode in with the load under his arm, cocking her an exasperated eye. He tilted the board against the back of the box office door and asked her to stand watch while he checked the toilets and auditorium for stragglers. Lea watched the foxy grandpa shuffle off across the street to a champagne Mercury parked a couple spaces from her rental. He took his time starting the engine and then took his time driving away. There were old men just like this, content at a slower pace, in Antwerpen.

Harvey returned with the all-clear and, with a twist of his jangling keys, locked the entrance doors.

"I can pick up the auditorium later," he said.

"Let me help!" she insisted. "It'll go twice as fast."

And so she followed him into the auditorium through the left set of doors. Harvey brought a barrel with him, coasting it effortlessly with one hand. All sixty feet of screen stood out in a wan off-white, the houselights hitting it from the ceiling with five parabolas of warmer light that faded away as they stretched lower. Masked simply in black curtains, whatever continuation of baroque decoration she expected was not to be found. Perhaps this was a good thing, every film speaking its own story without decorative incursion. Row upon row of seats graduated before them at a soft slope, strips of blue lights lining both sides of the aisle. Though the balcony hung overhead, it did not block out the screen unless standing at the very back, a negligible inch or two cut off from the top.

"She's bigger than she looks from the street," he said on his way down a row. There were, he informed, seven hundred eighty-six seats on the floor of the auditorium and another two hundred eighty in the balcony, for a grand total of one thousand sixty-six patrons on those ecstatic nights the house sold out—a rare event.

"*Transformers 4* only had six-fifty-seven for the midnight premiere." He returned to the barrel and deposited a cup and a wad of candy wrappers, which called Lea to action. She ran down to the right aisle and leaned to look down each row. The houselights were soft but aided the eye in spotting lazy leftovers carelessly left on the floor. Complicating discernment slightly, the concrete floor had been painted gray long enough ago to now be chipping in piebald patches—she headed down more than one row ready to cantilever into a reach for what turned out to be a mirage. No bother.

"Someone dumped a drink at the back," she called over, "and it's spilled all the way down."

"Happens every show. S'fine."

Quick to adapt, Lea was soon returning to the barrel with pinched boxes of Milk Duds and bags that rattled with old maids. Watching him go about it so simply, as if he were an orchard keeper bringing in the harvest, she thought about how he did this every night, alone. The pimply concessionists left around ten each night, leaving him to the solitude of the silent cinema after the last show. But not tonight. She hammed it up for his benefit, making certain he took notice. As a performer she was so eager to please. But maybe he would remember this and feel something nice on some future night when it was just him picking up after the last show and she was who-knows-where, hopefully filming who-knows-what. They worked in the same business, after all, just at either end of the supply chain. She made a game of it then, hurrying down the rows, grabbing as much as she could in a single trip, grinning at him as she chucked pompons of trash into the barrel. For this he smiled and shook his head, his pace steady. And though her pace held swift, efficiency all but died when she got to a seat near the front, just off-center. Fetching up a large cup she found it nearly full. And warm. She swished it in a tight circle and watched dark bits swim to the frothy surface—and then the smell—sour and dank and bright and earthy. She gagged and, holding it at arm's length, marched it up the aisle.

"Harveyyy!"

He raised his face to her from across the auditorium.

She held it high over the barrel, now approaching full. Lea had been so careful about not spilling any, not on herself or the seats, the floor, the carpeted aisle. "This is full and I don't know what it is but it smells like sick."

"Spit cup?" His voice carried the concern of true empathy.

"*Spit cup?* It's warm in my hand and kind of minty."

"Wintergreen," he explained. "Chewing tobacco. Go ahead and just let it go."

Reluctant to spill it even into the trash, not allowing it to tip, she set it into the middle amid a nest of popcorn bags and buckets and watched it sink from its weight.

"Absolutely disgusting!" She shuddered and he returned, tossing a few more cups in after it.

174

"That should do it." He wheeled the barrel back into the lobby and she followed. "You should get a merit badge for that... Actually, are you still cold?"

"A bit."

"How about an employee shirt?" Leaving her side, Harvey lifted a panel in the concession stand counter and slid behind it sideways, vanishing into the back room for a moment.

"Ladies Medium?" he hollered.

"Sounds right, yes!" she hollered.

He emerged with a black garment draped over his forearm and came out from behind the stand and gave a butlerly bow, offering it. She accepted the black tee as if bestowed a high honor and unfolded it. Over the left breast in gold embroidery and Arnold Böcklin font it read:

The Schwarzwald
Est. 1932

"Oh Harvey." She thrust herself into it, claiming it like new skin. She ran a finger under each sleeve hem, smoothing them flush with her arms. "It's my favorite shirt! I can keep it, yes?"

"Yes, of course!"

"Good because if you want it back you'll have to take it off of me."

He forced a chuckle to keep from blushing—that's how she read it anyway—and lowered the panel in the concession counter flat. "Thirsty? I can put the pop heads back in. Agri-Cola? Diet Agri-Cola? Mug?"

She craved Diet but spotted the coolers full of bottled

water and heard Hollywood urging her to hydrate. "Water?"

He retrieved two bottles and handed them over to her. "Now then. Can I show you the booth or would you prefer to wait for me in the balcony while I thread up?"

"With that Balthasar ghost haunting this place? I'm coming with you."

"Very well. Please follow me! But wait—which staircase? Siegfried or Brunhilde?"

"What?"

He pointed to the bannisters she had noticed earlier. "On the left is Siegfried. On the right is Brunhilde."

She took a better look at each of them. Siegfried, in armor, had his sword ready, his attention cast up his staircase. Brunhilde had gone sorrowful, wringing her hands, a few of her fingers missing, broken off, as if in anxiety, and then lost. She gazed from the base of her staircase across the concession stand at Siegfried ready to climb, as if to say, "I'm only right over here, you nabjaar."

"If we're going up, why not go with Siegfried?"

Her wish his command, he led the way, unfastening the velvet rope that girded customers from ascension. On approach she saw that this bannister bore a heinous crack running from helmet through shoulder to waist. Stain attemptted to hide this fissure and when Harvey noticed her touching it he explained the dry winters were likely to blame. When they reopened a woodworker was brought in, an Irish lady who came over for a residency at Living History Farms and ended up marrying one of the professors at Aylesbury University in town, and she helped preserve the statues from further damage.

"But only so much can be done," he explained. "Poor

Brunhilde's missing fingers are pure vandalism. She didn't have them when I was a kid. I can remember."

She lingered at the cloven Siegfried but with the alternative path being a deliberately maimed Brunhilde, she held to her choice, stepping up, her hand rippling over the oak leaves carved upon the railing. It was dark above so Harvey skipped ahead and flipped a switch, giving light to their direction. The landing, opening also from Brunhilde's staircase, bowed in with a curved wall bearing a prodigious dragon carved in relief. With its arched back and equine snout and tail wrapped in a snail's shell spiral it loomed with a surprising presence. One she had not anticipated. Billowing smoke-curls leaking from its lips complimented the spin of its tail at the opposite end. The archway to the balcony seats, curtained off in sable velvet, stood as a portal between the front and hind legs of the ferocious reptile, essentially challenging all balconygoers to pass beneath the dragon's belly to get to their seats. You could see, the scales polished smooth along the lip of the entryway, where an act of belly-rubbing appeasement had long been practiced by outstretched fingertips as people made their way into the auditorium.

"Hardly anybody gets to see this anymore."

She made for the monster's front end as if she were some kind of dragon whisperer. After a careful approach and offering her open palms so it could snort her scent, she was stroking its snout as if it were a red pony.

"Never seen him take so quick to somebody before."

"How do you know it's a him?" She cocked Harvey a glance while scratching under the jowls. "Maybe it's a her."

"It can be whatever it damn well needs to be, in this day and age."

Lea didn't know how to read that but feared there might be an uncomfortable conservatism behind it—uncomfortable for her. Was that ironically un-PC or genuine mild exasperation on his part? She asked nothing, preferring a Harvey with an unblemished veneer—at least for now. She could live with finding out he was an asshole later.

A wall opposite the dragon masked the creature from the lobby below and here, with framed photographs of the Three Stooges, Brando, and John Wayne throwing a punch, stood a door painted the same color as the wall. Harvey unlocked and opened it, reaching in to flick on another light.

"The booth is higher still."

She followed him in and up the set of utilitarian stairs, her guide's dress shoe soles rising before her in a scuffing jog. The temperature spiked with trapped, stuffy air. The walls here were unadorned cement block painted a sickly peach. At the top stood an open archway on the left and a locked door on the right—both directions humming with noise at their own specific vibrations.

"Balthasar's private quarters," he indicated toward the shut door.

"Where he died? Why's it make that noise like that?"

"He's entombed in there, as per his final wishes. Cryogenically frozen—like Walt Disney and Ted Williams' head. Was on ice to begin with, since cryogenic freezing wasn't around yet in 1932, so he kind of got a bit of freezer burn and went off but when they managed to actually *invent* cryogenics—"

Lea shoved him, hard. "I'm gullible!"

Smirking, he changed his story. "Sometime in the past they gutted the rooms and turned it all into the air conditioning-slash-furnace room. Probably in the sixties. The cooling unit is a dinosaur—I gotta watch it doesn't leak and ruin the lobby ceiling below."

"Dragons and dinosaurs," she muttered. "And ghosts—let's get out of this creepy hallway."

"Right."

They stepped through the narrow archway into the booth. The room was broad and dim but for a tiny lit bulb within the projector, illuminating its gears. A harmony of fans blew an undistinguished chord, the fraternal internal bellows of projector and sound system accompanied by a freestanding one oscillating the hot air, as if it were a heliotropic flower scanning the dark for the sun.

"Watch the cord there," he said, pointing it out along the floor, flipping on the overhead lights.

To the right of the projector stood a tall black box—the digital amplifier stack—blinking a few tight rows of red and green LEDs. The projector looked, as projectors often did to her, as if it were shouldering in at a lean to peer with its one eye, stretched wide open, through a keyhole window in the wall. An introverted firefly, its lamp house abdomen could only arc inner illumination; the light's only escape was through its eye. Like old theories of vision, long debunked, this animating piece of machinery could see from within, beaming light, blinked apart twenty-four times a second by an inner lid, through coursing panes of stained celluloid, enlarged and warped one-hundred-eighty degrees through its crystal lens, to create camera-obscura vision on the screen across the dark, cavernous auditorium. A titan of twentieth-century ingenuity, the projector was a blind, light-bringing Cyclops casting fluid motion on the mysterious terms of persistence of vision.

"Polyphemus and Prometheus in one," he announced and went bashful. "I minored in Classics..."

The projector's name, printed in white cursive on the glass window over the film pathway compartment, was *Century*.

Harvey explained the projector was outfitted to show both 35 and 70mm prints, being otherwise typical of the last of the pre-digital machines with its rise of three broad platters standing just behind it. The bottom one held a 35mm print lying on its side, a spooling of stock wound from the center ring, more than a mile and a half long, its tail tucked flat under the outside edge and labeled with a strip of masking tape in black marker: *LOVE ME.* The middle platter had another film spindled upon it, more than three miles there though it made more sense to the eyes to judge it like a tree, so much bigger with its many more rings, its broader girth. It trailed a slack tail of print stock that looped upward and lolled through a series of pulleys before curling limp to the floor.

Harvey tended it, again with the stewardship of a farmer, turning a switch and spinning the middle platter a few turns to draw up the long tail. It wimpled over the rollers and joined the massive coil. He tucked in its end, labeled *TFORMS.*

"You can see," he said, hands busy, "that boarded up panel there." On the wall, somewhat behind the sound stack, was a large square of plywood, painted slate blue, bolted into the cement. "The other window's covered up, from back when they used twin projectors, like you did in *ciné rex.*"

She went over and touched the panel. Just a piece of painted wood. That blocked portal had served as the aperture for one half of who knew how many films. "So what happened to the other projector?"

"Hell if I know." He lifted the core gear of rollers and dancers—the brain—from the middle of the top platter and slotted it into the center of the bottom one. "I'd love to see this booth restored to its original glory but with everything going digital and the whole no money thing..."

A workbench in a corner stood decked tall with bobbins of movie trailers and rolls of yellow and clear tape. A film splicer—the bastard offspring of a three-hole punch and a tape dispenser—sat at an angle beside a large pair of scissors with the paint worn off the grips. Next to those a portable bench, sporting dials and a cord and a great empty reel upon it—the makeup table—squatted under a clear face shield, welding jacket, and heavy-duty oven mitts hung upon the wall. Several dented metal film canisters sat on the floor, out of the way, yawning to reveal empty two-reelers marked with film ends. A hodgepodge of standees leaned against a side wall, Bill Murray's head peeking over Spider-Man's shoulder, obscured for the most part by a Dark Lord of the Sith, upstaged by Disney's second-newest princess. Beside the amplifier stack was a small end table with a corded phone—Harvey had set their bottled water here when they walked in. Behind the sound system, an alcove held a toilet and sink. Lea tiptoed to peek; the bowl was bone dry.

"If you gotta go, downstairs is your best bet. That hasn't been hooked up since before I got here."

"No, no." She backed away. "I just remember Ronny telling me that's for the projectionists. When they couldn't leave their projectors their whole entire work day."

"Ronny's exactly right." Harvey stood up straight. "What

do you say then? Are we gonna do this?"

"*Love Me Tonight!*" She felt the truth in the way she'd blurted out the title, too much truth, enough that she had to dilute it by dorkishly adding, "Let's do this yo."

"Well seeing as you're officially on staff now at the Schwarzwald, and given your past experience, how about you do the honors of threading up?"

"Oh no!" she balked. "I barely remember—that was like six years ago—it was a totally different kind of projector—"

"The projector wasn't that different," he said, being one to know. "But look who's here to make sure you don't chew up the print. Come on over." He popped the center ring from the print on the bottom platter and reseated it on the top one.

Lea, being open by profession to direction, joined Harvey and, following his instructions, sutured the start of the clear film leader through the mechanical brain and carried it over and under the rollers stationed up and down the platter system's steel trunk. She startled when the platter, triggered by tension, spun of its own volition, suddenly alive. Gently amused, he did not say anything to make her feel stupid—like Wouter would have—but simply indicated the high wheels that would arc the leader into the projector's reach. She stretched to hook the highest one, and unfurled the ribbon longer with the assured yank of a rhythmic gymnast. He had her bring it back to the platters, through more pulleys along the trunk, and up to the top one to catch its folded tip in a groove in the center ring. A few spins of the bottom platter provided a long garland of slack, which lifted off the floor with a few spins of the top.

"You're making this look easy," he said. "Now open the projector there."

She pulled the small compartment door open, revealing all of the toothed cogs the film had to negotiate. This actually did look familiar to her, but not in a way inspiring confidence. It was more that dread of confronting lost knowledge. Harvey, sensing and reacting to her anxiety, stepped in, maintaining a distance comfortable to himself by crossing his arms and covering his mouth. To start, he had her lift two locked gates and twist a large silver knob to open the path over the projection plate. Next she was to tuck the clear leader through the DTS sound reader above, introducing it to the inner tract it must traverse. Her hands, thankfully, remembered the feel of the plastic leader with far less worry than her head. Harvey spoke her through the turns, every snugging of the film against a new sprocket, each locking of the five gates, both sets of two-finger loops.

Their faces close, she had that thought, of him reaching into the mechanics and untangling her fingers and guiding them with his hands. Like in scenes where American guys fold themselves around their dates to show them how to bowl or golf.

Harvey didn't do that. He just advised step by step, his voice easy and steady. And when it looked good to him, and he brought his face in and squinted over his glasses and stuck his fingers into each set of two-finger loops, he declared, in that quiet, assured tone, "Perfect."

"You should direct films," she said.

He raised his eyebrows at her as he gave the top platter a turn.

"You're better with actors than all the directors I've worked with."

He shook his head, bemused, and drew her to the black

box mounted below the booth window.

"Ready?"

She nodded.

"Press that button."

She did and the house lights on the other side of the glass fell.

"Press the green one."

She did and the projector chattered into action, shutter clattering like the chewing of cartoon fingernails, trapped light igniting and spilling on them from unseen pores, platters whooshing as if jogging to catch up with the rest.

"Now," he said louder, waiting for the clear leader to give way to black film, "press that one."

She did and the dowser opened with a *shhk* and the screen through the window lit with Jack Nicholson, in plaid flannel and hair on his head, breaking up a fight at an oil well. The image also hit the back wall of the booth, blown up large, bouncing off the glass and blotted by the projector's own shadow.

"Trailers," he said over the noise. "*Five Easy Pieces* next week, *My Dinner with Andre* week after that, and Friday midnight shows of *Howard the Duck* all month."

When he reached out at the lens and adjusted the framing she again saw the gleam off his wedding ring.

She imagined—not by choice—this man's wife at their home in this little city, already in bed, not waiting up for him, sent to sleep with the text he'd sent earlier. <working late. don't wait up> or <projector acting up. go on to bed, hon> Though he didn't seem much the sort of American who would use "hon." <Don't wait up, honey> And who was she, and what kind of woman? Supportive? Doting? Vivacious?

184

Was theirs a living marriage or merely functional? Was she a Spanish teacher on summer holidays or a mortgage analyst or a civil rights attorney or an astrophysicist or internet psychic or firefighter or what? Why no kids? Just the Cockapoo. Whose idea had that been and who saw to its walks and shits the most? Was it asleep beside her right that moment, warming Harvey's half of the bed, or did they make it sleep in a sad little crate? If it was asleep in a sad little crate, whose idea was it that it sleep in a sad little crate every night? Would Harvey make his dog sleep that way? Would Piet get along with Consuela?

"We ought to head down." He said it with genuine anticipation, grabbing their bottled water from the small table. His eyes twinkled behind his glasses with colored light reflected off the booth window. He really was excited about this.

So was she.

They hustled down the stairs, Lea leading the charge, and at the dragon, knowing very well what she was doing, she held her hand out behind her. When he shifted their water bottles to the crook of his elbow and took it, she spirited them both under the dragon's belly, through the velvet curtains, and found the star-crowned Paramount peak shining on the enormous screen.

"*Welcome to the movies*," she sang, the song from John Huston's *Annie*, "*welcome to the show!*"

Down to the front row she pulled him, front and center she pulled him, and as the credits opened, down into the seats she pulled him.

The spring-backed cushions, tipping them with a creaking *twang*, astonished.

"Godverdomme!"

"Rocket chairs!" He handed over a bottle.

"Jesus!"

"Quiet, quiet, I don't want to have to throw you out for rowdy behavior."

"You would do that?"

"I can and would."

She turned her head away from his sweet sarcastic face toward the silver screen, prepared to prove to him she could enjoy this on her very best behavior.

They watched Paris wake in black and white, delighting as the sounds of morning syncopated to create a rhythm for Maurice Chevalier to sing along to. Unsettled beside her, after Harvey pointed out a shot of a smoking chimney as the first use of a zoom lens in cinematic history, he suddenly stood.

"Be right back. The focus is bugging me."

"Looks fine though," she said but he was gone in the dark. She watched on, the romantic atmosphere perishing as she was left alone for nigh on the entirety of the first reel. First she allowed herself a frown. Checking over her shoulder at the archway every minute, she crossed her legs tightly with disappointment. Then as exposition gave way to the song "Isn't It Romantic," she allowed herself a full crossing of her arms. Finally, as Jeanette MacDonald emerged upon her own balcony singing the song, Lea was utterly haunted by Harvey's disappearance.

Then, as a ladder swang into view against the balcony on-screen, one appeared before her at her balcony. And as Charles Butterworth climbed his in black and white, the one before her shook with each step taken upon it until two hands appeared and then Harvey's face.

"I just came up to join ya," said Butterworth and Harvey in unison. Butterworth had a rose between his teeth, Harvey a pack of licorice that he bestowed upon her. He climbed over the railing and took his seat beside her again, withdrawing from his breast pocket and rattling a box of Junior Mints.

"You're mad!" said Lea.

"Always wanted to do that," said Harvey.

When Butterworth failed to win over MacDonald onscreen with a fife, falling off the ladder to the ground, Harvey gave his own ladder a comic shove, never minding the resulting crash across the seats below.

"Ohh, I'll never be able to use it again!" he again said with Butterworth.

Harvey held up his hand—"Wait for it"—and dropped it with Butterworth's next line:

"I fell flat on my flute!"

She had, of course, seen the film before. But never in a cinema. Never with a fellow romantic. When Maurice and Jeanette finally met, his car broken down on the open road and her carriage run into a ditch, Harvey took up the tailor's role, turning to Lea, acting along with reflected screen-light brightening his left side.

"I didn't know you existed," Jeanette said.

"You don't exist either!" he and Maurice exclaimed in an out-of-tune French accent. "You're a dream!"

He seized Lea's Twizzlers-clutching hands in his and sang to her: "Mimi, you funny little good-for-nothing Mimi, am I the guy...?" He had Chevalier's lower lip mastered even if the voice was off and his hands were soft and firm around hers. It was the sincere glimmer in his eyes behind the glint on his glasses that made her stop and swallow her licorice. Just this sweet gentle attention, being sung to, as simple as the framing of the head-on shots of Maurice and Jeanette on screen, stirred what needed stirring.

When tears sprang and one fell to her cheek, he did not stop singing or smiling, but kept up both while folding down one of his sleeves. He lifted the horn-rims from her face and floated the loose fabric above the cuff before her face.

"Maar mijn mascara..."

He went ahead and dabbed her eyes with gentle presses, singing, the shirt bunched by the fingers of his other hand. Harvey did not shush or quiet her, carrying on. He let her feel what she felt in what genuinely seemed to be the safety of his presence.

Dabs and tears.

Dabs and tears.

And then the singing had stopped and was over and she found herself alarmed by Maurice shouting as if ringing the hour:

"I love you! I love you! I love you! I *LOVE* YOU!"

Lea put her hands over her nose and, watching the lines change on Harvey's face, dissolved in a fit of laughter. She sniffled back her congestion and knuckled the wet corners of her eyes and stood from her seat, the pack of Twizzlers sliding onto the floor. Harvey held out his hands, her glasses open in one of them, and stood, too.

"I need the little girls' room," she said in nasally mock-American.

"Ah! Downstairs—next to my office!"

"I remember," she said, already at the aisle, waving off the glasses outstretched to her.

Lea hurried out of the auditorium, under the dragon, and down the stairs—careful about not losing a glass slipper there or tripping over the velvet rope. She swung 'round Brunhilde's waist, launching across the lobby and through the door labeled LADIES.

Expecting panda eyes in the looking glass, she found clarity. Where were the grey watercolors around her eyes? On Harvey's sleeve, of course. She leaned in close to herself, opening each eye wider in turn, and yes they were red in that I-was-just-crying way but also unblemished by bruise-like smudges. Her lashes clung in spaced radiations, arcing over and under, making starbursts of her eyes. She also found color lingering in her cheeks.

That was her there.

For the sake of absolute clarity, she fetched some toilet paper from one of the stalls and blew her nose.

The bathroom, she suddenly realized, was a pixelated casualty of nineteen-seventies interior decoration, walls and floor all done in small brown tiles, the grout gone grey with time. She couldn't imagine this being the original design, incongruous as it was with the attention to detail administered everywhere else.

She returned to the balcony and when Harvey saw her walking sideways down the row, he stood again.

"Can I get you anything?" he asked.

She shook her head. When she sat, he sat. So polite.

She clumsily stuck her arm through his and patted his shoulder, laying her head on it. "You're wonderful," she told him.

She leaned up, found her glasses in his breast pocket, and retrieved them herself. "Did you try these on while I was away?"

"Of course I did. I couldn't waste my chance to see the world through the eyes of a Belgian starlet."

"Good." She pinched the bridge on his glasses and took them off, unfolded the temples on her own and perched them on his nose. Then she put his on her face and turned to the screen. Maurice et al warped as if entunneled at the peak of a boozy night.

"We're blind as moles! Both of us!"

He grimaced. "You actually *drive* seeing the world like this?"

She squinted at him over the rimless lenses. "Oh you're very handsome, sir," she said about his sweet face.

"This is my European look," he said, faking seriousness. "Do I look European right now with my European look?"

"*Very* European."

She reset glasses to rightful faces and gathered herself against his arm again.

"How old are you, Harvey?"

"Forty-two."

Six years older than her. A good age for a man to be.

They enjoyed the movie's big hunt sequence, with its early use of sped up and slow motion footage, relieved, though they both knew it was coming, when the short little stag was found eating oats out of a pan under Maurice's pro-tecttion in a cottage.

And when they came around to the late-night garden meeting and Jeanette's three-point expression of love for the Parisian tailor, Lea spoke along with her, squeezing Harvey's bicep with each clause:

"Whoever you are, whatever you are, wherever you are, I

love you!"

She spied up at his face and caught him grinning at that.

And when Maurice was challenged to redesign Jeanette's riding habit in two hours, did so marvelously, and fessed up to being a lowly tailor, Lea cracked, "Yeah right, she's worried for all the wrong reasons. So what if he's a, a—a common man? She should be more worried about falling for a guy who can give a princess a two-hour makeover that comes out right!"

"Pfffff!" said Harvey.

And yet, when Maurice fled and Jeanette took after him to win him for herself, chasing his train on horseback, cutting it off by standing on the tracks, Lea felt the gallop within her, brought out by the sudden connection with the gentleman beside her. She held onto him and he nuzzled the top of her head with his cheek.

And so as this old film of a princess and a prince charming—who wasn't a prince—but *was* charming—ended, the closing horns and Paramount peak fading to black, Lea felt herself willing it to last longer. Being of a time when credits preceded the picture, the projector abruptly stopped projecting and the house lights lifted.

There they were, quite wrapped together. She felt the both of them breathing. In the moment before it all went awkwardly self-conscious, she felt her lack displaced by him, so that the lack was a love. He smelled good to her, felt good.

When reflexivity kicked in again, the sensation was less a falling, more a plunking.

They would have to part soon.

Harvey took a deep breath, which she felt through her hair.

"It's strange I came here," she said, "isn't it."

He let out a one syllable laugh without opening his mouth. "I don't get a lot of actors visiting. You're the first."

"I just, I dunno."

"You can tell me."

She kneaded his arm with her cheek. She didn't look at him though. "You were saying earlier, about the real-est experiences happening in a cinema auditorium, like this, like we just watched here."

"Mhmm."

"I hadn't felt that for a while."

He nodded against the top of her head.

"And I've never just...shown up somewhere."

"So it's a bit out of character for you to be here like this."

"It is."

"What got you on a plane?"

"I worry," she admitted.

Harvey shifted, wrapped his arm around her and gathered her closer to him. "What are you worried about?"

"My worst worry," Lea said, holding nothing back out of thanks for finally being asked, "is to end up some sort of Xanaxed lady who has no children and no love."

Harvey, to his credit, let that be said without naïve reassurance. He offered no judgment either, not even a sigh.

"You're married."

"I am."

"She's a lucky woman."

"I appreciate that, thank you. He's—"

Her eyes bolted. She sat straight. *"He's!"*

His smile lopsided his dear face.

Her mouth gaped and she grabbed his cheeks and kissed

him on the mouth, kissed him with all of the relief of a disappointment she could accept, and felt nothing truly electric transferring back from him.

"It's even better when you help," she chastised.

Harvey sputtered and laughed and coughed. "*To Have and Have Not,*" he wheezed, back of his hand to his lips.

"How did you throw my gaydar, man? I'm an actor—I have great gaydar!"

"Well..."

"You can get married! I didn't know you had that here!"

"We were the third state."

"What's his name?"

"Pablo."

"Picasso!"

"He's from Guatemala."

"You married a Guatemalan! Hablo español. ¿Hablas español?"

"Un poquito..."

Lea asked Harvey many questions about his husband and he gave her all the answers. She found between them something she had not expected to find when she walked out of that rented house in California earlier in the day. Everything she had needed was found. And when he asked where she was staying and would she come stay the night at their house, she told him to make sure it was okay with the mister.

"Hi sweet cheeks," Harvey said into his phone, waking his husband in the night. "Um, I'm on my way home—I know you work in"—he looked at his watch "—the morning, but you might want to take the day off. Well... Well, you're not going to believe this, but what would you say to me bringing a Belgian starlet home with me?"

Lea snuggled under the granny quilt with Consuela circling in a pre-sleep routine down by her feet. The guest room was done up simply with more posters on the walls: *El Topo* and *Fitzcarraldo*. Lea had been granted pajamas from Pablo's wardrobe—boxer shorts and a t-shirt that said Simpson College—perfect for a summer night, although now it was already getting light outside. They had all stayed up drinking coffee and talking about how great a friendship this was already before collective yawning took over.

Harvey stood in the doorway like an American dad seeing to it that his daughter was going to sleep. "Everything good?"

"If you ever need a surrogate womb, I have one!" she declared.

"Okay." He was shaking his head, smiling.

"I'm serious!"

"Alright, alright, we'll remember that."

"And you'll come visit me in Antwerp? Whenever you want!"

"We will, we will. Never got to take a honeymoon, really, with work and all."

"Done, you're coming to Belgium. On me."

"Good night, Ms. De Wever."

He shut the door and she was left with Consuela and her long, long lashes already falling asleep on her shins.

Real quick, just out of curiosity at the messages she'd ignored, Lea turned on her phone. And immediately it rang. Cécile in Brussels.

"Hello?"

"Where are you! Are you okay?"

"Yeah, fine!"

"I've been getting calls about you not answering your calls, not being home, something about you feeling ill and the producer worrying about that, Trenise can't find you—"

"I went on Walkabout," Lea said.

"But you're alright?"

"Grand!"

"Alright, well look," her agent said, "there's been a fucking nightmare accident on the set. TMZ and Reddit already ran away with it—did you hear?"

"No?"

"Garrison broke his ankle."

"Oh no!"

"Well, more like, the door to the time machine broke his ankle. So I'm told. It wasn't his fault. The hydraulics came down real hard on it—he got airlifted to the hospital—producer's freaking out—but basically everything's getting all scooted around. So your scenes just got bumped up—and they need you day after tomorrow, bright and early, for the cavewoman scene—I'm sure Trenise will be on the phone to you as soon as you're off with me, if not the producer himself."

"I've got to send him flowers," she thought aloud. "Sweet peas."

"I already did that. On your behalf since you were nowhere to be found."

"You sent sweet peas?"

"Yes."

"From me?"

"Yes!"

"Cécile," Lea said. "You do know me."

"Listen, you sound tired. Go to sleep already and don't pull any more of this disappearing act bullshit and I'll let the people over there know you're fine and just resting and you'll be there tomorrow morning like they want. Okay?"

"Thank you, Cécile. You're wonderful."

"Good night, Lea."

"Good night."

Lea hung up and switched her phone off before another call had the chance to interrupt. She contemplated not going and staying here with Harvey—her Harvey—his Pablo, and the sweetest canine mascara model she ever met.

"I've a feeling I'm not in Belgium anymore," she said, knowing full well that she was being awfully silly in saying it.

Consuela jolted her head from her paws. The dog-tired Cockapoo blinked twice at Lea, her pretty head swaying, and dropped off to sleep again. Lea ignored dawn and, with a final jaw-stretching yawn, followed her lead.

Lotus

had the dream we met up @ my bros place on the lake n we did the "deed" w each other

u got moves liek a real woman

yr pussy lips were cryin for my wet tongue lashes

peace

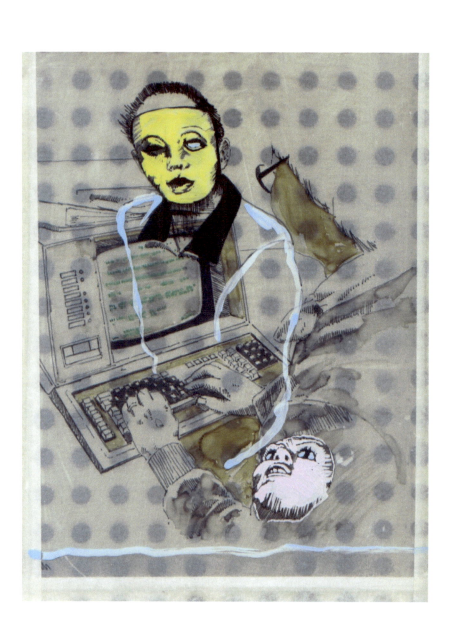

Fuga Mundi

Nearly thirty brothers, separated seventy-nine years from eldest to youngest, stand outside in the snow. The fire alarm continues to trill. No smoke, just a tincture of roasted barley on the crisp pre-dawn air. Brother Moriarty wavers his forefinger over the roster on his donated iPad, bouncing the whorled tip against each name of each man present. The monks stifle their grumbles for warmth, thankful for the also-donated winter coats. Brother Cobalt, one-hundred-and-two and in finer fettle than some half his age, shifts foot to foot in the abbey doorway.

"Wasn't even looking at the toaster this time," he says through the alarm.

"This is just a drill."

Brother Moriarty, the abbot, bifocals on down the candent list.

One missing—where is Brother Ambrogio?—and the others anxious to return within Mendips Abbey's limestone walls. He invites them to follow inside only after he disarms the alarm and heads in alone, shaking flurries from his white chrysanthemum of hair.

Before tending to the trilling, he swifts to the dormitory.

He sees the one closed door.

"Brother Ambrogio?"

He opens the door fearing a sudden view of cardiac arrest and finds the Black Madonna pulling her skin off, thumbs in at the waist, shimmying to shed. Beneath the sleeves of dark fallen-away skin is white, drooping flesh and white hair made whiter with powder. Blue robes wrap like a Christmas tree skirt round her tangled feet.

The alarm trills high to low.

She sees him—

—and falls to the twin bed as if shot to the head, the face still as mask as icon. Can't blink, can't open her mouth. Only a pout ushers out of that dark face with raspberry red lips and blue eye shadow. The hair and crown shine, cheap plastic. A brown baby doll, in small red robe, also crowned, perches regally on the pillow.

He sets the iPad on the nightstand and grabs the face, rolling the meat of his palms into the cheeks. They cave, vacant rubber. The neck rolls up, with effort, revealing Brother Ambrogio's teeth biting his lower lip. The sixty-eight-year-old isn't breathing. The mask, under the castoff wig, laces like a boxing glove up the back. It comes off with a loosen and Brother Moriarty shakes the man's clenched face, gives him, after a hesitant pat, a reluctant smack.

Brother Ambrogio sucks air, eyes flaring on the abbot's pectoral cross swinging into his nose.

The alarm trills high to low.

❖

Brother Ambrogio sits off the corner of the long table in the vaulted refectory, his bald head dropped in humiliation. Brother Moriarty stands behind him, hands on the man's limp shoulders, and looks around at the monks, seated like tame badgers in their black and white habits. Their untouched mugs of herbal tea and cocoa murmur swirls of steam on their silent behalf.

"I think we've all received Brother Ambrogio's resignation e-mail."

"I don't e-mail."

Brother Cobalt sits serenely at the far head of the table. Brother Cobalt was once the abbot.

"Yes, well, he Cc'ed all of us."

He pulls out the chair beside the disgraced monk and sits. He tends to Brother Ambrogio's mug of rosehip tea, wringing the teabag on his spoon and setting both aside. He resets the hot drink in front of Brother Ambrogio, who won't lift his head.

The monks stare.

"About this matter about resigning?"

The monks reach for their mugs.

"To paraphrase, I suppose, if I may," Brother Moriarty says, "the resignation offered details of my encounter with you this morning, during the fire drill."

"I didn't read it," Brother Cobalt says again.

"He expressed his habit, if we will, of dressing as a doll."

"And I take prayer in word-finds," the eldest monk shares. "So he plays with dollies."

"No," Brother Ambrogio says, "I become one."

Brother Cobalt's mouth spreads to a long thin line.

"It's called rubber masking. It's an outfit. A silicone outfit. Hypo-allergenic." Hearing his own voice, Brother Ambrogio cowers.

Brother Moriarty, aware that his posture might be construed as anxious, takes an anxious sip of chamomile. "How did this come to be?"

"My little nieces' dolls. They weren't much younger than me, my nieces. You've all met them—they do corn casserole for the Saint Claude Day potluck every year."

"Forgive me, I should be clearer on this point." Brother Moriarty, squinting, ruffles a hand through his shaggy petals of hair. "How did the costume or what-have-you, or, rather, when, no, no—*how* did you obtain the rather elaborate outfit?"

"When I obtained an iPad, when we were all brought up to date on technology by Brother Babatunde—"

All heads turn to Brother Babatunde. The youngest monk takes cover behind his peppermint tea.

"And so you ordered the accoutrements through the iPad."

"I received them, gifts from other maskers, much like we receive clothes here from charitable parishoners. After discovering masking is a path beyond myself. This masking, I thought about since I was a boy. It's a path that isn't just my own. This masking I thought so perverse—when it *isn't* perverse—and here I dedicated my soul to monastic life. For fear of it."

Brother Moriarty tries to chuckle the chuckle he has long practiced since joining the cloister—muted but sincere—and fails mustering it again. "And, and when I interrupted you, there, earlier there, in your cell there, I thought I was in vision of the Black Madonna."

"You see, I didn't know there were others like me. Just like me." Brother Ambrogio has wet eyes now. Soon, two wet cheeks. "I've lived a lie in your midst. I've always been open with our Father about it, always in prayer, but I've deceived you. My brothers. I've let you all down."

"Let's not—"

"I vowed *stabilitate sua et conversatione morum suorum et oboedi—*"

"And you're *grand*." He sets his open hand at the monk's collar. "You didn't Cc or Bcc the Bishop on that e-mail. Did you?"

"No."

"Good. It's a riddle, holding authority after his effort to hide what occurred in Davenport—but he holds the Cardinal's favor."

Brother Cobalt, abbey cooper emeritus, brushes the tabletop of nonexistent sawdust in three strokes. "The cardinals nesting in our Grotto live closer to God."

Brother Moriarty nods decisively, flowery hair wimpling. "I have reviewed the Rule and find no conflict to engender excommunication. You have my leave to possess the costume."

The bald monk covers his face to hide the sudden swell of tears.

"No one carries out wort separation as faithfully as you. The men and women who love Mendips Abbey Beer need you. We, your brothers, need you. The Church needs you. Our Father needs you."

The mum cete of musteline monks peer at him with lowered chins, gentling their eyes in case he uncovers his face to any one of them.

"But there's a bigger problem here and it isn't howsoever we worship in our cells. It's the presence of *these*." Brother Moriarty shoves his iPad an inch away with his fingernails inline like a snow plow. "Our cells aren't the places of meditation they once were. The whole world is there with us now, thanks to devices."

"Thanks to a glorified newspaper-stroke-typewriter," dismissed the least Wi-Fi savvy monk.

"Maybe computers fit that description a quarter of a century ago, Brother Cobalt, but, as my recent online survey of Bob Dylan songs recorded since I joined the monastery in 1981 has revealed to me, *things have changed*. Brother Babatunde is able to communicate with his family in Benin, in real time, in fluid video. This is certainly and without question a miraculous era, the immediacy of interaction across great distances boggling with its ease. But we live in cloisters. The world has a new way of imposing itself amidst our flight from it. Our cells are places for sleep, prayer, and quiet contemplation—however that may manifest. When each of us returns alone to our cell and closes the door, *each of us*, all bets are off, so to speak. It is us and the Lord, our Father, in that cell. As the Vicar of Christ here at Mendips Abbey, it is my duty to uphold the Rule of Benedict and see it is carried out in our community of brothers. As such, I have decided that computers and tablets are not to enter into our cells from now on. We may use them, as we may, in common areas during communal recreation times. I do apologize to those who have taken meditation in reading on an iPad or Kindle in bed—I myself am included in this group—but unfortunately, due to the inherent invasiveness of the world through these machines, reading in privacy can only continue if it is done out of books. You all know I'm quite lenient when it comes to approving reading material, and I see no reason to change our policy in that regard. Just, from now on, reading in privacy will commence only from printed pages."

"And incunables?"

"And the odd, rare incunable we have in the library, Brother Cobalt, yes."

None of the monks look at any of the other monks, their mugs low or empty.

"Five minutes to eight," Brother Moriarty says, standing. He does not know the exact time but wants to end this delicate meeting softly, like a whisper.

The monks respond as he hopes, rising and pulling up their pointing hoods. They file past the two open dishwashers and deposit their mugs on the way out.

Brother Ambrogio steadies onto his feet, drawing a slow breath. The abbot takes both of their mugs and slots them into the closest top rack at jaunty angles.

The rack won't slide in.

He resituates some mugs.

It slides this time without issue.

He turns around and the unsteady monk is steady, eyes looking down from their corners at the iPad's blank black screen, left on the long table.

"Come along, Brother Ambrogio," he says. "We need you at Compline."

Brother Moriarty and Brother Ambrogio, side by side, are last to step out to the cloister walk.

Gary

to LovelyLotus   8 July 2011

I'm not racist but in this dream of you I had this big red frog with
the face of a black man was terrorizing you. He won't let you alone
and its got your life all out of whack. It's a dream so I think my
landlady would take care of this for you but she's not around so its
up to me to rescue you. I grab him which isn't to hard and I gave
him a good long look. He's all pudgy and crazy but grinning. I take
him to my landlady's jail in the boiler room of the apartment
building here. She's got this wall of metal cages and throw him in
one with this great big lock on it needing a special key. There's this
series of gas burners hooked up under them cages and I'm dead set
on ridding this creepazoid from your life so I fire it up. He's barely
effected by the heat and the bars going all hot and just sits there
giving me a stare.
Whatever. He was trapped. So I went back to you and we went out
to have fun. I tell you the bastards locked up and we relax about it.
We go to a museum of magic andthere's a huge dark hall where we
watch a man come up from a water porthole and leap out of it like
a dolphin. He swam through the air to another porthole and
disappeared on into it. Then he reappeared at another one and
repeted the air swimming. There's four of the portholes and he
does his thing going in and out of them in different patterns. Its
pretty neat.
When that's done we walk out and are in line with other people
who came to see the magic. A younger woman bumps you and
looks around and recognizes you and says this real snooty HEY. You
nod and I can tell your troubled.
When the younger woman disappears up the line you explain when
you were a girl living in Africa that girl always terrorized you and
teased you and hurt your feelings. I say we don't need to be
around that kind of negativity so I get us out of there and take you

straightaway to Paris to go dancing.

We see Steve Martin there and follow him for a bit. Turns out he's going dancing to. So we dance a bit and then you get to dance with him and if it were any other guy I'd be pretty uncomfortable about it but its Steve Martin so its aok. He had on this yellow fedora low on his forehead so it covered his eyes. Was a pretty good dancer. Better than me anyways.

When we had our fix with that, I got us back home to my apartments thats now huts, like a village. I get you to mine and set you down for a rest and when you are asleep I got to check on the frog man in the jail.

He's gone!

My heart just sank. He wasn't in the cell where I left him. And I seen where the metal floor bars are burnt through in a melted circle. So I turned off the burner and heard this grumbling.

And he was there! In another cell!

The toad was all covered in soot and sweat and he gave me the meanest scowl. I started to worrying because I'm not sure I could contain him no more and I sure don't want him terrorizing you any farther.

Then I woke up.

+

GARY HOBSBAWM

Rug & Carpet Cleaner

Tiles & Grouting

Car & Bike Detailing

+

Email pics for quotes!

+

The Other Life of Pat Cottons

Every Christmas, I check my ex's dad's Facebook page to see if he's left them yet.

He has not.

And it's a wonder he has not, because there's no good reason to stick around.

I met Mr. and Mrs. Cottons the way you meet your girlfriend's parents when you're twenty: on a weekend, when she took me home with her for the first time. I'd been seeing Kelli for, oh, four months at that point? Somewhere in there. We'd met in uni at the Fornication Under The Sea Dance, this deplorable American-style night out at our college's bar. The idea behind the event was to take the piss out of American culture, a favorite English pastime, but the fact that it marked the beginning of at least one rather serious relationship really does complicate matters a bit. Out of a piss-take is born something like love that one or both of us took rather seriously at the time. What're we to make of that then?

Anyhow. As I recall it, and this was years ago, mind you, we got the train from town, switched over at Preston, and got off at the station in Formby. Awaiting in the carpark was the girl's father himself, ready to flip open the boot soon as he saw his daughter and the dashing young gentleman she'd brought home. He wore a tweed cap tight on his head, the kind that hugs the crown of the skull in a bland beige weave, and his arms were too long for both shirt and jacket cuffs. The effect, I noticed as he insisted upon taking and shoving my bag into the boot, was that he'd over the course of the day experienced an alarming spurt of growth.

'Thank you, Mr. Cottons,' I said.

He asked me to call him Pat.

Kelli and I sat in the back of the family Nissan Almera and he drove us posthaste to the Red Squirrel Reserve along the coastline there. I'd not anticipated a stroll through the pines but it was a nice thing to do for a visitor and I've thought since about how I ought to do something similar if I ever have a daughter who brings a fellow home. The National Trust has there on the edge of Formby's beach dunes a maze of trails in the woodlands where red squirrels have been ghettoized to protect them from the invasive grey squirrel. Grey squirrels are another thing we curse the Americans for.

Pat, gent that he is, fixed us up with little sacks of squirrel feed and we had quite a civilized afternoon there showing off our gentler natures, kneeling and extending palms full of monkey nuts for close encounters with ginger tree-dwellers. The squirrels were habituated to humans, something that made me feel rather sorry for them, but I can't deny it was a delight having one accept a well-meant offering. The tufts of their ears and the flutter of their tails were charms no hardened undergraduate hoping to impress his girlfriend's dad could resist. I think Pat got a kick out of the way I gushed over the little bastards.

Kelli, as would come to be a more prevalent feature of our relationship, was a tad impatient. She'd wanted to go straight home from the station. This was a diversion she felt could have waited and had no qualms voicing repeatedly.

Pat drove us to their house in Little Altcar, a redbrick suburban enclave much like the one I came from myself.

'I've brought the chap from Hereford!'

That's how Pat announced my arrival in their home.

He dashed to start dinner and I got to meet Sandy, the unpleasant miniature Dachshund I'd been made to look at countless times on Kelli's phone, and Christine, her mum. She held court in the sitting room, sizing me up, passing me brie and dry roasted nuts. I cracked a hilarious joke about their feeding me squirrel food.

'Quite moreish,' she observed from the other sofa. 'Like you.'

'Mum!' Kelli then punished me for her mum's flirting by retreating to the other end of our sofa with Sandy.

Mrs. Cottons—insisting on Christine—was quite like her daughter in temperament and hair color—bottle blonde—but her face was entirely plain. Her flesh was almost grey. It was a mystery that Kelli had such a grasp on makeup and cosmetics while her mother had seemingly never dabbled. Not that a woman needs to do that. She doesn't. It's just the sort of thing you tend to notice if you happen to be sighted.

She was drinking white wine and whenever she needed a refill she'd call and Pat would emerge to pick the bottle up off the coffee table and top it off for her before dashing back to tend to the meal. I didn't understand why she couldn't lean forward and fetch for herself the bottle before her. Even more baffling was her refusal to let me pour for her.

'It's Pat's job,' she said with some vehemence that signaled I should just play along.

Dinner was fine, although I've no memory of what it was we ate. Pat prepared it and I can't recall repulsion at what was put before me so it must have been fine. I tend to recall offensive meals I've been made to eat under pressure of politeness. Honestly what I was most concerned about was where I would be sleeping in relation to Kelli and whether or not we'd manage to rendezvous somewhere within the house to consummate what we'd been consummating daily since that Fornication Under The Sea Dance.

Before they went to bed and we could get to it (in the downstairs toilet under the stairs), Christine saw to it that he set us up with pudding in the lounge before excusing himself to his study. We were left to make nice with GOGGLEBOX on the telly until Kelli's mostly inebriated mum went to bed.

'Ugh,' Christine said. And I mean it when I say she said that. 'Ugh. Off to his Other Life.'

I didn't think she could mean that he plays around on Other Life, so I asked what his other life was all about? Reading or was he an aspiring writer?

'No, it's his computer game. Some *thing* called Other Life. What is it, Kelli?'

Kelli was on her phone.

I told Mrs. Cottons I knew what it was, that I sometimes went on there and goofed about.

'Ugh,' Kelli said, just like her mother. 'You're a weirdo

just like my dad.'

I asked if he was a designer, making his own skins and playing architect and whatnot. Neither of them knew. Sensing I knew a thing or two about it, she gave me a grilling as to what it's all about. I asked if she'd ever read *The Three Stigmata of Palmer Eldritch*—not expecting she'd be a Philip K. Dick fan—and I was right, in that she hadn't read it and didn't know who Dick was. So I made this rather tedious analogy about how in that book Martian colonists are so bored with life that they take this drug called Can-D and imagine themselves living the lives of dolls they play with on mats and how Other Life is like that except it's with avatars on a computer and people needn't be high to sink the better part of their days fully engrossed in it. Channel 4 did a late night special on it: SECRETS OF MY OTHER LIFE.

'But what is there to be bored about as *my* husband and father of *my* child?' She sipped her pinot grigio. 'Pat's living in Small Altcar, not *Mars*.' She laughed then, implying that, of course, life in Small Altcar could be rather mundane.

The next night, he did the same thing.

And Sunday afternoon we had to pull him away from it to drive us to the railway station to head back to uni.

From then on whenever I logged onto Other Life to be a bit of a griefer, just for 'the lolz,' I'd wonder if he was on, too. It wasn't anything I ever got too involved with, but I did have a bit more sympathy toward the concept than Mrs. Cottons. For the rendering enthusiast with a bit of time and creativity on his or her hands, it was a rather astonishing piece of software. Prior to it, socializing online in real time fell on the text-based shoulders of instant messaging. The boon of being able to customize one's avatar and wander around any number of 3D environments designed and maintained by their fellow users—and being able to chat with them—made it a community building platform. I did not find it strange or odd that people enjoyed chatting about their homemade skins that made them look like a Ken doll or a puffin or even a big walking penis. Some of these can actually be quite astonishing, I have to say—I once saw an iguana who pretty well took my breath away for its realistic looks and movements. The user on the other side turned out to be a really quite stunning young woman, American, who I'd fail to bed during her internship in London a few years later. You never can tell who's driving that iguana, so it's best to leave things open.

Any new means of gossiping, socializing, and becoming emotionally involved will be embraced. Other Life is that with the option of accessorizing.

I had fantasies each time I signed on of tracking old Pat down.

I tried to imagine what his user name might be and what avatar he would choose. Found myself keeping an eye out for man-sized red squirrels in wool caps.

I seriously pondered which servers he might frequent, too. There were plenty devoted to cybersex but I didn't see him nipping off daily for the likes of that. More likely he was involved in the Other Life arts scene. There were countless virtual pubs there, in environments spanning the gamut of Caribbean beach bar to faerie glen to zero-G asteroid belt, and most sported nightly gigs. Musicians streaming from home would play songs for anybody gathered. Pretty cool, actually, and a decent way to make some friends with your taste in music in other parts of the world. I, in my own charming way, occasionally used these gatherings as play-grounds for gentle trolling. Nothing cruel. I'd just show up in a Dalek avatar and wheel about the dance floor typing, <EXTERMINATE! EXTERMINATE!> For added amuse-ment, I'd plow right into dancing couples, park right on their virtual toes. Immature but harmless behaviour from a young man with an internet connection and far too much time on his hands.

I didn't anticipate this kind of involvement from Pat's end. One can never tell though. What's not—or oughtn't be—mysterious about bored white people with a computer at home is that the mysterious aspects of their inner personal-ities can find expression. Why is anyone ever surprised by the precipitation of this, that, or the other niche subculture cropping up online? Everyone's a weirdo in some capacity they often fear to be utterly unique. As if. Think up the most outlandish hobby, interest, or kink and Google it. You'll find a tribe. Nowadays the weirdos of like-stripe are able to find each other and carry on and make that personal side of them-selves communal.

I'd not seen so much as a glimpse of Pat's study and, with Christine clearly in control of home décor as well as opera-tions, I'd not picked up clue one regarding his leisure. Even Kelli seemed to lack any knowledge of her father's interests. Left to guess, I reckoned he was into virtual kite flying. And why not? There was simply nothing to go on.

Next time I went for a weekend visit was bank holiday.

In keeping with his theme of sights to see in the area, Pat drove us toward Ormskirk so we could see, at Rufford Old Hall, the squirrel topiary in the garden. Not directly upon ar-riving, no, he waited until Saturday to take us. Christine and

Sandy went along. Pat's year membership for the National Trust got us into the grounds and while I appreciated what he'd done in keeping with his arboreal rodent sightseeing theme, the other Cottons thought it daft. Which it was. But what's life without a touch of imposed daftness now and again? I'd hate to see it outlawed from family outings.

While the ladies were inspecting the home's sixteenth-century carved oak screen I had the opportunity to mildly interrogate Pat. So I told him I like to faff about on Other Life sometimes. He was quite forthcoming about his own involvement, letting on without the least bit of reservation that he was the owner and proprietor of an establishment called the Dappled Tablecloth. Pat explained it as a virtual B&B/café/art gallery. Off the IT clock he put his coding skills to artistic use, playing architect and decorator. His grandparents, he told me, had run a B&B in Blackpool when he was a child. The Dappled Tablecloth was his attempt at recreating it.

When he asked what I got up to on there, I just told him I was a pedestrian, taking in the rendering accomplishments of others.

What I did notice, without thinking much of it at the time, was how quickly he changed the subject as soon as the ladies returned—back to the clipping techniques necessary to sculpt the likeness of a squirrel from a shrubbery.

Why should he be so open with me about something he kept to himself within the family?

After tea that evening, while grey-faced Christine was having him serve her a cheese and wine course in the lounge and Kelli saw to it that I load up a dessert plate for her, he gave me a look on his feet I'd never really received before but could read plainly:

Get out now, young man, before it's too late.

It actually gave me pause, the message in that woeful face, but it passed when Kelli kicked me from her side of the sofa to remind me to hand over her brie.

No sooner had Pat retreated to his study than Christine asked if I could show her "how to do the Other Life?" I figured I'd try. This lady was a noob if ever I saw one—but she was frightfully determined and in this she adapted rapidly. Withdrawing a laptop from under her sofa, she'd gotten as far as installing Other Life but needed assistance getting everything set up. So I helped her pick out a beginner avatar—one of several bland doll-like choices—and took her shopping for new skins, new outfits.

'So is this something you and Pat plan on doing together then?' I asked.

'You're joking,' she said into her wine glass. 'I don't want him to have any notion I'm on this thing.'

We decked her out at the free shops and got her all set up. I showed her how to walk around, how to interact with others. I'd had no expectations as to her getting it, but get it she did. The woman took to it with something like avarice, it's hard to explain.

The user name she chose for herself was Regreta Grigio.

She'd clearly thought about this for some time.

Kelli, mortified, snapped pics of me teaching her mum how to use Other Life, exchanging messages with her girl-friends from uni. Her patience with Christine getting so much of my attention wore terribly thin terribly fast. She tolerated it with sneers up until her mum made sure my user name was added to her friend list. That was the most she could handle. Sharing me did not fall within the bounds of my girlfriend's emotional repertoire.

And so that was the extent of my Other Lifing with the Cottons there that second and final occasion I spent time with them in their comfy middle class home with that snarling little pup who never took to me the way even the most cantankerous of dogs often will to a temporary house guest.

I'm speaking of the dog, Sandy, there. I'm not alluding to Kelli being a dog out of bitterness for breaking up a couple months later. Kelli's alright. Not all breakups devastate, you know.

So whatever, Kelli and I went back to uni that bank holiday Monday and things were fine, except of course she expected me to wait on her hand and foot and I just couldn't be bothered most of the time. One thing I did that I was chuffed about: I taught her how to drive manual. That was a triumph. Saved Pat the pain and abuse of doing it himself.

One thing I did when I remembered it was check out the Dappled Tablecloth. It was late at night, well past midnight midweek, so I expected neither Pat nor Christine to be on. And they weren't. The location was revealed by a simple directory search and when I teleported there I found a somewhat convincing mockup of an old rowhouse seafront B&B without its row or the sea. There stood a body of water, sure, but nothing like the English coastline or a town like Blackpool, which Pat had invoked in describing his project. A dozen users milled about in the ground floor café/art gallery, Other Lifers logged in a quarter of a day behind us in North America.

It seemed the man's gathering point had drawn a devoted following, a hangout with signs of life in it. Most places you could visit in Other Life stood empty, totally devoid of participation, virtual ghost towns. Every now and again I'd go exploring these spaces, just fly-throughs, to see what people had designed and left along the way. Cyber tombs containing nothing like a treasure—although once I did come upon, in the heart of a big office building, a trio of furries conducting some kind of mostly text-based sexual experimentation in a room with this big ray gun and Frankensteinian slab in it. There was a cartoony dog, a blue hippo, and a pink penguin and it was the penguin who was on the examination table. And they were all typing out in chat what they were supposedly doing to the penguin, with her typing <ooooooooooh> whenever cranking up the ray supposedly tickled her bits a bit better. I don't know. They offered me a go but I left them to it.

Anyhow, yes, the Dappled Tablecloth had nothing of the sort going on at the premises. It was a local hangout for local people. It's an odd thing, building a make-believe B&B on a platform people used only when they were awake. I couldn't see the point in going to the trouble to do up eight guest rooms in detail down to the doilies on the dressers when no one would actually be sleeping over. I had a roam of the place in my most nondescript avatar, you see: a built guy with a tan, feathered brown hair, wraparound aviators. I rarely used it, reserving it for those instances when I didn't want to draw any attention to myself. The vast majority of users had these bland human avatars, wandering around in these variations on Action Man and Barbie that probably had less to do with their real lives than a more outlandish avatar would.

I understand that's a bit judgemental. But come on.

You've seen the same documentaries I've seen. You know people are presenting themselves in idealized forms—or what they perceive to be idealized. One fellow's idea of perfection is another fellow's idea of freakishness. That goes for ladies, too.

But anyway, I was happy enough to find, dancing on the café countertop, a hedgehog in white shades and feather headdress and a chipmunk wearing a backpack holding tinier chipmunks chucking acorns. With everybody else loitering in their own private conversations it was nice to see a couple of people having a bit of fun. The art on show this month consisted of boat paintings and paintings of faces with massive black oval mouths—trite stuff you might actually see for sale on the walls of an English café.

Had a look out back and found, empty though it was, a tea garden boasting a touch that should not have surprised me. There, in the middle of the terrace with tables arranged around it and a privacy hedge on all sides, stood a digitized replica of the squirrel topiary he'd shown off at Rufford Old Hall.

No sooner had I taken note of it than a user with a female avatar addressed me. She had followed me out—the tea garden was empty of people—and I'd already noticed her inside. Her name was Dr. Lola Cawfee. She had on a voluminous pink bouffant, diaphanous silk that trailed her as she walked, and black stilettos that sparkled little dissipating silver stars.

<Can I get you anything? Cup o' joe?>

I declined but thanked her for the attentiveness.

<Hospitality's the name of the game here.> she typed. <So few of us get it elsewhere.>

I checked her profile while we chitchatted. It claimed a

cubicled career in Connecticut, a love of classical music, and Anglophilia. She told me that she helped run the place with a real life Englishman, who had designed everything.

<I'm Polly to his Basil.> is how she put it.

<Who's Sybil then?>

<We manage without one.> she typed back.

Before ducking back indoors to tend to visitors' imaginary beverage needs, Dr. Lola pointed out a special feature. There was a sign posted in the tea garden that read KEEP CALM AND FEED A SQUIRREL. When clicked upon, a wee little red squirrel would bound out of the hedge and beg a nut from your hand.

Ah, Pat.

I didn't inquire after him or hang around hoping to glean his user name. I did, however, entertain a vague but present curiosity about the plot of property he'd leased to recreate his grandparents' Blackpool B&B.

I knew that one's allotment, in renting a prime plot of real estate in Other Life, was not restricted to what you see at ground level. Some maps you could visit failed to fence off their edges, which meant your avatar could fall off, which would result in a seemingly endless drop. By the same token, each map went up the equivalent of miles and miles and miles. Taking full advantage of this, users buying building privileges would often enough, for the sake of their own privacy, construct enclosed structures far above ground level. Often they were simple rooms, decorated on the inside, drab on the outside—a place to go and hide whilst online, to invite other users in and have some one-on-one time. They were called skyboxes and, knowing they were a thing, I followed my hunch and gave the atmosphere high over the Dappled

Tablecloth a look.

Sure enough, farther up than Other Life will render, I found a shape with the dimensions of a two-pack of mansize tissues. Pat's skybox.

There was a trick to them, see, whereby if the coding wasn't quite cricket, and you hovered your view at one of the corners of the skybox, you could finagle this flickering key-hole peek inside.

I know—it's intrusive behaviour, voyeuristic, unseemly. You'd not want your daughter to be dating a snoop, a creep, a peeping tom. It's a tendency that calls into question a young man's character. I'm aware.

I also know you'd likely sneak a look, too, were you in my position.

What I saw inside Pat's skybox was what suburban white men refer to these days as a man cave. Here, unbridled, flour-ished the masculinity Pat could not bring about in his own home. One wall was done in stone with a built-in waterfall, the others oak panel. Orange carpet on floor and ceiling. A bar with three stools and lit shelf of liquor bottles behind it. Jukebox. Grand piano. Dartboard. Nearly wall-sized telly with cinema-style seating in front of it. Seven electric guitars hung along other wall. Green German sports car, parked with nowhere to go. Aquarium stocked to the gills with neon tetras that spelled out motivational words every so often. And in the corner, under a mirror on the ceiling, a circular bed dressed in red bedsheets. No pillows.

I'd seen those beds before in Other Life. They sport op-tion menus by which you can select any number of preset animations that, if I might be frank about it, simulate adult activities.

There's no other purpose for them in Other Life.

And then, to my great surprise, I realized Pat was there. Pat was present. His back to my vantage point, seated in a tall chair set before the mouth of a polar bear rug stretched out upon the carpet.

His name, floating over his head, was Red Rufford.

A moment later and Dr. Lola appeared out of a swirl of pixels, teleported into the skybox by invitation.

He rose to greet her—and he'd done that thing Other Lifers sometimes do: he'd rendered his avatar as a facsimile of himself. The avi even had the same beige cap plastered to its head. They activated a loveseat I'd missed, their avatars sitting upon it and assuming an embrace of intense passion.

I'm pretty sure I laughed. But in that laugh at my computer screen, what I recall most was the unease in the pit of my stomach. It wasn't anything like—how might I put it—like a pang of responsibility to report to anybody what I'd seen. I didn't feel burdened by witnessing what was clearly some kind of emotional involvement Pat had cultivated outside his marriage. I knew people did far worse than that, jeopardizing the family's stability in more destructive ways. If this was the way he'd found to keep himself from drowning in Small Altcar, who was I to judge? Had he not been pleasant to me and rather pathetic in his efforts to appease his wife, I'd not have felt what I felt, which was the unshakable urge to protect him by keeping my mouth shut about the whole thing. Besides, I couldn't even imagine how I'd bring it up with Kelli. And I think in some odd way it was this realization, that I felt a greater loyalty to Pat than I did to the girl I'd been seeing for half a year, that signaled the beginning of the end of the relationship for me.

A few times there I saw Christine logged on. I typically left this alone, not sending her any messages. Eventually, however, she grew pretty adept at how it all worked, sending me greetings. A couple times I went ahead and accepted her offer of a teleport to accompany her. Kelli's mum had revenge on the mind, that much was clear, with her trying to coerce me into poking around her husband's pet project. I never did join her for a wander round the Dappled Tablecloth, though I know she wanted to glean my take on it along with whatever tips I had regarding the user interface.

I found the whole ballet rather exhausting. Have you ever primarily been a potential source of information to somebody? I was as much as that to Christine and nothing more. Knowing that and seeing through her attempts at pleasantries cast the whole thing in a rather desperate light. I had no intention of breaking this family apart, of being the Nick Carraway who reintroduced people who ought to have never crossed paths again, though that's what was wanted from me. And so it was that my casual hobby of taking the piss on Other Life became dominated by the marital strain of a couple whose daughter I was losing interest in quickly. She even commented once upon how it seemed I talked more to her mother than I did to her—a grotesque exaggeration of the truth that nevertheless held a grain or two of insight in it.

The night I deleted Regreta Grigio from my friends list was the night she pretended to be Kelli. I'm rather certain about this, though I can't be sure. Kelli had gone home to Small Altcar for the weekend—I was invited but declined, it being late autumn and courses ending soon and my devotion on the wane. Regreta signed on quite late and sent me messages claiming to be Kelli sneaking a midnight go on her mum's account. She tried to coax me to a sex club—one of many on Other Life, full of large-breasted pole-dancers who are most likely men acting out closeted fantasies.

<Come onn give us kitten licks luv> she said, her typing inebriated. <give your girl kitten licks>

Kelli couldn't give a shit about Other Life. I knew this for a fact. And not once in our almost entirely sexual relationship had she once asked for anything of the sort. It was a decidedly un-Kelli manner in which to request virtual cunnilingus.

By way of a test, I sent Kelli a message on her phone and when she didn't reply, likely asleep, I told Regreta Grigio to go to bed and promptly deleted her. After that, I didn't bother with Other Life until Christmas day. I was thoroughly off-put by the Cottons. And things with Kelli kind of just funneled off after that.

And then she calls me on Christmas with the most ridiculous story, shouting it down the phone to me. I was at home in Hereford. Had to excuse myself from the Xbox tournament my brothers set up so I could catch the gist of what Kelli was on about.

Apparently Christine had made good use of my Other Life lessons and gone and stalked her husband for some time. From what I could gather from Kelli's mostly incoherent rant, her mother's tracking of his activities revealed that Pat spent an inordinate amount of time with a woman whose avatar changed back and forth from winged angel to pink-haired dominatrix.

Dr. Lola Cawfee, no doubt.

I still don't quite see why this had to be such a bad thing. The Dappled Tablecloth could have gained its Sybil if she'd only taken a more continental view of things.

Anyhow, it was apparent to her that he was conducting an affair with another woman and a bit more investigating revealed he'd build a secret room—that's how Kelli described it—where he and this other woman carried out their emotional affair. She lacked details of the skybox but I could imagine what had happened, presuming that Christine had done as much as I had in terms of snooping on his activities. I refrained from asking questions but it's quite possible that she Catfished him, rubbing up to him without his knowing Regreta Grigio was his actual wife. This is the more dramatic possibility of events, with her playing a part, infiltrating his other life on Other Life, coercing him into cheating on the woman he was cheating on her with. The woman was driven enough for something like that. I just have a feeling she gathered her evidence from a distance, seeing as I'm pretty sure she was the one so unsubtly impersonating her daughter online the night I washed my hands of the Cottons. Kelli had some of the details about his bachelor pad though, relaying in condemnatory fashion the features on his skybox bed. You'd think the man guilty of crimes on par with Josef Fritzl the way she described it.

Christmas day, then, that day, the Cottons had done their Christmas thing, whatever that was—she didn't tell me—and ate their Christmas dinner, after which Pat excused himself to his study. Christine waited twenty minutes, not letting on to Kelli or the Dachshund what was at stake, and then marched upstairs with the roaster pan with turkey carcass still in it. Kelli, stuffed on the sofa (I imagine), was suddenly alarmed by sounds of great calamity coming from that room. A short time later her mum came back downstairs empty handed and, drinking straight from a bottle of pinot grigio she actually fetched for herself, told Kelli that her father was conducting an affair with an American whore on Other Life, that she'd just been upstairs to check on him and found him at his computer in his study enjoying a sit-down virtual Christmas dinner at a virtual dining room table with his virtual mistress. His sweet enjoyment of the holiday with his girlfriend was then interrupted by his wife's bashing in his monitor with the roaster pan, whereby it lost the turkey carcass, which became dispersed upon Pat and throughout his study.

Kelli was calling to blame me for teaching her mum how to use the program. And sure, I felt a bit shitty about that. It isn't nice. I didn't know quite what was going on really. Was just making myself of some use to my girlfriend's mother, you know, when she asked me to help her out with something I knew a little bit about. Anyway, with Kelli tearing into me on Christmas day like this—seeing to it that I was the recipient of her unrestrained venom—I couldn't not see Pat's face, that look he gave me, the one that said to get out while I still can. And taking the advice he'd given me then, I told her to fuck off and consider herself dumped.

Which really wasn't the most tactful way of doing it.

Especially on Christmas.

But it's alright really. She found a new beau next term and, I can only assume, went about blaming him for the things she used to blame me about. Chiefly: her problems.

And like I said in the beginning, I check his Facebook each Christmas and he's still there in Small Altcar, still with them. Next time I was on Other Life, whenever that was, I did pay a quick visit to the landmark I'd saved for the

Dappled Tablecloth. It was gone. A big sign there read: FOR LEASE. So much for any kind of lasting monument to his grandparents' B&B. He likely isn't allowed access to a computer at home anymore. I wouldn't be surprised if his study hasn't been gutted, converted into Christine's shoe gallery.

Is this it then?

The preservation of the family at all costs?

Is Pat made noble for sacrificing all his involvement in Other Life?

What happened to his girlfriend in Connecticut? She either deleted her account or changed her name—Dr. Lola Cawfee was stricken from the directory. I imagine she was quite hurt, losing not just him but the Dappled Tablecloth, too.

I never told anybody at uni the details of what happened. I felt guilty—still do, I guess—but there was no reason to embarrass Kelli. This doesn't make me a nice guy, I know. I do hope, selfishly, that it might make me less of a jerk.

I never saw Pat without his wool cap on his head. His avatar wore it and he's wearing it in his Facebook pic. Is he bald under there? Being bald is a fine thing to be. I hope he learns that somewhere down the line.

If I ever win the lottery though—and I've thought about this—I am going to liberate him. When Pat Cottons goes out to feed the squirrels at the reserve, someone will be waiting for him with a Venezuelan passport, a briefcase full of cash, a one-way ticket to the eastern seaboard of the United States, and a hug.

I shouldn't email you from this address but it's kind of an urgent deal. Had a dream I had to get my wife's dad a birthday present. (He died in real life seven years ago so I should have known this was a dream.) She said (my wife) that he wants a pair of bacon shades. I go to a store and buy some. They are sunglasses made of bacon. I go to his house to give them to him and his wife is you! You both have an eleven year old son I did not know about. He opened the present and asked what they were. He put them on and could not even see out of them because they were bacon. I felt so foolish for giving him a bad gift but you said they looked cool on him.

If I were still in therapy I might ask my counselor about it but since you were there in it do you have any ideas what all this might mean?

--

Dave McGarvey, Ed.D
Superintendent
Des Moines Public Schools
3232 Grand Avenue
Des Moines, IA 50312
(515) 229-4875
b.mcgarv@dmschools.org

"The secret in education lies in respecting the student."
–Ralph Waldo Emerson

```
*********************************************************
```
Barry's Quest
Walkthrough
By Ethan Alderyard
```
*********************************************************
```

```
                        NMMMMMMMMMMM.
                   MMMMMMMMMMMMMM77MMMM
                 MMMM77MMMMIIMMMMMMMMMM.
                 MMMMMMMM7IMMMMM7IMMMMMMMMMM
              MMMMMMMMMMMMMI7.          M77MM.
              MMMMMMMMMMMMN.                 MMMM
              MMMMMMM8D.              .888..MM
              MMMMMMM88,              .888..NM
              MMMMNN88888888880          88MM.
              MMMM8O8.                       MM.
              MMMNO8    MMMMMMM ..  MMMMMMM  MM.
           8DD8DMM.  MM                      MM778888
           8  DD88.       +=MMZO       +=MZZ  DD  D8
           8    DD.  8888      D.   8O  D8  DD   ..
           88D  DD.    O8888880D.   8D88D   DD  ND
           DDD  DD.    88888888D.   88808   DD  DD
            DD DD.            D.    88       DD  ,
             DDDD8N           M.    88       DDDN
              8D..          MMD.  MM         DD
               8D.        MMMMD8            DD
               88.                          ...
               88.                        DN.
               888.      DDMMMMMDD        88.
               8O8.                       88.
                D.                        88.
                 88.                    DD.
                 88.          ND      DD.
                N8.                  8.
                 DN.   DDDD     8.
                  DD88DDDDD8888.
```

```
```

```
* * * * * * * * * * * * * * * *
GAME INFORMATION
* * * * * * * * * * * * * * * *

Title: Barry's Quest
Developer: Gingle Gaming
Publisher: n/a (never published)
Platform: Anima 2000
Release: n/a (never officially released)
Genre: Graphic Adventure


* * * * * * * * * * * * * * * * * * * *
Document Information
* * * * * * * * * * * * * * * * * * * *

Document by: Ethan Alderyard <Alderyard@gmail.com>
Document size: 133 KB
Document version: 1.000
Document hosted by: retrowalkthroughs.com
Document © 2010 Ethan Alderyard - DO NOT STEAL MY WORK!


* * * * * * * * * *
DEDICATION
* * * * * * * * * *

This walkthrough, which has been toiled over with joy,
grief, and obsession, is dedicated with love to my wife,
Wei. 我爱你。


* * * * * * * *
CONTENTS
* * * * * * * *
```

```
CHAPTER 1 - INTRODUCTION
CHAPTER 2 - CHARACTERS
CHAPTER 3 - MAPS
CHAPTER 4 - WALKTHROUGH
        4.1 - OVERTURE
        4.2 - FATHER'S DEATH
        4.3 - PERCIVAL INSURANCE
        4.4 - GINGLE HOME COMPUTING
        4.5 - CANCER
        4.6 - HOSPICE
```

        4.7 - ANOTHER FUNERAL
        4.8 - FAILINGS
        4.9 - THE END
CHAPTER 5 - ITEMS
CHAPTER 6 - THE MANY DEATHS OF BARRY
CHAPTER 7 - EPILOGUE

****
CHAPTER 1 - INTRODUCTION
****

While I have written many guides to computer games (all
thirty-seven of my FAQ/walkthroughs can be found catalogued
at retrowalkthrough.com), this project is unlike any I have
undertaken or even encountered. That we have Barry's Quest
at all, let alone that Barry Gingle created the computer
game singlehandedly in the early 1990s, is a miracle on par
with anything you'll see at the Des Moines Art Center or
even the building of Saylorville Dam. When the archaeology
of home computing comes of age, dissertations will
certainly be written on this specific game, scholars will
resurrect Freud and Jung to explain its mysteries,
cybermystics will sift through its programming code hoping
for eternal answers.

My own job is of a far more humble sort: I am merely
here to help players win the game. By some providence I am
the first to have done so. My own hope, if I am allowed
such a luxury when dealing with another man's masterpiece,
is that this walkthrough will provide a lantern to those
stuck in Barry's Quest - and answer, albeit eighteen years
too late, Barry Gingle's cry for help.

In releasing this game for free download online, there
will be questions about its origins. I offer the following
as honorary executor of Mr. Gingle's legacy. A friend of
mine (who wishes to remain anonymous) approached me in
August of 2010 with the following story:

On a visit to Valley Junction, an old rail-stop-turned-
boutique-row in West Des Moines, Iowa, my friend was
disappointed to find not a single chicken at the Pink
Farmhouse Thrift Shop. A collector of chickens, she is no
stranger to that or other resale stores in the area, ever-
questing for poultry-themed kitsch. What she did find,
however, was a circa 1990 Anima 2000 desktop computer with
a post-it note on the screen reading "TAKE ME I'M FREE!"

The retired women who run the shop had it propping open the front door on the porch. My friend inquired about it, having immediate inspirational plans of gutting the monitor for a henhouse diorama of her own design and making, and the ladies were very happy to have it carted away for free. None of them remembered where it had come from initially, just that it had always sat in the shop without catching anyone's attention. An eventual nuisance, they had put it out on the porch just that morning hoping it would disappear, which, thanks to my friend's spotting it, it did not.

Another reason to be thankful: when she got home, my friend turned it on before her carrying out the crafting-induced disembowelment. There, staring at her from the middle of the humming screen, was an icon that said CLICK ME. And in so doing, she became the first person after Barry Gingle to launch the autobiographical videogame he designed about his lonely, despairing life. The next day, knowing my passion for old computer games, she invited me to take a look. The rest, as they say, is home gaming history.

Not much is known about Barry Gingle. He apparently designed and programmed Barry's Quest singlehandedly during his terminal battle with pancreatic cancer, as the game illustrates. The only photos we have of him are those found in Rosewater High School yearbooks, years 1971-74. He appears to be the same age in all four pictures, one of those unfortunate adolescents who could pass for forty. He did not sit for photos in college but did attend Iowa State University from 1975-79, majoring in Computer Science. His obituary, which ran in the *Des Moines Harbinger*, says he was Iowa's first Commandant and Anima home computer retailer, noting that his shop was located in Valley Junction and tersely adding that the business failed. His shop, interestingly enough, stood right across the street from the Pink Farmhouse Thrift Shop in Valley Junction, which leads me to believe Barry probably left his computer with them for resale shortly before he died, the game on the machine being his version of a message in a bottle.

Barry Gingle was born November 11, 1956 and died April 11, 1992. He was thirty-five at death. He left no surviving relatives. Or friends. Or even, so far as it seems from my research, acquaintances.

```
* * * * * * * * * * * * * * * * * * * * * *
```
CHAPTER 2 - CHARACTERS
```
* * * * * * * * * * * * * * * * * * * * * *
```

```
* * * * * * *
```
* BARRY *
```
* * * * * * *
```
Barry is the hero of his own game. He depicts himself with
a pensive face, always looking to the side, never looking
head on at the player. Indeed his face matches up with high
school yearbook photos. Is it not amazing how much despair
he fit into a face only twenty-two by twenty-seven pixels?

```
* * * * *
```
* MOM *
```
* * * * *
```
Nora Gingle is shown as an older woman with fluffy brown
hair. She wears blouses and slacks through most of the
game, switching to nightdresses when she falls ill. Her
real life obituary in the Des Moines Harbinger reveals that
she was born Nora Spaulding in Centerville in 1925.
Remarkably, her obit reveals that she had been engaged to
her high school sweetheart, Bartholomew Murray, but he was
killed in the Battle of Peleliu. Moving to Des Moines, she
worked as a florist and married Art Gingle in 1951. After
Barry was born in 1956, she became a homemaker.

```
* * * * *
```
* DAD *
```
* * * * *
```
Art Gingle is depicted as a pot-belied man with black hair
like Barry's. His obit tells us that he was born in 1921
and raised in Des Moines, that he served his country as a
sapper in the European theater during WWII, that he went to
college at ISU on the GI Bill and became an agent for
Percival Insurance in 1949. It also mentions ice fishing as
his passion, and if you look around in the garage in the
game, you will notice his auger, tackle box, tent bag, and
poles propped next to the lawnmower.

```
* * * * * * * *
```
* GRAMMA *
```
* * * * * * * *
```
Hazel Gingle is Barry's paternal grandmother. Her sprite
portrays her as wearing a long checkered dress and having
her gray hair pulled back tight in a witchy bun. Her obit

reveals that she was originally from a farm near Cedar Rapids, lived her adult life in Des Moines as a telephone operator, and was widowed two years after her son Art was born.

```
**************
* MR. BLUBAUGH *
**************
```

The one person who knew the Gingles, who might be able to answer some of our questions about Barry, is Marshal Blubaugh, both Art and Barry's boss at Percival Insurance. Tragically, he, his wife, and two of their grandchildren were killed in 2007 when their car was struck by a drunk driver. Barry portrays him in the game as a kindly man in a blue suit with white hair and a smile.

```
*****
* DEB *
*****
```

I WOULD LOVE TO TALK TO DEB. Seriously. If anyone knows who she is, please e-mail me at Alderyard@gmail.com. Deb works in the cubicle next to Barry at Percival Insurance and is his only coworker we ever see apart from Mr. Blubaugh. Despite it being a stretch to say they have even a working relationship, she is still an important presence in the game. Barry must have been fond of her. He depicts her with big blonde hair, always dressed professionally in pantsuits.

```
************
* DR. COKELY *
************
```

This is the doctor who operates on Mom. He looks more than a little like Dr. Fred Edison from Maniac Mansion, though he wears OR scrubs instead of a lab coat. I tried to contact the real Dr. Cokely, who retired to a warmer state, but received no response.

```
********
* SANDRA *
********
```

It is unclear what kind of specialist Sandra is, probably a physical therapist or physiologist of some kind, but we meet her in the hospital following Mom's surgery. Barry depicts her in a white coat. She has red hair that swoops over one eye. All efforts to track her down in real life have failed.

```
*******
* BETTY *
*******
```

Betty may be Betty Hannigan, who worked for twenty-two
years as a hospice provider before her own battle with
breast cancer came to an end in 2002. Hers is the only name
we receive of those working at Peckinpaugh House. Barry
portrays her with curly grey and black hair, and wearing a
sunshine yellow shirt with matching pants.

```
****************
CHAPTER 3 - MAPS
****************
```

MAP 1: HOME

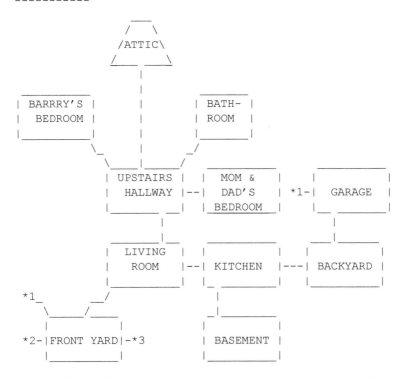

*1: Leads back and forth between FRONT YARD and GARAGE.
*2: Leads to TATE'S GROCERY STORE
*3: Leads to ROSEWATER HIGH SCHOOL

MAP 2: DES MOINES

```
 _____      _____      _____      _____      _____
|DAVENTRY|    |SCHWARZ-|    |PECKIN- |    |WAVELAND|    |GLENDALE|
| APART- |--|  WALD  |    | PAUGH  |--|  GOLF  |--|CEMETERY|
|_MENTS__|    |_CINEMA_|    |HOSPICE |    |_COURSE*|    |_____|
     |            |                           |
   __|____      __|____       _____      __|____       _____
|IMPERIAL|    |BOUNDARY|    |GRAMMA'S|    |CUM N GO|    |DONNE'S |
| GARDEN |--| BOOKS* |--| HOUSE  |--| STATION|--|FUNERAL |
|_____|    |___ ____|    |_____|    |____ ___|    |_HOME___|
                   |                           |
 _____      __|____       _____      __|____       _____
| IVOR'S |    | TATE'S |    |        |    |ROSEWA- |    | GREEN- |
| GAMES  |--|GROCERY |--| HOME  |--|TER HIGH|--| WOOD  |
|_____|    |_STORE__|    |_____|    |_SCHOOL*|    |_PARK*__|
                   |                           |
 _____      __|____       _____      __|____       _____
| DEB'S  |    |BASSMAN |    | USA   |    |LUTHERAN|    | NUB'S  |
| HOUSE  |--|PHARMACY|--| UNITED |--|HOSPITAL|--| NOVEL- |
|_____|    |___ ____|    |_BANK___|    |____ ___|    |_TIES*__|
                   |            |            |            |
 _____      __|____       __|____       __|____       __|____
| GINGLE |    | TACO  |    | ST.   |    | IOWA  |    |PERCIVAL|
|  HOME  |--| JUAN'S |    |IGNATIUS|    |CAPITOL*|--| INSUR- |
|COMPUTNG|    |_____|    |_CHURCH*|    |_____|    |_ANCE___|
```

* Seven of the twenty-five screens that make up the game world of Barry's map of Des Moines never play a significant role in the game. Most intriguing for me, on a personal note, is the inclusion of Nub's Novelties, Des Moines' premiere independent toy shop. Why, you ask? It was my first job in high school and, as of December 31, 2009, I've been the manager. Why did Barry include these places without using them? Was it for the balance of a five-by-five grid of the city? Had he intended to make them vital to the game but ran out of time, his life winnowing away by each precious hour, to incorporate them? We will never know. Our only avenue, as is the case with so many aspects of this singular piece of folk art software, is speculation, which of course can lead us only into more and more questions. If Barry sought to provide his ideal gamer with the stuff of his life, a byproduct of the early exit meted upon him is unsolvable mystery.

```
************************
CHAPTER 4 - WALKTHROUGH
************************


4.1 - OVERTURE
--------------
```

The first screen, saying only GINGLE GAMING in EGA
blue, hints at none of the splendor about to unfold in the
opening sequence. When that goes black, we hear the first
notes of a song perfectly chosen to encapsulate the essence
of his despondency, The Marmalade's "Reflections of My
Life." The song hit #10 on the Hot 100 Chart in 1969 when
Barry was twelve years old. As with all songs in the game,
it is splendidly rendered. Seeing as his computer lacks a
modem, it is likely that the music in the game is his work,
not fetched from a local BBS. This would have taken great
skill and time.

At the entrance of the flute, a haunting substitute for
the song's vocal melody line, we see one, then two orange
leaves waft down the screen. Then appears a forked maple
tree, identical in branching and detail to the one growing
in the yard of his childhood home, and then that house
behind it (The house and yard are rendered beautifully, and
only with use of thirty-two colors. A bit of detective work
revealed the actual house and, though painted grey now
instead of brown, one gains immense respect for Barry's
attention to detail. The wood shingle siding, the railing
up the stoop, the slope of the roof are all as they are in
life.).

We get a closer view of the second floor window. Its
black-and-white check curtains part and we see Barry for
the first time, in profile.

The screen cuts to his bedroom, where he is seated at a
computer with his back to us. It looks like a child's room,
what with the poster of the Big Red Cheese on the wall and
the shelf of tin robots, the stuffed moose doll on the
dresser. He stands and walks to the window. "*wince*," he
says. "Time to rake the yard, I guess…"

He turns and we see that his face is disfigured, just a
field of pink with two wavy wrinkles across it. No eyes,
nose, or mouth. He walks out of his bedroom, down the hall,
and down the stairs into the living room. He winces again.

Now you take control. Barry's Quest is a text-based
graphic adventure, so you control him by typing keyboard

commands. In this walkthrough I will render the commands
you need to type in caps. Movement is simple enough; he
walks up, down, left, and right using the arrow keys. Walk
over to the door and note the jar on the stand there.

GET FACE FROM JAR and PUT ON FACE.

There we go, Barry's got a face now. It's one of the
few poetic touches in the game really, as well as a nod to
that certain song by those certain lads from Liverpool
about loneliness.

If you fail to put Barry's face on and go outdoors, you
will hit Death #1.

OPEN DOOR and walk outside into the front yard. "All
the leaves have fallen," he says. "Is it already October
again?" Walk around the house to the garage and OPEN GARAGE
DOOR. Walk to the long-handled garden tools hanging on the
wall and GET RAKE. Now return to the front yard and RAKE
YARD.

Watch as Barry's back is turned, raking away, and a dog
walker passes without notice of him. When the leaves are in
a small pile, he says, "Guess I should do the back, too…"

Go to the backyard and, again, RAKE YARD. As he goes
into motion, he says, "Almost twenty years now…"

4.2 – FATHER'S DEATH (1973)

A younger Barry is raking the backyard. Dad walks on
screen and says, "Hey bud, Gramma's yard needs raking and
I'm beat. You think you could go over and take care of it?"

"But I'm going to the matinee at the Schwarzwald," says
Barry.

"How many times have you seen whatever they've got on?"

"I'm not gonna rake Gramma's yard."

Dad lowers his chin and walks off screen.

Walk to the garage and stand by the bicycle. PICK UP
LOCK from beside the bike. RIDE BIKE. (If you try to walk
beyond the house Barry will whine, "Too far to walk to the
cinema…") Ride to the Schwarzwald, which, incidentally, is
a real place, the oldest cinema in Des Moines. It's
unfortunate the scale Barry had to work with in this game
doesn't allow for the ornate face of the building,
decorated as it is in statues of characters from German
folklore, still intact since the theater was built in 1932.
I ache to wonder how Barry would have rendered them in

thirty-two colors. The vintage marquee reads AMERICAN
GRAFITTI. GET OFF BIKE and LOCK BIKE TO BIKE RACK. Walk to
the old-fashioned freestanding box office and BUY TICKET.
"Enjoy the show," the girl says, handing you a Ticket. OPEN
DOOR and walk inside.

TWO HOURS LATER…

Young Barry walks out of the lobby and blinks. "Just as
good the sixth time as the first…" UNLOCK BIKE and RIDE
BIKE one screen down. A siren sounds and then an ambulance
drives across the screen. "Hey, that ambulance came from
Gramma's street!" Ride one screen to the right to Gramma's
house, a small single-story home with a crab apple tree in
the front yard. Mom's car, a brown Oldsmobile by the look
of it, pulls up to young Barry and she shouts out the
window: "YOUR FATHER'S HAD A HEART ATTACK – GET IN, WE'RE
GOING TO THE HOSPITAL!" GET OFF BIKE. Young Barry turns to
Gramma's yard, sees the fallen rake, the small pile of
brown and orange leaves, half the yard free of debris and
the other half still covered. He says, "It's all my fault…"
GET IN CAR. Mom drives off screen.
     Walking into the hospital waiting room, Mom yells,
"WHERE'S MY HUSBAND?"
     The nurse behind the counter, visible only as the top
half of a head, says, "When was he admitted?"
     "HE JUST CAME IN," Mom shouts.
     "My son collapsed raking my yard," says Gramma.
     "The doctors are with him," the nurse says. "Please
fill out this paperwork."
     Mom takes a clipboard and starts to fill it out.
     Barry asks, "What can I do?"
     Gramma says, "Too late to rake my yard…"
     Mom yells, "OH LEAVE HIM ALONE! HE DIDN'T MEAN FOR THIS
TO HAPPEN!"
     The desk nurse says: "Please take a seat and wait over
there."
     Gramma walks to the right hand side of the screen and
sits in the first of three chairs. Follow her and SIT IN
CHAIR. Notice he takes the one farthest from her. Now WAIT.
You have to WAIT a total of forty-two times. On the
thirteenth WAIT, Mom hands over the paperwork and sits
between you and Gramma. On the twenty-second WAIT a medical
team rushes a stretcher across the screen. Mom stands and
asks, "IS THAT MY HUSBAND?" No one answers and she sits
again. Finally on the forty-second WAIT a doctor comes out

241

and stops at the desk. "Shirley," he says, "before I forget, no need for intake on the guy doing yard work. DOA." He walks off. Mom stands and runs after him. Gramma turns her head and says, "I sure hope the matinee was worth all this."

Screen goes black…

A small group is gathered around Dad's open grave at Glendale Cemetery. As people slowly walk away, Mr. Blubaugh walks over to young Barry and shakes his hand. "Your father was a good agent, Barry," he says. "Once you go to college and think about what you might like to do with your life, I want you to know you'll have a job waiting for you at Percival Insurance."

"Oh, thank you, Mr. Blubaugh," Mom says. "Thank you…"

4.3 - PERCIVAL INSURANCE (1980 - 1985)

Mr. Blubaugh walks with Barry, now in dress shirt and chinos, onto screen: an office showing two cubicles. The one on the left is occupied by a blonde woman; the right is empty.

"Barry, Barry, Barry," says Mr. Blubaugh. "You are going to put that computer science degree to good use starting TODAY."

"Thank you for the job, Mr. Blubaugh."

"It's great to have a Gingle back under our roof here at Percival."

The blonde stands and walks over. "Is this my new neighbor?" she asks and extends her hand. They shake. "Barry, this is Deb. Deb, this is Barry. He's going to revamp our databases and bring Percival Insurance into the '80s!"

"A man of the future," she says. "Did you just graduate?"

Barry nods. "ISU."

"Oh jeepers, you two. Oh boy," Mr. Blubaugh says, "We don't need a Cyclone/Hawkeye rivalry stirring up here on the eighteenth floor now. HA! Listen, Barry, I've got a meeting I'm late for but welcome home!" Mr. Blubaugh walks off screen and Deb returns to her cubicle. "Let me know if you need anything," she says.

SIT AT DESK and USE COMPUTER.

WRITE CODE. He types.

WRITE CODE. He types.
WRITE CODE. He types.
Deb stands and walks over. "Can I buy you lunch on your first day?" she asks. "Fishel's Deli in the Skywalk does the best dessert: a piping hot bagel with peanut butter and chocolate chips melting on top…"
A window providing options of YES and NO pops up.

YES leads to Death #2.

Select NO.
"Actually my Mom packed my lunch and I have a lot of work to do," says Barry.
"Okay, maybe tomorrow then." Deb leaves.
EAT LUNCH. Barry empties a sack and eats a sandwich, chips, and drinks a can of pop.
Deb returns. "I brought you a half of one of Mr. Fishel's bagels anyway," she says and hands it to Barry.
EAT BAGEL. "Thank you," he says.
"You're welcome." She goes to her cubicle and sits.
WRITE CODE. He types.
WRITE CODE. He types.
WRITE CODE. He types.
Deb gets up and says, "Time to go home. Good first day?"
"Yes."
"Good. See you tomorrow." She walks off screen.
STAND and walk off screen like she did.

Barry emerges from the ground floor doors of Percival Tower on Grand Avenue downtown. Notice the snow on the curb. During this portion of the game, all of Des Moines is shouldering winter, what looks to my native eye to be the dirty slush days of February. And again, his attention to detail astounds me. The amount of time it must have taken to render the same environments in four seasons must have taken considerable energy and time, especially for a sick man. So never fear, though it is winter now, spring will arrive – just not for some time.

The green Datsun B-210 miraculously parked in front is Barry's. GET IN CAR. When you move the arrow keys the car obeys, just as if you're walking. TURN ON RADIO and you will get more of Barry's musical renderings of oldies, mostly from the late fifties through the sixties. That's because the station he loves is Des Moines' very own KMOI, which played the songs of that era without a whiff of irony for fifty years. Nowadays it's a husk of its past self, bought out by some out-of-state company with no regard for Des Moines or its identity. Most of us natives stopped listening the day they put songs recorded after 1973 into daily rotation.

If you don't TURN ON RADIO whenever you get Barry behind the wheel, you will drive right into Death #3.

Now don't drive to the house but to the Daventry Apartments, which form the uppermost left screen in Barry's virtual map of Des Moines. The building is depicted as an uninspired cliché of 1970s apartment architecture: aluminum-siding and the predictable personality of an eyesore. GET OUT OF CAR and walk inside the front door. Now you'll notice you're in a hall with mailboxes on the right and a door numbered 4 on the left. CHECK MAIL. If you don't Barry will complain at bedtime that he forgot to do something. There's no mail – in fact, he never receives a piece of mail in the whole game – but you must check every day anyway. "Nobody loves me," he says. Walk to apartment 4 and UNLOCK DOOR. OPEN DOOR and walk in.

This is Barry's apartment. It consists of a living room with kitchenette, half-bath, and bedroom. I read an interesting book a year or so ago all about what you can tell about someone by looking at their living space. With that in mind, what does this apartment tell us about Barry Gingle? The living room portion of the first screen shows us green carpet, a brown couch, a window behind said couch with blinds permanently drawn, and a painting on the wall I've positively identified as Grant Wood's "Woman with Plants" (1929. Oil on upsom board, Cedar Rapids Museum of Art). Wood, Iowa's most celebrated artist and one of the world's best-known painters for "American Gothic," did this portrait of his mother. What did the painting mean to Barry? Did he know its story? Was it really hanging in his apartment? His relationship with his own mother is indeed the most significant he ever had with anybody, at least as depicted in the game. Not Norman Bates close; I don't want to risk sensationalism. Anyhow, when it comes to the painting's significance, we will never know.

The kitchenette, taking up the left portion of the screen, is lackluster, functional, with matching green oven and fridge.

The next screen to the left reveals first the half-bath, entirely utilitarian and gray. Then the bedroom. Given that all Barry ever does here is sleep, its lack of character makes it less than a motel room with free cable TV, as advertised. Another window whose blinds are closed – granted the view is probably just a parking lot in Urbandale, hardly an inspired landscape, but does not the sun shine even in places like Urbandale?

What I am trying to say is this: Barry's apartment is dreary.

Go to the kitchenette and OPEN FREEZER. GET FROZEN DINNER. SHUT FREEZER. TURN ON OVEN. OPEN OVEN. PUT FROZEN DINNER IN OVEN. SHUT OVEN. SET TIMER. Go to the living room and TURN ON TV. Note how the television set has knobs, no remote control. SIT ON COUCH.

The TV talks: "The president says blah blah blah… The Soviet Union is blah blah blah… Pollution and nuclear weapons and heart disease and cancer findings and blah blah blah…" This is always what the national news reports, in varying orders.

The oven timer buzzes so STAND and go TURN OFF TIMER. TURN OFF OVEN and GET OVEN MITT. OPEN OVEN. USE OVEN MITT TO GET HOT DINNER. SHUT OVEN. OPEN REFRIGERATOR and GET POP. Go to the living room and PUT HOT DINNER ON TV TRAY. SIT ON COUCH and EAT HOT DINNER.

The TV talks: "The governor says corn subsidies blah blah blah… There was a shooting today blah blah blah… The weather forecast is blah blah blah… Sports blah blah blah…" This is always what local news reports, in varying orders.

Finished eating, STAND and GET EATEN DINNER and go to the kitchen and THROW EATEN DINNER IN TRASH. Go back to the living room and SIT ON COUCH.

The TV talks and by what it says you can tell what show he is watching and what day of the week it is – and now is as good a time as any to discuss temporality in Barry's Quest: Time cycles in this game in a five day week without weekends. More on that soon.

On Monday, the TV will say: "Tenk you veddy much!" "Oh Latka!"

On Tuesday: "We-hell we're movin on up, to the East Side, in a dee-luxe apartment in the sky-y!"

On Wednesday: "Mallory, I think you should give Skippy here a chance." "Alex, I'd rather die."

On Thursday: "NOOOOOOOOOOOOORM!"

Barry falls asleep on the couch and snores, "Zzzzzzzz…
Zzzzzzz…" Then he wakes and says, "I'm hungry…" STAND and
go to the kitchenette and OPEN FREEZER and GET ICE CREAM.
Oh, get SPOON and SHUT FREEZER, too. SIT ON COUCH. EAT ICE
CREAM.

The TV talks: "Here's Tonight's Tops List!" or
"Ready for some Silly Animal Tricks?" or "This is the first
ever full-body Velcro suit!" or "Your parting gift is a
canned ham."

Barry says, "That Pressman is the best thing on
these days." He yawns. STAND. TURN OFF TV. Go to the
kitchen, OPEN FREEZER, PUT ICE CREAM IN FREEZER, and SHUT
FREEZER. Go to the bathroom and FLOSS and BRUSH TEETH. Go
to the bedroom and CHANGE INTO PAJAMAS, green-and-blue
plaid flannels as it turns out. GET IN BED. On the bedstand
is a book. GET DUNE and then READ DUNE. He flips some
pages. GO TO SLEEP and the screen goes black.

Morning sees him waking in bed. STAND and go to the
bathroom. TAKE SHOWER and a black box covers Barry's body,
censoring his nudity. When he gets out he's in his pajamas
again and you are not required to grab a towel, even though
one is there, to dry off. Is this Barry's own discomfort
with his body? Was he uncomfortable portraying himself
bathing? Or was he rushed in programming and just left out
the meticulous process here that you have to endure
elsewhere in the game?

We will never know.

COMB HAIR and BRUSH TEETH and PUT ON DEODORANT.

If you don't shower and do those three things, you will
experience Death #4.

Go to the bedroom and CHANGE INTO CLOTHES and leave the
apartment. LOCK APARTMENT on your way and outside GET IN
CAR and drive to Mom's house. Mom is waiting on the porch
and when you stop she will walk to the car and hand over a
sack lunch. "Have a great day at work," she says. Drive on
to Percival Tower and GET OUT OF CAR. Walk inside and…

Repeat.

Everything described thus far in section 4.3 is pretty
much what you will do over and over for a total of 235 full
days. There are a few variations and they require that you
remember what day of the five-day week it is, which can
grow pretty confusing if you don't keep notes on where you
are. I recommend tallying the days on paper as you work

your way through this grueling stage of the game. If you forget which day you're on, you will traipse into one of Barry's deaths.

Regarding the schedule you need to keep track of, and you do need to keep track of it:

Every Monday you need to go to Ivor's Games and BUY COMICS on the drive home from work. Ivor's was a real shop once upon a time, run by an old African American man with a big beard named, you guessed it, Ivor. I used to go there as a kid myself and can't tell you the number of times I've wondered if I ever ran into Barry there. He has rendered it much the way I remember it, with a rack of comics on the left and books and lead miniatures, with paints to paint them, on the right. You just need to go to the rack and GET COMICS and then BUY COMICS from Ivor at the glass counter, where you can see the green, purple, and blue power crystals he used to sell. When you get home, READ COMICS before making dinner.

Failure to get and read new comics on a Monday results in Death #5.

Every Tuesday you need to gas up the car at Kum & Go. Drive to the gas station and pull up in front of the pump. GET OUT OF CAR and UNSCREW GAS CAP. PUMP GAS. Wait while he pumps. SCREW ON GAS CAP. Now walk into the station – it looks like every other in the country, complete with a huddle of kids ramparting the Astro Chicken arcade game in the corner. Walk up to the guy at the counter, PAY FOR GAS, and go about Barry's business.

Failure to fill the fuel tank on a Tuesday will take you to Death #6.

Every Wednesday you need to make a trip to Tate's Groceries on the drive home from work. Once upon a time, there was a neighborhood supermarket called Tate's. It was located at 42nd and University in the Uptown Shopping Center, an eclectic gathering of shops around three sides of a parking lot: Russ' Uptown Optical (Still the best shop in the world to buy glasses. [A loyal myopic walkthrough-author, that's me…]), Showtime Video (It moved to Beaverdale in the nineties and there it sadly died.), Heller's Coffee, a Percival Insurance agency, a

gastrointerologist's office, and J. W. Place's general
store (Where my mother used to buy me Star Wars action
figures if I was good.). There is still a supermarket where
Tate's once was, a satellite of a franchise and now
complete with liquor section and digital photo lab, but
Tate's it is not. Barry shows it as it was back in the
'80s. Outside its front wall is tall glass windows with
specials painted in red and white on the other side:
PORKCHOPS $2.40/lb. and SWEETCORN 6 EARS/50¢. Inside it's
cream linoleum floor, half-stocked shelves, Drake students
at the tills: the land of plenty.

    Once through the sliding doors, head to the freezer
section and GET FROZEN DINNERS and GET ICE CREAM. Now to
the pop aisle and GET POP. BUY FOOD in the checkout line,
which always has three people ahead of Barry, in varying
orders. When you get Barry home, PUT FROZEN DINNERS IN
FREEZER and PUT ICE CREAM IN FREEZER and PUT POP IN
REFRIGERATOR.

    Failure to go to the grocery store on Wednesdays
results in Death #7.

    Every Thursday Barry must TAKE THE TRASH OUT. No idea
where he puts it, as once you type that he just goes
outside carrying a big black garbage bag. He reenters
without it.

    Failure to take out the trash takes you to Death #8.

    Every Friday everything after work changes as we take
Barry to spend the evening with his mom. Most important is
to remember before going to work those mornings is to GET
DIRTY LAUNDRY from the hamper in Barry's bedroom and when
Mom gives Barry his lunch, GIVE LAUNDRY TO MOM. After work
drive back home-home and Mom will have dinner ready in the
kitchen.

    Let's just take a moment and consider the feel of the
living room, even though we've been here already. Yellow
and brown, that's the palate, probably redecorated in the
early to mid-seventies. The staircase running from left to
right along the back wall is wallpapered in vertical
stripes and boasts, yes, another Grant Wood painting:
"Death on the Ridge Road" (1935. Oil on masonite, Williams
College Museum of Art). The composition is a study in
inevitable collision – a car passing another at the crest
of a hill is about to crash head-on into an oncoming red

truck, all while a thunderstorm builds in the sky. Not the cozy sort of picture one would expect in a widow's living room. Again, there's no telling if this painting really hung there, if Barry only used it for the game, or what. We will never really know what to make of it. But I'd guess that couch below the picture is upholstered in tweed. And, twinned to Barry's apartment, note the TV trays set up and, across from them, a rolling cart sporting a black and white TV with rabbit ear antennas lolling.

Your job is very simple on these evenings. TURN OV TV and SIT ON COUCH in the living room and Mom will bring dinner out and set it on the TV tray before you. "Go ahead and eat," she says – so EAT DINNER - before returning with her own dinner, which she eats beside Barry on the couch from her own TV tray. The news will blather its usual vague themes while you both eat. When finished, she gets up and takes the dishes to the kitchen. She returns with dessert: apple pie with a scoop of vanilla ice cream. EAT PIE. Mom will ask, "What time's Fawlty Towers on?"
"Right about now," Barry says.
She goes to the TV and changes the channel but the reception goes. She will fiddle with the antenna to no avail until you do something. STAND and walk to the TV set and ADJUST ANTENNA. "Oh there it is," she says, and then, "It's so nice to have a man in the house."
SIT ON COUCH and the TV will talk: "Don't mention the war!! Don't mention the war!!"
"Hee hee," Mom says. "I just love that Manuel. Hee hee!"
When the show is over, STAND.
"Don't you want to stay over tonight?" Mom asks. "It's such a long drive to your apartment and it's late. You can sleep in your old bed…"
Barry responds, "I better get going, Mom."
She gets up and goes to the kitchen, returning with a basket. "Here's your laundry. Cleaned and folded."
TAKE CLEAN LAUNDRY and she will walk you out. OPEN DOOR and step outside. She waves from the porch and doesn't stop. GET IN CAR and drive off to the Daventry Apartments. Once inside – don't forget to CHECK MAIL – be sure to PUT LAUNDRY IN CLOSET when you get to the bedroom.

Failure to take your laundry to Mom will result in Death #9.

Failure to go to Mom's house on Friday night will result in Death #10.

After day three, Barry's coworker Deb won't invite him to lunch again, but she will always wish him a nice evening. We never get to meet any of Barry's other coworkers or even a supervisor at Percival, and we only see Mr. Blubaugh one other time.

At day 203, Deb will stand and come over from her cubicle after the first time you WRITE CODE. "Barry," she says, "Notice anything different about me?"

Barry shakes his head.

She holds out her hand and a big diamond sparkles on top of it. "Brad and I are getting married! I'm having a party at my house on Friday. Please come. Here's my address." She writes it down on a piece of paper and hands it to Barry.

That Friday, take laundry to Mom like usual and go to work and go through the motions. After work drive to Tate's and go in and GET WINE and then BUY WINE (apparently there's one kind?). Barry, looking twenty years older than he is, isn't even carded. Now drive to Deb's house. From Tate's it's one screen down and one screen left.

Deb's house looks like many you'll find on the west side of Des Moines, built in the first decades of the twentieth century to its own character. I've not pinned down the actual house or even the street it might be on, and one wonders if Barry took care to duplicate her actual house or if he merely put something together from loose memory. Given the game's complexity and the idiosyncratic details of the roof's three visible gables, red tile roof, and stucco front, I'm willing to bet this house is depicted as it is. In game, silhouettes of many people move in the front windows. GET OUT OF CAR and walk toward the door. Barry stops and says, "…" Just then Mr. Blubaugh walks onto the screen.

"Hello, Barry!" he says. "You just arriving, too?"

A window providing options of YES and NO pops up.

YES leads to Death #11.

Select NO.

"I'm just leaving actually," Barry says.

"Sure you can't stay?"

"Wish I could. Good night, Mr. Blubaugh."

Mr. Blubaugh says, "You, too, Gingle!" He heads inside.

GET IN CAR and drive to Mom's house. When there everything proceeds as a usual Friday night. Strangely, there's nothing you can do with the wine he bought. It will remain from now on in the inventory, and if you type DRINK WINE he will say, "I don't have the right kind of glass for it." There is nowhere in the game, to my knowledge, that you can find a wine glass. If you find one, by all means, please let me know and we'll update this walkthrough.

Like I said before, you will have to diligently grind through Barry's five-day work weeks paying careful attention to the rhythm he has orchestrated. In all you must complete forty-seven of these weeks at Percival Insurance. It takes discipline and a lot of patience, for this part of the game is long and grueling. And that's part of the brilliance of Gingle's representation of his first job just out of college. We experience all of the monotony, boredom, irritation ourselves by having to send him through his vacuous routine. After a while the environment itself inspires claustrophobia and profound loneliness. Despite working in Percival Tower, the tallest building in Des Moines, hosting more employees each day than most towns in Iowa have residents, all you ever see of its interior is Barry's and Deb's drab and dreary cubicles.

This, paired with the lack of people on the streets and Mom being the only significant source of social interaction, makes for a profoundly isolating life. The few times he is offered time with others, Barry sticks to himself. Where one might expect to develop friendships over the course of a decent job, Barry is friendless. And does he secretly love Deb? There's no hint in any direction, the man betraying nothing about his feelings. He doesn't express interest, doesn't give any clues as to his sexuality or any fantasies bouncing around in his soul, save for the thirty-five imaginative – dare I say mythic – deaths. Granted, he made the game while terminally ill, but even then he comes off as having absolutely no sexual or romantic motivations, just an ever-present, recurring death wish throughout a numbed existence. Barry simply programs code and watches TV, over and over, for a span of condensed years.

Finally, sitting at his desk at the end of day 235, Barry will announce, "I can't sit at this desk one more day. What Des Moines needs is a shop selling personal computers for home use…" There's been no hint of this ambition up to now. We can only guess if it was on the books all along or if the idea really did strike Barry one day out of the blue.

A window asking "WANT TO QUIT THIS JOB?" pops up providing options of YES and NO.

NO leads to Death #12.

Select YES.
Barry stands on his own and walks to Deb's cubicle. "Goodbye, Deb," he says.
"See you tomorrow, Barry," she says.
"No, you won't," he says as he walks away.

4.4 - GINGLE HOME COMPUTING (1986 - 1990)

Here begins what is the happiest part of Barry's Quest. "Happiest" may be a tenuous description, sure; perhaps I should say it's the "least soul-crushing" portion of the game. And notice how springtime has suddenly sprung all across pixelated Des Moines. Gone are the filthy snow crusts on every curb, the icicles from every eave of every building; arrived are the green grass and leaf buds on trees, even daffodils and tulips in the odd yard.

The screen lights on the exterior of a nondescript storefront I've tracked to the north end of Valley Junction. Barry stands out front and a man on a ladder next to the new sign, which reads GINGLE HOME COMPUTING, asks, "How's it look?"

"Like I thought it would," Barry says.
"Alright," says the man, who descends and picks up his ladder. "I'll send you the bill." He walks off.

A brown delivery truck arrives and backs up, its lights blinking orange. The delivery man appears: "You Barry Gingle?"

"Unfortunately."
"Got a lot of boxes for ya."
Walk to the shop's glass door and OPEN DOOR. Now sit back and watch as the delivery man opens the gate on his truck, drops the ramp, and wheels box after box into the shop. When he is done, he will hand you a clipboard and pen. SIGN FORM and he will give you your copy. "Have a better one," he says and leaves. When the truck pulls away, walk into the shop.

This is the storefront in which Barry will try to sell

computers to central Iowans. Stacked high with boxes and walls that appear to be faux wood paneling, it doesn't look like much. "I guess this is it," he says.

Mom walks in and looks around. "I've brought your lunch," she says. "And after you eat, I'm helping you with all this."

"Thanks, Mom," he says and the screen goes black.

1 WEEK LATER…

Barry and Mom stand in the shop, ready for business. A desk on the left, set up with a computer and a till, serves as Barry's sales counter. Set in the middle of the room is a table displaying a Commandant 64 computer with keyboard and floppy disk drive and next to it a Anima 1000 with box, keyboard, and mouse. There are two rolling chairs for customers while test-driving either computer. On the right side of the room is a stack of boxed dot matrix printers and a rack of software, and where you will find so many classic games for sale, including those that inspired this one. Atop a filing cabinet next to Barry's desk, sits a potted green plant named Chuck.

This is Gingle Home Computing.

Mom walks to the door and turns the sign around so it says OPEN. "Your dad would have been proud," she says.

"Thanks, Mom," he replies. "And thanks for the loan."

"It wasn't a loan," she says. "It's what your father left us. Now sell some computers!" She leaves and Barry is on his own.

This is a strange moment in the game. There is no clear path forward, no telling what this venture entails. Without customers there is little to do, and so you are left to keep Barry occupied during the down-time. SPOILER ALERT: It's almost all down-time for this portion of the game. There are a number of things you can have him do to soak it up though, and the order in which you do them isn't rigid like it was in the coding job at Percival Insurance. For instance, you can COUNT TILL or WATER CHUCK or TIDY SHOP or BALANCE BOOKS or WRITE ORDER or TAKE INVENTORY or MAKE BANK DEPOSIT or, Barry's favorite, PLAY GAME on one of the computers - in no specific order. As a result, this part actually has a touch of dynamism – and a hint of danger, too, because it's easy to lose track of time.

Regarding the structure of the shop's work day: Before lunch and after lunch each consist of three units of time.

That is, you can conduct three tasks before it is time to EAT LUNCH and three tasks after. All tasks take up a single unit of time – except when Barry plays computer games. When you PLAY GAME it soaks up two units of time.

That means you must be mindful when starting to play a game, as doing anything beyond will throw off his hours at the shop and lead to Death #13.

The temptation, of course, is to play computer games all day because the time flies by, but that tactic spells death. Every week a number of tasks need to be fulfilled.

Regarding the deposit, it's easy. Simply FILL OUT DEPOSIT SLIP at the end of a day when Barry's made a sale, PUT DEPOSIT SLIP IN DEPOSIT BAG, and when you leave drive to the bank, which is the USA United Savings Bank on Ingersoll Avenue (More on the bank later…). It's a drive thru there, so just pull up and the drive thru teller behind her pane of glass will send a canister over through the pneumatic tube. OPEN CANISTER and PUT DEPOSIT BAG IN CANISTER and CLOSE CANISTER. It will suck back to the teller, who will then send it back. OPEN CANISTER and GET RECEIPT and GET SUCKER. CLOSE CANISTER, it'll go back to her, and she will wish you a good day. PUT RECEIPT IN DEPOSIT BAG and EAT SUCKER if you like (They will accumulate if you don't, with no harm to gameplay). Remember the next day to ADD RECEIPT TO FILES at the shop.

If you don't do a deposit run to the bank every day you make a sale, you welcome Death #14.

If you don't TIDY SHOP three times in a week, you will get Death #15.

If you don't BALANCE BOOKS once a month, you hit Death #16.

If you don't WRITE ORDER once every two months, you reach Death #17.

If you don't TAKE INVENTORY once every three months, you invite Death #18.

If you don't LOCK DOOR every afternoon when you leave the shop, say hi to Death #19.

If you don't WATER CHUCK or, conversely, if you water
him too often, Chuck the Plant will die and remain dead.
Chuck the Plant's fate, as far as I can tell, bears no
effect whatsoever on the outcome of the game.

You are free to balance it all however you like, until,
of course, a customer enters the shop. Then the real work
begins.

The first customer doesn't arrive until the third day.
It's none other than Mr. Blubaugh. He comes in after lunch
in his gray suit and says, "Gingle! We hated losing you but
look at the setup you've got here. Making a success of it,
I see. A man carving his own path, taking the road less
traveled, and that'll make you all the difference. I know
it's done me wonders, made all the difference. So help me
out here. I want a computer for the home, something for the
grandkids to toodle around on…"

As with every customer seeking a computer from here on,
a window with two options opens:

> A) PITCH COMMANDANT 64
> B) PITCH ANIMA 1000

Now, some customers will be impatient and you will only
have time to show them one model. Luckily, Mr. Blubaugh is
easy to please and will buy whichever computer you show him
first. I like to pitch the Anima 1000 because it retails
for more and can do more besides. Best to set up the old
boss with a state of the art machine, right?

If you pitch the Commandant 64, Barry sits the customer
down in front of it and goes into his lukewarm spiel: "The
Commandant 64 is the most affordable option in home
computing these days. Sixteen colors and 64K of RAM, yada
yada yada…"
The customer will ask one or some or all of the
following questions. You choose how Barry responds to each
with a weak or weaker answer (a natural salesman he is
not):

> 1) "Can it do word processing?"
>
> A) This machine was made for word
> processing.
> B) It can. You'll toss out your

255

typewriter in no time, I guarantee.

    2)   "Can it play games?"

     A) There are literally hundreds of games for this machine.
    B) Are there more pigs than people in Iowa?

    3)   "I heard Commandant is a European company or something?"

    A) That's right: the continent that brought us Einstein, waffles, and D-Day has now come up with affordable home computing.
    B) Don't be fooled by the imperious name. Your hard-earned money will stay right here in central Iowa.

If you pitch the Anima 1000, Barry sits the customer before that machine and delivers this somewhat more lively spiel: "The Anima 1000 is your choice if ingenuity is your desire. Four thousand and ninety-six colors and 256K of RAM, with expandable slots, yada yada yada…"
Then the following questions and possible responses arise:

    1)   "What kind of name is Anima for a computer?"

    A) Anima is "soul" in Latin. Isn't that nice?
    B) The makers tried calling it Lorraine but weren't moving any units so they renamed it something with more pizzazz.

    2)   "Can I do the graphics on it?"

    A) Can it ever. The amount of RAM in this machine is almost obscene.
    B) Ever seen a computer do this before? (He puts on an animation of a bouncing ball.)

    3)   "Can it play games?"

    A) There are literally hundreds of games for this machine.
    B) This machine was conceived of as a gaming platform, believe it or not. She'll handle everything you're eager to play.

Depending on what kind of rush they are in, the

customer will eventually interject with THE question: "How much are we talking here?"

If it's the Commandant 64, Barry will say, "$595."

If it's the Anima 1000, Barry will say, "$849."

Sometimes the customer will stand and say, "Well, Mr. Gingle, I really ought to think this one over. Thanks for your time." When they leave Barry shrugs his shoulders.

Sometimes the customer will say, "I'm sold. Do you take personal checks?" Barry will turn to face the screen and a cash register Cha-Ching rings out. Then a new set of options will pop up:

A)   Might I interest you in a printer?
B)   Are you interested at all in gaming?

The customer may well say no to both questions, but then again he or she may reply with a question of their own.

Regarding printers: "I've heard about the paper jams on those things..."

A)   A thing of the past. The guided holes on either side of the page keeps things easy.
B)   Yeah, those happen...

They will either decline or say, "Might as well get a printer, sure."

In response to the gaming question, they will say one of the following:

1)   "Nah."
2)   "Got anything with puzzles?"
(type MAHJONG 3000)
3)   "I like adventures."
(type MANIAC MANSION)
4)   "Sports are my deal."
(type LEADERBOARD BADMINTON)
5)   "Take me to the high seas."
(type PIRATES!)
6)   "Always dreamt of being an assassin..."
(type MASTER NINJA 1)
7)   "Anything about space?"

(type SPACE QUEST III)
     8)   "Got any games about scoring chicks?"
(type SOFTPORN ADVENTURE)
     9)   "I've always fancied myself a bit chivalrous…"
(type KNIGHT'S QUEST)
     10) "Do they got a Wild West kind of thing?"
(type AVENGING CUSTER)
     11)   "I have deep seated law enforcement fantasies."
(type POLICE QUEST)

If you recommend the proper game for their interest, they will always buy it, saying, "Yeah, I'll take it."

Once printer and software offers are exhausted, Barry will say, "To answer your earlier question, we do take personal checks. Or, if you prefer, I accept all major credit cards."
The screen goes black and relights with the customer exiting, carrying a stack of boxes that obscure his or her upper half.
Mr. Blubaugh, bless him, will buy everything you offer. Other customers are finicky. After that first sale they randomize; there is no telling who or when customers will come in, but I find typically two or three customers visit the shop over the course of a week. As time passes, repeat customers will show up looking either for printers or computer games, but no real relationship is ever a possibility. Barry is all business when it comes to shoppers.

Interesting to note: There are no deaths you can wander into by fudging a sale. If you fail to seal a deal, it doesn't affect much of anything at all. It's a curious detail for a game so focused on failure, where there are no fewer than thirty-five possible deaths altogether.

The other thing I need to point out: The post-work routine undertaken while Barry worked for Percival Insurance is carried into this part of the game. So after work, you need to do everything just like before, being sure to keep track of what day of the week it is, and so on. The only real difference seems to be what TV shows are being broadcast, which now are The Cosby Show, Cheers, Night Court, ALF, and, on Fridays with Mom, The Golden Girls.

The game runs thusly for 185 days, the seemingly most happy of Barry's professional life. He gave players the most freedom here in this section, letting us complete business-related tasks on a relatively relaxed schedule, possibly because then, on the 185th day, everything changes…

4.5 - CANCER (1990)

It's a Friday, everything going as usual, but after supper with Mom, after TV and receiving cleaned laundry, Mom sees Barry out with some startling news.
"I meant to tell you earlier but didn't have the chance," she says. "I went to see Dr. Cokely about that pain in my abdomen."
"You have a pain in your abdomen?" Barry asks.
"Surely I told you about it. A little ache."
"You didn't tell me."
"Well," she says, "they ran some tests and it seems I've got something called…" She pulls out a piece of paper and reads from it: "A-de-no-carcinoma."
"Carcinoma?"
"It's to do with my pancreas, just like Donna Reed, that's what Dr. Cokely told me."
"Donna Reed died from pancreatic cancer, didn't she?"
"I was hoping you could be a dear and take me to the hospital Monday morning?"
"Hospital?"
"Dr. Cokely scheduled surgery, just taking a look."
"I can't go back to the apartment tonight," says Barry. "I should be here."
"Oh it would be nice if you would come home," she says. "But go on tonight. You'll need a chance to gather what you'll need for your stay here."
Direct Barry back to the Daventry Apartments, CHECK MAIL and PUT LAUNDRY IN CLOSET. That night when you type GO TO SLEEP, you will notice that he is still lying in bed with his eyes open. You have to type the command GO TO SLEEP seven times before he finally falls asleep.

So begins what is arguably the hardest part of Barry's Quest. The cumulative effect of playing through more than 420 days with Mother Gingle providing lunch daily and dinner once a week deals an emotional blow to the player

259

that I neither anticipated nor knew quite how to
metabolize. I am still affected by the experience, for
these are not just characters in a computer game; they
actually lived life, and, whether I'm declared maudlin or
not, it's 100% true when I say I've yet to encounter a
video game that delivers a greater statement on human
suffering.

The game being weekendless, the next day is Monday, the
day of Mom's surgery. When Barry wakes, take him through
his morning routine up to driving to her house.
And look at Des Moines, shifted once again into a new
season. Summer has manifested in green lawns with brown
patches and leafy crowns on every tree. Spring's buds and
flowers have given way to summery Midwestern verdancy. You
can almost feel the sun. You can almost choke on the
humidity.
This morning, Mom comes to the car and says, "I made
you a lunch," handing it over and getting in. Drive on to
the hospital, park, and escort Mom inside.
This sequence has the feel of déjà vu, the waiting room
harkening back to Dad's death. Mom walks to the desk and
tells the nurse she has arrived.
"This way, Mrs. Gingle," another nurse says, leading
her away in a wheelchair.
"Mom," Barry says.
She looks back and says, "Eat your lunch when you're
hungry."
Now, just as before, sit in one of the three chairs on
the right side of the screen and WAIT. And WAIT. And WAIT.

If you leave the hospital, you will reach Death #20.

On the thirteenth WAIT, an obese woman and a man in a
bloody t-shirt will come in and sit down beside you. On the
twenty-second WAIT, a nurse fetches the man and takes him
away. On the forty-third WAIT, a stretcher and team of
nurses goes by. On the seventy-sixth WAIT, the obese woman
asks, "What're you in for?" Barry says, "My mother." The
obese woman goes into the very long, very unpleasant tale
of her brother, the self-destructive man who came in
wearing the bloody shirt. You are entirely helpless to her
long, boring account. There is no way to skip it either.
She drones on for eleven minutes real time, so if you need
a bathroom break or the dog needs a lap around the block,
here's your chance. Pledging fidelity to the game's

260

intended effect, I just grin and bear it. Finally she'll ask where the toilet is, get up, and stump off screen. Barry sighs.

On the 113th WAIT, Barry will rub his tummy. EAT LUNCH. He will say, "I hope that wasn't the last lunch."

After the 217th WAIT, Dr. Cokely walks by and asks the desk nurse, "Is Nora Gingle's son here?"

"He's sitting there." She points.

The doctor, in blue O.R. scrubs, approaches. "Your mother's fine, got her in recovery now, breathing's normal, was all rotten with adenocarcinoma, the head of the pancreas, but I got it out of her, she's looking at radiation therapy now, she'll start that real soon here, real soon."

"Today?" Barry asks.

"Today? HA!" The doctor laughs as he walks away. "She just had major surgery and he asks if she starts radiation today. HA!"

STAND and walk to the next screen on the right, which is Mom's hospital room. Walk past the first bed, occupied by an old lady with big red eyes staring straight ahead, to the second bed. Mom is there sleeping. SIT IN CHAIR at her side. A nurse will come into the room and check on her, saying, "Are you the son?"

Barry nods.

"We'll take good care of her," she says. "Don't worry."

"How long will she be here?"

"Probably a week, ten days…"

"The doctor mentioned radiation soon."

The nurse walks over and touches Barry's shoulder. "We'll take good care of you, too. We'll make sure you have all the information."

I find that small gesture to be one of the most moving moments in the entire game, precisely because it's one of the only times we see Barry being touched by another person. That he put it in speaks to how significant it was at the time. Whoever the nurse was - we never get her name - she really helped him with that expression of tenderness. Just doing her job, sure, but at the same time she transcends her duties by being so simply humane.

When the nurse leaves, Mom rustles and almost speaks: "… … … "

"Mom?"

" … … "

She does not wake and a new nurse appears. "Mr. Gingle, you can go on home and get some rest. We'll watch over her tonight."

"What time is it?" he asks.

"It's ten o'clock."

He looks left and right and asks, "How???"

"The world keeps on spinning, I guess."

STAND and walk past the other bed to the door. When you try leave Barry will turn around and say, "See you in the morning, Mom."

The red-eyed lady, still staring forward, will screech, "GET OUT! GET OUT! YOU DON'T LOVE ME! GET OUT!"

"Betty, what on earth?" the nurse asks, switching from Mom to the other patient. "Mr. Gingle, you can go on ahead…"

Mom nearly speaks again: " … … "

Barry turns and walks out. Leave the hospital. GET IN CAR and drive on to Mom's house (If you drive to the apartment, he will say, "Think I should check on the house maybe…"). At this point routine is defenestrated, so go into the house and up the stairs in the living room. From the upstairs hallway, Barry's old bedroom is the one on the left (For my map of the house consult Chapter 6). No need to change out of clothes or brush teeth in the bathroom. Just GET IN BED. You won't even need to type GO TO SLEEP before he passes out, exhausted.

Instead of going black, everything but Barry and his childhood bed go blue with white cloud edges curbing all four sides of the screen. A glowing computer appears and Barry sits up. The computer screen goes white and Barry is sucked out of bed and through the monitor.

He is transported to a low stone pillar in the lower left of the screen. Atop a taller stone pillar on the right is Mom in her hospital bed. Between is a bottomless chasm. "Help me, Barry! Help!" she says.

There is no way to get to her. Your inventory during this sequence is empty, save for a gas can, which is useless. There is no command for jump, so you must simply walk off the pillar and fall off screen.

Barry wakes up and it is the next day.

Don't worry about showering or doing the morning stuff – you won't die (If you try any of it he will say, "Got to see how Mom is."). Just go outside and GET IN CAR, TURN ON RADIO, and drive to the hospital.

She is awake when you walk in, sitting higher in bed, and her red-eyed roommate is gone, that bed empty.

"There's my son," Mom says. Walk to her bed and she will lift her hand out.

HOLD HANDS and Barry will reach out to her. "How do you feel?" he asks.

"The night nurse was very loud, a very loud Irish washerwoman," she says. "She came in banging things all around and making a terrible racket. I think I slept but she kept coming in and moving things. Just a terrible racket."

A nurse comes in, the nice one, with breakfast. She sets it before Mom and raises the back of the bed so she's sitting up more. "You think you can maybe have some food this morning?" Mom grabs a fork and takes a bite of food and the nurse checks her IV and heart monitor.

"I can't taste this," Mom says.

"It's good for you, Nora," the nurse says. "You just eat what you can, alright?"

The nurse leaves.

Mom takes three more bites and is done. "Ow," she says. "Ow, ow, ow…"

"What is it?"

"Need to lie down."

LET GO from holding hands and go around to the other side of her bed. USE BED CONTROL. A picture pops up of what the bed control looks like with its two buttons, an arrow pointing up and an arrow pointing down. PRESS BOTTOM BUTTON. The bed will lower and Mom will relax.

If you press the wrong button, it will lead to Death #21.

SIT IN CHAIR and HOLD HANDS. The nurse will return and remove her breakfast, saying, "Good job! You ate well!"

When she is gone, Mom says, "I'm thirsty…"

LET GO and GET WATER BOTTLE from the standing tray next to her bed. GIVE WATER BOTTLE TO MOM. She will drink and thank you.

If you don't give her water before the third time she asks for it, both here and later in the game, you will hit Death #22.

A woman in a white coat walks into the room with a folded metal walker and says, "Hi, Nora, I'm Sandra and I'm

263

here to get you out of bed."

"Oh do I have to?" Mom asks.

"We want to keep you strong," she says. "We'll just get you on your feet and take a few steps down the hall."

Watch now and learn because you will be accompanying Mom on these walks down the hall after this first day. First you will need to raise the bed (push the right button…) and UNFOLD WALKER. Then GIVE MOM WALKER. She will sit sideways in bed and stand. "Very good!" Sandra says this first time. "How about a step?"

Mom will take a step.

"How about a second step?"

She will step again.

"And another?"

"I'm so tired," Mom says. "So tired." She will whip around with the walker and step back to the bed and sit.

"Very good, Nora," Sandra says. "Tomorrow you'll be stronger. You did great."

She will leave and Mom will say, "Ow, ow, ow…"

Lower the bed for her.

"Barry," she will say, "I'm fine. You need to go to the shop."

"I need to be here," he says.

"You need to sell computers."

"I am staying here."

"Your father didn't leave us that money so it could dry up and blow away on account of me feeling a little under the weather," she says. "Go on. Work half a day. For your father."

LET GO and walk to the door. Barry will stop and say, "I'll come back after the shop closes."

She is already asleep again, " … … " afloat over her head.

Walk out of the hospital and drive to the shop. On the way, stop at the Taco Juan's drive thru. When the menu board says, "WELCOME TO TA-SHHHHH-N'S WHAT CAN I SHHHHH-OU TODAY?" order whatever you want. It doesn't matter. Just be sure and order something, drive to the second window, PAY and TAKE and EAT TACO JUAN'S MEAL there in the car.

If you don't, you will reach Death #23.

Drive on to the shop and, basically, fulfill a typical afternoon shift. Have you kept track of where you are in terms of inventory and bank deposits and whatnot? If not, you'll be screwed. Only working half a day halves what you can get done. So keep a list and check it twice. After the afternoon shift and closing up the shop, do a bank drop if someone bought something and then drive back to the hospital.

Mom will have a new roommate now, a woman with a family all around her: her parents, a husband holding a baby, a young son. Walk past them and SIT IN CHAIR beside Mom. She is asleep. The other family will talk, the ailing mother wanting to kiss her baby and little boy. She goes into a hospital bed soliloquy about love and fortune, culminating in the statement, "It's just so priceless what we have because so many people don't have families and never will or the ones they have don't love them and I'm just the luckiest woman alive to live with this love you all give me."

A nurse will walk in with Mom's dinner and raise her bed for her. When she awakens she says, "Barry... There you are."

"Hi, Mom."

"Is it time for breakfast?"

"Dinner," the nurse says. "And vanilla ice cream for dessert if you're good and finish your mashed potatoes."

Mom eats four bites while the nurse tends to the new roommate, drawing a curtain between the beds.

"How does it taste?" Barry asks.

"I want the ice cream," she says. "Will you eat the potatoes?"

STAND and EAT POTATOES.

"Good boy," Mom says.

The nurse returns. "Looks like someone's getting a bowl of vanilla ice cream!"

"Oh goody," says Mom.

The nurse clears the dinner tray and leaves.

"I'm thirsty," Mom says. GIVE WATER BOTTLE TO MOM.

The nurse will return with her ice cream, which she devours, and check her IV and heart monitor.

When she leaves, Mom holds her hand out. HOLD HANDS and she will go into, "Ow, ow, ow..." LET GO and lower the bed for her. She will hold her hand out again. HOLD HANDS and SIT IN CHAIR.

The family, who have crowded around the ailing woman as she ate her own dinner, clear out with loving embraces and so on. More talk of the importance of family, how some people have nobody. When they leave, Mom is asleep with, " ... ... " Barry is free to go for the night. LET GO – such a difficult command to type so many times - and walk out of the hospital. Go back to the house and crash, same as the night before.

Basically, from here, you will play out this last day, from the chasm nightmare, which recurs, to morning at the hospital, afternoon at the shop, evening at the hospital, and home, over and over. Mom is in the hospital for thirteen days total. There are a few changes as days progress:

Mom will be able to walk farther with her walker. You must ENCOURAGE MOM after each step. Soon she will be scooting out of the room and down the hall past the desk nurse. Eventually she does it without the walker, holding onto her IV stand for support.

If you don't ENCOURAGE MOM, you will strike Death #24.

Also, on the eighth day she gets a new roommate, another older lady who, thankfully, doesn't talk much. For some reason, the mostly-mute-but-prone-to-schizoid-outbursts patients are easier to take than the family that only talks about how great it is.

On the thirteenth morning, when you arrive, Mom is dressed and sitting on her bed, ready to be discharged. "Take me home," she says, hand out.
HOLD HANDS and she will stand. Walk with her out of the room to the desk nurse, who will have her sign a form. Note that you still hold her hand through this.
"Do we know when you have to come back?" Barry asks.
"We know," she says. "Don't worry."
"See you tomorrow, Mrs. Gingle," the desk nurse says.
Walk her out to the car, LET GO of her hand, and OPEN CAR DOOR for her. CLOSE CAR DOOR when she's in. GET IN CAR and drive home. When you get out OPEN CAR DOOR for Mom again and again CLOSE CAR DOOR when she's out. HOLD HANDS and take her into the house.
She will want to sit on the couch immediately, so LET GO and let her. "Oh," she says, "I missed my home. I missed my couch."
"What can I get for you?" he asks.
"Water, please."
Go to the kitchen. As depicted, this kitchen actually reminds me of my own grandmother's kitchen. This is

266

probably due to the green circa 1955 refrigerator that dominates the room. Its style, with the rounded top, lends a mid-twentieth century charm that offsets the big black microwave and coffee machine sitting on the counter. Note also the telephone on the wall, its spiral cord looping down to the floor.

OPEN CUPBOARD, GET GLASS, FILL GLASS WITH WATER at the sink, go back to the living room, and GIVE GLASS TO MOM. She will sip it and say, "I have those prescriptions. Could you go pick them up from Bassman's Pharmacy?"

"Yes."

"Oh, and have you brought your clothes over from your apartment yet?"

"Not yet."

"Do that, too." This is her way of saying he's worn the same outfit for two weeks…

"How's your stomach doing?" he asks her.

"What did you have in mind?"

"Chinese?"

"Yes, sounds good. Moo goo gai pan. Whenever."

"You don't need to go to the bathroom?" he asks. "You sure?"

"I'm fine, I'm fine," she says.

So. Go outside and drive to the pharmacy. Walk in and up to the counter. "Can I help you?" the pharmacist asks.

"I'm here to pick up some prescriptions for my mother, Nora Gingle," he says. "I'm her son, Barry Gingle."

"Gingle Home Computing!" the pharmacist says.

"Yes?"

"You sold me a Anima 1000," the pharmacist says. "Beautiful machine! My kids love the games."

He vanishes behind his counter and returns soon with a white paper bag. "Here you are," he says, "She should take these with some food." PAY and GET MEDICINE. "All the best to you and your mom," the pharmacist says.

Barry says, "Thanks." Walk out.

If you don't get Mom's medicine, you will reach Death #25.

Drive to Imperial Garden, the Chinese restaurant located one screen down from Daventry Apartments. Walk in through the big red doors with the golden Shishi guardian lions on either side. "How can I help you?" the hostess asks.

"I'd like to order some food," he says.

The menu pops up. Choose MOO GOO GAI PAN and whatever else you like.

If you don't choose MOO GOO GAI PAN, you will trigger Death #26.

"Half hour," the hostess says.

Walk out and drive to the apartment. Go in, remembering to CHECK MAIL, and when you get to the bedroom just type PACK CLOTHES. He will scurry about grabbing clothing from his closet. In the bathroom GET DOPKIT.

Leave and return to Imperial Garden. A large brown bag is on the counter. "I put in extra chicken wing," the hostess says.

"Thanks." PAY, GET CHINESE FOOD, and leave.

Drive back home and go into the house. Mom is on the couch doing her, " … … " thing.

"Mom!" He rushes to her side. "Mom, are you okay???"

She opens her eyes. "What? Just…resting. Just having a rest. I'm here, I'm here."

"I brought the Chinese food and your prescriptions."

"And you got your clothes?"

"I did."

Mom sits up. "I'll put them in the wash then."

"You just sit," he says. "It's time for some food."

Walk to the kitchen and UNPACK CHINESE FOOD. He will set the cartons out on the counter. OPEN CUPBOARD and GET PLATES and PUT CHINESE FOOD ON PLATES. OPEN DRAWER and GET SILVERWARE. GET NAPKINS. Go to the living room and Mom is sitting up, TV tray ready before her and yours beside it. PUT PLATES ON TRAYS, GIVE SILVERWARE TO MOM, and GIVE NAPKIN TO MOM.

"Thank you," she says. "Do I need to take the medicine with meals?"

"Yes."

"More water, please." TAKE GLASS and go fill it up in the kitchen. When you return she is eating. GIVE GLASS TO MOM and GIVE MEDICINE TO MOM. She will take her pills. "I think the Wheel of Fortune's on," she says.

TURN ON TV and sure enough, there's Pat and Vanna. SIT ON COUCH and EAT CHINESE FOOD.

After eating, Mom says, "Darling, I have to use the bathroom."

STAND and walk around the TV tray. Mom has her hand out

so HOLD HANDS. Unfortunately the only toilet in the house is on the second floor. Lead her to the foot of the staircase and ENCOURAGE MOM. "Let's take a step, Mom," he says, and she does. ENCOURAGE MOM on all fifteen stairs and she will make it up. LET GO and into the bathroom she scuttles, shutting the door.

Go downstairs and CLEAN UP DISHES. Barry will grab everything from the TV trays. Go into the kitchen and PUT DISHES IN DISHWASHER. TURN ON DISHWASHER. PUT CHINESE LEFTOVERS IN REFRIGERATOR. When you go out to the living room, the local news is on. Mom calls down from upstairs, "Barry? Baaaaaarry?"

"Yeah???"

"Can I have ice cream in bed?"

GET ICE CREAM from the freezer, just like at the apartment. Take it upstairs to her bedroom.

Floral bedspread, oak dresser, and lace curtains, Mom's room is pretty much the same as your sweet old granny's. Cozy is the word. The painting over her bed is, you guessed it, another Grant Wood. "Near Sundown" (1933. Oil on Masonite, Spencer Museum of Art) depicts the Iowa countryside in autumnal dusk, all hill slope and turning trees. Note, too, the two photos on her nightstand. The color one you will recognize as Barry's father. The black and white one, however, is a service portrait of Bartholomew Murray, Nora Gingle's first love who died in WWII. What are we to make of this? Clearly Nora was still in love with both men. Though she never speaks of Bartholomew Murray in the game, the inclusion of this detail raises all kinds of questions. Unfortunately, their answers are yet more we-will-never-know aspects of Barry's life.

Mom is in a nightdress now and sitting in her bed. GIVE ICE CREAM TO MOM and GIVE SPOON TO MOM. She will eat it right there on the edge of the bed. "Tomorrow morning at nine," she says, "That's when I have to be in for my radiation therapy."

"Alright."

"I think I'm done."

"Don't say that," Barry says.

"With the ice cream." She holds it forward with the spoon sticking out.

TAKE ICE CREAM.

"I'm very tired," she says. "I think I'll read some Miss Marple and turn in. If I need anything I'll call for you."

"Okay. Sleep well."

Walk downstairs and the TV will be showing that dreadful sitcom about a House that's Full. TURN OFF TV. Go to the kitchen and PUT ICE CREAM IN FREEZER. Go up to Barry's bedroom and PUT CLOTHES IN DRESSER. This is a good chance to have a shower and brush those neglected teeth. Go into the bathroom and follow the routine you're familiar with at the apartment. Pink tiles and yellow towels, that's Mom's bathroom.

Now back to the bedroom and CHANGE INTO PAJAMAS. Tread back into the hall now. Do you see the little door in the wall between Barry's door and the bathroom door? That's the laundry chute to the basement. THROW DIRTY LAUNDRY DOWN CHUTE. If you try to go to sleep now he will say, "I feel like reading," and if you try to read Dune, which he's been reading for ten years now, he will say, "I feel like reading something different." Lo and behold, there's a bookshelf right here in Barry's old room, untouched since he moved out. LOOK AT BOOKSHELF and a close-up picture will pop up, the titles standing out on the spines, alphabetical by author: Foundation, Something Wicked This Way Comes, John Carter of Mars, Stranger in a Strange Land, Brave New World, 20,000 Leagues Under the Sea, The Sirens of Titan, and The Invisible Man. Pick up Something Wicked This Way Comes (he won't read any of the others), read it after you have Barry GET IN BED, and our beleaguered hero will nod off.

Play through the recurring nightmare.

Now, this following day will be the same day, pretty much, for nineteen days. Note that as soon as Mom gets sick, the five day week, while progressing, is otherwise disrupted. Her illness, as illness truly behaves, has no regard for the structure of the week. Anyway, this next day will be played nineteen times and carries you through Mom's radiation treatment.

When Barry wakes, Mom is standing in his bedroom door. She is already dressed. She says, "Barry? Barry?"

"What is it?" he asks, blinky.

"We should go to the hospital in an hour. I've made you breakfast."

"You did what?" STAND. "Mom, you should be taking it easy here."

"It's just breakfast," she says, and walks out into the hall. Follow her downstairs. Breakfast awaits you on the TV tray in front of the couch. SIT ON COUCH and EAT BREAKFAST. Mom will stand while you eat, hands on her hips, watching a painting program on TV.

"You should sit down," Barry says to her.

"If I sit I won't get up," she replies.

He will take two more bites and say, "Thanks for the breakfast, Mom, but let me fix it from now on."

She picks up your dishes and says, "You'd better change. We have to be there soon."

STAND and go back up to Barry's room. CHANGE INTO CLOTHES and walk back downstairs. The TV is off and Mom is waiting outside already. Go out and HOLD HANDS. Escort her to the car, LET GO, OPEN CAR DOOR, CLOSE CAR DOOR when she's in, get Barry in and drive to the hospital.

At the hospital, help her out and HOLD HANDS again and head in through the sliding doors. Take her to the desk nurse and she will sign in, again while holding your hand. Another nurse will appear with a wheelchair. LET GO and Mom will sit into it.

"How long will it be?" Barry asks.

"Not long," the nurse says. "Half an hour?"

"See you soon," Mom says as she's wheeled away.

Sit in the usual chair and WAIT three times.

Mom is returned in the wheelchair and the nurse will help her up. "Thank you," she says to the nurse.

HOLD HANDS and walk to the desk. The desk nurse will say, "See you tomorrow, Mrs. Gingle," and you are free to leave.

Back to the car and through the opening of the door and whatnot for Mom. "What was it like?" he asks.

"Star Trek," she says. "They have me in this room and this big machine shot invisible beams into my abdomen."

"Did it hurt?"

"No."

Drive her home. Get the both of them out of the car and into the house. She will again swoon to the couch.

"We should think about lunch," he says. "What would you like?"

"Had a big breakfast," she says. "Go run the shop..."

"Mom..."

"Go run the shop. And I'll have a nap. Your lunch is on the counter in the kitchen."

Walk to the kitchen. There it is, the brown sack on the counter. GET LUNCH. Walk back to the living room and Mom will be asleep, saying, " ... ... "

Walk on outside and drive to work, EAT LUNCH, and
complete a typical afternoon at the shop. By this time,
going by the game's five-day week, it's a Thursday. Not
that it matters all that much. This is just a reminder for
you to keep track of your days.

After work, drive back home and check on Mom. She will
be awake but lying down, the TV set on and showing Pat and
Vanna again.
    "How're you feeling?" he asks.
    "What?" she asks, confused. "When is supper again?"
    "We can eat now if you like."
    "What's for supper again?"
    Barry turns to the kitchen and then back to her. "Um,
there's leftover Chinese?"
    "Yes, please," she says.
    Walk to the kitchen and OPEN REFRIGERATOR and GET
CHINESE LEFTOVERS. REHEAT CHINESE LEFTOVERS IN MICROWAVE.
GET DISHES FROM DISHWASHER. PUT CHINESE LEFTOVERS ON DISHES
and GET SILVERWARE and take dinner in to Mom. Serve her
just like the night before, give her medicine with a glass
of water just like the night before.
    When she's finished, take her upstairs to the bathroom,
HOLD HANDS and ENCOURAGE MOM every stair, just like the
night before.
    CLEAN UP DISHES, don't worry about saving leftovers
because they're gone now, and take ice cream up to her room
again, just like the night before.
    Turn off the TV, and return the ice cream to the
freezer, just like the night before.
    Now run through Barry's hygiene routine in the
bathroom, showering and brushing teeth, CHANGE INTO
PAJAMAS, and toss the day's outfit down the laundry chute.
Now you can settle into bed, reading Something Wicked, and
he will nod off.
    Play through the recurring nightmare.

And that's what the days will look like, with changes
to note over the coming weeks:

On the second day, Barry needs to go to the grocery
store after work and buy groceries. Stock these in Mom's
fridge like you would at Barry's apartment. The Chinese
food is all gone and Mom needs to eat. Serve her TV dinners
just as you did the Chinese food. Be sure to buy groceries
again on the fifth, tenth, and fifteenth days of radiation.

If you fail to get groceries, it will lead to Death #27.

On the tenth day, Mom is noticeably weaker. Morning seems her best time, with her perennially waking before Barry, making him breakfast, packing his lunch. She speaks less at midday and night, reverting to, " … … " before answering coherently. You will also need to ENCOURAGE MOM twice for each step upstairs in the evening.

On the sixteenth day, Mom is weaker still. Almost all of her speech now consists of, " … … " whether it's morning, noon, or night. Each step upstairs takes ENCOURAGE MOM thrice.

On the morning of the nineteenth day, when Mom is checking in at the hospital, she will tell the desk nurse, "I have some bleeding."
"Bleeding?" Barry asks.
"I have some bleeding," she repeats.
LET GO and let the wheelchair nurse take her away.
In your seat, WAIT seventeen times, and watch people drift in and out of the hospital hallway in slow motion between every WAIT.
When they wheel Mom out, she says, "They've called Peckinpaugh House and I can move in tomorrow."
"But that's hospice," Barry says.
"Yes. I move in tomorrow."
"Let me push you to your car, Mrs. Gingle," says the nurse.
"I'll walk, thank you." She holds her hand out to Barry. HOLD HANDS. She will stand.
"What about the bleeding?" Barry asks.
"Take me home," Mom says.
Lead her out to the car. Take her home. Help her indoors. Help her to the couch. She will lie down in a swoon.
" … … … "
Let her sleep. And forget about going to the shop this afternoon. Go to the kitchen and GET LUNCH from the counter.
"No," says Barry.
That sack lunch, the last she makes, will remain there on the counter for the rest of the game. Every time you try to pick it up from here on out, Barry will say, "No."

There is no guidance at this point and it took me forever to figure out what to do next, which is surely what Barry felt when living this. It is ingenious of him to imbue the game with the directionlessness he went through. Go down to the basement from the door in the kitchen. Like most basements, it's dark. TURN ON LIGHT and the proverbial cellar bulb hanging from a cord illuminates the basement, which is mostly cobwebs and boxes. The washing machine and dryer are in the corner beside a torrent of dirty laundry spilling out of the laundry chute from upstairs.

PUT DIRTY LAUNDRY IN WASHING MACHINE. PUT DETERGENT IN WASHING MACHINE. TURN ON WASHING MACHINE. It will start rumbling and you can go upstairs to the living room.

"Water…" Mom says from the couch. Go to the kitchen and GET GLASS from the cupboard, fill it up, and take it to her. She will take a sip. "I need to pack my things," she says.

"I can do that for you," Barry says. "You just rest."

"My suitcase is in the attic."

Walk upstairs to the hallway. PULL STRING on the hatch in the ceiling and a wooden staircase will unfold. Walk up to the attic. Cobwebs, a dressmakers dummy, and boxes clutter under the eaves. MOVE BOXES and there under the slant of the roof is a green suitcase. GET SUITCASE and walk back to the floor hatch. In the hall, LIFT LADDER and go into Mom's bedroom. OPEN CLOSET and PUT CLOTHES IN SUITCASE. He will grab a bunch of Mom's clothing and stuff them into the suitcase.

Go back downstairs and Mom is asleep again. You can run down to the basement to tend to the laundry. OPEN WASHING MACHINE and PUT WET CLOTHES IN DRYER. TURN ON DRYER. It will start rumbling and you can go upstairs.

In the living room, Mom is awake but not sitting up. "How about some food, Mom?" he asks.

"I've messed myself," she says. "I've messed the couch."

"We'll get you to the bathroom."

"I can't walk up those stairs."

CARRY MOM. Barry will pick her up in his arms. Now walk upstairs by typing STEP UP fifteen times. SET MOM DOWN and she will walk into the bathroom and close the door.

"You okay?" he asks.

"Mhmm," she responds.

Go to the kitchen. GET PAPER TOWELS and GET CARPET CLEANER from the cupboard under the sink. USE CARPET CLEANER ON COUCH and he will spray the foam onto the cushions. Now you need to let that sit so go back upstairs to Barry's bedroom. CHANGE CLOTHES and THROW DIRTY CLOTHES DOWN CHUTE in the hall. At the bathroom, KNOCK ON DOOR.

"I'm okay," she says.

"You sure?"

"Can you bring me a nightdress?"

Go into her bedroom and GET NIGHTDRESS from the closet. Back to the bathroom, KNOCK ON DOOR again and Mom says, "Leave it on the doorknob. Thank you."

HANG NIGHTDRESS ON DOORKNOB and walk downstairs. CLEAN COUCH WITH PAPER TOWELS and he will scrub up the foam. Go to the kitchen and WASH HANDS. Return and FLIP CUSHIONS.

If you don't flip the cushions you will get to Death #28.

Check on Mom in the bathroom, KNOCK ON DOOR, and she will emerge in her nightdress. "I want to lie in my bed," she says, "one last night."

HOLD HANDS. Lead her into her room. LET GO by the bed and she will sit.

"How about some food?" he asks.

"Ice cream, please."

Run and get it for her like usual. She will eat it and say, "I think I'll keep it here by the bed if I get hungry in the night."

"You going to sleep now?"

"Yes." She gets under the covers. Walk to the door and she will say, "Thank you for being so good to me, Barry."

Walk downstairs and fix dinner for Barry. Eat. Watch TV. Basically carry out a typical night like you've been doing, just without Mom.

In the morning, when Barry wakes, Mom is not at his door to wake him. Walk to her bedroom and she is awake but lying down.

"I'm so sorry, Barry," she says. "I'm so sorry."

"No need to be."

"I'm sorry for leaving you all alone," she says.

"I'm not."

"You will be," she says. "And I'm sorry."

A window pops up:

DO YOU FORGIVE MOM?
YES or NO

Of course, type YES.

If you type NO, you get Death #29.

"It is what it is, Mom," Barry says. "Please don't worry."

She swings her legs over the side of the bed and sits up. HOLD HANDS and walk her to the hall.

"Need the bathroom?" he asks.

"No," she says. "Let's go to Peckinpaugh House."

CARRY MOM and walk downstairs, typing STEP DOWN fifteen times. SET MOM DOWN in the living room, HOLD HANDS, and walk her out to the car. Go through the car routine and drive to the hospice center. It is located one screen left of the golf course.

4.6 - HOSPICE (1990)

Peckinpaugh House is a real hospice center, the oldest and most esteemed in Des Moines. Gingle has rendered its low-roofed, blonde-brick front entrance. The woods that sit behind it rise overhead.

Help Mom out of the car and in through the sliding doors. The lobby has potted trees, a white baby grand piano, and a desk with a woman behind it, almost the same as the one at the hospital. Walk to the desk and the woman will rise and walk around.

"You must be Mrs. Gingle," she says.

"Please, call me Nora."

"And call me Betty," she says. "May I help you to your room? Would you like to be wheeled there?"

"I can walk," says Mom, and she can so long as you are holding her hand.

"You must be her son then?" Betty asks.

"Yes," Mom says, "this is my son, Barry."

"Wonderful to meet you. Please follow me."

Betty leads you off screen right. The next screen is Mom's room, where she will die. Not yet, of course. She will live here for thirteen days before that eventuality. So far as rooms go, it is comfortable, muted brown and green: a twin bed, a couple of easy chairs, TV, wardrobe. The back wall is an enormous window looking out on woodland. A private bathroom is on the left.

Betty walks straight to the bed and fluffs the pillows. "Feel free to have a lie down. Please make this your home," she says, leaving.

Walk Mom to the bed and LET GO. She gets in and Betty returns with a tray. "Fresh cookies?" she asks. "Still warm…"

"No thank you," Mom says.

GET COOKIE and EAT COOKIE.

"Now Nora," Betty says, "are you in any discomfort? Any pain?"

"Some," she says.

"Okay, we'll take care of that. And have you brought your medicine?"

"Barry?"

GIVE MEDICINE TO BETTY.

"Thank you," she says, and, "I'll be right back."

You and Mom are alone for a moment. A cardinal comes to the birdfeeder outside the window.

Betty returns and gives Mom some medicine. "Can I take the things you've brought?" she asks.

GIVE SUITCASE TO BETTY. She will take it straight to the wardrobe and start hanging Mom's clothes. Then she hands Barry some forms with instructions to fill them out. "To the best of your knowledge," she says. "No rush."

FILL OUT FORMS.

When he finishes, Betty takes the forms and Mom lifts her hand. There is an easy chair by her bed. SIT IN CHAIR and HOLD HANDS.

The game now enters a series of days in which you have very little or no control over what happens. Almost cinematic, what is required of Barry is holding his mother's hand. Men and women in yellow come and go to check on her comfort, to offer whatever she would like to eat, to work the TV for her, bring blankets and change sheets, to help her in the bathroom (you have to LET GO at these moments so they can take care of her) and offer the lavender baths she declines. Out the window, a variety of birds come to feed, squirrels bounce by, even the odd deer makes an appearance. There is no waiting like in the hospital. There is just a day of holding hands.

When she falls asleep after suppertime, one of the volunteers will suggest Barry just stretch his legs for a couple minutes. STAND and take a walk out to the lobby, then outside for some air.

If you leave and go anywhere, it leads to Death #20.

Return to Mom's side and sit again. USE FOOTREST and
Barry will pull the lever that reclines the easy chair.
READ SOMETHING WICKED THIS WAY COMES and Barry falls
asleep, too.

No nightmare to play through. For whatever reason, it
does not return.

The days progress onwards, Mom eating less and less,
having less and less to say. The caregivers are always kind
and patient, their words always positive. Barry never
leaves the room except to stretch his legs after supper
each day. He stays the entire time, living on cookies.

On the eighth day, Mom starts on morphine drops. Her
appetite, what was left of it anyway, vanishes. She doesn't
speak any longer. When the volunteer suggests he stretch
his legs, Barry will say, "I should be here now."
    "I'll stay with her," the volunteer says. "We've got to
keep your circulation going, you know."
    This gives Barry the permission to LET GO and take his
short walk.

On the thirteenth day of hospice, everything progresses
as it has gone since the morphine started. But when he
returns to her room this night from his little walk, the
volunteer is standing by Mom's bedside. He will turn to
Barry and say, "She just went."
    Barry will fall flat on his back and the screen goes
black.

4.7 - FUNERAL (1990)

The screen opens on Barry in the coffin showroom at
Donne's Funeral Home. Three caskets stand on stilts, their
padded lids open. The funeral director, dressed in a brown
and gray suit, pitches each one: the brown one ("The finish
on this one brings out the grain of one's life lived with a
richness of hue and meaning. Though growth has come to an
end, life stands preserved."), the white one ("Purity,
sanctity, dignity."), and the blue one ("It's the color of
a clear sky, a robin's egg, one of the Great Lakes on a
calm spring morning. It says homecoming.").
    BUY BROWN CASKET.

If you buy the white casket, see Death #30.

If you buy the blue casket, see Death #31.

The screen goes black.

Open on the grave of Mom and Dad in Glendale Cemetery. The funeral director oversees the lowering of the casket via machine into the ground. Note, if you haven't wandered to this screen since Dad's funeral, that Gramma's gravestone stands on the left of Dad's side of their small monument. Barry never tells us when she died (The actual stone tells us she died March 18, 1982.), and we don't play through it. Given how she vocally blamed him for his father's death, is it any wonder?
There is no priest or clergyman here for the ceremony. No friends. Just Barry and the funeral director.
And no one speaks.
The screen goes black.

I can only say that the relative brevity of Mom's decline and death hammers home how painful this experience must have been for Barry. By stretching us through the monotony of his working life, on and on for hundreds of days, and then hitting us with her death so quickly, she really does vanish before our eyes. I think he superbly captured the daze and speed of losing a loved one, especially with the disjointed skips in time after she's gone with the leapfrogging to the funeral home and on to the burial. You may have noticed that Barry and his mother never say they love each other, and yet the care he shows her, the gratitude she shows him, they transcend whatever that word might signify.

4.8 – FAILINGS (1990 - 1992)

The screen opens on Barry in his shop. He now wears an ISU sweatshirt, no longer dressing up for work. A delivery man walks in pulling a hand truck stacked with boxes.
"Got a shipment for ya."
"Must be the new Anima 2000s," Barry says.
The delivery guy will cart in and build a pyramid of cardboard boxes. When he's done, SIGN FORM and he will give Barry his copy. "Have a better one," he says and leaves.
PUT AWAY BOXES. Barry will carry them one by one into

the back, all but one at the bottom. Now SET UP ANIMA 2000 and he will add it to the long table alongside the Anima 1000.

"I could use this empty box to move out of my apartment," he says. GET BOX.

It is now pretty much the end of the day, so lock up and drive to the Daventry Apartments. And look around: Des Moines has returned once again to autumn. Back are the orange, brown, and yellow leaves, the grass everywhere dead. Though spanning over a decade, Barry's use of the seasonal cycle in sequential order is an interesting touch. Here we see it representing not the passing of a year but the passing of a life.

Go into the apartment and PACK BOX. Barry will toodle around, fetching belongings and putting them in the box. When he finishes, LOCK DOOR and PUT KEY IN MAILBOX.

If you don't leave the key, you hit Death #32.

Now go home and when you get inside the living room, SET DOWN BOX.

If you don't drop the box, it leads to Death #33.

Don't bother to unpack the box. Like the last lunch Mom packed on the kitchen counter and the last pint of ice cream she ate on her nightstand upstairs, this box of Barry's stuff will remain here by the TV set for the rest of the game.

Your nights back at the apartment? Relive them. That's right, TV and sleep.

Everything is pretty well back to normal at the computer shop as well. Barry works full days again. The only difference is the Anima 2000.

If you pitch the Anima 2000, Barry sits the customer before that machine and delivers the glowingest spiel of them all: "The Anima 2000 blows everything else out of the water. Forget IBM. Forget Macintosh. This machine can handle everything, even video editing. Four thousand and ninety-six colors and 512K of RAM, with expandable slots, yada yada yada…"

The questions received will be the same ones Barry gets for the Anima 1000, suggesting that either Gingle had a lapse while programming the game or his customer base just couldn't grasp the full capabilities of the new machine.

Unfortunately, the Anima 2000 also carries a hefty price tag: $1500. Few will buy it.

And this reflects the national trend in home computing in the early nineties. Despite being a superior machine, easily outstripping PCs and Apples in its scope and power, Anima computers succumbed to the competition and soon vanished from the market. By 1993 you were hard pressed to find one of these machines for sale anywhere in the United States.

So along with the new model, you will notice a drop in customers. Fewer and fewer people wander into the store as the weeks pass. When they do, they don't often buy anything.

Lunch, now that Mom has died, is Taco Juan's. Every day.

Thursdays are basement laundry nights. Also, you won't be dressing from the dresser in his room anymore. Barry now wears his clothes right out of the dryer in the basement, meaning you will have to PUT ON CLOTHES down there.

Friday nights without Mom are now spent eating Chinese takeout from Imperial Garden.

If you don't get Chinese food Friday nights, you will reach Death #34.

Other than that, we're back monotonously playing out the five day week. At day fifteen, after you clean up his Chinese dinner in the kitchen, Barry will complain, "I don't know who I am. This face isn't mine." He faces the player and takes his face off, leaving only creases like at the beginning of the game. Clearly, Barry is dissolving into disassociation. Go down to the basement. The shelf along the back wall has a row of canning jars. GET JAR, walk upstairs to the living room, and PUT JAR BY DOOR. He will place it on the small table by the front door, which you recall from the very beginning of the game. PUT FACE IN JAR. Remember to put it on each morning when you leave and remove it each night when you get home.

281

If you go to sleep with Barry's face in your inventory, you will reach the last possible death, Death #35.

At thirty days if you try to PLAY GAME at the shop, he will announce, "I've beaten all of these games. It'd be more fun to read their code." From now on you can READ CODE to pass the day. No doubt this is where he learned to design Barry's Quest.

After forty days, Barry will develop a periodic wince, like we saw at the beginning of the game.

After eighty days, no more customers will come into the shop. He winces with greater regularity.

At day ninety-nine, Barry, alone at Gingle Home Computing, will announce, "Soon I won't make rent for the shop. *wince* And this pain in my side. Maybe I should see a doctor…"
Drive to the hospital, as there is no doctor's office in the game as such. Walk in and TALK TO NURSE at the desk.
"What's the problem?"
"Persistent pain in my side here," Barry says.
"Go to your family doctor."
"Don't have either."
"Fill out these forms, sir."
FILL OUT FORMS like she says and Barry will hand them over to her. Take a seat in the usual spot and WAIT nine times. Another nurse will appear and say, "Mr. Gingle?"
STAND and follow her off screen.

FIVE HOURS, HOWEVER-MANY-MINUTES, AND SEVENTEEN TESTS LATER…

Barry walks back into the waiting room and winces. Walk out to the car and he says, "I want to take an Anima 2000 home."
We are very close to the end of the game here. Barry, for whatever reason, shares the doctor's results with us indirectly. If you look in the inventory, you will find a doctor's report. If you LOOK AT DOCTOR'S REPORT, you will see his brief synopsis of what it says:

> "Stage IV Pancreatic Adenocarcimona… 10% chance
> of living 12 months… Patient waives treatment

    options… Contacted hospice on patient's behalf…"

   Why does Barry withhold the scene when he received this
terrible news? After all we've played through, why doesn't
he show his players his death sentence? I have no answers
here. We can only speculate. We will never know.
   Drive to the shop. Go in and GET ANIMA 2000. Lock up
when you leave and drive home. Take the computer upstairs
to Barry's room and PUT ANIMA 2000 ON DESK. He will set it
up. He will wince.
   He says, "What should I do with three to six months?"
   Are you ready? This is the master stroke. This is it,
the firing of the proton torpedoes down the thermal exhaust
port, the casting of the One Ring into the Crack of Doom,
the climax, the denouement of the entire game: USE COMPUTER
and MAKE BARRY'S QUEST.

4.9 - THE END (1992)

Barry sets to work programming and the song from the
beginning, "Reflections of My Life," returns for a reprise.
While Barry is shown typing away at the computer, a window
pops up on the right:

```
 _____
|                                                          |
| CONGRATULATIONS! You have won Barry's Quest. What a       |
| long, drawn-out ordeal, huh? At least you didn't have     |
| to live it. Believe me, that was a lot less fun than      |
| what you just suffered through by playing this game…      |
|_____|
```

   Another window pops up:

```
 _____
|                                                          |
| Nothing to see here, folks. Nothing to see. You're done.|
| You did it. Gesundheit and thanks for playing!           |
|_____|
```

   Another window pops up:

```
         _____
        |          |
        | THE END  |
        |_____|
```

   Another window pops up:

```
 _____
|                                                |
| Seriously, we're all done here now. You're free to go. |
| I release you. Go on! Scram! You're not needed anymore! |
|_____|
```

Another window pops up:

```
 _____
|                                                |
| No, really, thank you. Thanks for playing. I appreciate |
| your time and effort. You're a trooper. Bang up job!    |
|_____|
```

A penultimate window pops up:

```
       _____
      |       |
      | THE   |
      |_____|
```

And then:

```
       _____
      |       |
      | END   |
      |_____|
```

   Knowing a thing or two about how these old school games
were put together, and the great temptation of programmers
to leave a special signature on a piece of software, I
found this litany of windows at the end suspect. On the one
hand, Barry Gingle seems genuinely reluctant to let us go.
Despite knowing that he would never meet anybody who plays,
let alone completes his game – if indeed anybody were to
find it - he still feels the need to reach across the void
with an awkward goodbye. On the other hand, he spent so
much time reading code and programming that I wondered if
his repeated insistence that the game is totally over might
not be entirely true.
   Sure enough, taking a close look at the code for
Barry's Quest, I found a most curious command buried in
there at the end. That's right, there is an Easter Egg at
the end of Barry's Quest – and it unlocks a real-life
treasure hunt, transcending the game itself for the most
interactive meta-experience I've ever had with a computer
game. If you want to know more, the story concludes in
Chapter 7 - Epilogue.

                        284
```
```

Item	Barry's Description of Item
FACE	"I keep it in a jar by the door…"
RAKE	"Dad died using it."
LOCK	"So my bike stays mine."
LUNCH	"The same lunch Mom packed for Dad all his years at Percival."
BAGEL	"Lightly toasted with the peanut butter and chocolate chips melted on top."
KEY	"Apartment Numero Four-o."
FROZEN DINNER	"It's frosty cold."
OVEN MITT	"Don't cook at home without one."
HOT DINNER	"Salisbury steak, sweetcorn, and mashed potatoes under gravy."
EATEN DINNER	"All gone."
ICE CREAM	"Anderson Erickson Vanilla."
SPOON	"Good for scooping food."
DUNE	"Sandworms, spice, and Fremen."
COMICS	"Been collecting since forever."
DIRTY LAUNDRY	"They smell like I wore them alright…"
CLEAN LAUNDRY	"What a fresh, clean smell."

DEB'S ADDRESS	"This is where Deb lives."
WINE	"It's red and has a French name even though it's from Sonoma."
DELIVERY FORM	"It's my copy for my files."
DEPOSIT BAG	"For the bank deposits."
BANK RECEIPT	"Better add it to my files."
SUCKER	"Watermelon's the best flavor."
GAS CAN	"If only I had a chainsaw…"
WATER BOTTLE	"Spills aren't a worry."
TACO JUAN'S MEAL	"There's a whole lot of Mexicali going on right here…"
GLASS	"We had these since I was a boy."
MEDICINE	"For Mom. To be taken with food."
CLOTHES	"We all wear them."
DOPKIT	"This holds my toiletries."
CHINESE FOOD	"They sure know how to fly lice like nobody else."
PLATES	"I grew up eating off of these."
SILVERWARE	"I think these were a wedding gift to Mom and Dad back in the day."
NAPKINS	"I'd just as soon use my pantleg…"
SOMETHING WICKED THIS WAY COMES	"Boys, October, and a carnival."
SUITCASE	"Didn't know Mom had one. We never went anywhere."
PAPER TOWELS	"Quilted for better absorption."

CARPET CLEANER	"I think it's the foaming kind."
NIGHTDRESS	"Mom's pajamas."
COOKIE	"Fresh baked chocolate chip."
FORMS	"Lots to fill out."
BOX	"You could fit a lot of stuff in
	a box this big."
JAR	"Like Mom used to can preserves."
DOCTOR'S REPORT	"Stage IV Pancreatic
	Adenocarcimona... 10% chance of
	living 12 months... Patient waives
	treatment options... Contacted
	hospice on patient's behalf..."
ANIMA 2000	"What could I do with a state-of-
	the-art computer?"

****
CHAPTER 6 – THE MANY DEATHS OF BARRY
****

Listed here in the interests of producing a complete guide
to the game is a summary of each of the thirty-five ways in
which Barry can die in the game. Enjoy!

****
* DEATH #1 *
****

Walking out of doors without wearing Barry's FACE results
in a Frankensteinian death. An angry mob carrying torches
and pitchforks attacks and kills him, by fire and poking
respectively. "FACELESS FREAK!" they shout. "MONSTER!"

| |
| Baring your empty inner self by not wearing your mask |
| is hazardous to your health, you dingbat! GAME OVER! |
| |

```
        * * * * * * * * *
        * DEATH #2 *
        * * * * * * * * *
```

Barry leaves with Deb and the screen goes black. Then she
returns alone and Mr. Blubaugh is waiting for her. "I got
the call! What happened?" he asks. "Oh, Mr. Blubaugh, it
was terrible, simply terrible!" she says. "He just…stopped
breathing!"

```
 _____
|                                                        |
| You fool, what makes you think lunchtime conversation  |
| is Barry's forte? He wasn't built for that. GAME OVER! |
|_____|
```

```
        * * * * * * * * *
        * DEATH #3 *
        * * * * * * * * *
```

Driving onto the next screen, an Aylesbury duck flies at
low altitude and smashes beak-first into Barry's green
Datsun B-210. Barry is thrown out the windshield and skids
across the road, his body coming to a bloody stop without
any witnesses around to call for help.

```
 _____
|                                                        |
| Driving without oldies is dangerous to Barry's health. |
| Remember, music helps keep the driver alert. GAME OVER!|
|_____|
```

```
        * * * * * * * * *
        * DEATH #4 *
        * * * * * * * * *
```

When Barry next goes out to his car, he is struck in the
chest with a harpoon and killed. A hunter, in bright vest,
walks out, puts a foot on Barry's back, and lifts his head
while his hunting buddy snaps a photo.

```
 _____
|                                                        |
| Oh yeah, that new law about hunting unhygienic people  |
| went into effect today. Whoopsie doopsies… GAME OVER!  |
|_____|
```

```
        * * * * * * * * *
        * DEATH #5 *
        * * * * * * * * *
```

That night after donning pajamas, Barry will pace back and
forth and say, "I forgot my comics! Ivor's might still be

288

open..." He opens the window. "I might have time if I fly!"
He jumps out the window.

```
|                                                              |
| Barry may enjoy reading about men and women who can fly |
| but he's hardly capable of flying himself. Way to wind  |
| him up, Dr. Cruel! GAME OVER!                            |
|_____|
```

```
* * * * * * * * * *
* DEATH #6 *
* * * * * * * * * *
```

When driving to work the next morning, the car will just
stop. "Out of gas," Barry says. "Guess I'll wait for help
to arrive..." He sits in his car, a long beard grows from his
face, and he turns into a skeleton.

```
|                                                              |
| I know it's a lot to ask, but isn't filling up the tank |
| regularly sort of a given with car ownership? GAME OVER!|
|_____|
```

```
* * * * * * * * * *
* DEATH #7 *
* * * * * * * * * *
```

When you open the freezer to make dinner, Barry says, "Out
of food! What now?" He staggers into the living room
saying, "Too weak...to get to Tate's..." He collapses.

```
|                                                              |
| Barry is a human being and human beings require a thing |
| called food. You should've bought some, Einstein! GAME  |
| OVER!                                                    |
|_____|
```

```
* * * * * * * * * *
* DEATH #8 *
* * * * * * * * * *
```

The next time Barry is in the kitchen, a giant cockroach
will peek out of the trash bin, grab him with its long
skinny legs, and pull him in.

```
|                                                              |
| You filthy stinker, you! Usually people make a healthy |
| habit of taking the trash out on a regular basis, not  |
| living with it till it decides to gobble them up like  |
```

```
| leftovers. GAME OVER!                                        |
|_____|
```

```
        * * * * * * * * * *
        *   DEATH #9   *
        * * * * * * * * * *
```

The next Monday when you park the car outside work and get
out, people with aerosol cans will approach and spray
Barry, saying, "Fumigate him! Fumigate him!" Barry chokes
in the cloud of spray and keels over.

```
 _____
|                                                              |
| Somebody forgot to wear clean clothes today. What are        |
| you, hard of smelling? Way to win over people's noses!       |
| GAME OVER!                                                   |
|_____|
```

```
        * * * * * * * * * *
        *   DEATH #10  *
        * * * * * * * * * *
```

When you arrive at the apartment, the light on the phone is
blinking. "A message on the machine," he says and plays it.
Mom says, "Is it too much to ask you over for dinner once a
week?" Barry falls flat on his back.

```
 _____
|                                                              |
| How could you go and break Mom's heart like that? She's      |
| all Barry's got on God's green earth. GAME OVER!             |
|_____|
```

```
        * * * * * * * * * *
        *   DEATH #11  *
        * * * * * * * * * *
```

Barry goes into Deb's house with Mr. Blubaugh. The
silhouettes in the windows tear Barry limb from limb.

```
 _____
|                                                              |
| Who knew Deb was marrying into a cannibalistic sect?         |
| You knew better than to go in there with all those           |
| people enjoying themselves in there. GAME OVER!              |
|_____|
```

```
        * * * * * * * * * *
        *   DEATH #12  *
        * * * * * * * * * *
```

Upon refusing to quit, two guys in suits come into the

office. One says, "Alright, there he is." They wrap up
Barry, sitting at his desk, in bandages like a mummy. They
leave.

```
|                                                              |
| Now there's a career move for the ages: Permanent            |
| entombment at Percival Insurance. GAME OVER!                 |
|_____|
```

```
                    * * * * * * * * * *
                    *  DEATH #13  *
                    * * * * * * * * * *
```
When Barry steps out of the shop it is night, the colors
gone dark. As he walk to his car, a shadow reaches out,
grabs him, and pulls him screaming off screen.

```
|                                                              |
| Stayed too late at the shop, did you? Who knows what         |
| evil lurks in Valley Junction after dark? GAME OVER!         |
|_____|
```

```
                    * * * * * * * * * *
                    *  DEATH #14  *
                    * * * * * * * * * *
```
Arriving home, before Barry can make it through the front
door a burglar in black eye mask runs out from behind the
car, thumps Barry on the noggin, and absconds with a
cartoon bag of money.

```
|                                                              |
| Does home look like a bank to you? There's a much            |
| better place for that hard-earned moolah, fool! GAME         |
| OVER!                                                        |
|_____|
```

```
                    * * * * * * * * * *
                    *  DEATH #15  *
                    * * * * * * * * * *
```
Entering the shop next morning, Barry meets a giant gray
blob with rabbit ears. "It isn't Easter," Barry says. "Is
it?" The fuzzball picks him up and eats him like a Kit-Kat.

```
|                                                              |
| Those dust bunnies sure can sneak up on you. You should      |
| have tidied the shop more often. GAME OVER!                  |
|_____|
```

```
          * * * * * * * * * *
          *  DEATH #16  *
          * * * * * * * * * *
```

Two men in black suits enter the shop. "Barry Gingle?"
"Yeah." One draws a pistol and shoots Barry in the head.
"Lunch?" one asks. "Your turn to buy." They leave.

```
 _____
|                                                     |
| Failure to keep track of the shop's finances inevitably |
| leads to the IRS hit squad showing up. Everybody knows  |
| this, you petty crook. GAME OVER!                   |
|_____|
```

```
          * * * * * * * * * *
          *  DEATH #17  *
          * * * * * * * * * *
```

Barry makes a sale but comes out empty-handed from the back
room. "Heh… So… It seems we're out of stock. Would you mind
waiting six weeks?" "SIX WEEKS!?!" The customer pulls out
an axe and dismembers Barry in full-on Battle Chess style
right there on the spot.

```
 _____
|                                                     |
| The reason we write orders has something to do with |
| fears of failing to please the unexpected axe-wielding |
| customer. GAME OVER!                                |
|_____|
```

```
          * * * * * * * * * *
          *  DEATH #18  *
          * * * * * * * * * *
```

A little green man in a spacesuit with a glass dome helmet
walks into the shop and says, "Help me, Barry Gingle,
you're my only hope." "Who're you?" Barry asks. "I'm the
Meteor Police and I've chased a deadly, nefarious meteor
from one side of this galaxy to the other. I've tracked him
to your planet but interference has made him hard to
pinpoint. By linking up your computers I should be able to
find him. Tell me, how many do you have?" Barry turns
around and says, "Um, how many?" "Yes, how many do you have
in stock?" Barry balks. "You mean you don't know?" the
alien asks. "Big help you are!" The pint-sized visitor
pulls out a ray gun and vaporizes Barry.

```
 _____
|                                                     |
| You never know when the Meteor Police are going to show |
```

| up these days. That's why keeping track of inventory is |
| generally a good idea, ya goof! GAME OVER! |
|_____|


```
* * * * * * * * * *
* DEATH #19 *
* * * * * * * * * *
```

Next morning Barry enters the shop to find it entirely
empty save for Chuck the Plant, whose pot sits on the
floor. Barry keels over.

| |
| Shop doors have locks for a reason, you know. One perk |
| is that you don't have to worry about coming to work to |
| find the place ransacked. GAME OVER! |
|_____|


```
* * * * * * * * * *
* DEATH #20 *
* * * * * * * * * *
```

Walking out of the hospital when Mom is there results in
Barry being struck by lightning, charred to dust.

| |
| Who raised you? You must never, ever leave your mother |
| like that. GAME OVER! |
|_____|


```
* * * * * * * * * *
* DEATH #21 *
* * * * * * * * * *
```

The hospital bed spasms and wrenches shut on Mom like a
Venus fly trap. Barry pries it open but it snaps shut on
him, too. Then the bed burps.

| |
| This modern day medical equipment sure is touchy. Who |
| knew it was also hungry? GAME OVER! |
|_____|


```
* * * * * * * * * *
* DEATH #22 *
* * * * * * * * * *
```

Mom's head falls and she says, "All I needed…was a sip…"
She swoons and a giant tidal wave crosses the screen right
to left, washing Barry away with it.

```
 _____
|                                                 |
| How hard is it to get the woman some water when it's |
| always available? GAME OVER!                    |
|_____|
```

```
* * * * * * * * * *
    * DEATH #23 *
* * * * * * * * * *
```

Not long after lunchtime, Barry will suddenly grab his
stomach, double over, stagger, and collapse. A buzzard
descends and eats his eyes.

```
 _____
|                                                 |
| Starvation isn't the way to go, not when Mom needs you. |
| Why didn't you get a taco or something? GAME OVER! |
|_____|
```

```
* * * * * * * * * *
    * DEATH #24 *
* * * * * * * * * *
```

Pushing a step without encouragement sends Mom to the
floor, where she screams, "AAAIIIIIEEEEEE!" A black hole
opens beneath Barry and into it he tumbles, falls, and
disappears.

```
 _____
|                                                 |
| A good son wouldn't fathom driving his terminally ill |
| mother like a mule. Make like Otis Redding and "Try a |
| Little Tenderness." GAME OVER!                  |
|_____|
```

```
* * * * * * * * * *
    * DEATH #25 *
* * * * * * * * * *
```

After eating, Mom will complain, "Oh dear, something…
Something isn't right…" She will clutch her stomach and a
baby alien will plunge out of her chest. It leaps from TV
tray to TV tray and then onto Barry's head. He tries
pulling it off but falls motionless on the floor. It
scampers into the kitchen.

```
 _____
|                                                 |
| That medicine Mom's meant to be taking is designed to |
| keep malignant things in check, Rasputin. Before you go |
| thinking faith alone can heal anything, give the pills |
```

```
* * * * * * * * * *
* DEATH #26 *
* * * * * * * * * *
```

When you serve Mom her plate of Chinese food, she says,
"They ran out of Moo Goo Gai Pan, did they?" Barry says,
"Uh… Yeah." A giant scythe falls from the ceiling and takes
Barry's head from his shoulders.

```
|                                                       |
| First you forget your dying mother's simple dinner    |
| request, then you lie to her? GAME OVER!              |
|_____|
```

```
* * * * * * * * * *
* DEATH #27 *
* * * * * * * * * *
```

Quite similar to Death #5, Barry will balk at the empty
freezer and go to the living room. "We're out of food."
"But I can't take my medicine without it!" Mom cries and
collapses. Barry unrolls a mat, kneels, produces a tantō,
and disembowels himself.

```
|                                                       |
| What were you going to feed the woman? Air? GAME OVER! |
|_____|
```

```
* * * * * * * * * *
* DEATH #28 *
* * * * * * * * * *
```

When Mom next sits on the couch, she worries over it. "Oh
what have I done? Must wash these cushions…" She takes one
and walks out to the kitchen and falls down the basement
stairs. A giant anvil falls and squashes Barry.

```
|                                                       |
| Most folks know to flip the cushions when something   |
| like this happens to a couch… GAME OVER!              |
|_____|
```

```
* * * * * * * * * *
* DEATH #29 *
* * * * * * * * * *
```

When you don't forgive Mom for dying, Barry slowly turns

blue with white sparkles, like cartoon ice. He falls over
and shatters into a hundred pieces.

```
|                                                           |
| How absurd, to not forgive Mom for things so far out of   |
| her control. You are a cold, cold person. GAME OVER!      |
|_____|
```

* * * * * * * * * *
* DEATH #30 *
* * * * * * * * * *

"You'll take the white?" the funeral director asks.
"Excellent choice." The white casket suddenly transforms
into a big robot, shoots the funeral director and Barry
dead with lasers, and flies off screen in rocket boots.

```
|                                                           |
| Now intergalactic robots are disguising themselves as     |
| caskets in funeral home showrooms? Des Moines is          |
| finally like everywhere else. GAME OVER!                  |
|_____|
```

* * * * * * * * * *
* DEATH #31 *
* * * * * * * * * *

Lights flash and confetti falls from the ceiling. The
funeral director says, "Congrats! You've won the grand
prize by being the first person to purchase this tacky
casket!" "What's the prize?" Barry asks. "You're first to
be buried in it!" The funeral director picks up Barry,
stuffs him in, and shuts the lid.

```
|                                                           |
| Uh, weren't you shopping for your dead mother's casket?   |
| Selfish, selfish… GAME OVER!                              |
|_____|
```

* * * * * * * * * *
* DEATH #32 *
* * * * * * * * * *

Once home there's a knock on the door. Barry opens it and
in walks a man in a blue Robin Hood cap with a red feather.
He socks Barry in the gut and says, "Where's the key,
Gingle? You don't live in Daventry anymore." "Here…" Barry
holds out the apartment key. The landlord knees him in the
gut and leaves him for dead.

```
 _____
|                                                 |
| That Graham King is a helluva landlord, isn't he. And |
| here you thought it was harsh only getting half of your |
| deposit back. GAME OVER!                        |
|_____|
```

                    * * * * * * * * * *
                    * DEATH #33 *
                    * * * * * * * * * *

Barry's arms will fall off his body, dropping the big box.
Then he falls onto it and bleeds out.

```
 _____
|                                                 |
| I realize you're able to carry an ungodly number of |
| things in your inventory, but even camels have a limit. |
| GAME OVER!                                      |
|_____|
```

                    * * * * * * * * * *
                    * DEATH #34 *
                    * * * * * * * * * *

When you open the oven to cook the frozen dinner, a Chinese
man reaches out and pulls Barry in, slamming the door shut.

```
 _____
|                                                 |
| Looks like the Red Chinese have done it: dug a hole |
| through the center of the Earth that comes out in the |
| oven. You don't have to get Barry shanghaied to get a |
| taste of China, you know. There's a restaurant right |
| here in Des Moines! GAME OVER!                  |
|_____|
```

                    * * * * * * * * * *
                    * DEATH #35 *
                    * * * * * * * * * *

When he wakes, Barry stands and feels his side. He pulls
his face out of his pajamas and shakes it. "My face is
flattened from sleeping on it!" He takes it to the bathroom
and washes it under the shower, then uses Mom's hair dryer
on it. As his face is flapping like a latex mask, it flies
into the shower. Barry grabs it and is electrocuted, his
skeleton glowing yellow.

```
 _____
|                                                 |
| Well then. I guess maybe it's just a bad idea to sleep |
```

```
| with one's face in his pocket, isn't it… GAME OVER!     |
|_____|
```

```
*********************
CHAPTER 7 - EPILOGUE
*********************
```

Barry's Quest does not end when you complete the game.
There is, I discovered, a real life ending that took me
beyond the graphic adventure and right into the streets of
Des Moines.
   At the end, when the windows keep popping up about how
the game is over, if you type YOU CAN KEEP THE EVERLASTING
GOBSTOPPER, a special window appears:

```
 _____
|                                                        |
| Well done, you've done it! You've really done it! But  |
| are you sure about this? Really? Alright then. The true|
| ending of this game is a bit of a wild goose chase. Do |
| you think you can handle it? Go to my parents' grave.   |
| Look in the base of the mounted vase on Mom's side of  |
| the stone. Seeing as you beat this game, you will      |
| surely know what to do with what you find there…       |
|_____|
```

   I got to this screen on a Sunday afternoon. I was meant
to be watching the girls while my wife was at work - she is
a pedicurist and wasn't due home for a couple hours.
   I couldn't wait. I simply couldn't. I already knew
where the grave was thanks to the Iowa Gravestone Photo
Project website, but I hadn't made the trip yet to pay my
respects. Now I had an urgent reason to go. So I got the
girls bundled up (it was February) and we stopped at Tate's
to buy some flowers. We got to Glendale and parked in the
general vicinity of where the website said Mr. and Mrs.
Gingle are buried. I told the girls that whoever spotted
the Gingle stone first would get bragging rights in my
walkthrough: it turns out Emily is the winner (Way to go,
sweetie!). I pulled one daisy free and laid it on the grave
of Hazel Gingle, AKA Gramma. Then I split the flowers into
two bouquets and handed each to the girls. But before I let
them decorate the grave, I examined the mounted vase on
Nora's side. There was some old leaf litter there that I
cleared out with my fingers. At the very bottom of the

298

metal vase, I found something small wrapped in sticky tape. The girls set the flowers in either vase on either side of the gravestone and I tore my gloves off and picked at the sticky tape with my thumbnail. Finally it began to unravel and when I'd peeled the tape like mummy gauze, I had a safe deposit box key in my hand.

And I knew where to take it.

Unfortunately, it was a Sunday so the bank was closed. But the very next morning before work, after a tossy-turny night, I stopped at the USA United Savings Bank on Ingersoll Avenue. I walked in. I told a teller I wished to see my deposit box, holding up the key. They led me right into the vault, despite lacking documentation and not even banking there, and let me open box 434.

What I found in that box, on that wet February morning, was a brown silk pouch, drawn tight at its mouth. Inside the pouch was a small pyramid with rounded edges, made of clear glass, the size of a shooter marble. Attached to the drawstring was a strip of paper, like a long fortune cookie fortune, with the following handwritten in pencil on one side:

"You win the GRAND PRIZE: The soul of Barry Gingle."

On the other side is written:

"Thank you for completing my life, giving me a purpose."

As I, Ethan Alderyard, am the first to beat Barry's Quest and discover this very special Easter Egg, I have kept Barry's soul for myself. If you decide to play through the game, you, too, can type the last command and go visit the Gingle parents' grave, but the key is there no longer. I share this ending because, as a gaming purist, I believe it was all part of Barry's intent in designing the game at the end of his life. He wanted the game to be found, he wanted the game to be won, he wanted the safe deposit box to be opened. Barry Gingle wanted to be found.

Barry's remains remain in the possession of Donne's Funeral Home. I tried to claim them for a dignified burial with his parents but as I'm not kin they won't release them to me.

Some might argue that I've exploited Mr. Gingle's

memory by uploading Barry's Quest and making it available
for free download. I couldn't disagree more. This game is
one of a kind, an autobiographical graphic adventure from
the golden era of the genre, and, more than that, a cry for
human connection and understanding. It was made to be
played.

Document ©2010 Ethan Alderyard - DO NOT STEAL MY WORK!

Freckles

to LovelyLotus   17 November 2012

I dreamed a dream and you were in my hotel room when I came back but you were on your way out and you kept covering your mouth, like hiding your teeth or something. You were in a rush but I asked where you were running off to and you said Cliff Huckstable convinced you to get a camera installed in your gums. I said WHAT! And you showed me where in your gums like it was above your teeth right n your gums like the little black square of a cell phone camera? Right above your teeth. And you said you were heading back to the dentist to get it taken out. It looked like it was just done to cause the gums were kind of swollen around it. And I just couldn't wrap mu head around that one so I let you go to the dentist. It was like you were so embarrassed. Just red about it. I didn't ask if it took video or just still pictures or what but I thought it was pretty odd you let anybody let alone a black sitcom doctor known for pushing puddin pops to talk you into that lol...

See you next tine your on. I'm gonna mow the lawn now and maybe get a ruben afterwards. A place down near me does them so good.

Keep Your Future to Yourselves

"Wait here a minute," she said to Kyler Bates, the camera operator, the publicist, the representative from Smithwick World Records, and Kyler Bates's bodyguard. "Till I announce you!"

She knocked on the open door and walked into the small room at the forfeited living community. There, sitting in his wheelchair amid framed mandalas and shelves of books, he was. The white hair on the back of his head fanned up flat, the untamable effect of pillowed rest at the end of a lifetime. Elza, in her own small room in forfeited living in Russia, was on his rickety old LED flat screen, living ten hours ahead.

"Uncle Noah?"

She heard her but he didn't. Was fiddling with his hand-held game.

"Uncle Nooo-*ah*!"

He perked, turned. "Well! If it isn't my favorite shiteen! Look, Elza, it's our shiteen!"

"Our little shiteen!"

Besterley, planting a kiss on her great uncle's freckled forehead, waved at the antique screen. It felt so old fashioned, having to lean in front of the cam in order for it to pick her up and let Elza see her.

"Just 'shiteen,' Uncle Noah corrected. "The '-een' means 'little.' So 'little shiteen' would be 'little-little shit.'"

"Okay, okay," she said. "Enough is too much."

"How you guys doing today?"

The shrunken scarecrow of a great uncle tilted the sun off the screen on his handheld into Besterley's face. "Just playing my Neural Plaque Crush Saga." Simplified for old folks, the display was just a grid representing neurons in the immediate vicinity of the molecular remote toodling around his brain. Scooting aside and zapping balls of plaque with finger swipes reopened blocked pathways, keeping Old Man Alzheimer at bay. "Unlocked level fourteen-ninety-three just after breakfast. What level you on Elza?"

"One-five-two-two." She held out her own handheld.

"She's beating you, Uncle Noah. You gonna let her win?"

"Hell, it's my fault. I sent her the setup, paid for the implant."

"And I love you for it, darling man."

"You loved me before though."

"So you say, so you say."

"She denies it," he grinned his tea-stained smile. "I have the e-mails. Going back to the start!"

"So you say, so you say."

He jabbed Besterley hard with his elbow. "Saved all the sexts, too!"

"Uncle Noah," she deflected, "I have a little surprise for you."

"Gin?" His eyes sharpened, trying to see around her. "How'd you sneak it past the disorderlies?"

"No, it's not gin. It's really for both of you. You and Elza."

He banged his forearm on the armrest of his wheelchair. "No, no, no. We don't want a holoprojector—do we Elza?"

"We don't need."

"We want to keep our screens *just* the way they are."

"We need."

"We've always talked like this, for sixty-three years!" Color rose up in his cheeks where it had no bothered to blush since his morning dispute over what he was brought for breakfast. "We met this way on the Roulette Cam. *This* is how we know each other. *This* is how we are—and it's dis*tress*ing to us, them saying this way's being phased out. We could live another fifteen or twenty years! We want it to stay this way, none of that 3D crap."

"Always remember doesn't worth," Elza clucked.

Besterley regrouped and reached for the lines the marketing coach fed her. This was a big deal—she understood that—and reminding herself that what she'd done had come from a place of love, she meandered into her semi-dictated spiel.

"Alright, alright, but alright. You two, you know I've always thought yours was one of the great love affairs of all time. And when your parents were growing up, how they grew up in this fear that the other country would nuke theirs to Armageddon but then the wall came down and it's like you're both the peace that could grow all the way across the world."

"More matter with less art," he said, swiping away. He never had been all that sentimental. Stubborn, yes, but not given to emotional outpourings.

305

She took a breath and redirected her rhetoric. "I won a contest," she said, "that's the thing."

"Congrats and salutations," Elza said from the old LED monitor. She was no babushka with the kerchief and round face. The woman had carried flair and styled hair and dangly earrings with her into her nineties.

"What I did was write a letter about you two to some people who are making advances in—"

"And we don't have any time for their advances," Great Uncle Noah crowed. "Do we."

"Let the shiteen finish her saying."

"Thank you, Aunt Elza." She knew he was listening even though he kept playing his game. "What I'm saying is that I'm not the only one inspired by your love and I'm not the only one who wants to see you two together at last."

"We're together right now."

"Yes, I see, but don't you want to know each other?"

"We never met," Elza instructed in her instructional tone, "but we know another."

"*Each* other," Noah corrected.

"What of it?" she shrugged.

"Dr. Spaulding? Dr. Galeyev?" Kyler Bates, at the door, was trying to invite himself in. "If I may?"

"Let me guess," the old carbuncle said through a squint below tufted eyebrows. "You're my new stool softener gofer. In that case, go for it. Lord knows my rectum sent for you days ago."

Kyler Bates certainly had that entry level age about him, being seventy years younger than the pair of international love buzzards, but he was also the CEO of a powerful conglomerate. Every company at the forefront of progress was run by a teenager who would retire at twenty-five if he or she wasn't assassinated before then. What with the best ideas being concocted by the youngest minds, plenty of yesterday's prodigies quickly fell into embittering irrelevancy. Today's fresh faced upstarts were tomorrow's disaffected, disassociated, and fully-armed nobodies.

Great Uncle Noah and Aunt Elza had both grown up in a transitionary time, when corporversities were called universities and elders were no longer respected but people had yet to begin revering and turning to the young for wisdom. As such, they were prone to showing less respect than they really probably rather ought to have.

"I've dropped not a sole single fewmet in a week, Gofer," old Noah said. "Be a hero and bring us a bottle of Proon-E-Vac. You can just put a rubber nipple on it—I take it neat."

"Shaken," Elza quipped. "Not stir."

They chortled, her with a rattle and he with a wheeze.

Kyler Bates, known for an easygoingness uncharacteristic of his station in life, took this generational gap in stride.

"You're both totes educated, respected in your fields, your articles still referenced and quoted beyond the borders of your countries," he started, camera lens peering over his shoulder. "You put like the *merit* in professor emeritus."

"Oh Chriminy..."

"You're also pioneers. You traveled the Oregon Trail on the Apple II and the Smithwick peeps tell us you're also like the longest online relationship in the entire history of the planet."

"Are we now." The old man didn't care, barely noticed when the representative from Smithwick World Records gamboled in gushing with too much rouge on the cheeks and a framed certificate certifying theirs was in fact the oldest online love in the history of the planet.

"Congradyoo*lay*shuns!" she gushed, holding it out so Elza could see it, too.

"The point is totes worth listening to," the young CEO went on. "I'm inviting you with your pioneering spirits to be the first two people in the history books to try out my newest gift to the people: YourHere2."

An engineer, wheeling over Besterley's shoe, carted in a big box made of white plastic, unseemly in its bulkiness for the modern era, where devices bigger than a baseball were deemed too inconvenient to ever catch on with consumers. Simultaneously in Russia, as seen on the screen, a counterpart delivered an identical case into Elza's forfeited living room.

"What we can do now, *right now*, is set up YourHere2 here and YourHere2 there and bring about something the old science fiction guys dreamed up like ages ago. Where hologram tech offered 3D interactions surpassing your beloved old school webcams, YourHere2 is the very first solid projecttion system, capable of rendering touchable, huggable, kissable avatars of both of you like to each other and stuff. It won't teleport your bodies or nothing but it *will* render them in fluid, entirely hi-fi wi-fi. We flip these boxes on and you'll meet each other. For the very first time."

The engineer scooched the hand truck out from under the box, set before Noah in his wheelchair. Elza clucked her tongue at the one left before her.

Kyler flipped his hair and smiled so his dimple showed. "Do you trust me?"

Besterley watched her beloved great uncle scrunch his

nose and knew a lecture was coming. "You fuckwits and the fuckwits before you and your great-grand-fuckwits never did get what those 'science fiction guys' were saying about these things they dreamed up before you could make them."

He smiled with his teeth. "What's that then?"

"Those 'science fiction guys'—the ones who gave a flying fuck about human beings anyway—were telling us *not* to make them. How's your mini-fridge there respect the dignity of the body? It *doesn't*."

Kyler Bates looked for his publicist, finding Besterley first, and gave her a look that said he'd behead her if he could. He was embarrassed, this almost post-adolescent billionaire in the room, and she'd brought that on him.

Her great uncle twisted his head around and found her, too. "These people aren't my friends. They're not anybody's friends. My loved ones are my shiteen and my Elza."

"So you say, so you say," the old lady on the screen, for once, said with conviction.

"We don't want the new crap!" he said, that color burning in his cheeks again. "We want the old crap! We like *our* stuff from *our* time, when we were living in the future, which is how we thought of it when our crap came about and changed our lives. You keep *your* future to yourselves and let us keep *our* future the way we got used to it already!"

Elza, doing something Besterley had never seen her do before, shot her tongue off in her first language, making points upon long fingers, emphasizing each with a fiery tone roasting those attendants who had barged into her room over there in Russia.

They were so suited for each other, these two.

She finished with a flourish of condemnatory laughter and Noah, already zapping brain plaque on his handheld, gave a hard nod.

"What *she* said!"

Besterley, though it was not her duty to do so, burst out in tears and started ugly crying—because Great Uncle Noah and his Russian sweetie had never met—would never meet—and didn't know what they were missing out on—content as they were with far less than they deserved—complacent in the decades upon decades of physical separation—neither of them brave enough to bridge the distance—both convinced this was enough—forgoing the courage of wanting something more. No one else gathered there seemed to know what had set her off but it was sad to Besterley. It was all just so sad...

Enkidu76

to LovelyLotus   23 December 2015

It'd been some time since I dreamed of you but there you were last night. Walking through college in a foreign city I found a moonlit graveyard by the Chemistry Building. There, laying in the open empty stone casket of an abbot, grass grown inside, you were. You seemed grand, sprinkling fresh fistfuls of grass over yourself, playing dead. I stalled and watched, like I used to. But then I went over, why not, and you weren't unhappy to see me. Said you were lonesome when I almost knew ye when. Presently you were building a pyre for yourself but I'd stopped that. You took my hand and hopped out the coffin—you didn't let go and we walked the college green in the dark. It felt so good to be with you, though I couldn't say I knew you, in that foreign city deep in the night.

Sure look, I'm sorry I fecked off when I did like I did. Are you still cross with me? I'm a stupid man. I showed far too much care.

I saw you hung up your 'camwhorin' heels' whenever that was. Do you even check this email? If you do, I'd love to hear how you've gotten on since ditching the sunk cost fallacy business model.

Yours faithfully,
Dr Aengus Moriarty

(yes, that's *really* my name, like your man on *Sherlock* but no, not like him—sure there's loads of Moriartys all through Kerry and none of us, I assure you, conduct ourselves nefariously.)
****
Senior Lecturer of History and Ecumenics
Pindle College
Flachester University

ACKNOWLEDGEMENTS

Great thanks go to those editors who published three of these stories: Rhys Evans placed "The Martyr Dumb" in *how to hug your ex* (30 Sep. 2011), Mathew Allan Garcia chose "The Pixelated Paladin" for the Artemis issue of *Pantheon Magazine* (July 2013), and Alexander B. Hogan and Cheska Lynn brought out "http://youareforgiv.en" paired with music by Nicolas Horvath in *The Flexible Persona* (2 Feb. 2015). Thank you all for giving these stories such fine homes.

Special thanks to Kent L. Norman, who granted permission to quote his work as the epigraph for this collection. He is currently finishing the second edition of his book *Cyberpsychology: An Introduction to the Psychology of Human-Computer Interaction*. I found an analog between my project and his when I read the first edition of his book. Readers who want to know more about what is happening to us through our computers, tablets, and phones should start with Dr. Norman's book (published by Cambridge University Press).

Thank you to the scholars who have transformed my relationship with short fiction: my PhD supervisor Philip Coleman, my Viva threshold guardians: Kasia Boddy and Melanie Otto, my creative writing lecturers George Green and Graham Mort, Ailsa Cox, Susan Lohafer, and the ever-so-great Mike Trussler.

Gratitude to Kim and Cameron Wilson, as well as his students and colleagues at William Jessup University, who hosted me in April 2015. It was wonderful, as always, to see Caitlin Powell—and, of course, Chris Caughey and family, too. You all made me feel so welcome and I had such a fine time discussing all that we discussed.

When it comes to this collection, many friends read drafts and/or put up with me yammering about ideas, dead ends, and narrative riddles for which there could be no right or wrong answers: Georgine Althouse, Dennis Baker, Lehua Ball, Mollie Baxter, Peter Brown, Kyle Brzezynski, Deborah Burke, Brian, Manuel, and Bianca Cornell, Priyesh Dave, Caitlin Crowley Dodd, Michael Domen and Annemie, Ronny, and Katinka (who, the summer of 2014, put up with me scribbling "Out of Character" all through the Black Forest on a draft shat upon by a pigeon outside the Jung Institute in Zürich), Vicki Goldsmith, Tiffany Hearsey, John Hudson, Niki Jaramillo, Heather Keane, Vanessa Keogh, Mary McAuley, Jane McMillan, Kevin McNamara, Alecs Mickunas, Mike Morris, the Murphys *and* the Sweeneys of New Ross and surroundings, Peter and Mary Nazareth, Paul O'Toole, Jr., Natalie Pfund, James Robinson, Sarah Shafer Rosenbaum, Caoilainn Scouler, Humble Prince Among Self-Aggrandizing Dukes: Benedict Shegog, Amanda Simard, Sarah Smith, Kate Smyth, Fran, John, Alaina, Xander, Theo and, yes, I s'pose, perhaps, even Kevin Storrar—Eunice Tiptree, Darlene Woodcock. Some of you don't realize just how much you helped me bring this forth.

My purest thanksgiving, as always, goes to my family.

www.ingramcontent.com/pod-product-compliance
Lightning Source LLC
Chambersburg PA
CBHW041149050326
40689CB00004B/707